The BEEKEEPER

MYRON BROWN

ISBN: 978-1-963569-58-2 (hard cover)
       978-1-963569-59-9 (soft cover)

Edited by: Amy Ashby

Published by WARREN Publishing
Charlotte, NC
www.warrenpublishing.net
Printed in the United States

*This work is dedicated to Charlene, the love of my life,
for patiently encouraging the completion of this work; our
wonderful children, Arianna Crank and Jarred Brown; and the
many who have and will benefit from the work of a beekeeper.*

In loving memory of Jarred Samuel Brown.

Acknowledgments

Storytelling has been called one of the most essential communicative and cultural activities of humans. In primeval times, oral storytelling provided a historical and cultural record, predating the written word. In modern times, it continues to be a valuable source of information that can deliver ideas and sometimes ring a chord to open one's eyes.

Today we're so barraged with information, it's numbing. On the other hand, telling a story reaches out, invites us in, and occasionally inspires.

I was one of those so reached when seeking a career. My brother, Dr. Martin A. Brown, never tried to tell me what I should do. Instead, he patiently revealed the story of his path and stirred my interest with a fascinating opportunity.

We traveled to Davenport, Iowa, where chiropractic began. He introduced me to Drs. Reggie and Irene Gold, Joseph Strauss, Thom Gelardi, and other giants in the profession. To Martin, for his effectual encouragement, I remain indebted.

Dr. Pamela Brown, professor of communication and journalism at Rider University, offered invaluable assistance when this story was in its most fledgling stage. As only a loving sister would, she put up with additional requests and provided constructive, valuable insight again and again.

Dr. Arianna Coe was the first to read the completed rough draft. Although that coarse iteration was surely a burden to sift through, she found something of value. Her encouragement emboldened me to bring it forward.

My friend and colleague Gene Zdrazil, MA, DC, was the one with whom the adventure to find D.D. Palmer's 1870s apiary, Sweet Home, began. Together we sleuthed around the side roads of history. Then, after about a year of sobering research and several attempts to find the site, we enlisted Connie Waltz Zdrazil, Timothy Zdrazil, Charlene Brown, and Jarred Brown. Together we finally made it to the actual site.

The following year, with the assistance of Carl Gillman, DC, and Sherri Borer, DC, we planted our flag of discovery at Sweet Home. The ceremony included placing a granite marker indicating where the beekeeper lived, loved, and worked.

My esteemed mentor and friend, the late Bud Crowder, DC, provided first-hand insights about the Palmer family personalities and arranged a valuable interview with the late Vern Gielow, author of D.D. Palmer's biography.

Life's experiences produce many connections. I've been fortunate in this regard, yet one stands out as an individual who has been a consistent friend, mentor, and role model. Thom Gelardi, DC, not only grasped the significance of the beekeeper's discovery but also possesses the courage, wisdom, resolve, and passion for taking the steps to make a difference. I'm grateful to have been influenced by him.

With unbridled tenacity, Todd Waters yielded a treasure trove of previously unknown material about the beekeeper's early life experiences. His love of inquiry reminded me a historical journey is fun.

Louise Newcomb, a life-long resident of Muscatine County, Iowa, provided invaluable assistance in identifying some of her forebearers as well as the country schools where they were students of D.D. Palmer, who became a schoolmaster after arriving from Canada.

My thanks also go to Alana Callender, MS, and Glenda Wiese, PhD, for their assistance and cheerful cooperation whenever called upon for information from the Palmer College of Chiropractic archives.

Trusted readers Lyn Garris, J. Cameron Bosch, Lorell Lovett, and Joe'Terrious Neal generously gave their time and talents as beta readers, providing vital insights and perspectives.

Prologue

A BIT OF CONTEXT

Incredibly, no one has ever told this story. Although bits and pieces are out there, by and large, the world knows little of it. Such a sublime event ought to be as familiar as the apple falling on Newton's head. Or as recognizable as when humankind soared into the twentieth century on the wings of a Wright Flyer at Kitty Hawk.

Momentous as those breakthroughs were, what follows is an even more remarkable story, one of how an obscure beekeeper changed the world, quietly, humbly, and unheralded ... until now.

Throughout history, great thinkers have proclaimed that power corrupts. Human nature, when clothed in authority, often steeps a curious brew. The infusion strokes the ego of persons in control. The weak-minded, drunken by their status, cast aside reasoning and righteousness. It's why the Wright brothers' momentous breakthrough of 1903 came and went without acclaim from the pundits of their day. Instead of accolades came derision. After all, everyone knew machines heavier than air couldn't fly. Despite ample substantiation, entrenched naysayers, mavens, and scientists leaped to discredit the aviators. How could humble bicycle makers do what so many credentialed, well-financed notables couldn't?

Nonetheless, the brothers' first flight resonates like the apple that fell three centuries ago. Sir Isaac may have opened our eyes to gravity, but Orville and Wilbur consummated humanity's age-old dream to defy it.

Our beekeeper's story echoes just as loudly.

Chapter One

A MOMENT IN HISTORY

"Life is either a daring adventure or nothing."
–HELEN KELLER

D aniel's discovery occurred in near silence, especially for
Harvey. Although it was an experiment, the outcome was
exactly as expected. The instant he removed his hands
from Harvey's neck, he knew history had been made. A wave of
astonishment rippled through the doctor's body. He shuddered,
speechless ... at least for the moment.

Harvey's recumbent body rested on the wooden bench with his
head turned to the left. The hairs on the back of Daniel's neck
were standing up as he tried to get hold of himself. After a few
seconds, he bent over to check on the patient. Turning his face
toward Harvey, the doctor gazed into the man's intense, dark eyes.
Finding no reassurance there, nor having anything useful to say,
Daniel called out, "Harvey?" as a wave of uncertainty chilled him
to his core.

The unresponsive patient neither moved nor uttered a word. His
stillness brought forth a shiver as another wave of chills rolled up
and down Daniel's spine. Fear soon percolated its way into the
doctor's mind. He stood back up as dreadful questions flashed

through his head. *Any louder, and I could've woken the dead, but Mr. Lillard doesn't bat an eye. Have I hurt this man? Is he paralyzed? Why doesn't he respond? Doesn't he know his own name? My God, what have I done?* Daniel pondered briefly and conceded that it was fear, his old nemesis. He'd confront it and beat it down. *No one has done this before. So what?* Harvey needed *help, and everyone else failed him. He didn't need more of that. I've given him something entirely different.*

Chapter Two
FEARING THE WORST

"History: gossip well told."
—Elbert Hubbard

Grasping for control, Daniel searched for calming answers. His first thought was, *Maybe I didn't say his name loud enough for him to hear.* He scolded himself. *Don't be absurd!* Then he rationalized, *Well, maybe he couldn't read my lips because of how I had my head turned.* Dan dismissed that idea too. *Am I both irrational and daft?*

Fearing the worst, Daniel knelt before the patient's face. Although Harvey seemed frozen, his dazed eyes were the size of saucers. *What an odd expression for such a dignified, intelligent man,* thought Daniel.

Harvey continued to lie on his stomach with his head turned to the side. Uncertainty seemed to take hold of the African-American entrepreneur who appeared surprised but not stunned. Slowly he tried to rise. The doctor quickly placed a gentle, reassuring hand over Harvey's head so the patient wouldn't immediately disturb what had been done. *Well, at least I haven't paralyzed him,* Daniel thought with relief.

Harvey's head barely moved a quarter-inch before Daniel's fleshy, warm hand guided it back down onto the thin cushion. To calm him, Daniel said, "Harvey, please be still a moment." He wondered if he had spoken loudly enough this time for Harvey to catch his words. It didn't matter though, because the gesture worked, and the man stopped moving.

Daniel watched as Harvey, far from paralysis, let the weight of his shoulders back down onto the table, a shudder rippling all the way to the patient's feet. Wonderment on Harvey's face told the doctor the man felt much different. Then another shiver undulated like a wave from Harvey's feet to his head.

About half a minute later, the doctor decided it was alright for Harvey to move. That decision lacked any particular criteria, only an intuitive sense about it. He reasoned that keeping Harvey's head turned couldn't be good or remain comfortable. Daniel waved in a circular motion, indicating it was time for Harvey to straighten his head, then placed his hands on each side of the man's head gently guiding it to a straight, forward position.

While trying to maintain a modicum of professionalism, he used his loudest voice, "Let's have you sit up now. Try to keep your movements easy." A curious thought flashed through Daniel's mind as he watched Harvey rise. *That gripping fear is gone.* He whispered his amazement to the universe, "It worked!"

Insecurity immediately sprung forth in a veritable geyser of doubt. *How do I know it worked? Harvey hasn't said anything yet. But I know it worked. I know it with every fiber of my being.* But he had no evidence. *How do I know?*

The answer came from a small voice deep inside. It rarely spoke, but when it did, it was always reliable. *I felt it move!*

Timidity faded. The doctor had felt a pulsation at the base of his left wrist near the pinky finger. The single vibration was unambiguous, like the proverbial "X" on a treasure map. Even though fear had tried to wash it from his mind, he had indeed felt it.

Now lucid, his thoughts rushed in with the clarity of a diamond. *The tiny quaver under my hand was in Harvey's neck.* The procedure had worked as intended!

His excitement intensified when Harvey finally did speak, and Daniel was dumbfounded rather than reassured by what he heard. Harvey said nothing about feeling good, bad, better, or worse. Instead, his eyes looked directly into and nearly through Daniel. "WHO ARE YOU?" Harvey asked slowly, stretching his shrill words.

Harvey's words were more rhetorical than interrogative. But Daniel retorted anyway, "Why Harvey, you've cleaned my office for years—"

Before the puzzled doctor could finish, Harvey persisted. "WHERE DID YOU COME FROM?"

Daniel searched Harvey's face for anger or antagonism, trying to fathom the man's reaction. Finding none, he breathed a sigh of relief. Although mystified, Harvey seemed to be as pleased with the outcome as the doctor was. In response the doctor said, "I've been in Iowa for many years, but that's not important now ...." Finally realizing that Harvey was expressing his astonishment with humor, Daniel laughed heartily, and Harvey soon joined in.

Daniel decided he mustn't get too caught up in the moment and shifted to something more mundane and easily assimilated. "Please sit for one minute, Harvey. I must record this."

Always a meticulous record keeper, he reached into his vest pocket. His fingers closed around a silver pocket watch, and his serious face broke into a smile. This was something that happened every time he grasped the timepiece. The date and time were trivial, but the information's ordinariness had a welcome, calming effect.

He began with a bold heading in the upper left about an inch from the top of a clean page:

Ryan Block, Davenport, Iowa. September 18, 1895, 5:45 p.m.

He skipped down a few lines and began his clinical notes.

Upon Mr. Harvey Lillard, a deaf man of this city, I performed a left lateral correction of a misaligned second neck vertebra through its spinous process using a light, quick movement. The correction was …

Daniel stopped writing, thought a moment, and struck through the word *correction* and replaced it with *adjustment*.

He looked at what he had written, shifting his eyes from the stricken word *correction* to its replacement *adjustment*. He glanced back and forth several times and decided the term *adjustment* said it best.

The adjustment was deliberate. I delivered it using my left hand's distal lateral carpal (pisiform) onto the left, inferior aspect of the patient's C-2 spinous process. The adjustment …

Again he stopped and nodded his preference for the word *adjustment*.

The adjustment was suitably light and quick. I directed it anteriorly on a vector running from the C-2 spinous process, inferior to the auditory meatus and toward the patient's left ocular orbit.

Next, Daniel pondered whether to stop there or record something about the results. On the one hand, he wanted to cling to systematic, scientific reporting of measurable information. On the other hand, this experiment was too profound to remain silent about the matter. He made an abstract statement for the record, planning to return later with more details.

The objective was to unlock an obstruction in his central nervous system.
The movement was detectable.
It seems we have made the anticipated change.

Having the technical information recorded on paper, Daniel felt he could relax. He smiled at the watch again, checking the time, which indicated 5:47.

The watch reminded him of a lucky day about fifteen years before, when providence had happened to shine upon him. A dozen people applauded as he, the unsuspecting grand prize winner, entered to shop for a gift for his wife, Louvenia. Daniel had won the pocket watch by walking through the door at precisely the right moment, becoming the fiftieth customer during the jewelry shop's grand opening in What Cheer, Iowa.

Daniel grinned, recalling the moment when he had presented Louvenia with a gold pendant he purchased for her that day. It was two days after visiting the jewelry shop. "Oh, how beautiful," she said, reaching for something under a throw pillow on the armchair next to him. She grasped a page torn from the weekly newspaper, which had arrived earlier that day. The element of surprise was subdued, but not their laughter when she gestured at the photo appearing in the center of page two. The picture showed a watch dangling at the end of a chain from her husband's right hand. A proud smile beamed across his face as the store owner held a large number 50 in front of Daniel's chest.

"Well, aren't you going to show me the watch?" she chuckled.

"Y ... y,"—his tongue stumbled as if caught in some nefarious misdeed—"yes, I was planning to do that next," he said, reaching into his pocket. He sheepishly retrieved it and passed it over to her.

She reassured him with a warm hug, and they laughed again.

Chapter Three

NEARLY A LIFETIME LATER

As important as putting the key in a lock

Eighteen eventful years felt like a lifetime since the grand, triumphant experiment with Harvey Lillard. Louvenia, the mother of Daniel's children was long gone now, and Alvilla, his third wife, had also gone on to the great beyond. After Alvilla's passing Daniel had married again, but that union was even more short-lived than with his first wife, Abba.

Daniel was staring at the bold 1913 atop the calendar resting on the end table next to the sofa. His fifth wife, Molly Hudler Palmer, sat next to him in their Los Angeles home's heavily furnished parlor.

"Next week will be our seventh anniversary," Molly said. "It's funny to think that when I asked Harriet to be my maid of honor, she warned me about you. 'He's been married four times before. Do you think it will last?'"

"I've married my first love last. And last it will! Well at least as long as I do," he added with a kiss on the cheek and a hug to reassure her.

His gaze returned to the calendar as though it held the clue to a riddle. He was struggling to put something into words. But all he could come up with was, "Ever since that first adjustment restored

Harvey's hearing, I've been able to conjure up that exquisite feeling just by thinking of the look in Harvey's eyes! That fast, light movement of my hands and their swift recoil away from Harvey was a little thing with a big effect."

He gazed at the thick Persian carpet below them, idly tracing the mostly red, dense fibers' intricate design. Following its many gilt brown and green variegations helped him concentrate on that distant, momentous bygone event. He continued, "Molly, whether I'm in a good place or bad, happy or sad, I can relive that intense sensation, and it feels good to have it flash through me. I've lived that moment of supreme triumph a thousand times. I can still picture the purple horsehair cushion on the bench we used to hold those big laundry tubs. It wasn't a fancy piece of equipment like we have today, but it got the job done! I remember Harvey's face, so full of amazement, even before he got up off the table."

Daniel looked up to see if she was still listening. Molly smiled encouragingly, and he continued, "Harvey's expression went from anxiety to astonishment, and then it turned joyful, all before his feet hit the floor!"

Molly sat back on the amply stuffed sofa and watched him speak. Her eyes welcomed his enthusiasm because he was so often downhearted these days. Daniel continued to describe that victorious feeling. "From time to time, I've thought all the world's great discoverers must feel something similar when they make a breakthrough or finally solve some great problem. I knew ecstasy, and surely Edison must have felt something akin to it. Imagine that instant when he heard his voice echoing, 'Mary had a little lamb ....' It may not be the greatest discovery to emerge from his Menlo Park laboratory. Still, for the first time in history, a man had created and replayed a recording of a human voice. Our nearly deaf wizard friend referred to the phonograph as his *baby*—it was his favorite!"

Molly, nodded agreeably saying, "You know, Beethoven also did some of his greatest work after he had gone deaf, and I'll bet you, even though he never heard it as we can, he knew and felt something special in every note."

Daniel raised his bushy eyebrows, sizing up her remark, and nodded his agreement as he tapped the index finger of his right hand into the center of the palm of his left. "That's exactly what I mean!"

This particular conversation with Molly raised his passion, a rarity since leaving Iowa. He admired individuality and inventiveness. Nothing gave him more satisfaction than studying a problem, advancing a solution, and changing how things got done.

Seconds later, his expression dropped. "I didn't do it for praise, but some appreciation from the boys in the field wouldn't hurt." It had been many years since his great triumph. Still, jubilation was nowhere to be seen, neither on his face nor in his sad heart, despite reliving that joyous moment.

Molly tried to reassure him. "Dear, it doesn't matter whether the small-minded majority understands what you've done. The important thing is you did it."

"I know." Daniel retreated within, reflecting on the meaning of his achievement. He knew his quirky personality had played a role in keeping his discovery relatively obscure. Moreover, in the beginning, it seemed like a good idea to keep it as a family secret for safekeeping—and financial gain. Born into humble circumstances and having grown up on his own, he had always had to scrape together the minimal essentials. Daniel saw the potential security this great innovation could bring its owner. But things simply hadn't worked out the way he expected. Finances aside, why wasn't Harvey's adjustment heralded from the mountaintops for the magnificent discovery it was? He often wondered why and, in darker moments, tortured himself about it. In recent years, he had developed the habit of reading about inventors, explorers, and great thinkers. He hoped to find solace by grasping their essence, dissecting their spirit, and coming to terms with their distinctions. *What made them different? What drove the people who drove the life-changing advancements of humanity?*

"Molly, this morning I found an interesting parallel and even some peace of mind in Robert Thurston's *The History of the Growth of the Steam Engine*. One fascinating statement hit home for me." Daniel reached to the end table and grasped the book. He had inserted a quill feather to make it easy to find the passage. He looked sidelong at Molly to confirm she was still listening and began to read aloud. "Thurston said, 'Frequently an important invention is made before the world is ready to receive it. ... Inventions only become successful when they are not only needed, but when mankind is so far advanced in intelligence as to appreciate and to express the necessity for them, and to at once make use of them.' His idea got me thinking a little differently." Daniel closed the book.

"I see what you mean," answered Molly, who didn't mention the shift into his schoolmaster persona and compelling tone of voice that emerged whenever he stood before a podium.

He continued, "Everyone knows the steam engine ignited this so-called industrial revolution going on all around us. It's changed the world in countless ways, but Thurston illustrated something often overlooked. We credit James Watt with inventing the steam engine and curiously forget many others came before him. Thurston rightly argued that invention is more than creation; it's growth. He points out that the ancient Greeks, Romans, and Egyptians experimented with the same principles Watt and his contemporaries put into practical use."

Molly watched his eyes, which revealed Daniel's passion for these ideas as he summarized: "My discovery also engaged principles in existence for thousands of years. After all, everyone else had access to people with subluxated vertebrae for eons of time. Yet, no one else had developed a clear, reproducible method to find and correct what was choking off life's expression. Freeing up creation may not be equivalent to creating, but it's just as important as putting the key in a lock! I found a sane, sensible way to get Harvey's life-force effectively and efficiently flowing again." Seeing a glimmer of uncertainty in her expression, he quickly added, "Molly, I know it sounds dramatic. But it's not an overstatement to use terms like life-force. The conveyance of information over the body's central nervous system is a life-sustaining current."

Molly looked squarely at him. "Actually, dear, I have no qualms about it at all. I've only lived with you for seven years, but I've known you for most of my adult life. I edited your manuscripts, sat in the front row countless times at your lectures, and crisscrossed the country to deliver this message. It's a vital message that people need to hear, so no, life-force is not an overstatement to me."

Chapter Four

FINDING GREENER PASTURES

Shrouded by the artificial, innate beauty
is revealed in things genuine.

D aniel was of the old school. He demanded the best of himself and settled for no less from others, especially his children. The worn hickory stick in the kitchen's corner was their constant reminder.

To the children, their father was one of life's greatest enigmas. They spoke of him as the most mysterious of puzzles, even long after his death. Bart loved his father but hated their relationship. He marveled at the brilliance and strength of Daniel, now known to all the locals as "Dr. D.D." So in 1896, at age fifteen, Bart adopted some of his father's panache by replacing his given name with initials. He not only liked the sound of it, but also thought the moniker "B.J." might speed him into adulthood.

B.J. was proud to be D.D. Palmer's son, particularly since the prior year's "great, grand discovery"—as his father often said. But seething below the surface were other mixed emotions. It was embarrassing when jousts between his father and local physicians took place on the pages of the newspapers. D.D. always found time to have B.J. read his book reports aloud, his father stopping him to discuss every reasoning or grammatical error. The same man was too busy to talk about the trivial things of interest to his son, yet there was always time for discipline if the lad's obedience was brought into question. As a result, not only was B.J. uncertain about his father's love for him, but he also wondered whether he deserved love at all.

Bart and his sister May often commiserated about their feelings toward their father. May summed it up in one word, "Disappointment!" She hastened to explain. "I don't think he wants to be mean, but he's just so insensitive. It's not as though I don't love him, but he tramples on everyone's feelings, almost as if he doesn't care at all."

"That's for sure!" B.J. agreed.

"I think about it a lot, especially since Mother died," she added. "Father never thinks about my needs. And he doesn't care about Jessie either. He doesn't hit Jessie much. He likes to take it out on me because I'm older."

"Well, I'm the youngest," B.J. said, "and I get my share from him!"

A string of mean stepmothers had only compounded the situation. The children received beatings for the smallest of transgressions.

"He never takes our side, no matter what. Does he think we're always in the wrong?" May posed.

"It's completely unfair," B.J. said.

B.J. was forced to learn and showed no appreciation for the ritual of study and nightly philosophic recitations for his father. May loved to study but wasn't given the opportunity because of her gender. She had the capacity for deeper reasoning and logic, but like one longing for forbidden fruit, she was not invited to the table. Meanwhile, her brother didn't even know why he hated it. Whenever pushed, he just naturally pushed back. As an act of defiance, the teenager would stay out late and often sleep in cardboard boxes in the alley when the temperatures were above freezing.

Father ruled the household and pre-determined that the girls had better learn to read his choice of aphorisms and the Bible. He also required a rudimentary knowledge of arithmetic and writing too. Anything more than that was neither encouraged nor supported because it meant a girl was neglecting her chores, a fault not tolerated in the Palmer family.

May tried to point out the hypocrisy of her father's gender-based tyranny many times, but his patriarchal attitude trumped her call for consistency. On this subject, her father was blind to reason. Repression tragically shut her down, depriving both parent and child of the rich interpersonal connection which might have been, yet was forever lost. She expressed her frustration in a secret diary containing lists of musings, brooding, and aphorisms.

Friday, September 18, 1896 (104 days left this year)

> *I found a gray kitten wandering in the Third Street alley today. She has white socks. I'll give her a name tomorrow.*
>
> *I wonder why Father doesn't like me.*
>
> *Why is my best never good enough for him?*
>
> *Does he think he is perfect? Well, I know he isn't.*
>
> *Jessie gave me a bouquet today. She said not to sniff them too much because dandelions aren't so fragrant.*

Saturday, September 19, 1897 (103 days left this year)

> *B.J. broke three dozen eggs on his way home today. What an oaf!*
>
> *I wonder what Father will do.*
>
> *Father doesn't live up to his own beliefs, especially when it comes to us kids.*
>
> *He's caught in a paternalistic pickle—and it's not just our family. Men think they should be in control because they have bigger muscles. If only they had bigger intellects.*
>
> *What would it have been like if Mother were alive?*
>
> *It would be a better world if only fathers could listen to their daughters.*

He's blind to me.
Father denies the obvious but still sees all the
shortcomings in everyone except himself.
Patients say how great he is. Why doesn't he have any
greatness left for me, Jessie, and B.J.?

Although written by a troubled child in flustered moments, her insights defined Daniel, especially when it came to his Achilles' heel: interpersonal know-how. That pattern would appear and reappear in relationships throughout his life. He loved humanity as a whole but would always struggle with individuals.

Born on the forested Canadian frontier in 1845, Daniel David Palmer was as rugged as the environment he came from. As a young adult, he had fancied the idea that his time and place of birth corresponded with the time and circumstances surrounding Henry David Thoreau's hiatus at *Walden Pond.*

Daniel had entered the world in a simple home out in the northern woods. It was a modest frame structure, although sumptuous compared to the ten-foot by fifteen-foot cabin Thoreau lived in at the time. Thoreau erected his one-room shelter along the shore of Walden Pond on land belonging to Ralph Waldo Emerson to experience simplicity, peace, and quiet. Daniel began to read Thoreau's *Walden: Life in the Woods* when he was a teenager, and he couldn't put it down. Natural beauty, genuine strength of character, and social justice all resonated with him, and he became an avid reader of the transcendentalists.

He identified with Thoreau's closeness to nature while he struggled to understand the esoteric references to the sacred texts of India.

Taken with transcendentalist thought, Daniel no longer prized ownership. As Daniel grew into adulthood, Ralph Waldo Emerson became his favorite author, and he easily related to Emerson's essay "Self-Reliance." He had read it reluctantly for the first time when he was twelve years old. Mr. Black, a strict Canadian tutor, forced him to read the assignment, but the study on individuality became the boy's favorite. Daniel studied hard and, when he was twenty-five, became nearly ecstatic to learn of the opportunity to hear Emerson recite excerpts from his writings.

Soon, it was 1870, and the aging Emerson was scheduled to lecture in New York. Daniel was a teacher in the country schools on the Illinois side of the Mississippi River, where he read about the upcoming lecture in the *Mercer County Advertiser*. Live appearances by Emerson had already become rare, and Schoolmaster Palmer knew these would become more and more infrequent. When he read about the prospects of attending this lecture, which the announcement said was open and free to the public, a strange compulsion pulled at him to make the arduous trip.

That day, Emerson taught that ideals weren't reached by avoiding conformity, but rather by striving to be genuine. His point focused on how inconsistency stifled an individual's ability to connect with his/her inner voice or act on those insights. The lecture had a poignant flavor as Emerson applied the point in his discussion of abolition.

Emerson had spoken out both before and after the war. While so much had already come to pass, the writer's passion for the subject hadn't faded. During the lecture, Daniel was thinking about something he had read in a pre-war speech by Emerson that focused directly on consistency: "I think we must get rid of slavery, or we must get rid of freedom." There Daniel would hear, without ambiguity, what the phrase meant from Emerson's lips.

A reception line formed below the stage, where enthusiastic attendees greeted Emerson after the lecture. It took nearly half an hour for 102 others to offer handshakes, praise, and well wishes before Daniel finally got his turn.

"Mr. Emerson," Daniel blurted as he reached for his hand, "Now that slavery is ended, can we say the country is truly free?"

"Young man ..." Emerson hesitated, like one trying to be patient. His gaze burned into Daniel's eyes, like an invisible energy aimed directly at his brain. The luminary continued, "I've just expounded for an hour and a half on consistency. Human morality and ethics demanded abolition then. Surely, we all know nothing less is demanded of us now. It was a first step taken at great cost to everyone. Yet none of us can be so naïve as to believe tight-fisted oppression ends abruptly. We will not be free to believe a sane, rational consistency exists anywhere until all men and women on this continent have the opportunity to express their freedoms unreservedly." Emerson accepted Daniel's outstretched hand and, while turning his attention to greet the next person, gave it a single solid and unmistakably dismissive shake.

Daniel reflected on the encounter later, feeling like he should kick himself for not asking a more thoughtfully composed question. Daniel forgave himself as he contemplated the look in Emerson's eyes and his crisp, incisive response. *I guess I was lucky enough to have had any face-to-face meeting with such an intellectual giant.* On the train ride to New York, he had wondered just what it might be like to be in the presence of someone of that caliber. Now he was just thankful to have had the experience.

Transcendentalist thinking felt intuitively right to Daniel, who never broke from his fundamentally individualistic nature. On the contrary, it cemented his feeling of kinship with Emerson and Thoreau both philosophically and politically. Returning from New York, he had plenty of time to ponder. Drawn into a peacefully contemplative mood by the rhythm of the coach bounding from rail to rail, he ruminated over the encounter. *I now know who I am, and it doesn't fit well in this world as it is.*

Unfortunate circumstances had helped Daniel put enough money together to purchase his ticket to New York. The school system had been late in paying teachers for the first 1870 instructional term. Disastrous at the time, the delay worked out well in the long run. The general store allowed the teachers to run a tab on clothing and incidentals, while families around New Boston took turns providing instructors with room and board. Then, when their pay finally did come through, it was like a small windfall. Daniel was frugal; first, he paid off his modest tab at the general store and still had plenty left over to splurge. Not only could he buy the train fare, but he was also able to afford a new suit, meals, travel incidentals, and a hotel.

Daniel's keen mind had unrefined, rough edges. To children attending school, he built the reputation of being strict but fair. Their parents, and other folks in the community, found him to be bright, well-read, highly opinionated, and very articulate. Some enjoyed those attributes, while others found it intimidating. Schoolmaster Palmer was affable, and he loved to hear and tell a good joke. Yet many found his enigmatic character crude, harsh, and rude on occasion. He seemed to excel at everything his inquisitive mind latched on to, with drive and determination that was often more like a yoke. Once he mastered a thing, the itch would become a burning, and he was ready to move on. This unfettered compulsion caused him to ask new questions, want to know more, and understand the why of anything that interested him. Ultimately those impulses never gave him rest, yet compelled him to find his place in history.

On his way back from attending Emerson's lecture, Daniel was one of the eighty-nine passengers aboard a westbound train. It had departed from New York the day before and was now traversing the prairies of Indiana. Rail travel dramatically underscored the changing terrain as the contrasts of the vast countryside unfolded before their eyes. Then, somewhere in mid-Ohio, someone lifted the entire landscape and shook it out, like spreading a blanket across a bed. The tree-covered Appalachians were gone, replaced with vast fertile plains.

To the western Illinois schoolteacher, the changing landscape inspired reflection. Absorbed in existential thoughts since beginning the trip to hear Emerson, he contemplated the unhealed wounds of the recent war and how it had shaped people's lives, especially his own. A particular question would give his mind no peace: *Why am I brought to this time and place?* His life had shifted radically fourteen years before when Daniel's family left for Iowa without him. But it felt like only fourteen days ago in many ways.

When Daniel was barely twelve years old, his father, Thomas, had sat him down and said, "Son, you're old enough to understand that hard times, not of my choosing, have befallen us. Your mother and I have made a decision. We're going south to find work in the United States. We just can't continue with what little we've got coming in. We'll take your little brother Bart and three sisters. I've mapped out our way to Iowa and a plan to get started there."

"Okay, father, I'll see to things here," was all the dumbfounded young man could think to say.

When Thomas's Canadian business had failed in 1856, coal and agriculture were booming in central Iowa. It was a great opportunity for Thomas to relocate the family since the Native Americans had been driven off some of the most fertile lands in the world. The prevailing wisdom suggested "civilization" was offering the chance of a lifetime. Thomas knew these prospects existed because of a heinous tyranny carried out upon native peoples. But he conveniently found a way to put it out of his mind, rationalizing that others had committed the atrocities in a foreign country. What was done was done, and as a Canadian, he chose to believe his own hands were clean.

Meanwhile, Daniel would never forget his father's words charging him to look after his nine-year-old brother, T.J. "Daniel, we can't ignore this opportunity. You're my eldest son, a young man now, and I trust you to watch out for T.J. and be sure both of you continue your studies with Mr. Black."

Stunned, the boy felt like he had been hit in the face with a brick. Shock and dismay left such a thick lump in his throat; he could not speak. Then his thoughts flashed to the task of continuing with the family's tutor. T.J. loathed Mr. Black because the man's strict demeanor scared him.

Thomas explained his plan for the boys, "Continue your work in town at the shoemaker's store and help T.J. get whatever work you can find for him. Then, when Mr. Black says you're ready, and you've put aside some money, sell this cabin, and you and T.J. can join us in Iowa."

It would be nearly nine years before that day would arrive. Daniel never asked his father why they couldn't just come along with the family. Instead, he told himself it was just about the money while quietly dreading there was more to it. He tried not to think about those possibilities, and when he did, there were more questions than answers. *Am I being punished for some particular misdeed? Perhaps Father just doesn't like me. Could it be Mother's decision? No, definitely not Mother. I know she loves me.*

Since those questions were never asked or answered, Daniel became used to carrying anger in his heart. Being left alone and in charge of his younger brother T.J. up there on the Canadian frontier was frightening. He thought of himself as a child, not a young man. Wondering why he was left behind fed the fear. *Why did they leave me? Are they mad at T.J. too? I guess they love Bart and the girls more. What did I do wrong?* As time passed, he dealt with his emotions by becoming so driven, people around him wondered why he never seemed to be at peace.

On April 3, 1865, Daniel and T.J. finally took to the road with two dollars and staunch determination to leave Canada, find their way to Iowa, and reunite with the rest of the Palmer family.

It was a turn of events for two young men to be traveling to a new life in the United States because, in those years, just the opposite had become the norm. Thousands of young men had been flowing into Canada from the United States, flooding Canada's job markets. The Civil War triggered the migration, spurring healthy young eligibles to move across the border to avoid conscription into military service. Daniel and T.J. had found their already meager earnings threatened in the short term, with little hope for job opportunities to improve in the long term.

Two weeks before, the die had been cast when T.J. lost his part-time job as a clerk in a stagecoach stop and general store by the lake. T.J. arrived home that day with his shoulders slumped and, in a dejected voice, said, "Mr. Song let me go today. He's putting on two full-time men from Pennsylvania. Men from the States will work cheap, so he just doesn't need me anymore."

"It just keeps getting worse around here," Daniel answered.

"I think it's time to head for Iowa. What do you think?" T.J. asked.

Daniel quickly responded, "I've been thinking the same thing for a while too. I don't blame them for coming here, but it's becoming impossible for us Canadians."

Now animated, T.J. was standing taller. His voice came to life, as he enthusiastically fired off, "When will we leave? What do we need to do?"

"I'd hoped to wait for the war to end first."

They knew they would be entering a war zone. The Confederacy was on its heels, and a Union victory seemed inevitable. Still, there was no telling whether it would happen in a week or a year. "I guess I should give notice. Barrel staves are in very high demand. But they shouldn't have much trouble finding a Pennsylvanian or a New Yorker to take my place in the factory. It's customary to give two weeks."

"Okay then," T.J. said, "I'll write to Mother to let her know we'll leave in the first part of April."

April arrived with a soft, warm, southerly breeze as their journey began. From their prairie home in Canada West, near Lake Scugog, it took all morning for Daniel and T.J. to walk south for the first eighteen miles to Whitby, on the north shore of Lake Ontario.

Chapter Five

THE ADVENTURE BEGINS

"At last, fortissimo!"

–AUSTRIAN COMPOSER GUSTAV MAHLER
UPON VISITING NIAGARA FALLS

Their first stop was a small bakery on the edge of Whitby. Daniel smiled and introduced himself and T.J. to a weary-looking man whose apron, arms, and beard were dusted with flour. Daniel's smile grew when the man said, "Welcome, I'm George Biscuit."

Seeing no reaction from Mr. Biscuit, he grasped that a baker with the name "Biscuit" had already heard his share of jokes about it. Daniel wiped the smile off his face and followed with a respectful, "Pleased to meet you, sir."

Donning a suspicious eye, Mr. Biscuit reached out warily to meet Daniel's enthusiastic handshake.

Daniel asked, "Is there something T.J. and I can do for you to earn a loaf of that great-looking bread?" He didn't wait for an answer to the first question before explaining, "We're on our way south to the Iowa territory. We'll be earning our way as we go." He followed the first unanswered question with another. "Mr. Biscuit, can you suggest how we might gain passage across Lake Ontario?"

Turning the minor annoyance to his advantage, Mr. Biscuit replied, "Right outside the back door, there's a wagon loaded with flour sacks from the mill. You have a deal if you boys can get it put up in the basement, neatly stacked, and not tear any open."

George dreaded that chore. He stored flour in the cool basement to keep it fresh. But the long, narrow flight of stairs and the basement's low ceiling forced him to duck so as not to bang his head. Awkward as it was with a heavy sack over his shoulder, he'd absentmindedly scraped the top of his head more times than he cared to admit. With each bag weighing a fatiguing eighty pounds, it had become an all-too-familiar occurrence.

Daniel happily reached out, offering his hand. "You won't be disappointed, Mr. Biscuit!" Then, smiling, Daniel added, "Of course you'll let us smear some of that molasses too, right?"

George smiled back. "Mr. Palmer, you drive a hard bargain, but a deal it is."

"He sure does," said a customer sitting alone at a small table across the room. On the table in front of him sat a thick sandwich made with dark, rustic bread, an inner layer of something unidentifiable, and a cup of black coffee.

Feeling obliged to make introductions, George said, "Young fella, this is Howard Griggs, the strongest man in town. He runs the blacksmith shop, and in his spare time, he carries anvils around, hoping the ladies will see him!"

It was a habit for the blacksmith to stop in the bakery for lunch at least three or four times each week. Mr. Griggs added, "If you're willing to help load grain into a ship's hold, we ought to be able to help you find passage with the Great Lakes Freighter Line over to St. Catherines. From there, it's only thirty miles to Buffalo, New York. Once you're in Buffalo, there are many ways to get around to the various states. You can probably find work on one of the Lake Erie steamers to get you out west."

Wide-eyed T.J. never spoke during the whole exchange. But Daniel was eager to continue the conversation with Mr. Biscuit and Mr. Griggs. "Mr. Griggs, how do we get started with the Great Lakes—"

George interrupted, "If you want to unload that flour, you better get to it because it can't sit in the sun all day."

In his most respectful voice, Daniel said, "Okay, we're on it." He looked back and saluted Mr. Griggs with a tip of his cap. Then, as the two boys walked toward the back door, he said, "Excuse me, Mr. Griggs, I'd like to catch up with you after we have the flour unloaded. We'll come by your shop to look for you then, okay?"

Howard nodded agreeably.

A short while later, the two hot, sweaty boys returned to find Mr. Griggs still seated at the table. The sandwich devoured, he seemed to be enjoying a chat with Mr. Biscuit while sipping his coffee. Daniel wondered how Mr. Griggs could take such a long, leisurely time out for lunch but thought better of verbalizing the observation.

Seeing the young men back from their chore, Mr. Biscuit reached for a whole loaf of bread and put it on the counter. Then, looking at the Palmers and pointing to the bread, he placed a small crock of molasses and a wooden dipper next to them. "Looks like you earned your lunch," the proprietor said. Next, he placed two China plates before them with a pair of forks and knives.

T.J. and Daniel simultaneously said, "Thank you." Then, Daniel took the bread from the counter while T.J. carried the plates and silverware.

As they turned toward the dining tables, Howard Griggs gestured at his tabletop, "Please join me."

"Don't mind if we do," answered Daniel with a smile.

They sat across from Mr. Griggs, who watched the two young men enthusiastically tear into their bread and molasses. Meanwhile, Mr. Biscuit stepped down to the basement to inspect their work. Pleased everything looked neat and seeing no sign of torn ends, Mr. Biscuit returned to the kitchen. A couple of minutes later, he reappeared and put a plate full of bacon down on the table in front of the Palmers, saying, "Here you go: a bonus for a job well done."

Daniel and T.J., both beaming, showed their gratitude by eating ravenously.

Howard said, "When you're done eating, we'll walk down to the dock, and I'll introduce you to Mr. Moot. He's not very friendly to strangers. But with my introduction, he'll treat you okay." The young men continued grinning and eating while Howard added, "Moot handles the freight, and I know he can always use some extra hands. I expect a few hours of work to earn your way across Lake Ontario."

Daniel managed to swallow and quickly squeezed in a response, "Thanks, Mr. Griggs—it's awfully kind of you to help us out." The platter that held the bacon was soon clean, and the loaf of bread fully consumed. T.J. and Daniel cleared their table and brought the dishes to the kitchen, where George gestured toward a large sink with an adjacent hand pump.

They made short work of the cleanup and returned to George with outstretched hands to express their appreciation. "Thank you, Mr. Biscuit. I'm so glad we found you," said T.J.

Daniel added, "Me too. I'd hoped we'd find folks like you along our way."

George shook their respective hands and said, "I don't think you fellas will need it, but let me wish you luck anyway."

Howard piped up, "We'd better be going now. I still have eight hooves to trim and shoe this afternoon before the light gets low."

When they arrived at the warehouse by the dock, a man was already loading a large wood-hulled freighter. It looked like there was a lot left to do. He was loading large burlap sacks, and it seemed like there must be a couple hundred more of them stacked up near the gangplank. Having recently earned their lunch moving flour, T.J. and Daniel gave each other a knowing nod. They could also see large stacks of milled lumber and many uncovered bushel baskets of oats. Daniel wondered, *Can they really ship those oats without some sort of protection?*

The man slowed his pace, continuing to work while Howard introduced them. "Mr. Moot, these fellas are Dan and T.J. Palmer.

They're brothers from up by Lake Scugog. We just came over from the bakery, where they helped George unload a wagon full of flour. They're strong, trustworthy, hard-working lads wanting to work their way across the lake."

Not looking any of them in the eye, he offered his hand to Daniel. "I'm Jon Moot, manager of Great Lakes Freighter."

Happy to break the ice and relieve the awkwardness, Daniel answered, "I'm Dan Palmer, and this is my brother, T.J. We're from just outside of Port Perry, right below the lake. Now we're making our way to the Iowa territory."

Still shyly looking down at the ground, Jon said, "She's due to shove off in two hours. I'll give you passage if you help Bob get 'er loaded in time." Mr. Moot pointed at a man rolling drums of metallic-looking rock.

T.J. asked no one in particular, "What is that?"

Howard chimed up, "That's iron ore."

In his most business-like voice, Jon instructed, "You boys stick close to Bob, and he'll show you where and how to stack and stow and how to keep the dry bulk separated." Mr. Moot's face softened as he unclenched his teeth and added, "Then if you stay on the other end to help unload, 'n load her back up, there'll be supper and an extra half-dollar for each of you."

Daniel answered eagerly, "We'll do it." He tugged at T.J.'s sleeve, nearly dragging him over to where Bob was now busily lifting wooden crates full of anonymous merchandise.

Wages earned in St. Catherines reloading the freighter for the trip back across Lake Ontario were sufficient to buy some food and incidentals to continue the journey. Wishing to have a few more coins in their pockets, they stayed working and sleeping in the warehouse at St. Catherines for two more days. Finally, at daybreak on the third morning, they set out on foot and reached Niagara Falls by midday.

T.J. stood near the great precipice, mesmerized. Looking straight out over the edge, he was spellbound by the heady scents, sound, and height to which the great mist rose. Then, catching his breath, he said, "Brother, we *must* stay here a while!"

Daniel, also taken by the spectacle, responded, "Well, let's find out what's going on. Maybe we can find some work here."

They found a lead in no time at all. Before the words came out of Daniel's mouth, T.J. was smugly pointing at a help wanted bill on a fencepost near the overlook. The poster read: Two days' work, this week only. Inquire at The Niagara Café. Then, in small print below appeared: Harry Leslie, "The American Blondin."

"All right then, let's find the café," Daniel said.

Many people were milling around. Some were tourists taking in the marvelous spectacle. Others were there distributing leaflets for various commercial ventures seeking the opportunity to provide goods and services to Niagara's many visitors. T.J. approached a teenage boy handing out flyers, accepted one from him, and asked, "Say fella, can you tell me where the Niagara Café is?"

The boy responded, "Oh, it's just up the rise." Then, pointing up the hill, he continued, "Follow that road a short while. You won't miss it 'cause it's the busiest place in the village."

T.J. thanked him, and they lingered a couple more minutes taking in the view. Then Daniel said, "Okay," placing his hand on T.J.'s shoulder. "Let's go find this job."

They walked up the gravel path the teenager had generously called a road, and soon, several frame structures came into view. The third one in the row of five buildings was the largest, with a prominent wooden sign above the door. Painted in bright green over a black background was the name, "The Niagara Café."

The pair entered, sat down, and were soon greeted by a middle-aged woman wearing a red-and-white checkered apron. "Good afternoon. What can I get you gentlemen?"

T.J. gave a dumbfounded second look when he noticed her apron was identical in color and print to the thin table cloths and the sheer curtains hanging over each window in the front and back wall of the building.

Noticing T.J. was preoccupied to the point of distraction, looking from apron to table, then to curtains and back again, Daniel took the lead. "We'd like two coffees. And could you tell us how to find Mr. Leslie? His sign indicates he is the American Blondin."

"Oh, that," she chuckled. Not wanting to seem rude, she quickly explained, "We get our share of daredevils here."

Without thinking, T.J. asked, "What's a daredevil? Is it some kind of mythical thing?"

"Oh no, it's no myth. They're real people doin' real dumb things," she retorted. "My name's Marjorie John. I've been running this establishment for sixteen years now, and I've seen my share of 'em."

"My name's T.J. Palmer, and this is my brother Daniel. I've just never heard that term before," T.J. added.

She offered a good-mannered, "Pleased to meet you," followed quickly with, "Well, just think of it this way, they're people who dare the devil, often at the risk of their own lives." Marjorie turned toward the kitchen as she added, "I'll get your coffees."

A few moments later, Marjorie returned with a round tray holding two cups of steaming hot coffee. Daniel was a little taken aback to see how dark the beverages looked, but he was pleased by the rich aroma. Marjorie placed their coffees on the table and said, "If you stop back for supper today, you're bound to meet Mr. Leslie. He's been in the village for a few days now and has had morning and evening meals here."

"What can you tell us about him, ma'am?" Daniel asked.

"It's quite simple," she answered, then paused to look straight into his eyes. "He wants to walk across the falls on a tightrope."

Daniel tried to hide the look of shock spreading across his face while T.J. came right out with his reaction, "My Lord!" His jaw dropped. "I've seen the falls. That's impossible!"

"No, it's not impossible at all. It's been done a dozen times by the Great Blondin. He crossed the Niagara Gorge right over the Whirlpool Rapids," Marjorie confidently retorted.

Daniel jumped in, asking, "So why is he going to do it again?"

Marjorie answered, "Oh, no. He's not doing it again. He's retired from the daredevil business and gone back to Europe. Last year, I read an article in the *Niagara Observer* which says he's now a successful actor."

"I'm sorry, but I don't understand," said T.J. "If he's working as an actor in Europe, how is he eating two meals a day here?"

"No, he's not here anymore at all. You asked me about the American Blondin! You see, Harry Leslie is what I guess you could call an upstart. He's comparing himself to the famous French daredevil." Marjorie's eyes flashed between the two brothers to assess whether they were following. Then, she raised her eyebrows, explaining, "The first person, and up till now, the only one who's done it and lived to tell about it, is Jean Francois Gravelot, the Great Blondin.

"Everyone around here remembers him. He was born in France, where he became known as the Boy Wonder." She pointed to a photo on the wall behind them, where a framed print hung above a small sign that read *Chevalier Blondin*. Marjorie explained, "That picture was taken during his craziest walk—the day he carried his manager on his back!"

Daniel blinked in disbelief, seeing the man was indeed walking a tightrope above the rushing waters while carrying another man. The pair would have looked ridiculous enough even if the man riding piggyback hadn't been wearing a stovepipe hat.

"So then Mr. Leslie plans to be the next Blondin?" T.J. asked.

"That's right," she responded.

Daniel, who now seemed to be grasping the whole thing, said, "I imagine our job would be as crew members to work on preparations and support for his walk across."

Marjorie, remembering her other customers, offered, "Enjoy your coffee. I'll see you in a couple hours."

The two finished their coffee and returned to the falls for a relaxing afternoon, viewing the falls and napping in the meadow. At suppertime, they returned to the café to meet Mr. Leslie. Marjorie saw them immediately when they entered and waved them over to the already seated Harry Leslie. "Mr. Leslie, let me introduce these two brothers, Dan and T.J. They were here earlier to respond to your handbill," she said.

"Wonderful," Mr. Leslie answered and hastened to add, "We've got the crew pretty well filled out now. The walk is Saturday, but we could still use a couple more hands for odds and ends that may come up. So all that's left is that one day's work, but you're welcome to it."

T.J. blurted out, "We'll take it."

Mr. Leslie said, "Very good. We'll all meet here for breakfast on Saturday at 7 a.m."

With a few coins still in their pockets, Daniel and T.J. were able to stay overnight at the village inn. The Palmers learned the plan on Saturday morning as Mr. Leslie reviewed the details over breakfast at the café. There were two teams, each consisting of three men and a crew leader assigned to respective sides of the falls. One of the brothers would serve as assistant to each crew leader. The other crew members seemed to have a thorough grasp of what needed to be done.

It would take about half of the day to position pulleys and hardware to rig the event's tightrope. As soon as everyone was on site, work commenced and progressed steadily, and the walk began at midday. Mr. Leslie advanced with his left foot, slightly bowing the eleven-hundred-foot rope as he lowered his weight onto it. His long balancing pole bent much more than the thick rope. The arching lumber wobbled ferociously as Harry Leslie's hands gripped for dear life before taking his second step. Throngs of onlookers shrieked, expecting the American daredevil to plummet 150 feet into the gorge after taking his first step. As Daniel gasped along with them, he felt the misty breeze tickle his nose and a shiver go up and down his spine. Yet neither the thundering water roaring like an angry summer tempest nor the sporadic gusts of air dogging his pole seemed to beset the determined man, whose steps continued unfazed. Fifteen minutes later, he was greeted by cheers, applause, and lots of back-patting on the other side.

As it turned out, the Palmers' roles were merely precautionary. Everything went as planned, and their only actual work was limited to serving as observers and keeping spectators away from the attachment points. Once it was safely over, the Palmer boys followed instructions from the regular crew members, who seemed to know how to retrieve and stow the gear.

T.J.'s team was on the US side and he planned to meet Daniel, whose team was on the Canadian side after the walk. From there they would continue their journey. Before leaving, T.J. asked his crew leader, "What'll you be doing now since the walk over Niagara's over?"

The man responded enthusiastically. "Next Mr. Leslie's gonna do gymnastics hangin' from a balloon high over Central Park in New York City. I'm goin' with 'im. I'll be spreadin' the word 'round the city. Ain't an event without spectators! Then I'll put a crew together."

"Well, my brother and I will be leaving for Iowa now. I hope the stunt in New York City is safe and successful for you and Mr. Leslie," T.J. said, tipping his hat, and starting down the path to meet Daniel.

Daniel's crew had already finished and dispersed by the time T.J. arrived back on the Canadian side of the walk. Daniel and T.J., each with an extra fifty cents in their pockets, started for Buffalo, New York, more than twenty miles south of the falls. They walked for the rest of the day, finally reaching Fort Erie, Canada, just across the Niagara River from the city of Buffalo. It was already dark, and they were hungry when Daniel said, "This should be a safe place to set up our tent and get some rest."

T.J. answered, "Okay. The backpack's got two parsnips, some salt, dried beef, and a hunk of bread. I'll hike down to the river and draw some water for a soup. Why don't you gather up a fire?"

"Good. I'll get started," Daniel answered. "You know this trip had me worried, but so far, it has been one of the most interesting experiences we could have asked for."

They cooked a meal over the fire, set up camp, and stayed overnight, getting well rested and ready to board the 8:00 a.m. ferry leaving for Buffalo, their first stop in the United States.

The brothers boarded the ferry, enjoyed the short ride across the Niagara, and landed in the city. Leaning on the wood railing, Daniel said, "Li'l brother, I don't think we should spend more than about a week in Buffalo. We need to keep our eye on the goal, and New York isn't it."

"I know you're right about that. We'll find some work—just enough to fund our travel out west," T.J. responded.

Because Buffalo was a center of grain mills, commercial shipping, and steelworks, they were confident it would be relatively easy to find work there. But they weren't fully prepared for life in a big city. With more than ninety-four thousand people, Buffalo felt like another world to the two country boys. They had never before experienced so much hustle and bustle.

Disembarking from the ferry, they began down Ferry Street. Passing shipyards and several saloons, they continued walking many blocks, turned south on Richmond Avenue, and followed it into what appeared to be the downtown center of activity.

They soon came upon a small storefront restaurant. A simple sign painted on the glass picture window read: Mame's Tearoom. Daniel said, "Let's spread out and look for opportunities. We can meet back here at noon for lunch."

"Okay. Good hunting!" replied T.J.

Looking southward, Daniel could see a small park at the next intersection. He pointed toward it. "I'll go that way."

T.J. turned toward the east and said, "See you for lunch."

T.J. spoke with the first person he encountered. Coming upon a man who appeared to be distributing a large stack of newspapers in the center of downtown, he said, "Hello, my name is T.J. Palmer. I'm from across the border."

"My name's Turnquist, Sonny Turnquist. Welcome to the US! What brings you over?" the friendly man asked.

"My brother and I are on our way out west to Iowa, and we're staying over here looking for some work to fund our trip," T.J. said.

"So many young men have gone into the army ..." he paused, then added, "or Canada." Mr. Turnquist rolled his eyes at the idea of an able-bodied man making such a seemingly unpatriotic choice. "I've been shorthanded for the past two years. I could sure use another distribution and delivery man," said Sonny.

T.J.'s response was packed with enthusiasm. "I can start today, right now!" Then, tempering his gusto, he added, "But it would only be temporary because we'll be moving on in about a week."

"I understand." Sonny smiled, pondered briefly, and continued, "You seem to be a decent man, so let's give it a try. You can start first thing in the morning. Just report to *The Courier* office on Ferry Street and ask for me. The news business starts early, so be sure you are there by five o'clock."

It was precisely twelve noon when Daniel arrived at Mame's Tearoom to find T.J. already seated at a table. Seeing him sitting there, the older brother chuckled, "Well, li'l brother, you've either found work, and you're keeping a straight face, or you haven't, and you're so hungry, you just couldn't go any farther."

"I got a job, the first one I tried for!" T.J. responded. Daniel reached for his brother's hand. Taking and shaking his hand enthusiastically, T.J. said, "I begin first thing in the morning."

"That's great news. What will you be doing?" Daniel asked.

"I'm not exactly sure, but Mr. Turnquist, who hired me, said something about delivery and distribution. Oh, and it's for a newspaper," T.J. clarified.

"I didn't get anything yet," said Daniel. "But I feel good about my prospects. I talked with a store owner who desperately needs help. He wasn't so sure about taking on someone who'd be short-term. But he told me to come by later this afternoon. Said he'd talk with his wife about it. I'll go over after lunch and see what develops. Meanwhile, why don't you check around to see where there's a good place for us to set up our tent tonight?"

The lunch menu was the same for all guests. Mame served corned beef, eggs, bread, pickles, and coffee, plus a choice of pie or crullers—all for eighteen cents. The food was delicious and relatively inexpensive, so they decided to meet back at Mame's for supper at six o'clock that evening.

T.J. walked all around the downtown for the first two hours and then back in the direction of the ferry terminal. He looked around the waterfront for likely campsites. Seeing what seemed to be the usual busy harbor activity and too many saloons, he decided it wasn't the most wholesome area for pitching their tent.

T.J. enjoyed the afternoon as he blissfully explored the city and witnessed many interesting activities. Every block offered its distinctive hubbub. He finally strolled back toward the central district and Mame's, their de facto headquarters.

Arriving back in front of Mame's Tearoom, T.J. heard another commotion. At first, he couldn't tell what the unusual sounds were. Looking up and down the street, T.J. scanned the second-story windows, not knowing what he was expecting to find. Then he turned his glance to the south, at the little park Daniel had pointed out earlier that morning. Many people were gathering around the wooden pavilion near the garden spot's center.

Discordant sounds were coming from musical instruments, suggesting they were just tuning up and readying themselves. It was only a few blocks away, so T.J. decided to check it out. By the time he arrived, the band had started to play. More people were gathering there, forming a small crowd. Their first number was a rousing rendition of "Glory Hallelujah," then the more sedate "Bonnie Jennie Lee," followed by "Aura Lea" and a succession of other popular standards.

It was a perfect way for T.J. to relax as he enjoyed the music and waited for his meeting with Daniel at six. Time quickly went as he watched the people, spoke with a few, and listened to the ensemble. It was so delightful, it occurred to him this park would be an ideal place for them to spend the night.

Daniel and T.J. met inside Mame's at the appointed time. "Good news! I've been hired too," the senior brother exclaimed.

"Well, I guess we've both had a good day," answered T.J.

"Yes, Mr. Tork, the store owner, said business has been brisk, and he just hasn't been able to get any restocking and cleaning done. So I guess that's what I'll spend tomorrow doing," said Daniel, who hastened to ask, "Did you have any luck finding a campsite?"

T.J. answered, "There's a great spot just down the street. It's that beautiful little park you discovered this morning. It's even got a well, so we can draw water and wash up right there."

"That's great," said his brother. "Let's get a bite and plan for an early night since we'll need plenty of rest for a full day tomorrow."

"That's right," responded T.J. "Mr. Turnquist wants me on the job by five in the morning."

Supper at Mame's Tearoom was just as big and tasty as lunch had been. First, the two enjoyed a hot plate of potatoes, sausage, corn, and kraut; then, after finishing with generous slices of apple pie, they were so full, they felt like they might burst. After consuming every bit of the large meal, Daniel said, "Let's go for a walk. I want to make sure I can still move!"

Leaving Mame's, Daniel noticed a copy of *The Courier* abandoned on a bench right in front of the café. He picked it up and shook it to remove any unseen debris before unfolding the front page. He flipped through as they walked along, offering T.J. an occasional snippet of interest. "It says here the *Courier* has been Buffalo's official voice since 1849. Now war news is the big story. And the bottom right quarter of the front page is a section called "From the hundred and fifty-fifth."

"Oh yeah, after I left Mr. Turnquist, I walked for a while and spoke with two ladies on the sidewalk who had a table taking donations to send packages from home to soldiers in the hundred and fifty-fifth," said T.J. adding, "They're called *Commissary in a Box*. I gave 'em a penny. The packages have nuts, candied ginger, molasses pulls, and cherry stain glass candy for sore throats. It looks like broken pieces of stained glass, and they let me taste a small piece. It's really good!"

"It sounds like you've been doing some digging," answered Daniel.

T.J. eagerly responded, "Well, Buffalo's the hometown of the hundred and fifty-fifth New York Volunteer Infantry. They're mostly Irish immigrants from around here. Behind the ladies' table they had a hundred and fifty-fifth battle flag. It's green with a harp and shamrocks. Amanda, the pretty younger woman there, held it out so I could see the other side with the seals of New York and the United States on it. She said her older brother was with them at Petersburg for ten months, and he came back with a bullet hole in his hand last week, but the siege was still going on."

Daniel interjected, "Yes, it says here sixty percent of the hundred and fifty-fifth are now listed as casualties."

T.J. continued, "Amanda's cousin, Clara, is the eldest. She said many people in Buffalo start every day searching *The Courier* and hoping not to see the name of their friend or relative in the hundred and fifty-fifth printed there."

They strolled around the downtown and, about half an hour later, turned toward the park. By the time they arrived, it was cleaned up and nearly empty. The last two musicians finished packing up their instruments as the Palmer brothers set up their tent. When everything was staked down, they turned out their bedrolls. Daniel looked around and said, "It looks like we have the whole place to ourselves."

T.J. answered, "This place sure got quiet in a hurry, but it's just what we need." Then, darkness settled unequivocally over the grounds, and the two turned in for the night.

T.J. arrived at *The Courier* early, but it wasn't long before Mr. Turnquist appeared with a wagonload of papers with the distinctive smell of barely-dry ink. It was still dark when Sonny Turnquist said, "Good morning, young man." Then, getting right down to business before T.J. could even return the greeting, he added, "Your first responsibility will be to unload the papers into the front room."

"Got it," T.J. said.

Sonny headed into the office, where he lit a kerosene lamp.

After dropping off the last stack of papers, T.J. walked out to the wagon. He checked to see if he had missed anything when Sonny appeared behind him, holding a canvas sack filled with newspapers and a map.

Sonny placed the strap of the sack over T.J.'s shoulder to begin his on-the-job training. It took less than a minute. T.J.'s assignment was to distribute the news. First, Mr. Turnquist circled five distinct areas on the map of the city, saying, "There's enough in here to cover your first zone. Every check-marked address gets one. Make sure you stay within your zones and plan your route carefully so you don't carry more than you need for each zone."

It wasn't yet sunrise, and the gaslights shed insufficient light to read a map. Beyond that, T.J. had no idea what volume the next zone might require. Nevertheless, he would not allow temporary inconveniences to dampen his enthusiasm. Eagerly accepting his task, T.J. said, "Every one of these papers will end up in the hands of the people of Buffalo."

T.J. began to walk his route before most city residents opened their eyes. The early start of the work day seemed to heighten T.J.'s sense that the work was both meaningful and important. By the end of the day, he had fallen in love with journalism. He noticed people responded well, seeming to be genuinely pleased to see him—at least most of them did. The exception was a particularly heart-rending encounter with a young woman who appeared to be about his age. She trembled as she handed him a penny and then swiftly began to scan the lower right-hand section of the front page. There was plenty of emotion in her eyes while the rest of her face was nearly blank. T.J. realized the content of that newsprint might impact the direction of her life from this day forward. She soon breathed a quiet sigh of relief as she folded the paper, smiled, and walked on.

At 6:30 a.m., Daniel reported for work in the dry goods store and was also quickly set onto his first task. After exchanging perfunctory good mornings, Mr. Tork, the store's owner, said, "The place needs a thorough cleaning. See what you can do," as he handed Daniel a broom. Then, pointing to a closed door, he said, "There's plenty of cleaning supplies in that closet. Just let me know if you need anything else. Meanwhile, I'll be getting the store open."

Daniel spent the whole day sweeping and scrubbing floors, washing windows, dusting dry goods, and stocking shelves. Mr. Tork was happy to have found a strong, sober young man who was willing to work.

There wasn't a lot of conversation, but he found Daniel affable when they spoke. He also liked Daniel's inherent sense of responsibility, noting Daniel immediately returned to his task without requiring reminders whenever asked to reach something down for a customer or carry a package out for them. Mr. Tork complimented Daniel at the end of the first day with an extra ten cents. "Daniel, if you work this hard every day, I hope you'll decide to stay here in Buffalo. You have a job here with me as long as you want it."

"I certainly appreciate it, Mr. Tork," said Daniel.

As the young man left, Mr. Tork handed him a small brown waxed paper package. "Here's some licorice if you get hungry in your tent tonight."

They met back at Mame's Teahouse in the late afternoon. Having worked hard and long that first day, both were tired and especially ready for a restful meal. Mame soon delivered water and coffee to the young men and asked which dessert they wanted, cherry cobbler or blackberry pie. Customers didn't struggle over their selection of menu items. Other than dessert, there were no choices. At Mame's, everyone received the same main course and trimmings. All options depended upon Mame's mood, availability of ingredients, and the amount of time at her disposal.

Mame returned to the kitchen. The brothers leaned back on their chairs and avidly shared stories of their day's experience. Then, after another substantial meal, including blackberry pie for Daniel and cherry for his brother, they leisurely sipped their coffee, visited with Mame's other customers, and shared a few jokes. Finally, Daniel rose and put his arm around T.J.'s shoulder, saying tongue-in-cheek, "Let's get on home and turn in."

The pair thanked Mame. "You put out another wonderful meal," said T.J.

Daniel joined in. "See you bright and early for breakfast!"

The woman of few words replied, "You boys be careful."

Exiting the restaurant, they decided to walk off their supper for a while. They ambled for several blocks, enjoying the waning late afternoon, and then turned toward the park. The Palmer brothers were pleasantly surprised to see the gazebo surrounded by onlookers enjoying another gathering for music and song. It was gratifying to have entertainment brought right to their doorstep. Afterward, they set up their tent and bedrolls, stretched out, and collapsed for a refreshing night's sleep.

On the northeast shore of Lake Erie, the two brothers planned to earn enough money to gain passage on board a west-bound ship. Two weeks in Buffalo passed quickly during which they ate many meals at Mame's Teahouse, worked long hours, listened to evening bandstand concerts, and saved every penny possible to complete the journey to Iowa. Then, opportunity knocked unexpectedly.

The *Empire*, a palatial eleven-hundred-ton steamer moored at Buffalo, was scheduled to leave for Detroit at 1:00 p.m. It was 8:30 a.m., and Daniel was sweeping the floor when the ship's captain came in to buy tobacco and pipe cleaners. It was Daniel's second Friday morning in the shop, and he was thinking about how much longer it might take for him and his brother to amass enough money for the next leg of their travel. Mr. Tork greeted Captain P.J. Munch warmly with a familiarity that revealed a particular friendship. "Well, how's the Old Salt?"

"I've seen better days," the irascible captain responded. "I hope we can get the *Empire* off today. Those three idiotic Haward brothers got drunk last night and didn't show up to stow the cargo. The last time this happened, we arrived in Detroit half a day late and lost a lot of paying traffic!"

"You need to quit hiring boozers," said Mr. Tork.

The captain didn't seem to appreciate the terse advice. "Yeah, well, they don't wear signs on their chest when they apply." He slapped a pouch of tobacco down on the counter in front of Mr. Tork. "I'll take this pouch and some cleaners."

Daniel waited for Captain Munch to leave the store and followed him out on the wooden sidewalk. "Excuse me, Captain." The man, who had already stepped down off the sidewalk, and was about to cross the street, stopped and turned to face Daniel, who continued, "I couldn't help but overhear your conversation with Mr. Tork. My brother and I are on our way to Iowa, and a ride to Detroit would get us a big part of the way west. We're strong and willing to work for passage."

The Captain answered without hesitation, "If you're there and ready to work in half an hour, you'll have found your way to Detroit."

Daniel ran inside, thanked Mr. Tork, and blurted out, "Captain Munch is offering passage to Detroit if T.J. and I are there in half an hour. It's short notice, so don't worry about paying me for today." The store owner barely had a chance to say his farewells to Daniel who bolted out the door. Daniel ran at full tilt over to the corner of Main and Park to grab T.J., who was dispensing newspapers there.

"Brother, we've got passage on the *Empire*, but we've got to be there to work in thirty minutes!" the out of breath Daniel barked.

T.J. grabbed his bag, ran back to *The Courier* office, and turned in his canvas sack to Mr. Turnquist. "Sir, my brother's found an opportunity for us to gain passage to Detroit. However, if we're to make the ship, I must leave immediately!"

His employer said, "You've done well, and I'll miss you," and handed him a prorated fifty cents due for his work.

T.J. gratefully shook his hand and said, "I'm going to be a newsman. I'll write to you!" as he ran out of the office.

"See that you do. You'll be a credit to the profession!" answered Sonny.

They squeezed out enough time to swing by the little restaurant to say goodbye to Mame. She gave each of them a motherly hug, from which they quickly broke and ran full speed up the block toward the docks with their jackets and backpacks flapping in the breeze.

Approaching the waterfront, they could hear music. The *Empire* was the grandest of the several ships coming into view. The two-hundred-and-sixty-foot long craft had a glistening white wooden hull with elegant railings trimmed in brass. The sharply shaped ship stood apart from the other lake steamboats' usual rounded and squared contours. Her colors were flying as smoke lightly floated through her tall, ornately fluted stacks. The Palmer brothers ran toward her two broad ramps, which they would soon learn were called stages, that connected her with the large wooden platform where people and cargo congregated. Amongst the assemblage were three musicians playing cheerful tunes on stringed instruments. Near each musician were prominently situated cases into which appreciative passersby tossed coins. The brothers also noticed another man standing on the ship's bow, playing his fiddle for the enjoyment of passengers already on board.

The two young men raced across the stage, positioned closest to chaotic piles of cargo. Amongst the heaps were many familiar-looking stacks that looked like the flour sacks they had loaded for George Biscuit at the bakery in Whitby. T.J.'s fast glance reminded him of some seriously sweat-producing work, but he couldn't tell if the sacks were full of grain or something else entirely. Once they were on board near the top of the stage, a man with papers on a small clipboard stepped up, blocking their way. He didn't speak immediately, preferring to allow his intimidating appearance to speak for him.

The young men's haste and their obvious lack of familiarity with the language and mores of the river seemed to feed the man's disagreeable side. Daniel spoke up in his most pleasant voice, "Good morning, sir. You appear to be in charge."

Then, impatiently interrupting to avoid further banal pronouncements, the man pointed to his right. "Passengers embark on that stage, but you two look more like a couple of deadheads."

Straining to sound respectful, Daniel extended his hand. "My name is Daniel Palmer, and this is my brother, T.J."

The unimpressed man in authority neither accepted Daniel's hand nor responded in any other way.

Hoping to get on with the journey and having neither need nor desire for confrontation, Daniel allowed the man his meanness and continued as though he hadn't noticed the hostility, "We're here to work our way to Detroit. Captain Munch told us to be here by nine."

Hearing his superior's name changed everything immediately. "Oh, well, nobody told me anything." The man's voice and demeanor instantly retreated from obnoxious to somewhat helpful.

An authoritative voice came from a doorway leading to the ship's interior as a man stepped out toward the three of them. "You've got to stop hiring idiotic boozers onto my crew." He was dressed in an impressively decorated uniform with gold fringe on the shoulders and gold trim around the pockets of his long waistcoat. His brass buttons sparkled, sending off blasts of concentrated sunlight that hurt whenever the sharp, blinding glints of light hit the eye.

When he drew closer, Daniel recognized Captain P.J. Munch, transformed. He also noted for the first time that Captain Munch was a very tall man. *I wonder why I didn't notice how tall he is?* Thinking back to that moment on the street, Daniel remembered that his own five-foot, five-inch frame was up on the wooden sidewalk, poised nearly a foot above the street. Consequently, they were positioned eye to eye.

Daniel now found himself extending his neck to look up at the captain. "Johnny," Captain Munch added sternly, "if the Haward boys ever show up again, give them what they're due and get rid of them toot sweet!" Then, unambiguously vexed, the captain warned, "If this happens again, I'll be replacing you too."

Captain Munch turned his serious look toward the Palmers, softened it, and said, "Glad you boys made it. We've got little time and lots of cargo to load. Johnny here will show you what to do." He turned on his heels and strode down the deck as one on a mission.

Johnny opened the door Captain Munch had recently come through and shouted something unintelligible to the interior. Moments later, two other men stepped out onto the deck. Johnny introduced them by pointing. "Steven, Bobby, this is T.J. and Daniel. We five will have to do the work of six. You Palmer boys stick close to Steven and Bobby. They'll show you where things go and how to get it all secured down. Everything gets loaded as quickly as possible." With that, the conversation ended, and sleeves were rolled up.

Curiously, no one saw anything more of Johnny again until all the work was done. Then, finally, T.J. mentioned it to Steven. "Say, whatever happened to Johnny? I haven't seen him since we started."

Laughing, Steven poked Bobby in the ribs. "Yeah, Johnny's like a blister. He's the annoying thing that seems to show up after all the work is done."

The work was hard, and they had to move fast, but the ship was ready to depart on time at 1:00 p.m. The Palmer brothers were happily aboard, about to continue moving toward their destination.

The *Empire* eased away from the docks, and four tired men watched from her stern as the city of Buffalo shrank into the distance. Leaning against the aft wall, wet and sticky with sweat, Steven, Bobby, and the two Palmer brothers had all wilted onto the deck where they sat with knees bent, enjoying the cross breeze.

Soon the elusive Johnny reappeared. "You men did well, and we're on schedule. There's hot soup in the galley. You've earned your fill."

Peculiarity aside, it was gratifying to receive praise from someone like Johnny, who didn't often give it out. The four ate and then returned to the same spot on the stern for more rest and to settle in for a peaceful, scenic cruise to Detroit.

Night was falling when Johnny returned to the aft deck where the four young men were still stretched out. He placed a large paper bag with bread, apples, meat, and carrots on the deck. Then this more genial Johnny said, "There's plenty to eat here. It'll get too cool to stay out here all night. You fellas can find empty bunks in the aft section of the texas." They didn't see any more of Johnny after that. The group enjoyed their evening meal out on the deck, nattered about this and that. They joked, mostly at Johnny's expense, then headed inside for the night.

On Saturday before sunrise, an immaculately turned-out Captain Munch began his customary crack-of-dawn walk. It served as both a constitutional and an opportunity to inspect the entire boat. He finished by stepping into the texas, where the young men were just beginning to stir. "There's room at my table for breakfast," he announced to the four of them.

"We'd be honored." Daniel, the only one who was already on his feet, quickly accepted on behalf of the group.

"Very good, please join me in thirty minutes," the captain said and closed the door behind him.

"He sure has a flair for formality," Daniel said to the room. The captain's stiff manner didn't seem to faze Bobby or Steven, but it felt odd to the Palmers, who raised eyebrows at each other before shrugging it off.

Food and service at the captain's table were first-rate, and to the Palmer brothers, Saturday morning at Captain Munch's table was an extraordinary occasion. A couple of weeks back, the two Canadian frontiersmen had had only two dollars to their name, and now they were dining like royalty. Coffee was served first from a silver carafe, and along with it came a matching silver platter carrying an assortment of pastries. The captain reached for a cherry tart and looked over at Bobby. "How long have you been working for the Troy Line?"

"Me and Steven started together six months ago. Before that, we were in Elmira working in the kitchen for the army," answered Bobby.

"You mean the prison camp?" asked the captain.

"Yes, there are lots of jobs available, what with this war going on, but most of them involve enlistment. We learned there's a lot of work to do around the prisoner of war camps, and since we preferred not to get our heads blown off or come home on crutches, it just seemed like a really good idea at the time," said Bobby. His cheerful expression faded, showing a hint of melancholy. "It's such a sad situation. Those boys may have chosen the wrong side, but they suffer just like ours when they encounter a minié ball."

Steven added, "When men are wounded, they become easy targets for disease. There's so much sickness in those camps. We got out before we became a part of it."

The captain responded, "Well, it's all horrible, and I'm thankful it's almost over, save that this country will take a long time to heal once it ends." His somber face turned toward T.J. as he asked, "So what's your story?"

"My big brother," he gestured toward Daniel, "and I are Canadians. We're here because of the war, too, but in the opposite way. There're so many men from the States, it's flooded Canada's job market. So work has become hard to find. I even lost my job to one of 'em."

"What do you mean? Are there that many men from here going up there?" the now wide-eyed captain asked.

"Oh, that's for certain, and the reason is easy to understand. People are free to come and go, and in Canada, we're not putting them on a bloody battlefield," answered T.J.

The captain was silent for a few seconds, apparently processing T.J.'s response. Then his eyes took on a much different kind of expression. T.J. wasn't sure if it was anger or simple annoyance, but it was surely one of displeasure. Captain Munch's response sounded more rhetorical than one for which he expected an answer. "So cowards are welcome in the land to our north."

Daniel, sensing a serious disagreement was brewing, stepped in. "I've worked alongside several of those men who have come from the south to the area around Toronto. Cowardice may afflict some, but not the ones I've met. I've come to believe standing by one's convictions is not for the faint of heart; on the contrary, it requires courage of a different sort."

Captain Munch looked at Daniel, sizing him up. The young man's muscular frame wasn't tall, especially compared to the captain's, but it was solid. His face, full of wiry hair, gave the appearance of a person more experienced than he was, and the no-nonsense expression on Daniel's face confirmed his sincerity. "Well, I've not walked or talked with any of them, so I'll take what you say until I see otherwise with my own eyes," answered Captain Munch.

After that, the conversation moved to other more mundane subjects and the superb cuisine before them. That elegant meal at the captain's table would remain a highlight of the Palmer brothers' trip.

The lake was smooth, and the *Empire* pulled into Detroit Saturday evening on schedule. Captain Munch stood at the top of the stage, ceremoniously thanking his disembarking passengers. The Palmer brothers waited until all the fare-paying travelers had gone before stepping up to the captain. "Thank you for allowing us to take the voyage with you, sir. It was so kind of you to share your table," said T.J.

The captain nodded and shook T.J.'s hand, saying, "You earned your way."

"Sir, do you know where we might find a place to stay for the night?" asked Daniel.

"Check with them over at the Mariner's Church, corner of Woodbridge and Woodward Streets. You might be able to stay there, or if they don't have beds for you, they'll help you get into one of the nearby inns," Captain Munch suggested.

They disembarked and began to explore the busy waterfront area. An open-air rail car hitched to two large, light-brown draft horses was taking on passengers about a block away from the docks. The men approached and asked the driver about transportation to Woodbridge and Woodward. "It's five cents each, and I'll put you within three blocks of the Mariner's Church," answered the man. So they paid the fare and boarded.

Detroit had the feel of a city where everything seemed to look large and new.

"How many people live here?" T.J. asked the driver.

"We've got 'bout fifty thousand in Detroit," an enthusiastic teenage boy sitting opposite T.J. answered proudly before the driver had a chance to think about an answer. After that, the boy, who identified himself as Timmy, pointed out every noteworthy building, statue, and intersection.

Nearly twenty minutes and several stops later, the car turned north and stopped. The driver pointed toward the waterfront and a road with rows of illuminated gaslights. "That's Woodbridge," he said, still pointing. "You turn right at the corner, and it's a stone's throw from there. Good luck to you."

Daniel wondered why the gaslights would remain ignited during daylight hours. *They must either be careless, or it's a very wealthy city.* He mulled it over but didn't say anything that might provoke more elucidation from the unsolicited little tour guide. Timmy remained on the rail car when the Palmer brothers exited. Neither said anything directly, but they both rolled their eyes, indicating their relief to be off the tour.

A short walk brought them to a large stone structure. Standing on the sidewalk before the Mariner's Church, T.J. said, "It doesn't look much like a house of worship." The front was divided into retail spaces, looking much like the rest of the busy downtown, except the massive second story had bays of large, gothic-style windows, vertically reaching toward the sky. The building's four corners were defined top to bottom by large octagonal buttresses that rose above the roofline, approximating the height of its central peaked gable. Overall, it was a commanding display of architecture.

There was no lock on the front door, so they entered, T.J. calling out, "Hello? Hello?" Silence greeted them.

A short while later, a man dressed in a black shirt with a white collar appeared. "Greetings, gentlemen. I'm the rector. My name is A.M. Lewis."

The older brother took the lead. "Good evening, sir. I'm Daniel Palmer, and this is my brother, T.J. We just worked our way over from Buffalo on the steamboat *Empire*. We're Canadians headed to Iowa to reunite with our family. Captain P.J. Munch said we might find lodging for the night here."

The clergyman's face expanded with a knowing smile. "Well, the Mariner's Church is neither a boarding house nor an inn, but we have had to put up a few people in crisis from time to time. Captain Munch probably remembers a particular night when he brought rescued shipwreck victims here. We already had several other guests who had come in with a woman named Moses to stay the night. What a whopper of a busy night that was." Noticing disappointment on the men's faces, he added, "Don't worry, I think we can get you a room and a clean bed next door at Mrs. Clinton's house. Let's take you over." Stepping between Daniel and T.J., he put his arms over the shoulders of each of the men and gently nudged them toward the door.

Mr. Lewis knocked on the door and began the introductions. "Mrs. Clinton, let me introduce Daniel and T.J. Palmer from Canada. Captain Munch sent them. Boys, this is Mrs. Iola Clinton."

Mrs. Clinton opened the door wide to welcome them in. Although it was late for a meal, she found some bread and root vegetables for them to eat before calling it a night. They stayed the next day and a second night at Mrs. Clinton's, learning about life in a growing city and the church founded to honor and serve mariners. Mr. Lewis took meals there with them, and he turned out to be an entertaining storyteller. When Monday morning arrived, the Palmer brothers were ready to settle up and continue the journey to Iowa. "Mrs. Clinton, how much do we owe for our keep this weekend?" Daniel asked.

She smiled at Mr. Lewis before turning back toward Daniel to answer. "It's our treat, young man. Save your coins. You still have a long trip ahead of you."

Enthusiastically T.J. said, "Thank you. We'll not forget your generosity, Mrs. Clinton." He hastened to add, "And you too, Mr. Lewis."

"Yes, thank you both!" said Daniel.

They hugged Mrs. Clinton and shook hands with Mr. Lewis, and were soon on their way.

The remaining money from their work in Buffalo and on Lake Erie was barely sufficient to secure railway passage on a west-bound train to Chicago. They arrived three and a half weeks after leaving home on the Canadian frontier. They marveled at the busy city where the downtown streets were full of what appeared to be endless throngs of people.

The first order of business was to raise funds for the remaining leg of the trek. Their experiences in Buffalo paid off as T.J. quickly found work distributing for a newspaper, and Daniel had no trouble finding a dry goods store that could benefit from an extra pair of hands. They worked for a few days for their respective employers and stayed in a boarding house central to their jobs. Unfortunately, neither of them was earning much, and staying in the city of Chicago was expensive. Their wages barely covered the lodging and meals, so it was beginning to look like it might be impossible, or at least take a long time, to get ahead.

On Thursday morning, good fortune struck while the young men were walking to work. On the opposite side of the broad street, they noticed a group of uniformed soldiers lining up outside the train depot. T.J. nudged his brother. "I wonder where they're going?"

"I was wondering the same thing," Daniel answered. "Why don't we find out?" The pair stepped across the street to where the soldiers were assembling in an orderly line. The elder brother addressed the soldier at the end of the line. "Would you be so kind as to tell me who's in charge?"

The teenage soldier pointed at another young-looking man. "You want to speak with Colonel Nash."

Daniel and T.J. went to the front of the line to address the impeccably dressed soldier. Daniel stepped before the colonel and respectfully offered his hand. "We're the Palmer brothers. "I'm Daniel, and this is my brother, T.J. We're from Ontario, Canada, and our family now lives in Iowa." The colonel's face was curious as he sorted out the inconsistency. Daniel explained further, "My brother and I haven't seen them for many years. They're in an Iowa coal town called What Cheer, and it's long past time for us all to get reunited." Waiting for Daniel to get to the point, the colonel nodded politely. "The town isn't officially called What Cheer. On the map, it's called Petersburg, but they're getting ready to change it. We arrived in this city last weekend, and we're both working to raise the fare, but the cost of living here consumes just about all we earn."

Colonel Nash took in Daniel's explanation and responded, "Gentlemen, this is a railroad depot, not a recruiting station. You know the tide has turned, and we may not be taking many more men anyway."

T.J. didn't like how the conversation was going and, reading indifference on the officer's face, decided it was his turn to speak up. "Sir, we're new to your country, and as a leader, you know what's what. So we're simply wondering whether you know how a pair in our situation, without means, can get farther west." The colonel said nothing as he began flipping through a stack of official-looking papers. His demeanor was both serious and managerial, to the extent that it carried a hint of intimidation. It left the Canadian brothers unsure whether they should quietly stand and wait or politely move on.

T.J. was nervously beginning to wonder whether they had violated some law forbidding people to interrupt soldiers engaged in official duties. *Should I just thank the colonel and apologize for taking up his time?*

But their story had somehow struck a chord with the battle-weary officer. He studied his long list of names, another sheet of paper below it and another one underneath. Finally, the colonel spoke, "One thing I've seen far too much of is families divided. In two days I'll have another transport leaving here for the west. It's nearing the end of the war, and I can allow the two of you to ride along in my troop carrier car bound for Rock Island. Be here at six o'clock in the morning Saturday, and we'll take you along."

Saturday morning came, and the brothers arrived at five o'clock, hoping Colonel Nash would remember them and his promise to help. The officer, already inside the depot, saw them first and greeted them courteously. "I see you boys made it. Wait here until my men are all out on the platform. For now, just stay out of their way. After they're all on board and accounted for, I'll wave you on." The next forty-five minutes were nerve-wracking. Daniel and T.J. watched the arriving soldiers report to another soldier who appeared to check off their names.

The steady flow of soldiers trickled down, and when it finally ceased, Colonel Nash waved them out to the platform. The last couple of soldiers were already climbing into the car by then, and the colonel said, "Okay, now you fellas can get on. We'll get you to Rock Island, and then Iowa is just across the river from there." The soldiers nearly filled the car, but the Palmer brothers were happy to find two empty seats. One was near the front of the coach and one close to the center.

The train ride was reasonably comfortable and relaxing. The trip from Chicago to Rock Island included several stops crossing the state of Illinois, and it took much of the day. It was a unique way to travel, not only being on a train in the States but the atmosphere of riding in a car full of soldiers. Daniel listened with interest when the younger, inexperienced boys spoke about the glorious adventures of war, while the eyes of those who had already experienced combat told an entirely different story. Their lips revealed much more by mainly remaining quiet. He feared for those younger men and what would happen when their innocence was lost in battle.

Thinking about those young soldiers a little more than a month later, Daniel would picture their naïve faces and ponder their fate. In an unexpected encounter with the US military, he and T.J. found themselves scrambling to find a way to pay a sizeable toll. Even though the Palmer brothers were Canadians, they were not exempted from the military draft. However, if it came down to it, they could opt out of military service by paying the tariff. Under federal law, conscription into an otherwise required tour of military service could be passed on to another individual for a commutation fee of $300. Those funds would subsequently go to the substitute as a bonus for enlisting.

Chapter Six

IOWA AT LAST

"A journey of a thousand miles begins with a single step."
−Lao Tzu

In less than two months, Daniel and T.J. had left the Canadian prairie with what they could carry on foot and two dollars to their name. They crossed Lake Ontario to St. Catherines and entered the US at Buffalo. From there, they had found their way to Detroit and then Chicago, finally arriving on the banks of the Mississippi River at Rock Island, Illinois. They had made their way on foot, by carriage, water, and rail, and were now so close to Iowa, they could see it across the river from the depot. But getting across was another matter. The Chicago and Rock Island Railroad ended on the Illinois side. The first bridge ever built to span the great river joined Rock Island, Illinois, with Davenport, Iowa. Westbound routes operated by the Mississippi and Missouri Railroad began on the Iowa side of the river. The bridge, only about seven years old, was still simmering with lawsuits relating to conflicts between riverboat interests and railroads. Foment had been triggered when the *Effie Acton*, a steamboat, collided with one of the piers of the two-week-old bridge. The ship caught fire, and the flames spread.

Both the steamer and the span of the bridge adjacent to the opened draw were consumed.

Weighty commerce issues were at stake as the drama had unfolded even before the bridge's construction began. The spectacle involved several larger-than-life players, including Confederacy President Jefferson Davis, serving under President Franklin Pierce as Secretary of War. Davis vehemently opposed the completion of the bridge, while Abraham Lincoln gained much public attention as the attorney advocating for the railroads.

The lawsuits found their way to the US Supreme Court, including allegations of deliberate sabotage regarding the steamboat accident, the struggle for economic clout leading up to the Civil War, and the rights of railroads to build bridges across navigable waterways. Lincoln's case included a topographical survey of the river made by Robert E. Lee. The railroads and the future president ultimately prevailed, setting a historic legal precedent with far-reaching implications.

Inside the Rock Island Depot, Colonel Nash was directing the soldiers to secure their gear and prepare to fall in. Daniel approached him and offered thanks. "Your assistance made a huge difference to T.J. and me."

"Will you be moving on to Iowa now?" the Colonel asked.

"Yes," T.J. standing beside his brother, responded first. "Do you know the best way to get across to the Iowa side?"

"There's a ferry every hour," he answered. "Nowadays, you can't just take a train across into Davenport because the bridge goes over the island."

T.J.'s puzzled expression begged for clarification, which Colonel Nash provided. "The river divides right above here at the foot of the rapids, leaving a large island in the middle. Fort Armstrong was built on the island right after the War of 1812. We've got a prison camp there for captured Confederates, so things are kept secure. A man can't buy fare from here just to cross, because they only sell tickets to go farther west toward Iowa City and Council Bluffs."

The Colonel watched T.J.'s face to see if he followed the explanation. When T.J. nodded his understanding, the officer said, "But you can take the ferry. It's about a fifteen-minute walk from here to its dock. Just go west, down this road to Eleventh Street."

Daniel took the colonel's hand, repeating his thanks, and the military man stiffly offered his best wishes. "You men have a pleasant reunion with your family. That'll be thanks enough for me."

So full of gratitude he couldn't help himself, T.J. placed a brief, but decidedly masculine hug, not too close, and up around the colonel's shoulders.

Colonel Nash, touched by this unexpected show of humanity, had no words fitting the experience, so he just patted T.J. on the back amiably and said, "Good luck to you both." Then he cleared his throat and added, "You better make tracks because that ferry doesn't run very late in the day."

They took off running and made it to the ferry just minutes before the day's last run. Twenty minutes later, they stepped off the boat onto the Davenport waterfront.

The state of Iowa was a mere teenager, having been admitted into the Union eighteen years before. Daniel and T.J. were still more than a hundred miles east of What Cheer, the busy coal town where the Palmer family had located, and their funds were nearly depleted. They spent their remaining coins for sustenance in a small general store about two blocks northwest of the levee.

Following their now regular pattern, Daniel asked the store owner, Mr. F.T. Burkett, if he knew where he and T.J. might find work. "My brother and I have been traveling from Canada to meet our family in What Cheer." He hastened to add, "It's been a couple of months now, and the last of our money just went into your cash drawer."

Mr. Burkett was originally from England, and his British-sounding accent seemed out of place in the western frontier setting. "Did you say 'watch here' or 'what's there'?" Mr. Burkett spoke slowly to exaggerate his pronunciations of the words, his accent sounding quite aristocratic.

T.J. clarified, "Our family lives in a small town way out west, beyond Iowa City. It's called 'What,'" he enunciated slowly and clearly with extra emphasis on the "t," followed by "Cheer," with emphasis on the "ch."

"I've never heard of it," the store owner responded.

Opening a creased map he pulled from his now worn canvas travel bag, Daniel stepped forward. "I can show you." He started by pointing at Davenport, then slowly slid his finger left, over to Muscatine and even further to the west, stopping it at Iowa City. He then dragged his finger further to the south and west of Iowa City to a much smaller circle labeled Petersburg. Someone had drawn a line through the name Petersburg and handwritten in "What Cheer" in its place.

Mr. Burkett said, "Oh, there've been miners through here saying they were coming from or going to Petersburg. I guess it's a real hot spot for digging coal." Then he asked, "So why are you calling it What Cheer?"

"It's written in on the map because the town's people changed the name. But it's not official yet. In her letter, our mother explained it all. The people voted, but the postal service hasn't cooperated yet. So now they call their town by its actual new name, but they have to address their mail by the old name."

"That's interesting," said the storekeeper. "It reminds me of a phrase I haven't heard for years now. Back across the Atlantic, the Scots will say 'what cheer' as a greeting like one might say 'hello' or 'good morning.'" Then, Mr. Burkett returned to the original question. "Now, on the matter of work, has either of you ever done anything around a store like this? It wouldn't be long-term, but I could use a strong back for some projects, and the outside needs paint."

Daniel was quick to describe his resume, emphasizing the bakery, his work for Mr. Tork in Buffalo, and their experiences as dock workers for the *Empire*.

"All right then, as long as the two of you show up on time, give an honest day's work, and realize it's not permanent, you can start Monday morning."

Almost before the last words got out of Mr. Burkett's mouth, T.J. answered, "That will be great!"

That night the two camped near the waterfront. Their conversation was hopeful, musing about what might happen next. "I like Mr. Burkett," T.J. said.

Daniel responded with a smile, "I think you like everyone." He placed particular emphasis on the word *everyone.*

"There're so many unhappy people," T.J. answered. "I don't need to be one of them unless circumstances force me to be."

"I hope you'll never have to be," his big brother said.

"I wonder how long we'll be in Davenport," T.J. said. "This place has a nice feel to it. I mean, it doesn't have all the constant busy energy like Chicago, but there's something special about this little city on the river."

"I don't know about that, but we two industrious men will need to work here and now, or we're not going anywhere," Daniel said with a smirk on his face. So they talked it through, leaving the conclusion open. But, for the time being, they agreed work might be easier to find nearer to the fabled great river anyway.

Sunday was relatively quiet around the levee. They made coffee over a small campfire and stretched out on the grass to sip the beverage and take in more of the sights, sounds, and scents of the Mississippi River. The feathered fauna were the loudest and most active birds they had ever seen, especially in the early morning at sunrise. Some were walking at the water's edge, foraging for whatever they might find to eat, while most were swooping, squawking, and plunging into the water after food.

Soon an old black man wearing a worn felt hat arrived. He carried a bamboo pole in one hand and a three-legged stool in the other. Claiming a spot at the edge of the nearby wharf, he soon swung the rod to drag his line through the rapidly moving water.

Daniel called out, "Hope you're lucky!"

Contemplating, then responding, he said, "I suppose if I were really lucky, I'd be home eatin' 'stead of fishin' for breakfast." Then he broke out into contagiously warm laughter, soon adding, "No, you're right. I'm lucky to have two arms, two legs, and this pole to fish with!" Again he chuckled and asked, "You boys had anythin' to eat yet?"

Daniel answered, "We just arrived here yesterday, but we found work, so we'll be earning our way to a good meal first thing tomorrow morning."

"Well, I'll make ya a deal. I see ya got a fire goin', so if you'll cook the first catch, I'll be happy to share it wit y'all."

"You've got a deal, sir," Daniel answered quickly.

T.J. chimed in, "I'm T.J., and this is my brother, Daniel. We're the Palmers."

The elderly gentleman responded, "I'm Smoke. Now folks're always askin' me why, and the answer's I don't know. People been callin' me that since I learned to walk. Momma say it was 'cause my sister said I floated from one thing to another. One time I axed my daddy—" He was interrupted by a pull on the line. It seemed like only a minute since he had set his stool down. Smoke carefully worked the pole, and soon he pulled the biggest catfish they had ever seen from the water.

T.J. said, "That fish can easily feed all three of us. I'll go gather up some more wood."

Smoke continued to fish, catching two smaller catfish while the Palmer boys prepared the large one. They enjoyed breakfast together while the Palmers learned some local folklore from the jovial man. Finally, Smoke picked up his stool and the pole with two fish tied to it and said, "Well, it's been a good fishin' mornin'. An' I've got lunch and dinner too. Maybe I'll see ya around," he said as he walked off.

T.J. and Daniel cleaned up the campsite and left for a walk to get better acquainted with the town. They walked all around the inner city, whose rows of buildings were mainly two- and three-story connected stone structures with storefronts on the ground floor and layers of offices and apartments above. To exhibit merchandise, many of the shop fronts had bay windows with awnings, and the newest ones featured larger glass display windows supported by cast-iron frames.

The downtown was bordered on the south by the river, with streets neatly laid out in a gridwork pattern extending several blocks. Then the downtown abruptly gave way to a steep hill, which replaced the business district with a pleasant tree-lined residential neighborhood as it rolled north. The Palmer brothers walked on up the bluff, exploring the community. The houses were mostly two-story wood-frame structures, and the farther up they walked, the larger and more opulent the homes seemed to become. Some of the most luxurious homes were three-story, had gaslighted sidewalks, were set back farther from the street, were surrounded by many trees, and featured lush, manicured lawns. Davenport revealed itself to be most affluent at the top of the hill.

Altogether they walked about twenty-five blocks north of the downtown, observing a prosperous community. Turning one block east and continuing north on Main Street, they arrived at an expansive park with a painted overhead sign labeled Scott County Fairgrounds. The park featured a large bandstand and several large wooden buildings. There wasn't much going on, just a few children running and playing. T.J. said, "It seems as though this park is on the city's edge."

"You seem to be right about that," his brother answered. "It's nearly noon. Let's turn back toward the downtown and river area."

The pair began the downhill leg along Harrison Street, and soon they encountered Mr. Burkett and his well-dressed family out for a walk. Mrs. Burkett was walking on her husband's right, and his hand rested lightly in the crook of her left elbow. As they neared Daniel and T.J., the store owner aimed his left hand toward them, saying, "Dear, these are the Palmer boys." When they reached the young men, he said, "I'm happy we ran into the two of you." Then gesturing toward his family, he said, "This is my wife Lana and our children, Mark and Sissy."

In unison, the two boys answered, "Pleased to meet you, Mrs. Burkett."

Lana let out a little chuckle at their inadvertently synchronized greeting. "Francis has already told me about you. It seems like you have traveled far and hard. Why don't you join us for dinner? We live just up the block."

They gratefully accepted the invitation and the group turned uphill with the Burketts leading the way. It was an auspicious invitation, especially considering Daniel and T.J. were utterly out of money. Although they had been fortunate to share breakfast with Smoke, there wasn't anything to eat for the rest of that day.

Sunday dinner at the Burkett home turned out to be an unexpected feast. The food was abundant and well-prepared. The two brothers were treated like family, especially by Mark and Sissy, who peppered them with questions about Canada, traveling to the US, and their adventure at Niagara Falls. Later that afternoon, they left their employer's home satisfied and grateful.

The Palmers began work early the following day, assigned to various projects, including window repair, stocking shelves, and painting the whole exterior of the store. The latter project took most of their first week.

Knowing these men were living hand to mouth, Mr. Burkett paid them by the day, enabling the two brothers to immediately move into a boarding house. It was just a short walk from Burkett's General Store. In the evenings, they explored, learning their way around the rapidly growing little town on the big river.

They were preparing to finish the day's work on Friday evening when Mr. Burkett reminded them the store was open on Saturday. "We're getting pretty well caught up on the deferred tasks which have been on my to-do list for a long time. I appreciate the hard work you boys have been doing all week." His eyes scanned the room, taking in the numerous projects they had tackled already. "Now, let me remind you we took this on as a short-term arrangement for the store and me. It has exceeded my expectations, and if this were a larger business, I'd consider keeping you on permanently."

Daniel spoke up, sensing Mr. Burkett was feeling awkward about the uncomfortable truth. "Don't worry, Mr. Burkett, we understand, and you have been great. You gave us a chance to get on our feet when we needed a start, and we'll always appreciate that."

Mr. Burkett said, "Tomorrow, we'll get the basement and storage room cleaned up and reorganized."

"Will you need both of us tomorrow?" T.J. asked.

"It will be busy here. Saturday always is, what with farmers coming to town to bring in produce, sell grain, and pick up supplies and things they need for their households. So yes, I'd like to have you both here all day tomorrow." Mr. Burkett continued, "I've been thinking about how much help you've been, and what I'd like to do is keep one of you part-time, let's say half-time, only in the mornings all week starting on Monday."

"That seems fair enough," said Daniel.

T.J. chimed in, "How about this? We both look for something more long-term, and whichever one finds a job first doesn't come in on Monday, but the other one does."

"You sound very confident, T.J.," said Mr. Burkett.

Smiling a knowing smile, T.J. answered, "We didn't get this far by being unsure of ourselves."

Daniel interjected to temper his brother's lack of humility, "Well, let's not overlook serendipity, nor do we want to tempt our good fortune!"

The good-natured F.T. Burkett noticed a last-minute customer walking up to the front door and quickly concluded the discussion. "Oh, Lana said she wants you to join us for dinner on Sunday. She and the kids enjoyed your visit at home last weekend."

Daniel said, "We'd love to," while the brothers gave each other a joyful smile.

On Sunday morning, T.J went by the newspaper office to inquire about a work opportunity there. Despite what T.J. thought was vast experience in the field, not everyone was similarly impressed. While waiting to speak to someone in the small reception area for what seemed like an eternity, T.J. noticed a sign on the bulletin board near the door, so he took a closer look. It was a recruiting notice from the school district whose bold text across the top said: Schoolmasters Needed. The smaller text below continued: Muscatine County Schools is seeking qualified teachers for the upcoming season in Montpelier and Fairport. For more information, contact Mr. Frank Forest at the Davenport Daily Gazette.

T.J. contemplated the eligibility criteria for "qualified" teachers. Wondering what that meant exactly, he thought about his and Daniel's education and decided they were surely qualified.

The Palmer brothers had been rigorously tutored back in Canada before and after the family relocated. T.J. was six years old when he had joined Daniel in his studies with the harsh taskmaster, Mr. John Black. Tutoring was strictly organized, and their work was severely evaluated. When their family moved, the tutoring schedule was modified so Daniel could work in the nearby stave and match factory.

When they were younger, most of their lessons took place at home. After the family left for Iowa, Mr. Black required the boys to walk the two miles over rolling hills to his own home. T.J. didn't like taking lessons there because Mr. Black seemed to be especially mean in the comfort of his own home. The course materials included the classics, Latin, Greek, mathematics, philosophy, and natural sciences. Their teacher's weighty expectations and their diligent study paid off. It soon became apparent, as the Palmer brothers interacted with other boys their age, that they were receiving a superior education.

T.J. turned from reading the handbill at the doorway back toward the counter of *The Gazette* office. Finally, a tall man wearing an apron and a weary expression appeared behind the counter and icily asked, "Yes?"

T.J. began, "My name's T.J. Palmer, I've worked in the newspaper business before, and I'm wondering—"

The man behind the counter interrupted, revealing his irksome tone. "We're not hiring," he said, then added a disingenuous, "but best of luck to you." The tall man didn't invite any further conversation. Instead, he turned and stepped to the desk opposite the counter and bent to make some notes.

When he looked up again, he was annoyed to notice T.J. wasn't leaving. Instead, the young man appeared to be scrutinizing the bulletin board on the wall by the door. T.J. returned to the counter, where the man was now wearing a defensive look.

T.J. politely said, "I'd like to speak with Mr. Frank Forest."

"I told you, we're not hir—" the man began.

T.J. interrupted, "I understand the *Gazette* is not seeking help. However, I wish to speak with Mr. Forest on an entirely different matter."

The man holding authority over the front counter tipped his head and looked suspiciously over the top of his glasses at T.J., pondered fleetingly, then decided he didn't really care either way. "I'll ask him if he can see you." The man looked sternly at T.J., saying nothing at first, and then after an uncomfortable moment, impatiently asked, "Don't you think you ought to give me your name?"

"Oh, tell him Professor T.J. Palmer is here," T.J. reflexively shot back.

The man shook his head in denial and uttered "Humph" as he looked T.J. up and down, then turned toward the closed door of the inner office. He gave a short, quick double knock and gently turned the knob. "Excuse me, Mr. Forest, there's a *Professor* ..." he drew out a derisive emphasis of the word before completing the phrase, "... Palmer here to see you."

T.J.'s face turned beet red as he listened to the contemptuous clerk and silently chided himself for using the unearned title. He had been caught! Frantically analyzing his own words, T.J. was faced with the guilt of having hastily told a lie. He tried justifying it. *Well, it only happened because of the clerk's scornful attitude. But it was still a lie, intentional or not. It was just something that slipped out without thinking. I guess I better think more in the future.*

The ashamed, regretful young man had already turned toward the front door when he heard a cheerful voice. "Sir, I'm Frank Forest. Ricky says you're a teacher."

Relieved he wasn't going to be grilled about his impetuous claim of lofty academic achievements, T.J. was quick to answer with complete honesty. "Actually, I've never even worked as a teacher." The confession brought a sense of relief to T.J., but it did nothing for Mr. Forest as the room took on an eerie silence. T.J. awkwardly spoke again. "But I'm sure I could do it well. My brother and I have years of study in mathematics, writing, history, and Latin, and we've read many classics."

Frank studied T.J.'s eyes before responding warily, "You'll need to demonstrate reading, arithmetic, and writing proficiency."

T.J. answered immediately. "Gladly! Do I take the test now, or do you need time to get it ready?"

"We're already late to fill the Montpelier position. So, I'll have it ready for you after lunch tomorrow," answered Mr. Forest. "There are nine families there with eighteen students waiting for a teacher, so if you perform well on the test, we'll put you to work immediately."

"Where's Montpelier anyway?" asked T.J.

"It's a nice little village right on the river, about halfway to Muscatine," Mr. Forest answered. "There's not much money, but you'll get paid. Room and board come with it too. You'll have to see to cleaning the schoolhouse, hauling water and firewood. Maintaining the building is your responsibility, but there's usually some help from the families." He stopped to take a breath and added, "The parents will expect to see you attend church regularly."

"I'll be here tomorrow, and I look forward to meeting the people in Montpelier," said T.J., reaching to shake Mr. Forest's hand. As Frank grasped his hand, T.J. seized the opportunity to add, "My brother Daniel has a great mind, and he is the most methodical person I've ever known. I'm sure he would be a great teacher. Is it all right if he takes the test too?"

"We also need to fill the schoolmaster position in Fairport, another little village along the river on the way to Muscatine," Frank began agreeably. "Bring him along with you. If he passes the test, I'm sure our friends there would be happy to have a qualified man."

That afternoon at dinner, they informed the Burkett family. While passing the mashed potatoes, T.J. directed his comments toward the head of the table. "I spoke with Mr. Forest at the *Daily Gazette* this morning. He serves on the school system, and there is a great need for schoolmasters in the counties of Scott and Muscatine. He is going to give us both a teacher's test tomorrow. I hope you won't be disappointed if we get hired."

Lana giggled in response. "We wouldn't be decent friends if we didn't want the best for you. No one should be thought ill of for wanting to better themselves."

Her husband quickly added, "Lana's right. The two of you have helped immensely, and we appreciate that. We got into this thing thinking it was temporary, so perhaps you have found something."

Daniel interjected, "Well, we haven't passed the test yet. So I may be crawling back to you, seeking part-time work."

Lana was quick to quell the idea. "There's no doubt the Palmer brothers will pass. It's only been four years since I was a student in the Muscatine County Schools. I started at the one in town, near the button factory. Then, after we moved, I finished school at the Wapsinonoc Township School out in the country. I had four different teachers, and I believe they were all trying their best, but I can tell you they did not have your depth, Daniel. You will pass their test easily," she declared. She reflected momentarily and added, "I remember the quirky Mr. Vanater, a nice man who taught in the Muscatine School. He was a bit too proud that his uncle, Colonel Vanater, had originally laid out the town and named it Bloomington. I'll never know why it was such a big deal to Mr. Vanater when the town's name was changed. They changed it a year or two before I was in his class because our mail would often go to Bloomington, Indiana. I suppose people found sending their mail on an extra trip a few hundred miles east before coming to them just wasn't preferable." She raised her arms, palms up, shrugging her shoulder for emphasis. "The name Muscatine did not please him at all, especially when he found out the county name would change along with the city name. He said the name didn't sound fitting for a significant city, and not only that, he argued there were no other cities in the whole world named Muscatine, which to my way of thinking, made the change advocates' point for them!"

Everyone at the table gave their rapt attention to the normally reserved Lana. Feeling all those eyes focused on her, she added, "I think it was a good idea because the Indians, who have always been treated so badly, named the island in the river after their tribal name, Mascoutin. Mr. Vanater was fussing over it more than a year later, which made me curious. So, I went to the library to look up what I could about it. I learned the word meant fiery nation, and naming the city Muscatine honored the Mascoutin." She ended her commentary with, "The schools will be much better off with the two of you in them."

Mr. Burkett raised his glass. "Here's to Iowa schools and the Palmer brothers."

Chapter Seven

SCHOOLMASTERS

"If thou hast knowledge, let others light their candle at thine."
—Thomas Fuller

The teacher's test went well, revealing Daniel and T.J. were capable of performing the basics well above the standard required to teach. Within a few days, the two were school teachers in Muscatine County. They began to teach in one-room schoolhouses a few miles from each other. Daniel was assigned to Cranston and T.J. to Montpelier.

On Saturday, after their first week as teachers, the brothers met over corn and beans in a Muscatine café. They hugged, sat down at the table, and a serious-faced Daniel spoke first. "I'm in trouble!"

T.J.'s eyebrows rose as he prepared for the worst.

With a reassuring, broad smile Daniel said, "I love it!"

"You mean teaching?" his brother asked.

"Yes, I love everything about it. Much more than I expected. I even love the children!" Daniel paused briefly before jovially adding, "Well, most of them."

T.J. blurted out, "Well me too. It's almost like I was made to do this. It makes me feel good, like when I was distributing the news.

And it's a lot easier than carrying sacks of flour or loading cargo on a ship."

Puzzled, T.J. inquired, "So why did you say you were in trouble?"

"I tossed and turned last night. How am I going to tell this to mother and father? They probably think we're going to live in What Cheer," Daniel explained.

T.J. was quick to answer, "Well, at the end of the month, we get paid, so we can buy train fare to spend a weekend with them. They've managed this long without us, so we'll just tell them about the great jobs we've got here. I think that they will be happy for us."

When they began teaching in 1865, Iowa's public school system was barely twenty-five years old and became a model for other states introducing public education. Education as a profession was a novel idea, still being debated by Iowa's politicians. Indeed, the Palmer brothers helped pioneer public education. Over several terms, Daniel took on numerous teaching assignments in Muscatine County and Louisa County. T.J. also took multiple teaching positions.

One day while Daniel was sweeping the floor after school, Jimmy Viner and his father showed up carrying a wooden box. Daniel greeted them. "Hello, Jimmy. I'm surprised to see you back so soon. What's in the box?"

"It's a movable frame hive," Jimmy blurted. "Father and I made three of them, and we just finished this one."

"Well, that's fine-looking work," the teacher answered.

Mr. Viner spoke up, "Thanks, we were just wondering ... that is ... we really only need two, and we'd be happy to sell you this one. It would cost you three dollars, but by the end of the season, the honey you would get could bring in much more."

"Well, I sure wouldn't mind supplementing our income. I have a dollar and fifty cents in my pocket, and think I can get the other half from my brother T.J. to send home with Jimmy next week if that suits you," Daniel answered.

The two huddled briefly then Mr. Viner said, "You've got a deal."

The Palmer brothers began to study the art of raising bees for honey and were soon spending weekends as amateur beekeepers.

Then, after completing his second year as a schoolmaster, T.J. left to join the family in What Cheer. Having an itch to get back into the newspaper business, he took what he could scrape together from teaching and, with a bit of help from his parents, founded the *What Cheer Patriot*. He felt like he had found himself, happy to finally put his writing skills to work publishing a frontier newspaper.

Meanwhile, teaching in a Louisa County school near Lettsville, Iowa, Daniel had fallen in love. The now seasoned teacher had taken up residence in a small house on the outskirts of the tiny town where he met a sweet young lady named Molly Hudler. The eighteen-year-old worked in the local bakery, where she kept long hours and found time to sew on the side. Daniel's first glimpse of her was at the annual Independence Day Picnic.

It was 1870, and Daniel viewed himself as a worldly creature, although he was only twenty-five years old. Lettsville's big event was exciting, and it gave him the opportunity to meet more people.

Molly had entered the lard-baking competition for the third consecutive year. Determined to make a good showing, she placed six pies in the contest.

Standing behind a long table at the far end of an open metal-roofed building, she had already cast several surreptitious glances Daniel's way. Drawn by his striking features, muscular build, and intense eyes, Molly found him to be distinctively handsome.

The table was covered by at least a dozen pies carefully arranged on a red-and-white checkered cloth. Although the building shaded the table, she stood at the far end in direct sunlight, which glistened against her long, dark hair. Everything about her was as fresh and beautiful as a spring day after a soft rain. To Daniel, she was stunning, and he would soon fall for both the apple pie and Molly, but perhaps not in that order. Daniel's thoughts were simple: *I don't know if love at first sight is possible but ... wow!*

Daniel stepped right up to her table, and smiling, she offered him her hand. "I'm Molly."

He reached across the table to introduce himself. The mere touch of her small hand withered him. Daniel was enthralled, captivated, and so love-struck, he forgot his name. "Good morning, I'm ..." He was inelegantly stuck.

Pretending not to notice, Molly removed her hand gesturing toward the pies in front of her. "Pleased to meet you. These four apples with lattice crust are mine, and so are the two over there with the crumb topping."

Finding some confidence, he answered, "I'm ready to give 'em a try. Oh, my name is Daniel Palmer," he added to smooth out his earlier sputtering.

Smiling at his awkwardness, she answered, "I'm Mary Hudler. My friends just call me Molly."

"I'm pleased to make your acquaintance, Molly," said Daniel.

Now beaming with pride, Molly said, "Last year, I won second prize in the pie baking contest. This year, I'm after the blue ribbon!"

Daniel, spurred on by her enthusiasm, smiled and consciously donned his most robust look of anticipation while gesturing toward one of the crumb-topping pies.

Molly put her hands up, signaling it was out of her control. "I can't cut into anything until the judges do and have finished their deliberations. There will be plenty to go around then," she reassured him.

With his interest in pie having been raised to a fever pitch, Daniel spent the next two hours occupied with anything and everything that could and would keep him within eyeshot of the table full of pies.

While he anxiously waited for the judges to complete their deliberations, Dan positioned himself near the bandstand, wishing the minimally talented group might soon take a break. He was a bit indifferent to music anyway, but loud brass rubbed him the wrong way. Short on repertoire, the ensemble was playing its fourth rendition of "Aura Lea" when, just to make small talk, he spoke to another pie-coveting gentleman. "I don't think I can stand to hear that tune again."

The band began "Beautiful River" for the third time as if on cue. The fellow answered sardonically, "Just to show things can get worse!"

Daniel wondered why the other man was hanging by so close. However, he soon dismissed it, assigning the label *pie lover* to the man.

Finally, the judges had assigned all their colored ribbons. Then, an announcement came from the doorway of the metal-roofed building through a megaphone. "This year's blue ribbon for Best Pie goes to Lettsville's own Lulu Johnson. Pies are now available for purchase." The band answered the proclamation with a faster, louder *oompah*, hastening Daniel's movement away from them and toward the building.

He was first in line and noticed a red ribbon on one of Molly's pies with the crumb topping. "It looks like congratulations are in order!" he said enthusiastically.

Molly's gracious thanks was followed by, "Not the color I wanted." She broke into a big smile. "But I'll take it!"

He picked a plate off the stack and gestured toward one with the crumb topping. Taking his cue, she loaded a large slice on his plate. When Daniel eagerly sampled Molly's apple pie with crumb topping, he knew he was in love.

Over the next two weeks, the shy school teacher tried in every possible way to create chance encounters with Molly. He didn't speak much because he couldn't think of anything to say in her presence. He could hardly think of anything but Molly all the rest of the time. The tongue-tied suitor became a frequenter of the bakery and found himself eating far more baked goods than ever before in his life. Living with T.J. out on the Canadian frontier, Daniel had rarely tasted freshly baked bread or cake in his younger days. But, consequential to his interest in Molly, thoughts of her became indelibly tied to the aroma of baking.

It had been two weeks since the Independence Day Picnic, and on a Friday evening, Daniel was sitting on the front porch thinking about baked goods and Molly. *I never knew what I was missing! The smell of fresh bread is the best fragrance I know of—except the scent of Molly's perfume.* The pleasant, clandestine thought brought a smile to his face as he anticipated a visit to the bakery bright and early on Saturday morning. It was an imprinted memory, consisting of her scent at the Independence Day Picnic, mingled with the aroma of a table full of pies. Always questioning and probing, Dan continued to think about that particular scent. He anticipated it so compulsively, he could almost bring it to life while romanticizing it on the porch.

The following day he was about to step through the bakery's front door when a question occurred to him. *Why are smells tied so vividly to memories?* As he entered the building, he continued mulling it over, *It's hard to describe—sweet, yes, certainly sweet and mild, not overpowering.* Daniel wore a big self-satisfied smile as he closed the shop door, and his eyes met hers.

Behind the counter, standing in front of shelving that ran from floor to ceiling, Molly returned his smile. "Good morning, Mr. Palmer." The shelves were filled with loaves of bread and cakes.

He returned the greeting with a strong, confident voice, "Well, good morning to you, Miss Hudler."

He had finally worked up the nerve to ask her to accompany him to the upcoming church social. There weren't any other customers in the store until he began to speak, but the door opened when he started to talk as if on cue. "Miss—" It threw off his concentration, which was already teetering on edge, and produced an awkward pause. With a stressed intonation, his words now came gawkily. Finally, he continued in a slightly quieter voice, "I really enjoy speaking with you and always look forward to my visits to the bakery."

Fighting an attack of shyness, he chided himself, *Why did I say anything about looking forward to visiting the bakery? Come on, Dan, stop acting desperate and just come out with it!* Then, gathering his wits about him and trying to pretend another customer hadn't just entered the store, he got straight to the point in his normal voice. "I'm wondering if you might like to join me on Sunday afternoon for the social at—"

Molly, beaming an appreciative, kind smile, interrupted him hoping to avert embarrassment. "Oh, Mr. Palmer, how kind of you to invite me, but Pastor Young has already asked me to accompany him."

Daniel's lips were frozen. His self-conscious mind had already died, but the merciless inner voice spoke, *Her smile could even charm an angel whilst she innocently drives a stake through the heart.*

Neither could such a maladroit moment pass without her noticing. Although she betrayed nothing but utmost propriety, Daniel sensed a connection. Pastor Young notwithstanding, he was encouraged to see her stealing a nimble perusal by looking him up and down as she spoke. It sparked something hopeful in him.

His recent efforts to show up at every opportunity surely couldn't have gone unnoticed. Even a nun would have noticed his strapping masculinity. Firm, broad shoulders atop a solid albeit stocky frame, and long, wavy black hair edged with a full beard made his wide, sturdy face look like an intellectual's if not that of some kind of seer; and his gentle yet intense personality made him stand out from the crowd.

Daniel optimistically indulged a stray musing. *I wonder what it might feel like to lie with her?* Then, recognizing how ridiculously out of place such feelings were, especially since the woman standing behind the counter wearing a flour-dusted apron had just turned him down. He admonished himself. *I'm standing before her, with another customer just a few feet away. I should be more respectful.* His swelling ardor quickly lost the battle to a sense of shame.

Molly gracefully rescued him with a timid nod. "Pardon me, Mr. Palmer," and turned to shift her attention toward the customer. "How may I help you, sir?"

She had shifted the exchange smoothly enough, but her poise only emphasized his clumsiness. Daniel just stood there mortified.

The man glanced at the two of them and shrugged his shoulders, not particularly interested in the fact that he may have interrupted something. Then, pointing at a rustic-looking round dark loaf on the shelf behind her, he said, "That loaf of dark bread, please." Coincidentally, he was the same stranger who had tolerated the band with Daniel at the Independence Day Picnic while they waited for the judging to finish. They had not exchanged names nor developed any particularly great rapport, but this was the second time the man Daniel labeled, *pie lover* would witness Daniel's gawky side.

Molly answered, "Of course, sir," while she reached for and placed the loaf on a sheet of waxed paper, which she skillfully wrapped around it as she had done so many times before in the bakery shop. Her hands worked automatically.

Meanwhile Daniel's face revealed intense disappointment, as he waited.

Handing the wrapped loaf to the customer, Molly said, "Sir, that's our large loaf, so that will be two cents."

The man swiftly glanced at Daniel and curiously winked his eye before turning back to Molly. He took the loaf with one hand and nonchalantly asked, "Ms. Hudler, have you made any plans for the church social?"

Her answer came so fast, her words arrived almost before his finished exiting his mouth. "Why, thank you, Gabriel, but I'll be accompanying Pastor Young on Sunday."

Unmoved, he reached into his pocket with his other hand, pulled out two coins and handed them over to her. "Thank you, Molly. See you next time."

"We appreciate your business." The strictly mechanical rejoinder flowed from Molly, who had successfully navigated past offers from two hopeful beaus within seconds of each other.

Gabriel had invited Molly with confidence, and he smoothly accepted her regrets, which contrasted sharply with Daniel's unease. Once the man had exited the bakery, time passed in slow motion as Daniel stood naked in his ungainliness. Entirely unprepared for rejection, he finally managed to say, "Well, perhaps some other time."

He was still standing in front of her, as if waiting to be dismissed. So Molly nipped it in the bud. "Daniel ..." She waited for him to make eye contact then continued carefully and deliberately. "I'm very flattered, and I think you are a fine gentleman. But I must tell you, Robert Young asked me to marry him two weeks ago." She paused to break eye contact. "And I accepted."

Daniel was nearly overcome. In the face of such a huge letdown, he could barely bring himself to wish her well. A wave of nausea came over him when he tried to speak, and he stuttered, "I w ... I wish the both of you every happiness." But as he turned to leave, Daniel thought, *That's a lie. I don't wish happiness for Robert Young because that means Molly will be with him.* Disappointed and angry with himself for being disingenuous, he continued his retreat as politely and rapidly as possible. Nausea did not let up, and later that night, he lay awake in bed, unable to stop thinking about her. The powerful infatuation precluded sleep. He tortured himself thinking about her, his ineptness, and how he might never fall in love again. *If only I had spoken up sooner ... if I were better looking, smarter, or if my timing was better.*

During the day, he could barely focus on teaching, and the angst-ridden pattern repeated itself and intensified every night. The lack of sleep was catching up with him, and he felt too exhausted to read or adequately plan his lessons during the days. When Daniel walked through town to go to the schoolhouse, he would intentionally pass her house. He could not keep from watching the Hudler home closely in the off-chance he might see her in the yard or on the porch. His silly fantasy was she would see him and come running. She would fall into his arms, distraught that her relationship with her betrothed had collapsed, and he would be there to console her.

It was hopeless, yet a part of him wouldn't let go. It seemed as though being unattainable made her even more desirable. Unfortunately, the situation showed no sign of improvement during the ensuing weeks. Preoccupied with her, the usually enthusiastic Daniel, with his eclectic curiosity and exuberance, was becoming downright lethargic.

Chapter Eight

"Love is patient, love is kind."
– 1 Corinthians, 13:4 (King James Bible)

Absorbed to distraction over his unrequited love for Molly, Daniel knew his situation was pathetic. He was doing nothing well except slipping into despair. Then one day in early September, he met Abba Lord, a bright, outspoken girl from Rock Island, Illinois, who had been staying with relatives in Lettsville for the summer.

It was Wednesday morning, and Daniel was on his way to the schoolhouse, deliberately taking the long way through the center of town—a futile daily ritual in which he went past Molly's residence, always watching for a glimpse of her. It yielded one consistent effect: self-torture. But this time would be different.

A wooden gazebo was the focal point of the town. Curiously situated in the center of the intersection of Chestnut and Main, to encourage commerce, it served as a small bandstand for Friday evening get-togethers and Sunday after-church entertainment. People used it as a meeting place the rest of the time, and children enjoyed it for play and horsing around.

Approaching the gazebo, Daniel heard the familiar sound of kids frolicking. However, the sound of a stern but pleasing female voice momentarily stilled the banter. "You better slow down on those steps, or you'll fall and break your little necks!" Ripe for distraction, Dan was drawn to the alluring voice like a sailor to a mermaid's song.

The children were playing a revolving game of chase. It began on the dirt road, up the four steps to the bandstand, across the pavilion, down the stairs, to the other side of the intersection, and around again. The unlikely leader of the pack was a small dappled dachshund, who was patently enjoying the merriment, yapping and running at full speed around the structure from one side to the other. His four legs gave him a decided advantage over the kids, and when running full out, the canine's ears flapped up and down like the wings of a flightless bird. The dog, anticipating the children, made quick about-faces. Always wanting to be first, the silly, long, low creature's short legs moved so fast, they became a blur. Yet somehow he always adroitly got to the bottom of the steps before the children. The only thing questionable was who would wear out first, the dog or the kids.

Lettsville was a tiny town with little traffic, and the few riders and horses going by could easily see if people were coming to or coming down from the gazebo. Yet it still seemed unnecessarily dangerous to place an attraction that would draw small children right smack dab to the busiest spot in town.

An attractive young woman, seated in the gazebo reading a book, appeared to be in charge of the youngsters, but she was paying more attention to her reading. Distracting him utterly, the eighteen-year-old woman caught every ounce of Daniel's attention.

She appeared to be overdressed for a weekday morning in the small rural community, which along with her pretty, round face, made her look out of place. Her smooth white dress seemed to flow right out of her long, curly blonde hair. Daniel, gazing at the gazebo, saw a captivating vision of beauty with a book in her lap, which left him breathless as if a dream had come to life.

Molly's recent rejection was still fresh in his mind. But Daniel, determined to repress his usual shyness around attractive young women, walked right up to the gazebo. Dishearteningly, neither the children nor Abba noticed him. He stood there inanely, not knowing how to start. Feeling foolish, a wave of embarrassing warmth flushed over his face. Then, in a near panic, he caught his breath and spoke up loud and clear, voicing the first thing that came to mind, "Quite a long dog you've got there."

Abba, a little startled, wore a puzzled expression, which grew into a protracted gaze. Beginning over the top of her book, she slowly scanned up the exceptionally masculine physique and then back down, ending on a pair of clean black leather boots. His strong-featured, manly semblance highlighted by a full beard, rounded cheekbones, and long flowing hair under a large, wide-brimmed black Stetson hat immediately appealed to her. Now, realizing the scrutiny had gone on a bit too long, she blushed. Then, looking him in the eye, she answered, "Not my dog. Not *our* dog. He just showed up when the kids started playin'."

"Are these your children?" Daniel asked.

Abba laughed an irrepressible short chortle before continuing to giggle out her response. "Do I look old enough to be this brood's mother?"

He sputtered, "Well, no, ma'am ... I mean, yes, miss ... I mean, I just wondered ...."

She rescued him. "It's okay. My name's Abba, Abba Lord. And this rambunctious bunch are my cousins. The three boys are Aunt Jane's, and the two girls are my second cousins."

Relaxing and pleased to have successfully broken the ice, he confidently offered his hand. "I'm Daniel Palmer, and ...," he gestured over his right shoulder toward the schoolhouse, "... I'm the schoolmaster here. I don't believe I've seen you around."

Abba shook her head. "No, I'm only here for a few weeks. I live in Rock Island, and my folks suggested I spend the summer weeks away from the city here with Aunt Jane and Uncle Maxwell. They run the livery stable." She gestured toward the opposite end of the tiny downtown.

Daniel's mind raced to think of something to say, but the harder he tried, the more he felt himself falling into the same old pattern. He was freezing up!

She broke the silence. "I hardly believe how quiet things are here!"

Nodding affirmatively, Daniel relaxed again, answering more naturally, "Yes, if there's anything Lettsville has a lot of, it's quiet. Nothing much ever happens, but folks around here seem to like it that way."

She smiled, holding up the book. "I guess that's why my mother thought it would be a good place for me to work on my reading."

Putting on his best consummate school teacher face—the one he tried to wear at meetings with children and their parents—he asked, "Just what are you working on?" As those words came out of his mouth, he self-consciously thought, *I really ought to check it out in a mirror some time to see what this expression looks like.*

The mental note was quickly discarded in favor of the sound of her voice. "Mom gave me this book. She said it'll help me develop my *own* values—that's her way of saying I don't have any." Abba watched his eyes for a reaction. Seeing none, she continued, "It's called *Woman in the Nineteenth Century.* Margaret Fuller wrote it before the war. You've probably never heard of it." Then, she ruefully added, "It's one of those idealistic, preachy things."

"I don't know that work," Daniel answered, "But I certainly know about Margaret Fuller. She was a member of the Transcendental Club. She rubbed shoulders with Emerson, Thoreau, and Hawthorne—all giants of New Thought. It's tragic how she, her husband, and baby all died in a shipwreck." He looked deeply into her eyes, adding a somber note. "One has to wonder what the cost to the world is when a great mind like hers is lost."

Still uninspired, Abba voiced her frustration. "I'm afraid it's all just above my head. Mother said this"—she waved the book in her left hand—"is an important book an' I should read it. And if I'd just try I'd like it. She wants me to write a letter an' tell her what I got from it." She looked up, locking onto his eyes before emphasizing her next point. "I don't think she'll be pleased when my whole letter contains but one word: *nothing*! I've read this paragraph over and over, three times now, and it makes no sense at all!"

Daniel jumped at the opportunity to help. "Why don't you read some of it to me, and maybe we can figure it out together. Sometimes reading a passage aloud makes it easier to understand."

Though she scowled at the idea of becoming one of his students, Abba found him appealing and was intrigued enough to accept his offer. As an eighteen-year-old, she'd be an unlikely candidate for his schoolroom anyway, so she began to read in a deliberately expressionless voice: "Meanwhile, not a few believe, and men themselves have expressed the opinion, that the time is come when Eurydice is to call for an Orpheus, rather than Orpheus for Eurydice; that the idea of Man, however imperfectly brought out, has been far more so than that of Woman; that she, the other half of the same thought, the other chamber of the heart of life, needs now take her turn in the full pulsation, and improvement in the daughters will best aid in the reformation of the sons of this age."

She shot an exasperated look at Daniel, who wore a neutral face while reflecting on the passage. Then, she impatiently added, "Balderdash!"

When he spoke, there were no explanations. Instead, he only came up with questions. "Did that part seem preachy to you?" he asked while searching Abba's eyes for a spark of something. Instead, he found a familiar look he had come to associate with students plowing through tedious narratives or overbearing morality.

She just shrugged her shoulders.

"Okay, let's break it down to see if we can make sense of it," Daniel said. Lowering himself onto the bench next to her, he asked, "What do you suppose the last two lines might mean?" Then, quickly realizing the question was only meeting with more frustration, he calmly added, "I think that part is fairly straightforward. I bet you know what it means."

Abba hesitated before deciding that talking with him was more interesting than trying to writhe through it in the gazebo alone. She began to play along. Defiantly rereading the last four lines aloud, she looked him square in the eye. "First of all, it means females are half of the world."

Taking that as a win, he tried to draw more out of her. "Do you mean the whole world in the material sense?"

Forgetting her exasperation entirely, she engaged the question with growing interest. "No, the whole mankind." Looking again at the final two lines, she hesitated and added, "As the female improves, she brings males along too."

Continuing to probe her thoughts, he asked, "Then, in the bigger picture, what does it imply?"

Uplifted and empowered, she replied, "It's obvious. If women don't progress, men stay stuck, and the whole human race does too. It also means that when men oppress women, they are tyrannizing themselves, even if they don't know it!"

Gratified to see her become caught up, Daniel encouraged her, "I believe Fuller would have been happy with your interpretation."

Abba countered, "What about the Greeks? Why's it gotta be so complicated?"

Again he answered with a question. "You seemed to know the characters were Greek. Have you studied Greek mythology?"

"Not really," she said, "but they sound like Greek names."

Smiling confidently, he said, "I don't know why Fuller used Greek examples, but we can figure this out." Abba's expression was blank as he continued, "I remember their names well because Mr. Black, our tutor, loved Greek stories. The story of Orpheus and Eurydice is one he selected for my brother T.J. and me because it had lots of symbolism in it."

Abba rolled her eyes. "Ancient symbolism, oh, how exciting," she added sarcastically.

Daniel, unaffected and mildly amused at her renewed resistance, said, "Let me tell you their story. Orpheus, the son of Olympian god Apollo, was a famous musician and poet who could charm animals and people with his music. There was a tragic event in which his young wife died suddenly after being bitten by a viper.

He loved her so much, he couldn't accept losing her. So he decided to find her in the underworld of the dead. He used his music to woo his way past many obstacles until he found her. The powerful charm of his music convinced Hades to allow him to bring her back to the land of the living."

Seeing her eyes fixed on his and all traces of sarcasm now absent, Daniel took the opportunity to lure out her thoughts. "Now that you know more of their story, how could that work out in the first part of the paragraph?"

Bright enough to know his intellectual shenanigans were playing her, the young woman could have easily brushed him off with a simple, *Why don't you just go back to your classroom?* But curiosity got the best of her, and she played along anyway. Pointing at the first part of the passage with her pencil, Abba said, "So, if the myth says Orpheus saved Eurydice"—she glanced up at him to gain his nod of encouragement before continuing—"then Fuller's sayin' it's time to turn the tables. It's time for women of the world to save the lost men."

She watched the large beard in front of her become very broad as his face gushed into a satisfied smile. Not wanting to be bested, she renewed her show of irritation. "Is this how ya manipulate your students?"

Now becoming unnerved, Daniel yammered, "Oh, I'm sorry, Miss Lord. I'm not trying to manipulate you. As a teacher, it's my job to bring an idea forth. You already had the understanding in your head. We were just pulling it out of you."

Abba was comfortably in control and enjoying it. Finally, she stopped him with a giggle. "It's okay, Mr. Palmer. You've just watched Eurydice call out Orpheus! I just wanted ya to think about how it might feel to be in the other chair—to be the student. Besides, it's entertaining to pull your chain and see you sputter."

They laughed together, and Daniel said the phrase *pull your chain* wasn't in his usual vernacular. But it made him think, which sobered him, he'd better check the time. He pulled the simple timepiece from his pocket by its chain, and it flipped into his hand.

Glancing at the time, he knew he must run or he was going to be late.

As one who held the students to the strictest punctuality standards, being late to ring the bell just wouldn't do. Jumping to his feet, Daniel said, "I'm so sorry, Miss Lord, but lessons begin in five minutes. I must run to the schoolhouse, or the kids will be wondering. May I perhaps see you later?" His chest swelled with pride at his ability to boldly invite her out.

Maintaining decorum, Abba coyly looked down at her hands folded in her lap and nodded her head.

"That's wonderful," Daniel sang out. "I send the children home at two. Might we meet here after that?"

He watched her face for an answer. Her eyes circled the pavilion to check on the children as she thought it over, then said, "I'll drop the kids off at Aunt Jane and Uncle Maxwell's an' come back here then."

Meeting her had brightened his whole world. He felt like jumping and kicking his heels together in mid-air. Picturing how it might look, his mind conjured up a smiling leprechaun holding its bag of gold in one hand with a bright rainbow flowing over its opposite shoulder. Fate had taken such an intense weight off his chest, he felt lighter than air. Feeling a bit foolish, Daniel turned and ran gleefully toward the schoolhouse.

If Daniel had been lovesick over Molly, then Abba was a miracle cure. Perhaps it had something to do with his need to feel loved, appreciated, and accepted, but he quickly embraced everything about her. Life was now totally involved with and about Abba. Having discarded his obsession and anguish over Molly, he'd replaced them with a fierce passion for Abba. She had splendidly filled the vacuum in his heart, and a whirlwind courtship commenced.

Abba's infatuation with him was equally intense. They each seemed to be precisely what the other wanted and needed. His wit, his rugged, masculine body, and his style ... as well as his unconventional approach to just about everything, enthralled her.

He soon asked for her hand, and they were married in less than a month. However, the proposal didn't go as expected.

It was only a week after they met. But in such a tiny village, it didn't take long before Abba's Aunt Jane and Uncle Maxwell heard Abba was seeing a young man. So, naturally, they insisted on meeting him and invited him to dinner at their house.

After dinner and a bit of pleasant conversation, Jane sent the children upstairs to get ready for bed. That also meant it was time for Jane and Maxwell to practice their music. She played piano and he the guitar. "Maxwell and I will be performing at the church this weekend, and we've hardly had time to work on our repertoire this week," Jane said. "I hope you will excuse us." Then, rising from the table, she added, "No need to rush off, Daniel. We'll just be in the next room."

Daniel rose from the table and replied, "Thank you, Aunt Jane, it was a wonderful dinner." Then he turned toward Maxwell and offered his hand. "Thank you, sir. It's so kind of your family to welcome me into your home."

"Not at all," said Maxwell, warmly receiving Daniel's hand and shrugging toward the parlor. "Now Jane and I better get busy."

The young couple left the dining room too, choosing to sit out on the porch where they were least likely to disturb the practice session.

Sitting with Abba on the porch swing, Daniel was unusually quiet. Pondering something, he rested his arm across her shoulders, and his fingers gently stroked her upper arm. They pushed with their toes against the wooden plank floor to keep the swing in motion. While they slowly swayed to and fro, his thoughts ran full speed ahead.

He was stuck, even though he had decided before leaving for dinner. It was such a big step. He continued to hesitate. *We haven't known each other very long. Is this the right time? Am I ready to ask?*

Abba could sense he was struggling, and finally, she spoke up. "Daniel, our lives are gonna change now." She gazed straight ahead, not needing to see his reaction, which she knew would be innocent, confused, and curious.

His knee-jerk response was, "What do you mean?"

Abba answered, "I know precisely what's on your mind."

Since he hardly knew himself, he laughed. "Okay, since I barely know, please tell me!"

She responded matter-of-factly, "You think you're ready to spend your life with me."

Daniel jumped to answer, "How did you know? You shouldn't be too surprised, but how did you?" He stumbled over his words, "You mean the world to me, Abba, but how could you know my thoughts?"

"I've got a gift," she responded. "It's not always there, but it's always right when it comes. Aunt Jane calls it clairvoyance, but mother says it's the devil an' I shouldn't do it."

"There's a lot I don't know, but one thing I do know is you are heavenly, and there's no devil about it!" he answered.

Abba's tone became serious. "There's times when I can tell a person what's goin' on; or why they are sick, how to get better, all that. I wouldn't understand why drinking some herb or eating a certain root I'd never even heard of before might heal them. But when a person needs something, and the answer comes to me, I just gotta tell 'em. Sometimes they're angry because they're afraid of where the insight comes from. And when they ask me that, I have to tell them I have no idea. It just comes. I dunno when these words and feelings will come or if they will, but it's always the right answer for that person when they do. Sometimes it frightens me—and others too."

He stayed quiet while it all sank in. Nor did he wish to belittle what must be a heavy burden to Abba.

Then he spoke, "This is quite a turn of events. We started with me helping you with reading comprehension and you turn out to be a great intellectual. Then falling in love with you, and now I learned you are gifted. And it seems that I'm the one whose mind is a silly open book!"

"Not silly at all!" Abba protested. "You're the man I want. You're strong, handsome, and smart; you study science; you've learned Latin and understand Greek philosophy; you speak French and English. And I'm just a simple girl from Rock Island."

He hastened to say, "You may be from Rock Island, but no one can accuse you of being simple." Then the words tumbled out of his mouth, "Abba, will you marry me?"

With tears in her eyes, she rapidly nodded an affirmation, threw her arms around him, and kissed the word "yes" into his mouth.

Their wedding was simple yet large by local standards. Most Lettsville weddings were family events held in the home of the bride or groom's parents. Often, a "bride's recognition" would be held at the church the following Sunday, formally announcing and consecrating the marriage before the congregation. However, Abba and Daniel sought simplicity, so they decided to have their wedding at the end of the month, leaving a little more than two weeks to organize.

They planned to have the wedding ceremony performed at Aunt Jane and Uncle Maxwell's home by Arnas Pranty, Justice of the Peace. Aunt Jane and Uncle Maxwell enthusiastically agreed. But then the couple began counting persons to invite, and the list quickly grew too long for a wedding at home to accommodate.

Finally, they decided to ask Pastor Young to repeat formal vows in the church on Saturday afternoon.

Daniel announced their plans to his parents in a telegram:

Mr. and Mrs. Thomas Palmer, What Cheer, Iowa.
My wedding Saturday after this.
Please tell the family it's time for a grand reunion.
D.D. Palmer, Lettsville, Iowa.

Daniel's brother T.J. was to stand up with him. So, to spend some time together, T.J. stayed at Daniel's house during the preceding week. Their parents arrived the day before the wedding, along with their younger brothers Thomas and Bart, and three sisters Lucinda,

Hanna, and Catherine. The seven began from What Cheer and took a train to Davenport followed by a Chicago, Rock Island, and Pacific Railroad connection right to the little station in Lettsville.

Abba, an only child, was presented by her parents, who arrived by rail from Rock Island only an hour before the wedding. Also with Abba were Maxwell, Jane, and their children.

The church, a small white wood-frame structure, was filled with family members, Daniel's schoolroom kids, church members, and local friends. Best of all, the Palmer family grand reunion included the addition of a new family member.

Everyone socialized after the service; shared hugs, cake, and lemonade; and sang songs. Soon everyone was lining up along the sidewalk inside the churchyard, surrounded by a white picket fence. While they all watched and waved, Daniel realized he had no idea what was supposed to happen next. So he looked at Abba for the answer.

When she saw his perplexed expression, her sweet face erupted into a great big smile. "So you're wondering what to do now, aren't you?" she asked.

Embarrassed, he sheepishly nodded and shrugged his shoulders. "I guess I didn't think this wedding through very well," he answered. "So what *do* we do now?"

Abba had been smiling for so long, her facial muscles ached, and it felt doubly good to switch to a relaxed, sultry expression. She inched forward, reached up around his big, broad shoulders, clasped her hands behind his neck, and put her lips against his left ear. "Now we're goin' to Aunt Jane's house, and you're gonna get my suitcase. It's all packed, and you're gonna carry it to *our* house." She glanced at the assemblage standing on the other side of the gate and lightly licked the firm part of his ear while pulling her body closer and closer against his. Then, with her breasts and hips pressed tightly against him, she added, "Then you're gonna …," she tortured him, grinding her hips back and forth against his swelling groin.

Daniel's face turned red as he thought about where they were and how everyone was watching. His only solace was thinking about how his beard covered most of it. On the other hand, Abba was enjoying one of her most playful moments, slyly arousing him while disguising her lustful movements behind a large, flowing bridal gown. She was sure she simply appeared to be a bride whispering in her groom's ear.

Family and friends applauded, anticipating the couple's first married kiss. Giving his ear another caress with the tip of her tongue, she continued, " ... You're gonna take every stitch of clothing off of me—and there's a lot of 'em." She whispered a sexy chuckle into his ear. "And then you'll take me to the bed." Abba stopped, thought for the briefest moment, and changed one word while raising corners of her mouth and eyebrows into a wicked smile. "*Our* bed and show me what's goin' on there." She emphasized the word *there* with an extra hard grind of her pelvis against his.

Then in a clear, strong voice, Abba spoke so all could hear. Her lips were so close to his ear, it startled him. "Now you're gonna walk me through that gate, down the street, carry me over the threshold, and show me our home." Then she pressed her lips to his, holding the kiss long enough to justify the applause. Abba was in control of everything, and everyone in the churchyard gave another ovation, cheered, threw confetti, and wished them well as the couple walked hand in hand through the gate.

Starting for Aunt Jane's house, Abba gripped Daniel's hand and swung their arms cheerfully as they walked. Arriving at Aunt Jane's, they climbed the five wooden stairs, and she pointed at the suitcase on the porch near the front door. He dutifully picked up the oversize piece of luggage, and she grasped an adjacent little duffle bag containing toiletries and personal items by its rope closure. They proceeded four blocks to Daniel's three-room house at the edge of the village. Abba had a grand jovial spring in her step, swinging the duffle bag in her right hand and his arm in her left. Meanwhile, anchored to the hulking suitcase in his left hand, he was barely keeping up.

Their house was tiny. The parents of the school children paid the low rent as a part of his teaching stipend, but to Daniel, it was his castle, a place to proudly share with his new bride. When they arrived on the front porch, he was relieved to put the heavy suitcase down. As he reached for the doorknob, she startled him again by placing both hands on his shoulders and spinning him toward her. Before he had time to think, Abba impetuously leapt incredibly high, vaulting her hips nearly as high as his shoulders. Her stomach bumped into his forehead, and her spread legs bounced off his chest as his unprepared arms urgently scrambled to catch and hold her. It took all his strength to remain upright as he stumbled backward, barely managing to regain his balance.

The day the circus had come to Muscatine flashed through his mind. "You remind me of the time I saw an acrobat fly from a high trapeze into the waiting arms of her catcher. It was frightening and amazing. The whole crowd screamed, expecting her to fall to her death. Instead, everyone breathed a sigh of relief when they saw a perfectly planned and timed catch. They were graceful and polished, but if anyone had seen what we just did—I was so surprised and clumsy, it's a wonder I'm still on my feet."

Pulling his shoulders close and again placing her lips right up to his ear, she spoke softly, "Why were you surprised? Weren't ya listenin' to what I said back at the churchyard?" She punctuated her question with the tip of her tongue, giving his ear another light lick, and his blissful smile grew larger.

He responded. "Oh, I heard one thing very clearly. Now it's time to do everything else, exactly as you said."

Still holding her, he bent his knees and managed to push the door open with his left hand. Dan carried her across the threshold, delicately lowered her petite body onto her feet, and then intensely pulled her to him for an impassioned kiss. Abba broke the embrace first, asking, "Aren't we forgetting something?" Confounded, he looked into her happy eyes as she nodded toward the open door and her luggage out on the porch. He hastily stepped out, snatched the grip with one hand, the duffle bag with the other, pivoted back into the house, and kicked the door shut. Dan dropped the luggage, turned to Abba, and stopped short. Transfixed, he looked her up and down, drinking in the beauty of the woman dressed in pure white standing before him. Finally, beginning to feel self-conscious, she encouraged him, "Well?"

He lifted her purposefully, glided to the bedroom, sat her on the bed, and hastily started for her buttons without a word. Daniel's left hand reached behind her head, pulling her close for a kiss while the other frantically worked the buttons. He quickly realized this was a two-handed chore and, while trying to hold the kiss, put both hands to work on the row of buttons, which ran from her neck down her chest.

With tight loops of fabric surrounding each button, they securely formed high friction closures, which did not easily yield to his large fingers. It seemed the faster he worked, the gawkier his hands became, and by the time he managed to unlock just five of them, he broke the kiss, took a breath, and smiled. "How many buttons does this thing have?"

Abba knew precisely how many buttons adorned the gown. Enjoying his frustration, she chuckled, "The ten you're handlin' here in front hardly gets you started because they've six mates on each sleeve—and I won't have you tearing my dress, so you better tend to every one of 'em. Aunt Jane wore this dress, and she kept it perfect, and I'll do the same. Oh, and then there're forty small buttons down the back!"

Thinking only of the reward soon to be his, Dan chortled back, "I better free you from all of this." Then tickling her upper lip with the tip of his tongue, he engaged her in another fervid kiss while diligently returning to the chore as she had ordered.

Every fabric-covered button resisted his struggle to slide the white loop over it. After finally undoing the fourteenth button, he decided he had earned some recompense. Hinting it was time for dalliance and having an object in mind, Daniel folded back the fabric from below her neckline, broke the lingering kiss, and with intense anticipation, glanced downward. He took a deep breath and softly whispered, "Oh my." Instead of the expected glistening bare skin and soft feminine features, he discovered the magnificent prize continued to elude him despite his most fervent efforts. Yet another hindrance dashed his high hopes immediately below the dress's bodice.

In a nearly comical irony, he beheld an additional row of buttons running down her chest under the dress. Like a pianist stroking a row of ivories, he rolled his fingertips up and down a dozen shiny shell buttons, and a stupefied "What's this?" escaped his lips.

"A lady doesn't go naked under her wedding gown!" Abba responded playfully. Emboldened by her friskiness and encouraged to see her chest rising and falling more rapidly now, his left hand took a detour. His hand covered her right breast through a lacey part of the lightweight cotton corset. She gasped, not in surprise but at how unfamiliar the touch of a man's hand felt there. She expected it to feel rougher than her own but hadn't thought it would be so large, warm, and fleshy—even through the lace fabric, it felt much better than she imagined. He could distinctly feel the outline of her nipple, which suddenly became much more erect as he lightly glided his hand over it. A flush of warmth ran from her chest, up her neck to the tops of her ears. She hadn't been expecting such an intense, dizzying sensation. *I'm glad to be lying down,* she thought, then decided not to try to think, *at least for the moment.*

Accepting her unpreparedness, she brought her lips to his. Continuing to gently stroke her, he explored the exciting world of her form, moving his hand to the other side of her chest while her body seemed to be doing things her mind couldn't control. Intense warmth arose from below her belly, and she felt strange involuntary sensations there, too, without any touching. Daniel was pleased to discover so little was concealed, thrilled to feel her pounding heart and rapid breathing. He also noticed his trousers were getting too tight. The two virgins, so totally immersed in their magical encounter, knew only each other. For those moments, the rest of the world no longer existed as they embarked toward an unconstrained consummation of their craving for each other.

Daniel was breathing heavily. Despite his arousal, the unexpected undergarment layers thwarted him—not to mention forty more of the world's most challenging buttons still ahead. He tried to take a shortcut by reaching under her skirt. Awkwardly fumbling with yards of slippery white fabric proved his arm was far too short to get hold of the hem of the long bridal gown. Abba, whose heart was thumping rapidly, broke the kiss and, between breaths, cooed, "Do you even know what you're doin'?"

He answered only with a silly shrug of his shoulders. Instead of making headway, he was confounded again, self-conscious and speechless. Finally, Abba decided it was time to take action, and the answer wasn't to let him just pull her skirt up—picturing how ridiculous she might look with her lower half exposed while layers of skirt and petticoat covered her face.

Amused at his tongue-tied discomfiture, she giggled and decided to take charge once again. Abba bent her right knee a bit to raise her leg just enough to press her thigh firmly against the bulge between his legs and slid her leg in a tantalizing tease from side to side. She looked deeply into his eyes and, having gained his fullest attention, shaped her mouth into a devilish grin. "Let me help." She continued to rhythmically maneuver her leg to keep his full attention while she reached for her neckline, where a delicate ribbon tied in a bow secured the undergarment. She pulled the white ribbon, easily untying it, and deftly undid the row of shell buttons in a jiffy.

Abba loved having him so under her control and, with the slyest look on her face, majestically pulled open both sides of the corset, like one raising the curtain off of a great sculpture. Continuing to unwrap, she was gratified to hear him gasp upon seeing her breasts for the first time. They kissed passionately, and he lightly explored her upper half with his hands while they enfolded and squeezed against each other with their lower halves.

Minutes passed, and the temperature rose. They were working themselves into a frenzy, and something had to give. This time

Daniel, finally resigning to the task of the forty remaining buttons, broke the kiss. "Okay, let's straighten this out!" Her eyebrows went up, wondering what he meant by that. He sat up and declared, "I love you, Abba Lord Palmer," then reassuringly took her hand and pulled her up to a sitting position.

Abba answered softly, "You're my man, Daniel Palmer, husband and life." Then with a knowing smile, she turned her back to him and pointed over her shoulder at the row of buttons. It was time for an intermission.

Their passions for each other ran high that day and every day. It seemed like an attraction that would last forever. Abba couldn't get enough of him. She ached for his body during the day and looked forward to his return every afternoon. She would often jump into his arms when he came through the door of their little house and order him to carry her directly to the bedroom. Over the first few months, Daniel frequently wondered how he would manage to keep up with her. It seemed like it would go on that way forever.

Chapter Nine

SWEET HOME

*"Only that traveling is good which reveals to me
the value of home and enables me to enjoy it better."*
–HENRY DAVID THOREAU

The train lurched while traversing a sharp curve, abruptly jolting Daniel so unexpectedly, his head bounced off the adjacent window. *That may have been a shock, but I guess I should be used to surprises by now.* He was thinking and journaling about his marriage to Abba and how it had shaken the course of his life. Like a grease fire, their union burned hot but sadly, didn't last. Their short courtship didn't give enough time to really know each other beyond infatuation. But life together soon demonstrated that aside from sensual attraction, they had little else in common. She had left him six months ago, on July 26, 1873.

He closed the journal and focused on the present. *Returning to Sweet Home today feels no less triumphant than the victorious Charlemagne must have felt while being crowned by the Pope. He too went off to fight for what he believed.* Daniel was now better armed with determination at twenty-eight years of age than he could ever be with a sword. *True, my marriage to Abba failed miserably. It shook me to the core. For months after that, I was profoundly sad. It was a frightening darkness everyone could see. I wondered if life was worth going on during the worst moments.* His thoughts wavered as his body swayed with the train's movement. Then, to examine the experience, he journaled in a new section of the notebook:

I've come out of it and moved on.
I'm glad I'm a beekeeper because the bees taught me so much.
Being close to the soil, and putting his hands to work, can save a man.
I'm not the same person I once was.
Scarred, but better for it.

When Daniel had his heart broken, he felt like a real nobody, lower than a serf. Now, with more money bulging from his pocket than he'd ever seen before, he felt like royalty.

The thick roll of currency testified to his valor. He had earned it through hard work and tenacity, having just delivered a carload of honey, honeycomb, and apiary products. Vincent Titone, a wealthy New York produce distributor, had gratefully handed over $2,000. Titone had his agenda too—by the time it was fully distributed as assorted food and wax products, the raw material would net him nearly $3,000 in profit.

To Daniel, taking home $2,000 cash was a huge victory—sweeter than honey—because his colleagues in the school system had adamantly assured him the beekeeping enterprise would fail. Amongst those who voiced an opinion was William Burges, first headmaster for Mercer County and New Boston Schools. Burges, a mentor to Daniel, had floored the younger man when he voiced his opinion about Daniel's plan to become a beekeeper. Instead of encouragement, Burges raised his eyebrows and looked over his thin eyeglasses in disapproval and said, "No one has ever turned a profit from an apiary in this part of the country. So what makes you think you can do it out there in the middle of nowhere? Why not just walk over to the Mississippi, stand at the edge, turn your wallet upside down, and shake out what little you have into the current! The outcome will be the same, and you'll save yourself a lot of distraction and hard work."

The land in question was barely eight miles from town, but Burges made it sound like Daniel had proposed growing tomatoes in the middle of a desert. Nevertheless, the elder's predictions of failure only drove Daniel to higher levels of determination.

Daniel felt sure it could be done and argued, "Mr. Burges, my brother T.J. and I started a small apiary over on the Iowa side while serving as schoolmasters near Lettsville. It was before I was married, and we two shared—"

Burges, wondering why Palmer had asked for his opinion if all he wanted to do was argue, cut in. "You're really coming into your own in the schoolhouse. Why ruin it all?"

Daniel responded without hesitation, "I love teaching the children, but you must admit, no one ever made their fortune in education. We spent only three dollars on a little stand of bees and turned a profit, bringing in fifty dollars in honey sales. If we can do that in one season in Lettsville, shouldn't we be able to do much better here in Illinois?"

William, still seated behind his desk, placed his elbows on the large, padded blotter and rested his forehead on his hands, covering his eyes as if not seeing Daniel somehow made him go away. But Burges's frustration did little to dissuade his mentee.

Daniel unrelentingly argued, "T.J. and I stayed together when we first came to Lettsville. I was teaching in the Concord Township Country School, and he at the schoolhouse on the edge of Lettsville, so we were working just a few miles apart. It was easy for each of us to put in less than half an hour a week caring for the hives. Just imagine what a serious apiary could do!"

Mr. Burges tried to reason with him. "You're a good teacher. Why not leave farming to the farmers who know what they're doing?"

Daniel hadn't originally planned to start an apiary at Sweet Home. *The natural combination of locust trees, bees, and the Mississippi Valley were a perfect lure*, he remembered. *The positive experience T.J. and I had with it on the other side of the river whetted my appetite for more. But what sold me on it was discovering the mystical behavior of the fascinating insects, the amazing qualities attributed to honey, and the potential to be paid well for their products.*

Of course, D.D. Palmer could never be like his neighbors, content just to raise a few hogs, grow a little grain, and keep a few bees. Once stung with an idea, he couldn't rest. Daniel wondered whether it was a blessing or a curse. *Why couldn't a Palmer be satisfied with the ordinary? T.J. is like that too. Why is a Palmer driven to have all the answers? Why must we excel?* These questions would never be answered, and they gave him no peace.

So he studied every word he could find written about bees. Hard work, research, experimentation, and simple doggedness brought experience. On a quest to find out how to provide the best raw materials and environments for the bees to work their natural miracles, he quickly expanded the apiary and gained expertise and notoriety. After Abba left, Daniel worked sunup to sundown. He was elected to an officer's role in the apiarian association and became the author of a regular column in the beekeeper's journal. By the beginning of 1874, Daniel Palmer was the leading producer of honey in the country.

It was an odd quirk of fate that the honey production was doing so well since he'd begun his first efforts, and much more energy had been directed into the raspberry business. Daniel had also developed the Sweet Home raspberry, a particularly hardy new strain of the fruit, and he was proud to have hundreds of nursery stock growing on the farm, ready to ship to distant parts of the country.

His vision had been inspired by an innovation that was changing the face of how homemakers handled food. He had expected the option of canning fruits and vegetables to catalyze the demand for his black cap raspberries and nursery stock. So to that end, he had developed a disease-resistant strain of the plant that bore a sweet, juicy large blackcap raspberry unlike any others. Stacks of favorable testimonials from satisfied customers whose shipping addresses stretched from Connecticut to California attested to his product's quality. He advertised in newspapers, catalogs, and almanacs, proudly citing their testimonials along with his fanciful poetic acclamations for the berries. Convinced he had produced the best raspberry in the country, he was disappointed that despite its superiority and his marketing efforts, there just weren't enough orders to justify the investment of time, work, and money the Sweet Home raspberry deserved.

On the other hand, Sweet Home honey took less effort since the bees did the most intricate work—theirs being the essential part of production. It seemed ironic the honey was working out better than the raspberry business since he originally intended his beekeeping to bolster the pollination of raspberry plants. Mr. Burges had either missed that point or simply disagreed when Daniel explained how one horticultural practice sustained another. "William, I mean the bees play a critical role in producing the raspberry—"

Knowing Daniel could argue any point he believed in until he wore a person down, William shook his head and walked away.

As a beekeeper, Daniel was uniquely first a Palmer, and as such, he was driven, often to the point of compulsion—striving for excellence, not recognition. That, in addition to an inventive streak and a penchant for being a nonconformist, rounded out his personality. He was not one to blather, but Daniel would not shrink from the role of an opinionated proponent of his point of view once he had his facts. He reflected on the disappointing exchange with William. *I wonder if Mr. Burges thinks I'm big-headed? People often tell me I'm articulate, but I still don't seem to communicate well.* He scribbled a note in his journal: *I must be more careful in choosing my words.*

The train ride provided ample opportunity to relax and pursue such reflections. His thoughts strayed back six months to an instance when he had had a chance to display prowess as a beekeeper. The occasion was a visit to the Essley family. Daniel had purchased his acreage from the family patriarch, Elisha Essley. *I enjoy Elisha's company. Although quite wealthy, the Essleys are unassuming, warm, and friendly.* The Essley's were amongst the nearest neighbors, living only about a mile and a half from the apiary. Most of the land along that portion of the bluff belonged to Essley, and Daniel was able to strike a good deal with Mr. Essley when he decided to enter into horticultural activity.

It was beneficial for both of them because Essley, having acquired extensive tracts of land, wished to sell off the less tillable sections. Having steep overgrown hillsides, a feature central to that section of land, made it undesirable for most farmers who wished to work larger, level tracts. Dan liked the terrain for its rugged character that reminded him of the forested Canadian frontier of his boyhood. It also featured a stream that flowed between two hills, providing plenty of water, and from the summit, the plot offered a beautiful view of the Mississippi River Valley.

He had developed a liking for the whole Essley family and occasionally enjoyed visiting there. On that particular day, right before things had come to a head with Abba, several of the other neighbors who made up the rural community were sitting down to an afternoon tea when the subject of honey happened to come up. Afternoon tea on the edge of the prairie was like an oasis in a vast desert, but that was one of the things that made visiting the Essleys so interesting. Their home perched on top of the bluff featured a magnificent view of the river, at which Elisha gazed while dripping a spoonful of honey into his tea. "Honey is a marvelous substance. It never spoils, and it's always sweet for us. It renders me well when my throat is raspy, gives me energy when I'm tired, and sheds light when I burn its wax. As the good book said, the Lord promised his people a 'land flowing with milk and honey'—it really is a gift from heaven." No one was surprised by Elisha's occasional flashes into poetic oration, a style that fit his personality well.

Daniel gazed with pride at the familiar jar bearing his Sweet Home label. It sat next to the pitcher of cream, and he wondered if his friend was giving him a cue to follow up with a commercial message for his product. However, the group had already discussed the meaning of various dietary customs, particularly those odd restrictions passed down from ancient times, adhered to by certain groups while ignored by most others. The small jar of honey in the center of the table moved Elisha to goad his neighbors into a deeper discussion. Mr. Essley relished this kind of conversation. "Daniel, you're the school teacher, so tell us why the Jews can eat honey. They never eat pork because it's not kosher. Now insects aren't clean meat, so why can they eat honey?"

There weren't many, but the few Jews settled in the Mississippi River Valley stood apart because of their peculiar customs, like keeping the Sabbath on Saturday and rigorously observing the delineations between kosher and non-kosher foods. Daniel was quick to respond authoritatively, "I don't pretend to speak for other groups, but the answer seems obvious enough to me. When you eat honey, you are not eating bees or any part of them. Honey is the juice of the flowers! The bees transform the nectar, but it remains the product of the Lord's flora, not his fauna."

Eyebrows went up around the table approvingly.

Then the consummate school teacher took the opportunity to recite one of his favorite Emerson quotations. "My friends ..." He paused, strategically making eye contact with each individual. "We must be mindful that consistency is crucial to finding truth in our world. Any philosopher will say so, but we should be careful not to lurk in the bushes watching for any apparent inconsistency as an excuse to denigrate."

Reading their faces, he saw only puzzlement, so he tried to clarify. "I was paraphrasing Emerson. He put the idea well when he said, 'A foolish consistency is the hobgoblin of little minds.' I think that while the Jews may look and act slightly different than us, we should remember they're industrious, hard-working people who aspire to the same values we do." His neighbors' discomfort was obvious, so he tried to inspire them. "Distrust of others is usually based on fear. It stifles new ideas and enlightenment itself." However, the silence around the table was deafening. His words were too preachy for their comfort, so he searched for a mood changer.

"You know what else? I eat about a pound of honey a day!" Dan exclaimed. His moralistic remarks had lowered eyebrows around the table, but now they were raised in amazement. The thought of a person consuming such a large quantity of the thick sweet stuff seemed improbable. He continued, "The honey provides abundant vitality, and I burn a lot of energy in a long day of farm work. I work from before sunrise until long after sunset during the weekdays. The only exception is for school sessions, and these twice a month tea-and-talk get-togethers here with you folks. If it weren't for our handyman, Gene, I wouldn't be able to be sitting here with you friends enjoying this delightful respite."

"I don't trust him!" the usually reserved Ava Essley chimed in. Elisha's wife, Ava was the embodiment of propriety and good manners, so coming from her, it was a notably strong comment.

Dumbfounded by her comment, Daniel's mouth was agape as he tried to take in the unexpected remark. Wishing she hadn't said anything, but with everyone now looking at her, Ava turned toward Daniel to explain, "Your Mr. Horvath won't look a person directly in the eye, and I don't count on shifty-eyed rascals."

Embarrassed by her terse comment, Silas, the Essleys' twenty-five-year-old adopted son, tried to soften the mood, "He's just shy, Mom, that's all. But he's okay; he helped me load salt into my wagon yesterday in town, and I didn't even have to ask him."

Standing her ground, Ava growled, "That may be, but it probably was because he thought there'd be a reward in it for him."

"Well, I gave him a few coins after we were done," Silas conceded.

"It's not hard to find faults in people," Daniel offered, then continued in a defensive tone. "I'm not wealthy, and I can't afford a crew of farmhands. But the workload's grown to more than one man could handle, and I don't know what I'd do without Mr. Horvath. Right now, he's filling orders for Sweet Home raspberry nursery stock, which can't wait while I socialize. I was pleasantly surprised when I first saw him fill out address labels because he has the most beautiful penmanship I've ever seen from a man's hand. Now, as a school teacher, that means something to me. He pushed me to break away and come here—and said I needed to take a breather. I appreciate he's with us. Nor do I like to leave Abba alone at home. She said there was too much on her to-do list to come to tea with us."

Ava's retort was swift. "Just be sure to count your silver!"

Daniel laughed heartily. "Well, that won't require any higher math in my house!"

A hint of waggishness began to show around the corners of her mouth, but she quickly reverted to the solemn face that stubbornly refused to join his lighthearted expression of levity.

It seemed like something more was bothering her about Gene Horvath. With an awkward smile, Ava stood, and reached for the fine porcelain teapot. "I'll fix some more tea." She retreated from the room, taking her mixed emotions with her.

While renewing the aromatic pot of tea, Mrs. Essley gazed out the kitchen window at her favorite backyard feature. The pergola, a trellised walkway covered with flowers, led to a gazebo in the backyard. She had sat there with Mrs. Noble yesterday and heard an earful of disturbing news about their neighbor, Abba Palmer.

Abba, who was somewhat insecure socially, did not invite folks into her home, nor did she try to build friendships with the other ladies living out along the bluff. Although not intentionally snobbish, Abba didn't much care what the neighbors thought anyway. But to that small cluster of women, a high and mighty attitude, intended or not, was a clear provocation. So when rumors started to fly about the standoffish Abba having an illicit relationship with her handyman, they stuck like glue. It seemed like Daniel Palmer was the only one kept in the dark, and Ava pitied him for it. Her thoughts shifted from yesterday's conversation in the gazebo to a disturbing image of what Abba and Gene might be doing right now with Daniel safely out of sight.

Some part of her wanted to warn her naïve neighbor, but it didn't seem like the right thing to do. After all, it was just a rumor, and she had no evidence. Maybe Abba was utterly faithful, and perhaps

Gene Horvath was just a loyal employee. Then she remembered the first time she had seen him about three months ago.

She was in town at the dry goods store picking out some fabrics when he entered the shop. Her first impression was negative when she saw the young man wearing a brightly colored red-and-blue silky scarf. *It's not cold today, so the cravat is just a clumsy fashion statement.* Sandra Noble, who had accompanied her to town, said, "Oh, Ava, let me introduce Mr. Horvath. He's staying with the Palmers—their new farmhand."

Partially bowing while reaching out his hand to hers, it struck her he was trying to put on a European air, which failed to impress. Instead, it just came across as phony. "Pleased to meet you, miss." What he said wasn't offensive, but the way he looked her body up and down gave her an unpleasant chill, particularly when his gaze seemed to get stuck on the way back up, as his eyes dashed horizontally back and forth, scrutinizing her breasts. Ava might have otherwise been flattered to be the object of a man's admiration and desire. But Gene's way of sizing her up was unnerving, and she felt only distress bordering on disgust.

The smirk on his face would have been enough to annoy her, but how he continued grasping her hand while addressing her as *miss.* It all vexed her right from the get-go. *He's up to some kind of skullduggery,* her little voice inside said. *Definitely not trustworthy. Steer clear of this one.*

Ava wasn't sure of many things in life, but she had learned never to ignore what her mother had referred to as "that wee small voice inside." Trying to brush off that feeling, she told herself, *Well, calling me miss was an understandable mistake because Sandra didn't introduce me as Mrs. Essley, and maybe he was just trying to be polite and didn't know.* But the rationalization was quickly shut down by the creepy feeling she got from his overt inspection of her body. Now, with her eyes still on the gazebo, her thoughts came full circle, concluding out loud, though softly, "My first impression was right. He's sleazy."

She tried to force herself to think about preparing a wonderful fragrant tea—a far more comforting thought than the one she had just relived. But, stubbornly, a perverse scene grew in her imagination. Flashing through her mind, Ava remembered a particular day several weeks before when she and Carrie Andrews, another neighbor, had helped to hang drapes over the windows in Abba and Daniel's house. Although they hoped the gesture of friendship might engage Abba in neighborly dealings, thus far, there was no evidence of it breaking her out of her shell.

Picturing the light green curtain they had hung in the Palmer's bedroom fostered an unwelcome image that gave Ava a chill. As she failed to suppress it, her distaste for Gene evoked an even more vivid depiction in which a bouncing bed's headboard tapped out a cadence against the adjacent wall. She even conjured up a colorfully complete scenario to that same rhythm, with squeaking springs under the adulteress, whose audible moans recoiled from her in time with each bounce.

Her yelps encouraged the pale-skinned naked man, whose thinning, wispy red hair, short stature, and pudgy shape were his key features. Ava's embarrassing imagination wouldn't quit, including smacking slaps of flesh, gasps of heavy breathing, and that base creature atop enjoying the ride. Worst of all was that same sly smirk she had first seen on him in the dry goods store. *It must be his trademark*, she thought. Envisioning all this might be going on right now, just a stone's throw down the road, made her say, "That sleaze!"

Cleansing her thoughts, Ava gazed into a colorful picture on the tin container of tea. It portrayed a festive tea party with three young children wearing party dresses. The little girls, obviously occidental, were seated around a table in a room of oriental style. They were being served biscuits and tea by a Japanese woman formally dressed in a beautiful, ankle-length kimono. It's ample, brightly colored fabric had exceptionally loose-fitting sleeves and was fastened at the waist with an elegant wide sash. Everything about the décor was traditional Japanese, from the massive hanging lantern above the table, copious accents of glossy red lacquer trim around paper wall panels, grass mats on the floor, and even a stand of bamboo alongside cherry trees visible through the window. Yet the blonde-haired young girls seated in their blousy pastel dresses didn't tally with the overstated setting. The artist had created a cliché advocating a Japanese tea party as just the thing to please wealthy young westerners. At the bottom of the graphic appeared the decree Drink O & O Tea! Studying these details in the illustration freed Mrs. Essley from the distasteful chimera, bringing her no small relief.

Meanwhile, Silas had been the next one to speak after Ava left for the kitchen. "Mr. Palmer, how can a person possibly eat a whole pound of honey?" While Dan reflected on the question, Silas added, "I can eat a teaspoon of honey and enjoy it, but if I take another spoonful right after, I feel sickly, and that's just a tiny portion of what you're talking about."

Wearing his helpful school teacher's smile, Daniel answered slowly, "In running an apiary, many surprising things come to light." He paused, checking to see everyone was listening, then continued, "I've learned a person's body can adapt to different kinds of food remarkably well. While honey is no exception to that rule, it is the most exceptional of substances. No one understands how honey gets its mysterious properties, but as Elisha said earlier, it is a miraculous food." Then he picked up the pace. "I never tire of the amber stuff, and I can take it in a way that would sicken most. It used to be that a few drops were all I could swallow at one time. Then the more time I spent with the bees, the more honey I wanted and the more I could manage. Now the more I work with them, the more I crave that food. I guess I've bonded with the bees!"

"Bonded?" Silas asked.

Daniel's enthusiasm spilled forth. "If honey is shelved and thickens too much, the warmth of my hands transforms it to run clear again. It seems faster than how my mother used to do it by placing it in a pot of warm water. Silas, something changes in a person when he dedicates himself. I'm not just running an apiary for gain. I've become an apiculturist—a caretaker for the bees."

Silas grappled, "An api ... what?"

Daniel loved being the center of attention, especially when he knew the most about a subject. With his trademark broad smile, he said assertively, "Silas, I'm an apiarian who breeds and cares for bees. It's a grand calling with a great reward, and I'm proud to call myself a beekeeper. That means much more than just farming their labors for profit. I have a relationship with these special creatures. I depend upon them, and they do me."

Silas answered unassumingly, "I didn't think there was so much to it. I know you wear that special suit and netting mask when you take the honey, and I figured that was about it."

Now the lecture was on. Daniel took on an academic tenor. "Silas, I can understand it doesn't look like there's much to it from the outside. That's one of the reasons I am so fascinated with beekeeping. I have learned many new things, from science to history, the supernatural, and even folklore. I would never have believed the charms of a beekeeper could be anything but superstition—until I saw them work."

With a concerned look on his face, Elisha interrupted, "What do you mean by charms? Isn't that what witches use?"

Daniel said keenly, "No, it's got nothing to do with evil spells or those sorts of things. I've read everything I could find to learn about beekeeping, and there's a lot out there. Yet, the more I discovered, the more apparent it became that I didn't know much." Daniel watched Elisha's face. Then, seeing no reaction, he added, "Elisha, think of this more like I've been digging up history and even a bit of archeology."

Elisha's eyebrows lowered as his countenance softened, implying he was comfortable with an educational analysis, so long as it avoided the mystical.

Daniel shifted into storytelling mode. "It seems these charms have been used to protect and nurture the bees for hundreds of years. It's recorded that eleventh-century monks at Winchester, England had an abiding faith in the value of one particular charm they put into the ground. A Columcille's circle consisted of concentric circles around a stake driven into the ground at the center of the area designated for their apiary. The original text, which still exists in the monastery's archives, contains explicit instructions for crafting the piece. An apiculturist I met in Nauvoo brought the instructions with him from his earlier home in the mountains of New York. He showed me a copy of the passage, which he pulled from where he kept it, safely inside the front cover of his family Bible."

Daniel glanced around the room at his friends' faces to ensure they were all keeping up with the story.

"The inscription was written by his father's hand on a large fine-linen paper and folded in half to fit in the book. I distinctly remember his father's missive included the following words and a diagram. *The monks would inscribe these words onto a soft, indigenous stone with a blade: That the bees may be safe and in their hearts.*

"This stone was placed over the stake so only the stone was visible at the ground level. An accurately placed charm is thought to protect the bees from theft, harm, or getting lost during the swarming.

"Even today, many serious-minded beekeepers seem to pay heed to the protective consequence of a charm for their apiary." Daniel paused again to allow his rapt audience to reflect on the device's usefulness.

At that moment, Ava returned with a fresh pot of hot tea, and without interrupting the quiet, she began to refill each cup.

Then, breaking the silence, Daniel asked, "Do you want to know something more?

"I think it's fascinating," answered Silas.

That was all the encouragement the schoolmaster needed. "You may be surprised to learn there were no honeybees in the Americas before colonization, just wild bees. The colonists brought honeybees, along with known methods of husbandry, including charms. The Native Americans called the bees 'white man's fly' and found great symbolism in the bee sting. They would say, 'Like the bee, which produces sweet honey, the white man can be an obliging friend who can turn on you swiftly and painfully.' I think that's where the analogy ends, because unlike our treatment of the natives, bees have been kind to humans." He directed his gaze unequivocally at the young man. "By the way, Silas, did you know the stinger of a honey bee is ripped from its body, and it dies when it stings?"

Silas, singled out for that bit of knowledge, only reacted with a silent shrug.

Daniel was on a roll, and the dissertation continued, "These amazing things I've been learning about bees don't just go back hundreds of years, but many thousands. Ancient Greek coins have been found with honey bees on them, and Aristotle wrote about the habits of bees. In Scripture, John the Baptist lived in the wilderness largely on locust honey. Egyptian tombs, sealed for thousands of years, have been opened to find honey—still edible! So it seems there was truth in their yarns of immortality; it exists in the honey that never spoils. The one thing that puzzles me is this insect can produce food for humans yet was completely unknown to the Indians."

Stopping only to take a breath, he continued the lesson. "Furthermore, history tells us beeswax has been used for skin creams, lip balms in winter, and candle making throughout recorded history. And science is only beginning to understand why honey is sweeter than sugar. Entomologists tell us a single pound of honey involves two million visits to flowers, that each honey bee will visit between fifty to a hundred flowers per trip, that a honeybee has five eyes and four wings, that the females do all the work and the males are merely drones for procreation, that the buzzing sound we hear is made by their wings stroking more than ten thousand times per minute, there's only one queen ... and I could go on!" He took a deep breath.

Spellbound, Silas just looked on wide-eyed at the display of knowledge.

Elisha broke the silence. "You have made quite a study of this, Mr. Palmer."

Daniel, nodding assent, toned down his enthusiasm, "They have a fascinating culture too. I have learned each bee has specific duties or assignments. Some are guards protecting the hive, others are housekeepers, some take on the role of nurturers, others tend to the queen, and some bring home the necessities. A handful scout around the environment, and others are assemblers. They're a most complex society. I had no idea how much would be involved when I started that apiary.

"They've taught me so much about so many different things in life. For example, winter beekeeping is entirely different from summer, but the planning goes year-round. Marketing product means you must learn to become a businessman in addition to caring for hives and their components. There are bee diseases, and you need to know the nectar sources and its flow. And I've had to learn carpentry to build structures, I've had to study pollination, and even dance! Yes, did I tell you bees dance to communicate?"

He didn't wait for an answer. "Extraction of honey is a complex art. I tell you, there is a whole lifetime of study for the person who wants to pursue beekeeping properly." Then, for emphasis, he lowered his arms, which he'd been waving through the air, and abruptly parked his thumbs in the small watch pockets of his double-breasted waistcoat.

His neighbors around the table remained surprisingly quiet when Daniel finally paused. Then, like a brick to the face, it occurred to him the sermon had gone on too long. A flush of embarrassment came over him, and he prepared to receive some jeering. But they had never before seen so much passion coming from him. Moreover, seeing and hearing a person so dedicated to his work was thought-provoking, so no jeers came.

Then Elisha summarized, "Now I'll know there's a big meaning to the little 'Sweet Home' sign whenever I pass by your gate."

Chapter Ten

INSPIRATION

"Let your dreams be your wings."

—Anonymous

T he name "Sweet Home" and the decision to focus primarily on the apiary were inspired by a dream. Daniel went to sleep one night with an angry frustration in his heart and mind. After putting his all into developing a unique blackcap raspberry, his plan to acquire income from it just wasn't working out. The raspberry nursery stock was everything he had hoped for *except* one crucial element: earnings.

Earlier that day, he and Abba had been going over the books. It was 1871, and they had been on the farm nearly a year. She had shown that at their current rate, they could not profit from selling nursery stock or even staying on the farm, for that matter. He finally fell asleep, exhausted after hours of tossing and turning. Ideas came, but none could answer the critical question: what would it take to make the horticultural business profitable? Then shortly before daybreak, he woke up in a cold sweat. A remarkable, arcane vision arrived in a dream.

In the reverie, Daniel held a piece of honeycomb and looked down one end of the multi-hexagonal structure as he had done hundreds of times before. Except this time, he was transfixed by what he saw. The sticky, geometrically perfect wax shimmered, intensifying its beautiful bright-amber color, and its lustrous walls surrealistically glistened until it grew to encase the whole bedroom. Standing in his bedroom, Daniel was aware he was dreaming but no longer in bed. He felt strangely detached, yet tranquil and secure.

Then his disconnected form shifted, no longer on his feet but in motion. He felt exceptionally light, a sensation unfamiliar to his stocky build. Then he noticed a familiar book cover on a shelf by the window. He had loved *The Arabian Nights* as a child and now shared that book with his students.

Queen Scheherazade's tales of "One Thousand and One Nights" fascinated him, and it won over his students too. They were so drawn in by their teacher's fervor for it, they didn't know they were studying literature. Stories like "Sinbad the Sailor," "Ali Baba and the Forty Thieves," "Aladdin's Lamp," and the others whetted their appetites for reading.

Like a character in *The Arabian Nights,* Dan effortlessly floated into the honeycomb as if soaring on a flying carpet. It drew him in with ever-increasing speed like a powerful magnet, and he wondered what might happen when he finally crashed. But inside the honeycomb, the motion slowed, akin to cold molasses sliding off a spoon. And he traveled slothfully through a sticky hexagonal tube.

Stirring montages of classical music played in his head as he floated through a beautiful mosaic of colors, gradually fading from bright amber to iridescent green, then various warm red-tinged hues. The dream was vivid and bizarre. Then it occurred to him, *I don't really like this music. It must be someone else's dream.*

Suddenly, he was soaring quickly. *Surely, there must be a demon just around the bend*, he reckoned. But there were no bends, just a never-ending hexagonal tube with lights, colors, and objects embedded deep in the walls of the comb. There were golden coins and a kaleidoscope of images leading to a barn near a two-story house. *This is Sweet Home, but what's that in the flat behind the house?* He blinked twice and could see rows of beehives, scores of them!

There were people in the honeycomb too. One of them was Molly Hudler, looking intently toward him with a mischievous gleam in her eye. *I wonder why I never saw such attentiveness from Molly after the Independence Day Picnic?* He mused. *Am I still pining for her?*

He blinked again. Molly was gone and he saw his parents walking between rows of beehives. *Why are they in this dream?*

Floating along, he saw himself in a lecture hall before the eager faces of many students. Unlike the usual one-room schoolhouses with children, these contained adults. *I love teaching,* he thought. *Did I hear or imagine those words? If that is what I love, why am I moving in a different direction? Why am I in this crazy place between sleep and awake? What's the point? I should be getting some badly needed rest. There's a lot to do tomorrow. It's already tomorrow!*

Movement through the honeycomb accelerated, and his thoughts raced to keep up. *Ideas are coming faster than I can think.* And that thought triggered something. *That Indian shaman!*

Has that rascal figured out how to create a dream? Daniel asked himself. The peculiar dream began to make sense. *Could one person possibly place a dream into the mind of another? If dreams are like handwriting, then this one has Wiseman written all over it. And I'm analyzing the dream while still in it!* he chuckled, wondering if the sound was actually audible.

Questions kept coming. *Isn't Abba here next to me? Where am I? Why is this dream so long?*

An object in the six-sided chamber came into view, and Daniel's movement slowed to a stop. Ahead of him was Wiseman, donning a big smile on his usually staid face.

The ascetic Wiseman claimed to be a descendent of Chief Keokuk and an Algonquin shaman from the East Coast. Daniel had met Wiseman during a Spiritualist gathering at Verdurette, the nearby estate of William Drury. The wealthy mogul, Drury, had built his home on the prairie near New Boston. Verdurette had an eerie look and feel about it, well-suited for their meetings. The first home in the state to have running water, gas lights, and steam heat, its Victorian architecture featured very steep, ornate gables, giving it a uniquely gothic flavor. These accents on the home and outbuildings gave the whole place an extra-spooky feel, as did the wrought-iron fencing, life-size lawn sculptures, fountains with running water, and an adjacent exotic wild-animal preserve. Wiseman fit in well as both a guest and an ornament there. Mysterious and outlandish, he was just the sort those odd gatherings attracted.

Daniel had been drawn to the Spiritualist ideals immediately when his two friends Will and Mary Kellogg first spoke about their religion. They were amongst the first people he met when he arrived in New Boston to take a teaching position in 1868. He soon came to value their friendship as righteous, enlightened folks who appreciated nature, which stood out in a culture racing to find artificial mechanistic solutions for every problem. Though practicing Spiritualists, Will and Mary had little use for séances and a special enmity for those who would turn a buck at the cost of bereaved family members.

Wiseman never referred to himself as a Spiritualist, but he regularly attended Spiritualist functions. Daniel once asked Wiseman why he didn't fully accept the Spiritualist religion. Wiseman responded, "Religion should not exist for its own sake. The people here use Spiritualism like society. It fills a social need, and they connect here largely to belong to something they like."

Wiseman's typically oblique responses tended to bring deeper reflection to the questioner. Daniel wondered, *Or does he simply do it to irritate and frustrate?* But Daniel was stubborn enough to persist until he got a more direct response. "Now, Wiseman, you're too smart to make such a generalization out of all these people."

Not altogether dismissing Daniel's entreaty, Wiseman explained, "My ancestors did not separate their purpose in life from their pursuit of life's experiences." Wiseman studied him as if to measure comprehension. "The essence of the Spiritualist's beliefs is already there within the tribal wisdom, but it remains only a small part of what my people know. They accept life as the expression of the immaterial through the material, the spirit through the body."

The dream frustrated Daniel. He had little love for music, wasn't prone to foolishness, and appreciation for beautiful, vivid colors eluded him. Yet there he was, floating through a fantasy, enveloped and mesmerized by things of whimsy.

Suddenly he wasn't floating but flying on the strangest contrivance, making a loop-de-loop motion. There was no music on this daredevil flight, just a high-pitched buzzing. The vibrant colors were dizzying, with lots of intense blue. It soared higher, and the colors became recognizable as huge flowers. Then he realized the flowers weren't large. He was tiny! And he was riding on the back of a honeybee.

Looking down over the vehicle, he noticed that covering the bee's thorax were rolling mounds of bright-yellow powder. The direction of flight shifted suddenly, nearly throwing Dan off and dousing his bearded face with the yellow ash. Unfortunately, it caused him to take an irritating breath full of the stuff. He brushed off his face with one hand, sputtering and sneezing while holding on tight to the insect's back with the other like a cowboy in a rodeo.

Finding a stable depression that worked like a saddle, he could sit upright between the hairy thorax, where the honeybee's wings attached, and the larger, smooth abdomen. Heaps of pollen clung to stiff straight hairs springing up from its body and more stuck on the creature's legs. It seemed like every nook and cranny was stuffed with yellow dust. Daniel's eyes got itchy, and his breathing raspy. *I don't have allergic problems. Why is this affecting me? Of course, I've never gone swimming in pollen before!* Annoying yellow droplets of it hung from his mustache like icicles.

The jerky flight suddenly smoothed out as the bee hovered inside the open cone of a bright-pink flower while its stamen dropped mounds of bright yellow dust of pollen on the honeybee's back—and Daniel. Pollen pressed his shirt to his skin, and it was surprisingly heavier than the previous piles. Now aware not all pollen was the same, he noticed the honeybee's head appeared clean. Then his gaze swept down the thorax, where he could see several different shades of yellow.

The bee wiped its proboscis on the inner portions of the flower, causing it to drop more of the pale yellow pollen. Daniel made a mental note. *Each type of flower has its distinct pollen, and the bee gathers nectar with its snout. So I suppose pollen and nectar are both essential to the hive.*

Finally, he was breathing freely, and the itching eyes and runny nose cleared up. Then he heard a question that was neither audible nor silent. *Why am I gathering nectar?*

The bee was gone. Neither lying down nor standing, the amorphous traveler asked, *Am I awake?*

No, we're still asleep, the answer came from some unknown place.

Still surrounded by iridescent colors of amber, red, and green, Daniel continued dreaming. *This is such a long dream. I wonder if it's already daylight in the real world?*

Feeling trapped, he tried thinking about time as a tether to reality. *It's just a measure of something that doesn't exist.* Grappling with time and place reminded him of Wiseman.

We were at Verdurette discussing Spiritualism. With a reverent look in his eye, Wiseman quoted an Algonquin tribal leader. "Big Thunder said, sometimes, dreams are wiser than waking." The circumspect Wiseman watched for his friend's reaction.

Daniel asked, "If you think wisdom is found in dreams, where do you think the dreams come from in the first place?"

Wiseman answered circuitously, "Big Thunder lived in the lands far to the northeast, so his dreams came from cold waters, connected to all the spirits that float on waters."

But Wiseman's recitation of the authority of floating spirits did little to enlighten Daniel. So he decided to dismiss Wiseman from the dream. That's when he heard some mysterious words.

The phrase seemed to bypass his ears, finding its way right to the brain. *Add honey to your life and make it sweet.* The mysterious call felt authentic, resonating to his core from neither within nor without. His first thought was, *I'm in no mood to trust Wiseman. But perhaps he's right, and dreams can provide valuable insights.*

Neither awake nor slumbering, he was moving again. Molly and Wiseman were far behind in the golden tunnel. Abba was standing nearby, waving at him. She looked like she had that very first day in the gazebo. He took her by the hand as they accelerated toward a bright spot, which grew larger and larger until they burst through the end of the honeycomb into a bright, beautiful sunny day. Daniel stood in the sunshine, but the hand that had held Abba's was empty.

He woke up shaken and drenched in a cold sweat. Then the words came to his lips. "Add honey to your life and make it sweet." It was a revelation, and he knew what he must do.

He would become a beekeeper.

The commotion woke Abba, who asked with a perturbed voice, "What in heaven's name? You are all wet. What are you doing?"

Dan calmly answered, "We're already living our salvation—I've just been too blind to see it. Those pesky bees swarming around the locust trees and my raspberry stock kept trying to tell us, but we wouldn't listen!"

Abba groggily dismissed him, "Go back to sleep!"

"We will sweeten our lives and save the farm," he insisted.

Abba whispered, "You're a fool," hoping he would stop and let her sleep.

Undaunted, Dan announced, "We aren't going to lose our home!"

With nothing more to go on than a vision, he was so sure of success, he already considered it achieved.

The half-awake, half-slumbering Abba paid little attention as he droned on, "Sweet Home will remain ours thanks to those rascal bees. They're going to give us Sweet Home honey."

He may as well have been speaking to the walls. Abba was dead to the world and his jubilation. He listened to her heavy breathing cadence, and his emotions quickly spiked from elation to melancholy. She simply did not share his enthusiasm about most things that mattered to him, especially his dreams.

He had never had the heart to confront her directly, but he knew she was lost to him. Abba, the clairvoyant, should have seen this coming. Had she used her skills as a medium to foretell the misery they would cause each other, then perhaps something might have changed.

Chapter Eleven

SOMETHING'S AMISS.

*"Set me as a seal upon thine heart, As a seal upon thine arm:
For love is strong as death; jealousy is cruel as the grave."*
— SONG OF SOLOMON 8:6 (KING JAMES BIBLE)

Now living in an empty marriage, Daniel and Abba remained under the same roof, but geography and material items were all they shared. Since the day Daniel had joined the Essley's for tea, it had been that way.

He left the tea and talk in a cheerful mood, having been the center of attention while sharing his knowledge of beekeeping. But upon returning home from tea, he learned things about her and himself.

He stepped inside the house, knowing something was amiss. It wasn't anything identifiable, just a powerful sense that all wasn't right. He looked out the windows in each direction and then focused on the large, glass-framed hive he had proudly embedded into the living room wall several months before. Abba hated Daniel's "great invention," while he thought it was brilliant. The hive, covered by glass on the inside for observation, was open outside. Abba appreciated his dedication to his work, but she felt that bringing it into the living room intruded upon her home life. Looking at the hive and thinking about the house without Abba in it gave him a sickly feeling in the pit of his stomach.

He walked around the yard to see if she was there, perhaps occupied with some chore or project. Staying down on the flat near the house yard, Daniel walked up and down the orderly rows of free-standing, wooden Thomas beehives, inspecting each of the first hundred structures as if expecting to find a clue. Reaching the center of the level, two and one-half acre plot immediately behind the house yard, he stepped up to the wooden platform before the door of their small bee house. They had built it the year before to support the raspberry operation. He recalled what Abba had said while they were working on it together, "Sweetheart, you work too hard and long. I think we should hire a farmhand to help you."

"The business has just grown enough that we can sustain and expand it, but if I have to pay a salary, I think it will just set us back," he answered.

Abba argued her case. "I know you are driven to do it all, but I'd like to keep you around for a while. Don't burn yourself out like some kind of woeful hero. If we can't hire skilled farm work, maybe we could find a simple handyman who you can train as he goes."

Building the structure was great fun for the young couple. They worked well together, often stopping for playful diversions, and Abba didn't even know about the baby growing inside of her yet. They built the structure large enough to serve as a workshop. Later, with the rapid growth of the apiary, it became the *bee house*, a practical workspace for repairing hives, various projects, and slinging honey. Abba liked the rustic little structure, and she mentioned she might want to have a chair out there for times when Daniel was engaged in projects, so she could be out there with him. Fortuitously, a few months after the Palmers had moved full-scale into the apiary business, the Essleys were replacing a fainting couch with a new lounger for their sitting room. Daniel asked if he might purchase the sofa for his bee house. Pleased not to have to deal with its disposal, the Essleys happily gifted it to him. Later that day, while Abba was preparing dinner, he hitched up his team and went to pick it up.

While he and Elisha were loading it on the wagon, Daniel said to Ava, "Abba will love this. I can't wait for her to see it!" Elisha rode along, ostensibly to pick up some honey, and together they slipped the couch into the bee house.

After dinner, Daniel asked Abba to come out to the bee house because he needed another pair of hands to help repair a stubborn honey frame. She quickly spotted the surprise when he opened the door, and she gasped. A great smile burst across her face as she looked it over, thrilled to behold the lush red upholstery, while he beamed with satisfaction. It looked out of place next to his rough-looking, unpainted workbench, but that didn't trouble either of them. Abba said, "Daniel David Palmer, you could have won my heart with a simple chair! You've outdone yourself." She scampered over, leaping onto it so hard, it almost turned over backward. He rushed to the rescue, but before he got there, the couch righted itself. Abba was safely stretched across it with her head and shoulders casually leaning on the raised end, positioned perfectly to watch him at his workbench. He would never forget the carefree, happy look on Abba's face, perched on the couch with her hands clasped behind her head, looking expectantly up at him.

It soon became their custom to retire to the bee house after dinner, she talking incessantly on the fainting couch while he, engrossed in some project, would mostly listen. On many occasions, when he got to a good stopping point in the task, he would carefully place his tools in their proper harnesses. Then, in a ritual which seemed to signal his intent, Daniel would dip his hands in an ever-present bowl of clean water, sprinkle them with some borax soap, lather them up, rinse, and dry. The game was afoot as he would inspect his hands for cleanliness, and when satisfied they were, he would turn to Abba, still sprawled out on the couch. Then striking a thoughtful pose by stroking his beard and lecherously looking her up and down, he'd slowly inspect her body like a connoisseur appraising a sculpture. Each would play out their role lightheartedly, he the aggressor and she the submissive damsel on the fainting couch. The game added spice and a touch of naughtiness to the young couple's lovemaking. It was the most carefree, happy time of their lives together.

Now, one year later, standing on the platform of the bee house, he reached for the doorknob and hesitated. Would she be on the couch napping? Or would she not be alone? A wave of nausea swept over him as he considered the possibility of misconduct on her part. His ears reddened, and he could feel and hear his own pulse. Anger fueled by jealousy owned him.

Finally unable to stand the anticipation, he turned the knob, opened the door, took a deep breath, and looked inside. To his relief, the bee house was empty, but so was the feeling inside him. He closed the door, stepped off the platform, and walked behind the structure. Another hundred hives arranged in rows stood before him, just like those in front of the bee house. He gazed over them and then up toward the top of the bluff whose steep hillside was thickly covered by native locust trees and the hundreds of nonindigenous trees his own hands had carefully added. Daniel walked past the rows of hives. If she was engaged in some manner of mischief, then at the top of the bluff is where he would get to the bottom of it.

Abruptly, his mood shifted. Angry with himself for the out-of-control paroxysms of ire inexorably taking control of him, Daniel stopped immediately before reaching the thick columns of raspberry stock, whose rows of sharp, thorny canes began just before the steep rise up the bluff. Then, feeling foolish and disloyal, he decided to simply return to the house and wait inside for a while.

He had already searched every room of the small, two-story frame house but decided to do so again. Finding no sign of her or anything untoward, he sat down in the living room, fidgeting while he waited. It was nearly half an hour since he had returned from Essley's to their empty home, and his fury grew again. *By late afternoon, she is usually started on dinner. I wonder if something happened to her. Maybe thieves came in off the road. I shouldn't have been gone so long. It's not right to leave her alone like that. But, no, she wasn't alone when I left for Essley's. Gene Horvath was here working on the hives. I asked him to build two more frames, but he couldn't be done yet. So where's Gene?*

Both Abba and Gene were missing at the same time. While he had never imagined anything might be going on between them, reality finally hit him square in the face when he remembered Ava Essley's derogatory remark about Gene.

It made sense, like finding two missing pieces of a puzzle, perfectly completing the picture. Amid growing fury, he took a mental detour. *It's like discovering the hidden object in one of those busy pictures made for children. Once you see the shovel drawn up in the leaves of a tree, or a coffee pot set sideways behind an oil lamp on a bedside table, from that moment forward, the leaves always fail to camouflage the shovel, and the oil lamp plays second fiddle to the coffee pot!* The diversion did nothing to quell an ugly, empty feeling in the pit of his stomach, as a steadily worsening vexation possessed him. Although he didn't have evidence, he could focus on nothing except Abba in an act of betrayal with Gene. *Where are they?* he asked himself. Dan decided to resume the search.

He walked briskly and then broke into a run, first to the shed, then the granary, the stable, and through each outbuilding. The intense disquiet grew with each step. Before, he had been worried about Abba's well-being, but concern for her safety was no longer driving him. Instead, he was consumed with anger and a diminished capacity for reason, leaving only rage and envy. The emotions looped around each other. Fear, distrust, and anger intertwined with disappointment drove him to the boiling point. "So this is jealousy." Daniel's lips uttered the words just loudly enough so he could hear them articulated. Gripped by anger, he was possessed, and the emotions concerned him. *I've heard jealousy is powerful, and such antipathy can drive a person to extremes, but I've never felt anything like this before.*

Having covered every possibility down in the flat, he turned toward the hillside. Climbing up the bluff, he threaded his way between thorny raspberry canes and reached the steepest portion of the path when a likely spot came to mind. Beyond the summit was a clearing with lots of sunshine and deep, thick grass. When their home was still under construction, he and Abba had frequented that secluded place. They would bring their favorite heavy blue checkered blanket and sometimes even a picnic basket. It was a romantic setting, just right for their most amorous moments.

Thinking about where and how he expected to find them roused a deeper, more primitive resentment. Fuming as he climbed, Dan again uttered, "So this is jealousy." Feeling empty, angry, and purposeless, it occurred to him he loathed these emotions. *People often turn to violence when they're jealous.* That thought sobered him. He abhorred violence, yet now his thoughts were of finding them together and beating Gene to a pulp. *What if I get so out of control, I kill him? Then what? Am I to unleash my fury at Abba?* That's when rational thought struck. *Even the basest betrayal won't bring me to that level of savagery.*

About a third of the way up the hillside, he heard a familiar giggle—it was one he hadn't heard in quite some time. His heart sank as he saw Abba gleefully swinging her arm, walking hand in hand with Gene. Sauntering down the path, they hadn't yet noticed her husband as they rounded the top of the bluff. The blue checkered blanket was folded over her other arm, and Daniel now knew all he needed to know. If infidelity weren't hard enough to bear, the thought of the tryst taking place on the same blanket where he and Abba had often enjoyed each other made the betrayal feel humiliating too. The shock of seeing him on the way up the path abruptly choked her giggles.

He had caught them red-handed. Abba instinctively yanked her hand out of Gene's, and the two hastily exchanged words Daniel could not hear. Seeing her panic-stricken recoil from Gene brought a strange relief to Daniel, lifting much of his pain and even quelling his fury.

The horrible jealousy quickly faded, and he replaced it with pragmatism. *Should I stay and send Abba away, or should I quit her and Sweet Home? I could move to What Cheer and reunite with the family. T.J. is there. I'd like to spend time with him again.* Either way, the sadness was genuine, but he could see himself getting through it because the worst part was over.

Ensnared on the path, they knew he knew everything. Their strained conversation became animated. Abba was pulling at her hair, and when she let go of it, she was gesturing toward the sky. Gene just stood there, nearly motionless, and saying little. They slowly began to descend the path toward Daniel.

They approached cautiously and silently, holding their heads down in shame. Daniel stood motionless with his arms folded across his chest. As she drew near, Abba gathered her courage. With her head held low, she looked up with her eyes, swallowed, and began to speak, "Daniel—"

He interrupted, "You could do much better than this weasel!"

The excitement of the fling had turned into a sickening disgrace, and she said nothing more.

Gene, frightened and silent, remained a couple of steps behind her.

Gesturing toward the farmhand, Daniel continued, "Tell him those frames are waiting for him." Then he turned and began back down the path, leaving the two behind.

Chapter Twelve

LIFE'S LABYRINTH: ANGUISH, BLISS, AWAKENING

*Is humanity more enlightened, or is our character
just as atrocious now as in ancient times?*

It was October 18, 1873, and the westbound train was largely
through Illinois, carrying Daniel back from New York to Sweet
Home. Recalling those moments on the hillside with Abba and
despicable Gene was painful yet liberating, like turning a page in
a book.

Now he was moving on. He had taken the train between New
York and Illinois several times in the early 1870s, and a long train
passage always made him feel like he was traveling in royal style.
Although the ride was fatiguing, hot by day, and cold at night,
it afforded safety and comfort, which contrasted nicely with the
hardships of walking, horseback, or stagecoach, which had been
the *only* options just a few years before.

Daniel reflected on travel through the Midwest in October. *It's a
good time to go by train—warm fall days allow for open windows.
Fresh air is a blessing because passengers confined closely, bouncing
along in this wooden box tend to develop a distinct pungency.
Making matters worse, passengers fall asleep in their seats in the*

evening. He smiled as he thought about what that implied. *Anyone who has experienced the smell of humans confined for too long knows the mysterious aroma uniquely given off by sleeping people! So open windows on a train provide welcome relief to one's distressed olfactory apparatus.* However, whenever a weak northwest breeze created a downdraft, westbound travelers had to choose between a coach filled with smoke from the engine's stack or closed windows and concentrated whiffs of human odors.

None of this "color" appeared in the brochure he was perusing. Instead, the pamphlet proudly depicted this last leg of the journey. The flier's face presented bold block letters *1873* at the top center, directly above *The Rock Island Line*. The text expounded on the role of The Rock Island Railroad as *the* innovative authority, boasting how the company had pioneered the first passenger service from points east to the Mississippi River. In addition, the Rock Island Line had recently coordinated with the Missouri and Mississippi Railroad, adding a new service between Davenport and Muscatine along the Iowa side of the river.

The booklet proudly proclaimed the railroad's achievements in bringing the cutting edge of civilization, culture, and commerce to frontier America. So Daniel was pleased that when he disembarked in Rock Island, he could board another smaller train, cross the river through Davenport, and continue west over to Muscatine. Then, a few steps from the Muscatine's *Union Station*, he'd ride a convenient ferry back across the Mississippi River and, on the Illinois side, catch a horse-drawn coach back to Sweet Home. The itinerary could get him home from Rock Island in less than half a day.

Sweet Home, his beloved little farmstead overlooking the Mississippi Valley, consisted of a wooded homestead of mixed terrain and a simple two-story white frame house. Typical of mid-nineteenth century rural Midwest architecture, the house had white clapboard siding, a kitchen, bedroom, and living room downstairs, three small bedrooms upstairs, and a covered porch across the front, suitable for sitting out. The house and yard, set below a steep wooded hill, stretched up, yielding to a vast expanse of level prairie at the top of the bluff.

The Mississippi Valley topography was characterized by a steep bluff paralleling the Mississippi River on both the Iowa and Illinois sides of the river. Distinct sloughs on both sides of the river, depending upon the season and proximity to the bluffs, extended up to several miles from the water's edge. These flood plains offered many thousands of acres of rich farmland—except for when untimely floods happened. Then the sloughs could be under water for weeks at a time. Immediately below Sweet Home, the slough stretched for about two miles before reaching the river's edge. Nevertheless, Daniel occasionally saw the river rise covering the bottomland, almost knocking at his door.

Located on some of the world's richest soil just a few miles north of New Boston, Illinois, Sweet Home better resembled the far-off frontier of Iowa than its more civilized Illinois counterpart. New Boston was actually located southwest of Davenport. Beginning at the west bank of the Mississippi, the Iowa territory occupied the next three hundred miles until reaching the next great waterway, the Missouri River. It's why Native Americans referred to Iowa as "the land between the rivers."

Travel to this part of Illinois involved a westward crossing of the Mississippi via the first railroad bridge ever to span the fabled river, joining Rock Island, Illinois, with Davenport, Iowa. Daniel thought about the recently martyred president and his impact on local history whenever he crossed the river here.

In 1832 the future president had served in Reynolds' militia during the Black Hawk War. Although he never saw action against the Native Americans, a courtroom drama that unfolded due to a maritime incident involving this bridge, a ship, and a fiery accident gave Lincoln the feeling of jubilation that comes with triumph over a formidable challenge. The case also established legal precedent for conflicts between railroads and waterways. Schoolmaster Palmer liked to discuss the lawsuit to show his students how Lincoln gained notoriety, confidence, and experience as a strategist.

As the train crossed the river, Daniel realized he could use its direction of flow to create a geography puzzle for his students. *The great river is often referred to as the gateway to the west. So why does the bridge crossing over the Mississippi River at Davenport run north to south? I'll throw in some practicality by adding what I'll be doing on this trip. Suppose one continues by train another forty-five minutes farther west. In that case, one arrives at Muscatine, where it will be necessary to cross the Mississippi River again to get back into Illinois. The students will use the map and the railroad schedule to figure it out.*

He considered what students solving the problem would learn. *The key to understanding this misdirection stems from a stubborn streak of the Old Man River. They'll learn the Mississippi flows from north to south for two thousand three hundred and fifty miles before it empties into the Gulf of Mexico. So the solution is that the only place where the Mississippi flows directly from east to west is a stretch of about fifty miles starting from a bit north of Davenport to just south of Muscatine.*

Homesteaders living in this part of the world were living way out west. Life was rugged and luxuries few. Abraham Lincoln had surveyed the fledgling New Boston about twenty years before Daniel came to the town. It grew steadily into a promising port community, showcasing a new two-story brick schoolhouse. New Bostonians proudly claimed their linkage to the slain president, believing being mapped out by Lincoln procured a higher level of validity for them. The locals never seemed to tire of recounting that fact to anyone who would listen.

The constantly changing views afforded to Daniel by the train ride kindled wide-ranging contemplations. Finally, his thoughts drifted to one of the many dramas that made up the rich legacy of these robust Mississippi River towns. *It's been fewer than twenty-five years since the largest city in the state shrank almost overnight into a small village.* It fascinated the Canadian who, soon after arriving in the Mississippi Valley, learned the great city of Chicago had actually played second fiddle to a lesser-known river town for several years. Nauvoo, Illinois, had reached its peak in 1845, the same year Daniel was born.

Exiled from New York, the Mormons who settled in Nauvoo had rapidly become a dominant force in Illinois politics and caused no little concern amongst their adversaries on the national political scene. Just sixty miles downriver from Sweet Home, Nauvoo had become the center of life for the Mormons. In 1846, violent anti-Mormon factions abruptly drove Brigham Young and the Mormons out of their homes in Nauvoo, igniting the great Mormon Trek. Three thousand souls destined for Utah began by tasting the bitterness of travel through Iowa during the piercing cold of winter, struggling westward despite difficulty and deprivations.

Hearing the train's loud whistle, and riding in the relative comfort of a car pulled by a powerful steam locomotive, gave Daniel pause. He reflected on the contrast between his situation and the suffering multitude who endured persecution and hardships on foot and in wagons as they crossed the country in those harshest conditions. It was his habit to develop lesson plans while pondering issues like this. So he reached for his notebook to jot down some concepts.

Is humanity more enlightened, or is our character just as atrocious now as in ancient times? Are we getting any better, or just going through the millennia in the same way? Are ignorance, intolerance, and violence so ingrained in our nature, it will always be this way? They were disheartening thoughts, and he muttered to himself as he penned: *Where's the evidence of human progress?*

No easy answers came, but something deep inside said there was at least the hope of enlightenment. Then, breaking the melancholy spell, he wrote: *Hopefulness itself makes a difference.*

The idea of hopefulness reminded him these were better times, at least in some ways.

Gazing at the landscape, he daydreamed with growing excitement about arriving home. He imagined bursting into the kitchen and putting his profits, along with the order for next season's yield, on display for everyone to pay homage.

The more he thought, the more anxious he became, and the more slowly the miles seemed to pass. Then he began to think along a whole different track. *Why is this so important to me? Why should I want to gather everyone around the kitchen table for a ceremonial unveiling of my success? Of course, Will and Mary will be there too! But why is it so damned important to me, I can hardly wait to show, tell, and exult?* He smiled and nearly broke out in laughter, thinking about his words. It seemed fitting since he liked to use precise language, but *exult* wasn't in his usual vocabulary. Beyond that, exultation was not a Daniel Palmer value, nor did he appreciate pretentiousness in others. *I put considerable effort into being my own man. I don't much care what anyone else thinks of me, and I occasionally go a bit out of my way to make sure everyone knows I don't give a hoot about other's opinions.*

He mulled it over. *Nobody thought I would succeed out there on the bluff—especially that witch, Abba! Everyone said, "Just be content to teach school to the New Boston children," and "Don't risk what little money you have on things no one has ever tried before." She just didn't have any faith in me.* These thoughts revealed something unexpected. The more he tried to convince himself, the more apparent it became. *Maybe I do care about what others think!* That revelation irritated him. Daniel unclenched his teeth and contemplated the circumstances leading to the deterioration of his relationship with Abba. It was painful, but he decided hiding from it was worse than going through it. He envisioned the beautiful face of a baby girl, and her memory brought something else into sharp focus. *Abba just never was the same since our infant daughter died.*

Abba never wanted to live out there along the bluff above the Mississippi. It was only about eight miles from town, but New Boston was a lifetime away when the snow flew. Midwestern winters could be so brutal. The ground froze hard like cement. The hillsides looked like a barren, snow-covered desert, punctuated by the occasional deciduous tree—hardly more suggestive of life than rocks projecting up out of the ground. Daniel had planted three long rows of red cedar along the western edge of the farm to create a wind block. But the trees were still small and looked fragile against the backdrop of this fiercest of Midwestern seasons.

The baby was nine months old when she took fever during an early February blizzard. Named Abba after her mother, their daughter was frail compared to other nine-month-olds in and around New Boston, and their delicate baby was particularly fussy.

Abba scolded Daniel for their situation. "Now we can't even get Doc Noble out here 'cause you refuse to live up in town like normal people. We're helpless out here!"

Daniel, already distraught, in addition to a jumble of other emotions, was not ready to be intimidated or conciliatory. Instead, he angrily shouted back, "That quack reminds me of a mule. He's got all the stubbornness, but no one would want to depend on him to heal anything!"

Like many, if not most, physicians of the day, Doc Noble had minimal education. During the Civil War, he served in the Illinois infantry and, without explanation, got assigned to help treat the wounded. He wondered if it was because of his poor marksmanship. It had been just seven years since he started learning most of what he knew about caring for patients in field infirmaries. The infirmaries were often tents or shacks not far from the front lines. Caregiving consisted largely of bandaging wounds and limb amputations. Survival rates were poor, and many patients survived despite, rather than because of, their medical care. After the war, doctors released from the military flooded towns all over the country. Doc Noble, like many others, was trying to figure out how to make a living with the skills he had learned as a medic. He was competent to amputate limbs and cauterize the remnant but rarely encountered patients with Minié balls in their arms or legs anymore. Instead, unsuspecting sick people became his most lucrative opportunity to carry on a gainful vocation.

Now, with a deep sense of regret, Daniel remembered how exhausted he and Abba both were after a day and a half of trying to care for the ailing infant. It was getting well into the evening when he finally said contritely to Abba, "Sweetheart, you need some rest, go to bed, and I'll take care of the baby." Then, feeling helpless, he added, "Maybe the storm will settle so Doc Noble can get out here in the morning."

It was the longest night of Daniel's life, worrying about the storm and much more so about his daughter. He tried hard to keep the house quiet so Abba could rest, but the baby cried continuously, and the only thing that seemed to help was holding her and moving. He paced around the living room, dining room, hallway, and back again while rocking her in his arms and softly singing to her. Holding her, moving, and singing was all he could do to soothe the misery.

He didn't know a lot of songs, but he sang the ones she recognized over and over again. "She'll be comin' 'round the mountain when she comes. She'll be comin' 'round the mountain when she comes ...." He kept singing, holding her, and pacing while he wondered how many renditions of "Camptown Races" and "I've Been Working on the Railroad" his voice could utter. He would swing her in his arms at fussier moments until they hurt, and he couldn't do it anymore. Then he would hold her close to his chest, still pacing and swaying more in his upper body to give his arms a break, all to the tune of yet another rendition of "She'll Be Comin' 'Round the Mountain."

It went on for hours that way. He found himself thinking about the meaning of the song. Even in moments such as this, Daniel Palmer's mind refused to rest. His quiddity was to analyze and overanalyze everything, even a trifling little tune. He held her close, trod the floor, and tried to minimize the noises that might disturb his wife by stepping on the rugs as much as possible. He had mapped the quietest floorboards in his mind's eye and trod most deliberately on them as he continued to sing faintly while pondering the song. *Why would she be driving six white horses? And so what if she was wearing pink pajamas? "We'll all come out to meet her" makes sense, but was it really necessary to kill the old red rooster?*

He decided he needed to change songs. So he created a musical medley. Softly he began, "She'll be wearing pink pajamas when she comes ..." which segued into "Li'l Abba's wearing those pajamas when she comes"—he dragged out the word *comes*—"and she's singing 'Polly Wolly Doodle' all the day." He even personalized it for her. "Abba went down South. She's a spunky gal, singing 'Polly Wolly Doodle' all the day. ... Fare thee well, fare thee well, fare thee well, my Abba gay, for I'm going to Lou'siana, for to see my Abba Danna, singing 'Polly Wolly Doodle' all the day!"

Daniel felt foolish singing silly songs with ridiculous words, but it mattered little to a man trying to help his ailing daughter through the night. Thinking it might help to add a serious touch to his repertoire, the next time the medley cycled through, he inserted the patriotic "Yankee Doodle." Again he worked Abba's name into the lyrics. "Abba and I went down to camp, along with Captain Gooding. There we saw the men and boys, as thick as hasty-pudding. Yankee Doodle, keep it up, Yankee Doodle dandy. Mind the music and the step, and with the girls be handy." Once the words came out of his mouth, it bothered him to realize the unlikely word *doodle* showed up prominently in two of the three songs in the medley. To improve an unsuitable lyric, he decided to alter the chorus with "Abba Dabba keep it up, Abba Dabba dandy; Mind the music and the step, and with *only* good boys be handy!"

Several more hours passed along with endless renditions of "Polly Wolly Doodle," "Comin' 'Round the Mountain," "Yankee Doodle," and whatever else his short repertoire offered. He was halfway down the hall, still pacing and gently swinging the infant in his arms, "For to see my Abba Danna, singing Polly wolly doodle all the—" when his wife startled him with a tap on the shoulder.

She commanded, "I'll take over now. Go get some rest." Too tired to speak, he tenderly passed the blanket-swathed child over to her and watched as she placed the child across her chest, walked to the couch, and sat down. He marveled at how she could take the infant and just sit on the couch with her, while he, on the other hand, had been unable to stop or sit without triggering tears and shrieks. Raspy little breaths were still coming from her, but she could be content in her mother's arms without all the pacing and song.

Daniel went right to bed, noting it was about an hour and a half before dawn. He passed immediately into a deep sleep for what seemed like only about two minutes when a harsh shake on the shoulder and the sound of Abba's voice woke him. "It's over."

Her unsettling tone was one he had never heard from her before. He struggled to open his eyes, and even in the faint light of early morning, she looked drained of color. He knew what it meant when he focused on her teary, contorted face. He jumped from the bed, instinctively opening his arms to reach out and comfort her. Unable and unwilling to accept his affection, Abba silently turned and walked out of the room. At that moment, consoling her would have been the only possible solace for him, but it was not to be.

Daniel stood in place, stunned in disbelief. He tried to assimilate that they had lost their child, and an invisible wall separated him from his wife. Clarity of thought wouldn't come, so instinct took over. He ran to the hallway, past Abba, who sat silently on the couch where he had left them a couple of hours before, and up the stairs to the nursery. Like usual, little Abba was tucked in her crib. The depth of despair vanished, and for a fleeting moment, all was okay. But the devastating stillness in the room told him it would never be okay again.

Silently time passed. Their baby had died in her mother's arms during that night's blizzard. But the young couple neither embraced nor spoke. Instead, dazed and confused, they suffered. She stayed on the couch, and he went to the kitchen, where he sat on a wooden chair, resting his elbows on the table and his head on his hands.

The young mother, in a semi-conscious stupor, was numbly aware as she stared blankly across the living room for the next two hours. Grief was new to her, and the longer she sat, the angrier she became.

She didn't *want* to blame her husband, but nothing about their situation made sense. In her anguish, anger was preferable to emptiness, and what ifs played in her mind. *If we hadn't been so isolated, then maybe someone could have helped. What good are psychic abilities if you can't save your own child?*

Finally, she went to the kitchen to make coffee. She poured a cup for herself, placed it on the counter, and then brought one to her husband, who gratefully accepted it. "Thank you ...," he began, but she had already turned and stepped away before he could add a word of endearment, so he stopped speaking.

His appreciative eyes met hers only for the briefest moment before she broke the connection. Proffering coffee was not a gesture of warmth or kindness; it was just something to do. No other words were spoken that morning. The day continued that way, each of them tending to their chores.

Daniel gathered several pieces of cut firewood at midday and carried an armful up to the top of the bluff, where he collected some brush and built a fire. He knew the ground was frozen, and hot coals would be needed before he could dig.

In the late afternoon, Abba found some relief in the mundane. Finally, sweeping the kitchen floor reminded her that neither of them had eaten anything that day. She mechanically poured cut-up vegetables from a glass canning jar into a cast iron pot, put it on the wood stove, and went to the basement to get a piece of salted beef. As she was climbing back up the stairs, it occurred to her that beef stew was one of Daniel's favorites. Stalled halfway up the stairs, she considered whether preparing something he liked would make an unintended statement of affection. Shrugging it off, Abba decided she simply didn't care what he or anyone else thought and returned to the kitchen. She added the meat, water, dried parsley, a parsnip, and a bit more salt, slid the pot over the fire, and stirred. Later she thickened it with some wheat flour and put a lid on it to keep it warm.

Daniel's chores kept him outside. He built a wooden box, returned to the top of the bluff, dug a tiny grave, left the shovel up there, and returned to the house. He entered through the mud room and felt welcomed by the aroma of supper on the stove. It was the first pleasant sensation since putting his head on the pillow the night before. He removed his boots and stepped into the kitchen, where he saw Abba standing by the stove. She held herself tightly, signaling her mood hadn't thawed.

He finally spoke directly to Abba, "Evening will be falling in about half an hour. I've beaten a pretty good path through the snow, but you'll need your snow boots."

Abba responded, "Take off your coveralls. I've made some stew."

Obediently, he removed his heavy outerwear, hung it by the door, and sat down at the table while she ladled stew into two bowls. They ate together without speaking, and each of them found that swallowing required extra effort.

Daniel was angst-ridden, not just with grief but also by the idea he was to sit there eating her stew in silence. He had only spoken two sentences to her that day but understood she did not want to talk. Her frame of mind could tolerate only the fewest words and only those that carried the least emotive content. So they ate little, each knowing the perfunctory meal was necessary.

When she stopped eating, he looked up at Abba and said, "We better go soon. There isn't much daylight left."

She barely nodded to acknowledge she was ready.

They left the dishes on the table and proceeded to the mud room, where they pulled on their boots and winter gear. Abba stretched gloves over her hands and picked up the Bible, which she had placed on the shelf near the door in anticipation of this moment. He walked to the nursery while she waited by the door. For once, it didn't seem to matter he was tramping through the house with his boots on. She had barely looked directly at him all day. But now, she did as he approached the mud room, carrying the still child in his arms. Tears poured from her eyes, making it difficult to focus. Then, blotting her eyes on the sleeve of her coat, she reached for a tiny, folded quilt on the shelf where the Bible had rested. She tenderly draped it over the baby, and together they turned and walked out the back door.

They buried their child up on top of the bluff above the house at Sweet Home. From there, one could see for miles. Daniel had always loved that spot. He liked the way he could fix his eyes on both Iowa and Illinois at once, and his spirit enjoyed rare moments of peace there. He could stand and gaze out at the valley with a view unobstructed by trees or the rooftop of their two-story frame house, just below the bluff.

Chapter Thirteen

BERTHIE

*"For everything there is a season, and a time
for every purpose under heaven."*

–ECCLESIASTES 3:1, KING JAMES BIBLE

Abba never forgave Daniel, and the warmth between them turned to ice. Even the birth of Lucy several months later did little to rekindle the flame of affection Abba had once felt for Daniel. To her, he was now contemptible, self-centered, and arrogant, but not loveable. She wondered what she ever had loved about him. She found herself despising him for her situation; the new baby was his fault and made everything worse.

Sitting in the living room rocking chair, silently knitting on a cold December evening, Abba contemplated her situation. While others enjoyed knitting and the satisfaction of creating something from nothing, Abba found no pleasure in it. Like everything else she did, it made her feel like she was fulfilling some kind of womanly obligation. Anything considered normal, wholesome, and productive seemed to rub her the wrong way and contributed to her irritability.

The longer she thought, the further she felt from her husband, and it reminded her of another thing she resented about him. *I know when little Lucy's conception took place, and it was the very last time I submitted.* Abba's thoughts haunted her, and she stopped herself at the word *submitted.* There had been a time when submission had absolutely nothing to do with it. Instead, that word triggered the memory of his scent when they would cling to one another in bed. It was a time when she couldn't wait to go to bed with him. She remembered how he felt strong and powerful. His scent was masculine, and he was desirable in every way. Entertaining those thoughts now sickened her, and she loathed herself for having ever felt that way about him.

Aside from the antipathy she felt toward Daniel, she was frustrated by and jealous of his unquenchable thirsts. *Why does he have to know the why of everything? Why does he always have to be different? Why must he ask questions no one else cares to ask? If no one else cares to ask unanswerable questions, what gives him the right anyway?* That last question bought clarity. She finally realized what she resented most was his *need.* His need to know, search, and persevere took precedence over everything, including her.

"Goddamn him!" she said aloud. She could abide by a lot, but she would not tolerate being second fiddle to her husband's obsessions. When they spoke, he said little. Often deep in his thoughts, he shut her out like she was an unfortunate distraction. She usually countered by shouting with spitting anger, which deteriorated into profanities. That drove him inward, further from her and her concerns. As a result, there was little peace in their home. He dealt with it by avoiding her when possible and drawing further inward when she pressed him with increasing frustration. She dealt with it by looking elsewhere for the caring, companionship, and emotional support she craved.

As it turned out, she did not have to look far.

Several months after Lucy's birth, Abba left in the middle of the night for a new life in far-off Minnesota. She and her lover Gene Horvath, farmhand to the Palmers, decided to slip away at night. They reasoned it would be prudent to avoid the possibility of rage or retribution. Daniel had already discovered they were involved, but he and Abba hadn't yet talked about it. A succinct note from Abba left no doubt that he was totally on his own.

Before leaving, Abba secretly met with Mr. Keele, one of the two attorneys in town. He would finalize her legal obligations, administer the dissolution of the marriage, and complete the sale of her half of the Sweet Home property. She did not allow herself to think about her child, but in rare, quiet sleepless moments, she couldn't repress her feelings of shame and regret she would not see Lucy grow up; nor would she ever again climb to the top of the bluff and visit baby Abba's tiny grave.

Curiously, the twenty-eight-year-old apiculturist took the shock of their flight under cover of darkness in stride and soon felt fulfilled in a way he never had before. True, he didn't have a wife, but Berthie had become a pretty good companion.

Abba's abrupt exodus had placed Daniel in a predicament. Schoolmaster obligations and keeping up with Sweet Home meant his hands were full, long before meeting the needs of an infant and running a home. The first problem to solve involved finding domestic help. There weren't many options in the small, rural environment, and he wasn't wealthy either, so the first person he thought of was Berthie. Everyone around New Boston called Henrietta Bertha Holcomb by her middle name, stylized to Berthie.

The morning after Abba left, he saw to morning chores, and at nine o'clock, he folded the note from Abba into his shirt pocket and took the baby over to the Essley's on his way to town. Daniel held the folded paper in his hand while speaking to Ava. "She's gone, Mrs. Essley." He began to get choked up immediately, surprised to find that saying it was harder than just knowing it. He looked down at the note as if it could provide courage. "Abba's not coming back ... ever."

Ava got the picture quickly, and in her most helpful, understanding voice, said, "We're here for you, Mr. Palmer, and I know you will be okay." She smiled warmly. "I know you don't feel good about it now, and that's understandable. Just remember, though, your freedom from her"—Ava emphasized *her* with the harshest, most negative tone she could muster—"is the best thing that could have happened."

"Thank you, Mrs. Essley," he said as he put the note back in his pocket. He felt silly. *Why did I bring that note along? Would she have asked me for proof? How ridiculous. I'm not thinking clearly.*

When Daniel arrived at Berthie's house, she was busily doing laundry for Mrs. Noble, who usually dropped off a basket full two or three times per week. Mrs. Noble was aware of Berthie's tenuous financial situation, so she happily gave her the opportunity to earn money, which the Nobles could comfortably afford to pay for the service.

"Hello, Mr. Palmer," she greeted him cheerfully before noticing his somber face.

"Hello, Berthie," he began, then took a breath before going on. "There's been a difficult change in my life that's not easy to talk about." Her concerned face and full attention assured him as he continued. "The long and the short of it is Mrs. Palmer has left abruptly, and she won't ever be coming back. I've got an infant daughter and a household to care for, so I'm wondering if you might consider taking on something like that."

Berthie's jaw dropped as she listened to the shocking news of his circumstance, and a mother leaving her baby. Like a student caught daydreaming when called upon in class, Berthie stood there just looking at him for an awkward moment.

Berthie's words stumbled out of her mouth. "How terrible! I mean, I'm sorry for your distress. I really haven't been courting …," she stammered, trying to think of the right thing to say. "I mean the thought of getting together with someone …" His puzzled expression stopped her in mid-sentence as it finally sunk in. Blushing with embarrassment about her presumptions, she'd understood he wasn't seeking a new wife, just someone to help run the home.

His bewildered look compounded the gawkiness of the situation until Berthie hastily came out with a simple direct answer. "Oh! I understand. Yes, Mr. Palmer, I can help you." Clumsy communication notwithstanding, her words lifted a weight off of Daniel's chest.

His spirit lightened, he began in rapid succession. "I need you as soon as possible. We live simply, but there's plenty of everything to go around. The baby can be fussy, and someone must watch over her. You'll get a large room of your own, right off the hallway—"

Berthie stopped him and offered some reassurance. "I'll need to finish this for Mrs. Noble, clean floors at the Kelloggs' home today, and cancel the Knots' housekeeping for tomorrow. Why don't you come by for me with a wagon this afternoon so I can bring some things along? I could be ready by four."

Only eighteen years old when she moved into the Palmer home, Berthie had learned to fend for herself early in life. Her father had died in battle at Gettysburg when she was nine years old. Four years later, she lost her mother to flu and found herself living alone in a tiny cabin in New Boston at age thirteen, with no relatives within a thousand miles and only limited education. Nevertheless, she worked hard and found it possible to continue her education while earning barely enough money for food and clothing by doing laundry and housecleaning in and around New Boston. Sometimes people paid her with coal to heat her cabin, or perhaps a chicken, whatever helped sustain her in the cottage on the edge of town.

At five foot ten inches, Berthie was taller than any of the young women she knew. She was physically strong, bright, and pretty in a unostentatious way, and people in New Boston liked her. Often, especially in the hard winter months, folks in the community would invite her into their homes for supper and fellowship. She was upbeat, smart, and poised. Those attributes, in addition to her stature, left most of the neighbors unaware of just how young she was.

She had been one of Daniel's students in the town's fine new brick school building only three years ago. He remembered vividly the day she came to him on a Friday afternoon while everyone else was filing out of the classroom. "Mr. Palmer, I'm sorry to tell you,

I'm afraid I can't continue in school any longer. There's just not enough hours in the day for me to keep up with everything."

Sharing her disappointment, he tried to suggest alternatives. "Perhaps we could reduce your homework assignments and—"

Before he could go on, she interrupted, saying with tears in her eyes, "I should have stopped last term, Mr. Palmer, but I didn't want to disappoint you. Maybe I can come back again, but for now, I have to put food on the table."

Berthie, a good student, was quiet, obedient, and had a strong work ethic. These qualities pleased Daniel, so she seemed like the natural answer when things blew up with Abba and he needed household help right away. It worked out well for both of them. He provided room and board, plus a few dollars a month, affording her a secure situation. For him, she was a godsend, enabling him to keep his schoolmaster position, in addition to the daunting work maintaining Sweet Home involved.

Mourning over Abba's departure just didn't fit Daniel's personality, and soon Berthie was accompanying him and the baby to picnics and social events in and around New Boston. She efficiently organized a more serene home than he had ever experienced before, and on a few occasions, they had even carried their relationship further.

It started innocently during a snowstorm one night. Berthie had seen to early evening chores and just finished putting little Lucy to bed. When she came out to the parlor, Daniel was sitting near the fireplace, holding a book illuminated by the light of the fire and the oil lamp on a nearby end table. He frequently sat this way and read after supper. But this time, he was just gazing into the fireplace. She knew something was wrong when she noticed the fire was dying down to little more than a few flickering embers. He was generally very attentive to such things and would have customarily stoked it up so it would burn strong until bedtime. But, as she approached, it was apparent all was not well. She discovered he was shivering, and there were beads of sweat on his forehead.

Never having seen any sign of weakness in Daniel, she became alarmed and sprang into action. The first thing was to get him focused. He wasn't delirious, but he did seem to be mildly confused. "Mr. Palmer, you're ill. We need to get you down to rest," Berthie said.

He looked up at her, wiped his brow with his shirt sleeve, and said, "Okay," but he didn't seem to be trying to do anything else.

Berthie positioned herself alongside his chair, bent her knees, and lifted his left arm across her shoulders. Then grasping his hand, she straightened her knees. Her tall frame and strong legs as levers efficiently helped pull him up to a standing position. That was the easiest part. But guiding his solid frame from there to his bedroom down the hall took every bit of her formidable strength. He couldn't muster enough energy to undress on his own, so Berthie said, "I'll support you." She clumsily steadied his left arm while dutifully fixing her gaze toward the hallway to assure decency and save both of them from embarrassment. He peeled off his outer layers, and she eased her grip, allowing him to collapse onto the bed. Then she helped him to roll straight onto his back and covered him with extra layers of blankets.

She brought him hot tea throughout the evening, wiped his brow, and kept vigilance. Finally, he fell into a deep sleep while she loyally stayed by her employer's side in an armchair near his bed.

Berthie checked in on the baby and was pleased to see her peacefully in deep slumber. Having been frightened to see Mr. Palmer so helpless, she decided he should not be left alone. She kept the oil lamp burning with a low wick, barely enough so she could see to read. As the night wore on, Berthie intermittently drifted off to sleep, reawakening with a stiff and sore neck from bobbing her head off to one side. Exhausted yet committed to keeping a close eye on the situation, she slid the chair close to the bed and dragged a pillow over to its edge. Now, still seated on the chair, she leaned over and placed her shoulder and head on the bed. Getting her head and neck perpendicular to her shoulders was a relief to her neck, which was no longer strained. Berthie soon drifted off into welcome sleep.

Slightly before dawn, the fever broke, and Daniel awoke refreshed for one who had just experienced such a feverish night. However, he was surprised to discover Berthie was still asleep and resting her upper body on the bed with her head on the pillow next to his.

Mixed emotions gripped him. She had shown caring and dedication beyond the demands of her employment. Without thinking, a sense of affection and appreciation compelled him to reach forward and lightly press his lips to her forehead. It unexpectedly awoke frightful feelings. Her alluring youthful presence, pretty face, and charming serenity inflamed and attracted him in a way that propriety forbade. In horror, he realized, *That appreciative kiss on the forehead of my slumbering employee betrays the ground rules of our relationship!*

Well, actually, the ground rules have never been spelled out, but they certainly exist. He argued with himself, carrying on an emotional tug of war. *Is there some way I can take it back? I'm not that much older than she.* Then he invoked a rationalization, *Well, we never really agreed to ...*

His thoughts were interrupted as she awoke to see him awake, no longer feverish, and with a yearning look that said more than he was just no longer ill. Berthie tilted her head upward and kissed him back. But her ardent kiss was on his lips. Unlike his tentative graze, hers had a zeal that took both of them by surprise.

Feeling a bit dazed and bewildered, he saw the smiling, confident face of a woman eagerly taking control.

Placing her hand behind his head, Berthie pulled him into another long, passionate kiss. Then, still in charge and without breaking the kiss, Berthie rolled her lower half from the chair, over him onto the bed. Grasping his shoulders, she spun, dragging him around and on top of her. Now there was no stopping either of them. Their lovemaking was warm and wonderful, fulfilling a thirst both yearned to quench.

It was well into the morning when Lucy started to stir. They both quickly dressed, and Berthie scrambled to her room, not wishing to be caught in Daniel's bedroom. Once in her room, she giggled quietly. "How would baby Lucy know which room I came from this morning? So ridiculous!"

No words of love were ever spoken between employer and employee. Strangely, neither of them mentioned the preceding night at all. It was cumbersome, even silly, how each of them found a multitude of mundane tasks to busy themselves, desperately finding ways to be in each other's company as much as possible. Neither of them knew how to express what the preceding night/morning meant to them. Nor did either of them wish to suggest that any kind of commitments were made or even implied.

Over the next few days, Daniel came to Berthie's room three times. She opened her arms to him, and they silently repeated their lovemaking. The fulfillment and excitement of those nights with Berthie were so intense, he couldn't help but think of how his experiences with Abba seemed pathetic and shallow in comparison. Nevertheless, he felt terribly guilty about the whole thing. Neither uttered endearments. During the day, they never spoke about what went on at night. The remarkable thing is the essence of their relationship never changed. They remained a young housekeeper and an older employer—who had temporarily seen to a few of each other's extra needs.

The whole thing passed in less than a week, and neither he nor Berthie tried to renew the intimacy again. Occasionally she had gentlemen callers, and Daniel was not jealous. On the contrary, the very idea of her friendships with young men eased his guilt. He looked forward to her striking up a steady relationship with someone because he secretly felt that once her future looked safe and secure, he could finally put the gnawing sense of remorse to rest. His need for absolution resolved when he stumbled upon a surprising occurrence several months later. Unexpected though it might have been, what he saw soothed his guilt-ridden conscience.

One afternoon Berthie returned to the Palmer home from the general store where she bought some fabric. Accompanying her was a shy young woman carrying a tattered gray carpetbag-style suitcase. Daniel, who had just come in from tending to the apiary chores, directed a puzzled look toward Berthie. Not waiting for him to speak, Berthie introduced them. "Mr. Palmer, this is my friend Lucinda Adams. Miss Adams, I'm pleased to introduce my employer, Mr. Daniel Palmer."

Lucinda wore a long skirt of light-green print fabric with small beige daisy-shaped flowers that looked as tired as she did. Above, her ivory-colored blouse was tightly laced at the neck.

They exchanged polite greetings. "Pleased to meet you, Miss Adams."

"The pleasure is mine, Mr. Palmer."

Knowing he would be ready for some rest and a snack, Berthie gestured toward the table. "Let's have tea." Not waiting for a response, Berthie began to heat water while they obediently found seats at the kitchen table. "Mr. Palmer, you will be interested to know Lucinda's husband died the day before Lee surrendered. It's disgusting. He was a hero who gave his all for our country, and she's been left struggling ever since. Now they've taken her little house away because she couldn't pay the taxes. She's been without a home for a week now. Lucinda slept on sacks of flour in Wells Willits General Store last night. Mr. Willits was kind enough to lend her a blanket and put some extra coal in the stove before he went home, but that's no place for a decent girl to sleep. I told her I knew you would let her stay until she could get some work and get back on her feet. There's still a lot of her things in that house. But it's locked up until a magistrate lets her in. So all she's got for now is what's in that suitcase." Berthie pointed at the carpetbag on the floor as she stopped for a breath of air.

Daniel seized the moment, speaking in a firm, helpful tone, "I've got a sister named Lucinda. She's living in Iowa, married to a coal miner in What Cheer. If something like this were ever to happen to her, I wouldn't want anyone hesitating to help. You're welcome to stay here. It isn't much, but we always have plenty to eat. The house is small, so you'll need to share Berthie's room for as long as it takes to get things straightened around for you."

Lucinda's small, round face softened with relief, and a warm smile appeared. The petite young woman seemed so delicate and vulnerable, Daniel couldn't imagine turning her away. He hated what war did to people and loathed the glorification of militarism with its parades and patriotic songs. Just thinking about the spectacle nauseated him. *If only those fools realized the truth about the suffering they cause. I'll never pledge allegiance to a flag.* Since the end of the war, it had become fashionable in public meetings, park dedications, and even public school sessions to open events with a pledge of allegiance. Whenever Daniel found himself at such gatherings, he kept his integrity while choosing not to make a scene. Realizing most people weren't thinking it through, he simply recited the words with an honorable modification. *I pledge allegiance to the* principles *of the United* ... Daniel made no mention of the flag because pledging allegiance to a flag implied an unthinking, unconditional nationalistic commitment to whatever those in power at the time decided. He loved the United States of America and its ideals, so he could enthusiastically pledge allegiance to its principles, but he would never go forth to blindly kill others on the orders of any man—to him, that would be immoral. He could commit himself to just principles, but not permanently nor irrevocably to any flag.

Lucinda's situation drove Daniel deeper into contemplation. *Furthermore, the country recently condoned and encouraged slavery of one person as the property of another. A vote in congress followed by a signature could do the same again. No, Daniel Palmer is a patriot who lives the principles to which this country is dedicated, and that's why he will not pledge allegiance to a flag.*

He recalled one of his first great challenges after arriving in Iowa. It had been a real struggle to scrape together three hundred dollars. That was the price required to exercise his right to buy out of military service. The money would later fund a willing enlistee's bounty for joining in his place. Even though he came from Canada-West, and was not yet a US citizen, the country was still at war. Conscription was the likely reality for healthy young men of his age. A lot was said to justify the conflict, but Daniel had his thoughts. *Yes, slavery was ended in the conflict, and it had to end. But did it really have to be achieved this way? What about all the joy stolen from Lucinda and her husband and the children they will never have? What will it take, and when will the human race evolve above the insanity?*

Daniel seemed to have withdrawn to his own world, and Berthie noticed a look of concern coming over Lucinda. Then, to shake him back to the here and now, Berthie said, "Mr. Palmer, the tea is almost ready. Would you mind taking Miss Adams's suitcase to my room?"

His attention to humanity's flaws and war's devastation notwithstanding, being lost in his thoughts provided no compliment to Berthie and their frail-looking young guest. He rose, gave her a big smile, took her hand, and offered a warm, "Welcome! I'm glad to share our home with you, Miss Adams. I'll see to your bag." Then, taking the bag, he strode out of the room. As he entered Berthie's room, he heard indistinct but cheerful chatter from the kitchen.

Lucinda had been in the Palmer home for a bit over two weeks, and Daniel asked nothing of her. The three of them agreed she was welcome to fix a soup, mend some socks, or do whatever she felt comfortable doing to contribute to the household. She busied herself with chores around the house and loved working in the garden. Since her arrival, the vegetable plot was quickly transforming into a horticultural showplace. Weeds didn't have a chance against her watchful eye while flowers and plants flourished. She went into town every second day to look for work opportunities and keep in touch with the lawyer who was supposed to be trying to get her house back.

On a bright moonlit Thursday night, everyone had gone to bed. Daniel was using one of the upstairs bedrooms so that Berthie and Lucinda could have the larger bedroom downstairs. Being restless that night, he reached to his bedside table to pour a drink of water. Then he discovered he had forgotten to bring his small pitcher of water from the kitchen to his room. It was his habit not to worry about burning lights when stirring around the house at night since he knew his way around and didn't want to disturb anyone. However, while passing down the hall toward the kitchen, the moonlight shining through Berthie's window into the hallway caught his eye.

It was customary for the bedroom doors in the Palmer home to be left about halfway open to allow natural convections of warmer air from the kitchen stove and the cast-iron wood-burner in the living room to provide heat. Open doors throughout the house kept things comfortably warm.

Normally, he would politely walk by her open door, focused straight ahead. But the unusually bright moonlight drew his gaze to the window on the opposite wall.

Daniel was somewhat confused at first glance. Berthie and Lucinda were sitting upright on the bed, facing each other. The night was still early, and the moon was rising. Positioned somewhat low in the sky, it shimmered brilliantly from across the horizon.

The effect was one of those rare, magical-looking moons that come only once or twice a year. Having covered this event in the classroom on Tuesday, he knew it wasn't supernatural, despite its intense appearance. In their science section, the children made paper models explaining why a certain type of perigee full moon can appear astonishingly large, radiant, and seem like you could almost reach out and touch it. They also learned about its impacts and folklore, how it could produce the highest of tides, and the Native American tradition of calling the first full moon of the year the wolf moon. The lesson included a discussion about celestial alignment and how the phenomenon can inspire poets to write, increase sap flow in trees, and correlate with bizarre human behaviors.

Consequently, the children learned the term *lunacy* was derived from Latin. Luna was the name of the ancient Roman goddess of the moon. Thus she became the namesake for things lunar. The students also learned the bright shine of the wolf moon had been known to wake people out of a sound sleep, and with good reason because during that phenomenon, the moon was approximately thirty-one thousand miles closer than its more typical orbital segments. In the classroom, Daniel praised the ancient Greeks' ability to make this calculation using the geometrical "Shadow Method" attributed to Aristarchus circa 270 B.C.

Even with this knowledge fresh in his mind, the moon's intensity on such a clear night was surreal, even hypnotic, compelling him to scrutinize another spectacle taking place right before his eyes. The window, Berthie's bed, and doorway aligned perfectly with his viewpoint from the hallway. Like a beacon shining through the window, the intensely bright moonlight framed the two women like a portrait and created an extraordinarily detailed silhouette of their forms. He watched Berthie's hand reach forward as her head leaned toward Lucinda.

Her movements were slow, and Daniel's eyes widened as he saw Berthie lifting Lucinda toward her mouth. He blinked, clearly seeing her lips and the distinct silhouette of a nipple vanish into them. His eyes were riveted in astonishment while his cheeks became warm, making him glad their redness was invisible.

Distinctive sensual energy emanated from the room. Its occupants didn't notice the motionless man unconsciously holding his breath while breathing inside the room was ardent. Lucinda was wearing a thin white nightgown, wide open at the front, and Berthie was undressed. Berthie's mouth remained as her hands rose, sliding the gauzy nightshirt off Lucinda's shoulders and slowly urging her onto her back. The delicate fabric fell, revealing the petite woman's striking shape. He was fascinated by the well-defined curves of her diminutive form, especially the forward curve of her low back, which soon disappeared as she was lowered onto the mattress. Berthie glided herself on top of Lucinda, and the two moved slowly against each other.

A strong compulsion suddenly struck Dan. *I must not be here! No, I can't be caught in her doorway! Of course, I never intended to violate their privacy, but how could I ever explain that?* The heat in his cheeks intensified, as did his embarrassment.

He silently backed away in slow motion, as though mesmerized by the intense image of the couple inside. Then, finally breaking free, he tip-toed up the stairs and padded back down the hall toward his room, hoping desperately that the floor wouldn't creak. It all happened in less than a minute, yet it seemed to last much longer.

Soon he was lying in bed, thinking about what they were doing just down the hall. His own body had responded to what he witnessed, and it annoyed him his pulse had quickened, his heart raced, and a warm, stirred-up feeling had come over his entire body. He wished his physical reaction would abate, because it worsened his compunction after invading their most private moment.

Regrets soon gave way to absurdity. In typical Daniel Palmer style, he mulled it over to the point of weariness. *Perhaps I should go back to Berthie's room and ...* The fleeting thought made him feel awful, so he crushed and cursed it. *They'd know I've been peeping. It's bad enough to have inadvertently come upon them, but deliberately returning is an entirely different message.* It struck him he wasn't even sure about the message within his flummoxed musings. It had been months since the affair with Berthie, and he was anxious to see her move on—not that he expected it to happen in this particular way.

Lucinda's stay in the Palmer home was never intended to be anything but temporary, and she was such a good-looker, he was sure it wouldn't be long before numerous offers came her way. On the other hand, Daniel had hoped the circumstances with Berthie would have permanence. Between lesson plans during the school season and all the demands of the apiary, he couldn't fathom handling the needs of an infant child. But heartbreak again visited the Palmer home.

It was mid-afternoon on a clear day. Berthie was inside seeing to household tasks, and Daniel was outside working to fill orders for Sweet Home raspberry nursery stock. Carefully choosing the canes, he walked through the rows. They grew the thickest and thorniest along the hillside, and there were long rows on top of the bluff, tied up on tall stakes for easier handling. He had developed an eye for the small plants that were just the right shade of green, telling him their roots were healthy and independent of the mother plant.

The plants proliferated when a cane cascaded over from a larger established one, touched the ground, and dropped down new roots capable of sustaining it as a separate entity. He would then gently dig around it to loosen the stem, leaving enough soil to protect the more delicate roots. After freeing and setting the new plant on the ground, he would inspect it to ensure it was worthy of the name Sweet Home. He would then cut the cane free from the mother and immediately wrap it in a moistened newspaper. Later it would get an outer layer of waxed paper to hold in several drops of extra moisture added just before sealing it in a shipping envelope.

Little Lucy was almost nine months old and not yet walking. Berthie was cleaning floors, so she placed the child on a blanket on the far side of the living room. The freak accident happened so suddenly, Berthie barely had time to think. She was sweeping with a corn broom when she turned, and something slick under her foot caused her to slip. The sock she'd stepped on glided so freely over the hardwood floor, Berthie went down hard and fast. Somehow the long handle of the broom was pinioned under her hip. Then as she fell, it came free and flew to the side, its end hitting head-on into Daniel's prized observatory.

The glass-covered hive was built into the room's exterior wall, from which it cantilevered to the outside, providing easy access for the bees to come and go. The unusual hive, designed for viewing the activities of the bees from the comfort of one's easy chair, was the envy of visiting beekeepers. But when speared by the high-speed hickory projectile, the glass seal shattered into a thousand pieces.

Moments later, Berthie was back on her feet in a room full of bees. Desperately whirling around, she grasped the newspaper from an end table and began swinging it at the insects. Soon, her reaction was like fanning the flames, and the swarm appeared to grow larger and angrier. Hearing Lucy's cries, she recognized the seriousness of the situation and knew the highest priority was to get her out of harm's way. Berthie rushed to the blanket, threw the paper over the baby, scooped her up, and ran outside screaming for Daniel.

Seeing no sign of him and still screaming, she held Lucy tight and ran to each side of the house yard. Still running and shouting for help, Berthie continued along one end of the many rows of hives in the flat behind the house yard, but to no avail. Then, finally, she remembered the warning bell and ran back to the porch. She balanced Lucy in one arm and began frantically pulling the rope attached to the large brass alarm. Then, with precious time passing, she decided to run through the flat toward the path that went up the hillside.

Daniel was up on top of the bluff when he heard the commotion. He came running through thickets of raspberry canes toward the main path down the hill. They were both out of breath when they met partway up. It had already been several minutes since the calamity, and Berthie was crying hysterically. He took Lucy in his arms and saw three stingers in her face and more in each of her arms. He knew he must remove stingers quickly to reduce the venom released. He also knew one must scrape at rather than pull on stingers, so he removed his leather work glove to use his fingernails.

He began with one of the stingers in her badly swollen face, and his heart sank when he touched her pale, cool skin. Lucy did not move, and she wasn't breathing, and like a shot blasting through every fiber of his being, it struck him the quiet baby was already gone.

Lucy was buried next to her sister Abba on top of the bluff. It was an accident, and although despairing and emotionally drained,

Daniel didn't blame Berthie. However, she had a harder time forgiving herself and quickly began to feel out of place living at Sweet Home. A few days later, Berthie said, "I believe it's time for me to return to New Boston. It's probably best if I live in town."

The only response he could muster in his grief-stricken state was a simple "I understand."

The next morning, Daniel helped Berthie load her clothing and other possessions onto a wagon and they drove the seven miles to New Boston together. When they arrived at the little house where Lucinda used to live with her husband, she came out to greet them and help unload Berthie's things. "I'm so sorry about what happened," Lucinda said.

Daniel, half smiling, nodded acknowledgement, and the women comforted each other with a short embrace.

Daniel said, "I'm glad to see you have your own home again."

"Me too," Berthie interjected.

"Yes, my lawyer is still working on it. I've given them letters from Washington, and the town says there are still unpaid property taxes. Meanwhile, I'm allowed back in my home until it all gets ironed out." Lucinda responded.

"Well, just let me know if there is anything I can do," said Daniel.

"We will," Lucinda answered for both of them, then turned to Berthie and said, "Now, let's get your things inside."

The three made short work of moving Berthie's things into the house.

Since he was already in town, Daniel thought about stopping at the home of his close friends Will and Mary Kellogg on his way home. But the tragedy was too fresh, and he wasn't in the mood for light conversation. He decided against it and said, "Berthie, would you please tell the Kelloggs I'll stop and see them next week?"

"Yes, I'll do it this afternoon," she answered.

Then Lucinda, Daniel, and Berthie exchanged hugs, and he departed for Sweet Home.

Chapter Fourteen

LOUVENIA

"Apparently there is nothing that cannot happen today."

–MARK TWAIN

The week quickly passed, and Daniel worked hard, all the while trying to think about the future. It was 1874, and he was now on his way to visit his friends the Kelloggs. Longtime residents of New Boston, they were the only ones to offer encouragement and helpful advice when he had decided to purchase Sweet Home back in 1871. Of course, Abba *knew* it wouldn't work, and before finally relenting, she tried to get everyone else to convince him not to do it. But the Kelloggs were friends, mentors, and family in a way his real family just never quite was to him. Daniel treasured his visits to their home and the long talks with Will and Mary when they discussed, argued, philosophized, and theorized together.

Daniel's study of reasoning in classical Greek philosophy had begun at six years of age under the rigorous watch of John Black, the tutor who came to his family home in Canada. As he grew, he developed a thirst to understand the *why* of most everything, but the frontier where he lived was far from libraries and museums and the answers to many questions. He had worked hard to overcome that handicap, and his multifaceted mind developed into an eclectic conundrum.

His was a coarse, sometimes crude personality without many social refinements, but he could think, write, and even speak on an echelon equivalent to individuals educated in the finest European universities. The Kelloggs offered sustenance for his intellectual hunger, and their Spiritualist religious beliefs stimulated his thoughts and questions about the nature of life.

Thinking about the Kelloggs on this occasion was uplifting. *Why do I always anticipate a visit with them with such delight?* He considered Will's ever-present sense of humor, Mary's warmth and intelligence, and their hospitality. A bigger reality struck him while making a list of their many qualities. They had invited him to dinner at their house. His enthusiasm wasn't just about seeing the Kelloggs. He was really excited because Mary told him Louvenia McGee would be joining them too.

His eagerness to see Louvenia reminded him of something his brother Bart had said about two weeks after Abba left with Gene Horvath. Bart thought he was offering a helpful tip to one who was still distraught. "Think with your head, brother. You can't afford to again be foolhardy when it comes to the ladies." Of course, it wasn't such a profound idea, but coming from Bart, any weighty comment was memorable.

Daniel didn't recall much else about the conversation with Bart, except how the statement stayed with him. *If anything, I'm too shy and cautious*, he argued with the passing scenery. *Like when I first met Molly Hudler at the Lettsville Independence Day Picnic. Hesitation didn't get me anywhere then!*

A furtive glance, followed by several others, was his usual tactic when encountering an attractive young woman. Assembling glimpses was enough to gauge his relative interest. Then he would hope for the opportunity to create conversation or simply retreat. *My hesitating moments of shy shilly shallying yield missed opportunities. It's silly and inconsistent with who I am*, he concluded. Next, he analyzed, *The normally assured and assertive Palmer style seems to melt when*

I come face to face with nice-looking, eligible ladies. I'm confident, easy-going, and always ready to take on the world. So then why do I transform into a self-conscious, awkward, ungainly hulk? He hated that part of his persona.

Shifting to a pleasant, crisp memory, he recalled the first time he saw Louvenia. That time had been different. The event intensified rapidly from a fleeting glance to near obsession in seconds.

He saw her on the crowded waterfront platform. Built by New Boston citizens to welcome the steadily increasing number of Mississippi River travelers, it also handled a formidable quantity of freight. The heavy cedar platform anchored to solid cypress supports was built to last, and creating it was one of those great communal experiences akin to a barn-raising. The project, which became a source of great civic pride, had begun on the same day Daniel Palmer arrived to become the town's newest school teacher. Participation in the work assimilated him quickly into the community, with which he soon felt bonded. The platform, which grew larger year by year to accommodate the ever-growing riverboat traffic, would become a crowded mass of humanity whenever a paddle wheeler moored.

Daniel was at the landing that afternoon, hoping a badly needed plow shear he'd ordered more than two weeks before would arrive. He didn't do a lot of plowing, but while breaking some new ground above the bluff in early April, he had hit a rock, fragmenting off a piece of iron. He was walking behind the horse and plow, holding the wooden handles of the implement, when it collided with something. The sudden obstruction startled both the horse and Daniel. An immediate unwelcome looseness followed the bump. Usually, the bolts holding the shear to the plow would have broken off first, making the repair a minor one and the delay short. But the angle of impact and mass of the boulder combined to break the point off the shear. So he wrote to the manufacturer in Moline and sent his payment along in advance, hoping it would bring the replacement part promptly.

Annoyed more time was passing, he stood there wondering, *Could there be some greater reason? Has providence prevented me from putting in that half-acre of tomatoes?* "Foolishness," he snickered aloud. *It's absurd to think that everything that happens is tied to some vast eternal plan. Sometimes things just break.* He shrugged and watched the considerable activity involved in mooring the large steamboat.

Passengers began to disembark, some with and some without luggage. Meanwhile, Daniel noticed the crew, who were beginning to unload cargo. Watching them reminded him of working shoulder to shoulder with T.J. on their trek from Canada. Now it seemed like a long time ago. *Maybe the idea wasn't as foolish as it seemed. When things don't work out smoothly, it's often better to take a pause. That's when some unlikely obstacle reminds me to slow down, change direction, think it through, and let things happen naturally.* Then his train of thought came to a crashing halt, stopped dead in its tracks by a face. "And there she is," Daniel said impulsively. He wasn't sure why he said it but was certain it was meaningful.

So moved by her unfamiliar face, he became unnerved and froze on the platform like a fixture. Reflecting on this troubling idiosyncrasy, the flustered man pondered. *Where is the adroit, clever, strong, and capable me now? Why did I instantly turn into mush in front of this stranger? Why can't I speak to her? I must introduce myself. I can't just let this pass.*

There're many single men in New Boston, and she's sure to be noticed and receive their attentions. In an all-too-familiar mental tug-of-war, Daniel was struggling. On one side stood a bold, charming fellow, eager to step forward and strike up a conversation, while on the other, a shy namby-pamby, fearfully predisposed to just watch from afar, cowered. Then fate took over, shoving him into action.

The woman's back was arched, her white knuckles revealing two tightly clenched, delicate hands straining at the handle of an oversized suitcase. Moved by the sight of her struggling, he damned his penchant to take shelter in the familiar waters of introversion and sprang into action. Boldly stepping forward, he tapped her hands and wrested the handle from her. "Welcome to New Boston. My name is Daniel Palmer. I believe that's the largest valise I've ever seen. May I help you with it?"

"It's a portmanteau," Louvenia McGee promptly corrected him. Her aristocratic tone, while inadvertent, played well under the circumstances.

He waited for her to give the go-ahead while she looked him up and down. The aloof, blasé look on her face either signaled disinterest or simply revealed her refined Southern upbringing. While not looking unclean, the hair flowing over his shoulders appeared to be an expansion of a broad bearded face. That, coupled with deeply tanned skin and covered with an extra-large hat, all gave him an individualistic look, befitting the stereotypical courageous lone wolf character as popularized in Western fiction.

The delicate young woman yanked her luggage back and began to proudly strut past him. Already stretched to the end of her physical capacity, she stumbled over her own feet. Falling forward, she let the suitcase drop, but before her face could be planted on the deck a strong hand caught her by the elbow. Now they were face to face and her eyes were unexpectedly glued to his. Louvenia turned her head and fixed her gaze on a horse and wagon parked a short distance from the pier. "My name is Mrs. Landers," she said.

He answered, "Is Mr. Landers still on board?"

His voice and unique appearance were disarming. "I lost him in the Battle of Baton Rouge," Louvenia said. Then she clarified, "We were only married for a couple of months. You may call me Miss McGee." The ephemeral conversation had now turned surreal, unnecessarily revealing more than necessary to a stranger, even denying her deceased spouse by offhandedly reverting to her maiden name.

"I'm sorry for your loss."

"Thank you," Louvenia said matter-of-factly.

The well-bred young woman yielded the suitcase to him while nervously shifting her eyes about the platform, taking in as much of her surroundings as possible. Then she brought the banter to a halt with a mundane question, "Where is the New Boston Hotel? A flyer in the ship's dining room said it was clean and comfortable."

"Please let me show you," Dan answered, gesturing toward the street.

"Wait, my son Frankie is on the gangplank," said Louvenia as she waved at the boy to urge him along.

Daniel scanned several people coming down the walkway, then zeroed in on a dark-haired eleven-year-old carrying a small carpetbag.

As the lad drew near, Louvenia said, "Frank, this is Mr. Palmer. He's going to show us to the hotel. Say hello to him."

"Hello, Mr. Palmer," the compliant boy said.

"Nice to meet you," Daniel answered, adding, "I'm sure you'll like New Boston." He turned and pointed to his left saying, "The hotel is this way."

The boy offered a shy smile and stepped beside his mother.

A formidable burden even for this brawny man, the oversized leather trunk took considerable effort on his part. Yet he was grateful it had provided him the opening to approach her. Making conversation as they walked, he said, "Portmanteau ... it has a certain French ring to it. Did you say you were from Louisiana?"

Warily, she gave an affirmative nod. "This is my first time in the North."

Enthusiastically, Daniel followed with, *"Parlez-vous français?"*

Louvenia, taking on the tone of an aristocrat reacting to a challenge, rolled her eyes and responded in French. *"Français et l'espagnol est les langues de la maison en que j'ai grandi, mais je parle anglais."* Her pronunciation of each word was crisp, clear, and effortless. He was impressed to learn she spoke three languages and felt rebuked by her mastery of one he could barely navigate.

He quickly accepted she wished to use English. "Your French is excellent. I came from Canada, and it's been a long while since I've spoken French with anyone. I've never been great with it, but it's comforting to hear you speak it so well."

Of noble birth, Louvenia was an aristocrat long before she had ever learned the word's meaning. Innocent as can be, the child was dangerously naïve, and her nanny, Keesha, frequently said, "She's born with a silver spoon in her mouth." Louvenia learned to speak primarily French at home. When she was five years old, Louvenia's mother insisted Keesha speak *only* English to the child. Her mother, a French Creole, was fair-haired with pale blue eyes and such light skin, her features were more in keeping with a Scandinavian. Her father, primarily of Spanish blood, contributed the dark hair and dark brown eyes, which, combined with the fair complexion, distinguished Louvenia's appearance. Even as a young child, she was a striking figure to behold. Although French was the dominant language of the household, she was also fluent in Spanish, owing to her father's persistence in speaking his native language with the child. Her English, peppered with a Southern accent, which she picked up from Keesha, was also flavored with a ring of confident snobbery, typical of the members of the aristocracy who frequently visited the McGee estate.

Louvenia's childhood was spent almost exclusively on the Louisiana plantation. The grand home was of classically Greek-revival design. About a quarter-mile off the road, its grandeur was accentuated by the long, wide stone walkway leading to the porch, whose dominant feature was its massive white ionic columns. The corridor was lined by grand oak trees forming a long, spectacular canopy.

One day Louvenia's eldest brother was passing the time by digging into the bark of one of those mature oaks with a knife, and Keesha muttered something under her breath in a disapproving tone. Louvenia asked her what she said, and Keesha looked around before answering to ensure no one else was within earshot. "Those oaks are more than a hundred and fifty years old, and they should be cared for and appreciated, not dug into and hurt." Louvenia understood, but she also knew, even when Keesha was right and a McGee was wrong, Keesha would never raise her voice or try to correct them, not even the children. More than nine hundred other slaves served and feared their masters on the vast estate.

The McGee's house servants were slaves, yet Keesha held a higher status than the others working in the house in a way Louvenia never quite understood. The house servants served meals to the children in the large kitchen, but only after serving their parents in the formal dining room. If the occasion included guests, the children would have to wait longer until everyone completed the main course in the dining room. Either way, it was only in rare moments the children dined at the table with the parents. It wasn't as though the children were to be kept from the affection of their parents, but formal lifestyle was in vogue on Louisiana plantations, and the McGee family chose to conform.

Unlike the other house servants, Keesha would usually sit with the children at mealtime, and she was adept at finding ways to use tabletop conversation as teaching moments. Louvenia often felt these were especially aimed toward her, but never heard anything directly confirming that from Keesha or her parents.

Her upbringing was typical for an antebellum child of privilege. Music and dance lessons, equestrian events, and dinner parties dotted the family calendar. The best teachers came to the plantation to educate the children. They grew up in a sheltered, false reality, being taught the slaves were happy to be there, and without the plantation to take care of them, the poor negroes would be out on their own, surely unable to fend for themselves. Keesha might not look like her and the McGees, but she had proven she wasn't any less capable, and in many ways, Keesha shared wisdom with Louvenia that her mother, father, and brothers lacked. This was especially evident in their treatment of animals. Keesha loved and respected them, even those used for food. But Louvenia's family seemed to lack all reverence for animals, and they seemed to take everything for granted.

The McGees were rich in money, land, and social status but poor in compassion, caring, and even basic morality. They weren't immoral in the commonly accepted ways like stealing or impiety, and they attended church regularly. But Louvenia gradually came to see the fabric of her family's lifestyle was immoral. She sensed slavery was wicked, and the success of the whole plantation—and her family's wealth—was all based on that immoral precept. Spending time with Keesha made it obvious, more by how Keesha lived than by anything she said. Louvenia didn't know how to articulate it, but she innately recognized the notion that whites were better than colored people was wrong. She had heard it said outright and intimated many times in many ways, and in every instance, the dependable little voice inside said, *It's a lie!*

Louvenia had come to love Keesha, and she generally spent more time with her than with her mother. When the insensitive Mrs. McGee finally did notice the depth of their relationship, it sparked malicious jealousy that grew to the point it was intoxicating. Finally recognizing the bonds between Keesha and Louvenia, she decided to remove Keesha from her daughter's life.

One morning when Louvenia was ten years old, she came down the long, curving stairs and went to the kitchen to get ready for breakfast. She was puzzled as to why Keesha wasn't there in her usual coarse linsey-woolsey dress and cotton apron. Before looking further, the ten-year-old stood still and gazed around the kitchen, thinking about how empty the large room full of culinary utensils seemed without Keesha's familiar, warm face. She also thought about how she liked Keesha's clothing. It was much different from her own wardrobe of fine English cotton prints, white linen, wool, and silks. Linsey-woolsey, an inexpensive blend of wool and flax commonly worn by slave women, would not be found in Louvenia's closet. Slave clothing was typically loose-fitting because it kept the arms and legs free to do work. It was a warm, strong material but wouldn't be considered a beautiful fabric. That particular textile was like a sign that said slave, but to Louvenia, it was strangely comforting because she associated it with Keesha. She had spent so many wonderful hours with Keesha, and always there was that loose-fitting linsey-woolsey dress.

Louvenia ran out across the orchard to the rows of small shacks where the slaves lived. She was concerned Keesha might be sick, so she knocked on Keesha's door to check on her, but no answer. The ever-present big white dog, Paddy, wasn't there either. None of Keesha's family were there, and the shack seemed nearly empty, save a couple of straight-back wooden chairs next to the old wood table where the family often sat together. Mr. Harold, a white-haired, wrinkled, dark-skinned man, lived in the next shack. He saw Louvenia knocking and called over to her, "They's gone ... master sold 'em."

Louvenia's eyes filled with tears of betrayal, and she uncharacteristically forgot to thank or acknowledge him as she turned and ran back to the great house. He took no offense, as he was aware of her fondness for Keesha. Mr. Harold merely gave his head an expressive shake while watching her flee.

Louvenia's pleading with her mother only increased Mrs. McGee's resolve that Keesha would never return to the plantation. Louvenia learned a bitter lesson that day, having suddenly become conscious of the horror of slavery. Keesha's dismissal also created an enduring wedge between her and her mother. Mrs. McGee's ire was always raised whenever Louvenia tried to ask about Keesha.

A few days after Keesha's family vanished, Louvenia tested her mother's resolve. "Mama, do you think I could go see Keesha on Sunday?"

"You can just get that thought out of your head! Keesha and her kind are beneath us. They're just property. It's natural, and you need to remember that. The good ones are grateful that we take care of them."

Louvenia didn't dare argue. But something deep inside told her that her mother's words were wrong. She worried about Keesha and wondered where she and her family were. *I hope that Paddy is okay and that Keesha's achy legs have gotten better.* The more Louvenia thought about Keesha, the more helpless, and hopeless, she felt. So, she tried not to think about her.

Louvenia grew to be a bright, attractive young woman with a warm, friendly personality. Many young men came to call, and she had more than one offer of marriage when she was only fifteen years old. Then, at age sixteen, she fell in love for the first time with Jeb Parsons from Baton Rouge.

Jeb lived just a few miles from the plantation and was a fine, well-bred young man. He seemed to agree in principle with Louvenia about the inequities of their culture, but he enjoyed his comforts and pragmatically argued it just wasn't time to change things. Whenever they spoke about it, he voiced a familiar contention. "For one thing, there just weren't enough whites to work the cotton fields, and the dark-skinned people needed more time to get educated and ready to be on their own." Louvenia disagreed with both sides of his argument, but she usually allowed him the last word to keep the peace between them. As deeply as she cared for him, she could not understand how this subject inevitably brought out his sinister side not reachable with logic or reason. Jeb's mind was made up, and all their discussions ever achieved were to bring out stubbornness in him and frustration in her. Gradually she became aware that the frustration was growing into anger, and she wasn't sure where to direct it. On the one hand, he was a purveyor of evil, therefore deserving of her resentment. But he had such a smooth manner and was so handsome, her heart fluttered whenever he smiled, and in most other things, he neither looked nor acted maliciously.

Every ounce of her being knew bigotry, whether his alone or of their whole culture, was indubitably wrong. Still, no matter how loudly her inner voice proclaimed the truth to her, she could never successfully explain it to Jeb. Whenever she tried reasoning with him, they both became irritated. It vexed her to think about it. *I love someone who can't understand that racism and hatred obstruct his ability to think. Why does this usually kind, funny, charming man turn into ice whenever the subject comes up?* What infuriated her was when he tried to rationalize those immoral convictions by talking about states' rights and the unfair Northern economic advantage. It was so transparent to her, there was no justification without racism to underpin it, and the rest of his argument failed.

April 13, 1861, started with a fine breakfast of eggs, toast, and hominy grits, followed by fresh fruit for dessert. Jeb came to call on Louvenia, and he was just beaming with excitement. "Lou, this is great! Did you hear?"

Puzzled, she looked at his strange expression, fearfully anticipating that whatever delighted him would not do the same for her.

Too excited to wait for her response, Jeb speedily reported the news. "Yesterday morning it finally started and went on all day at Charleston. Our boys on Sullivan's Island opened fire on Fort Sumter. They pounded it hard until dark! I don't know how many of 'em they got, but it was comin' in hard."

When he came up for air, the alarmed Louvenia asked, "Where's Fort Sumter?"

Jeb eagerly explained, "South Carolina! That's where Anderson's Yankee horde fled when we declared independence in December. Most of them were over at Fort Moultrie on Sullivan's Island, but they knew they were in for it, so they went over to the new fort on the little island at the entrance to Charleston harbor. Our big guns by the lighthouse on Morris Island joined in too, so we had them in a crossfire." Jeb beamed with pride, expecting Louvenia to share his delight and patriotic zeal.

She was horrified, but Jeb mistook the unsettled expression on her face for confusion about geography. "You remember Sullivan's Island. It's the place in the popular Poe story you liked so much. Remember the one about Captain Kidd's treasure? What was the name of it? Oh yeah, 'The Gold Bug.'"

Louvenia remembered the story well because she liked the clever secret messages and how the writer crafted cryptograms into the treasure hunt. It also reminded her of a big argument with Jeb over that same story. They were discussing Poe's work, and Louvenia mentioned she didn't like how Poe depicted Jupiter as a dumb, black servant. Jeb couldn't see why she had a problem with that, any more than he could understand her lack of enthusiasm for what was happening right now. Instead of fervor for armed conflict, Lou felt sick inside.

She hoped Lincoln's election would compel progress toward greater morality in the country. She and a decided minority of Southerners hoped for peaceful compromise, including a change in the social structure and the eradication of slavery. Geography placed her in the tiniest sliver of minority thought since most Southern Unionists were in the border states. It was nearly impossible to find sympathy for their position in Louisiana. In fact, in her parish, vocalizing such ideas was tantamount to blasphemy.

Louvenia also knew she was living in the lap of luxury and that the very fabric of society she wished to see change provided her lifestyle. She rationalized her inaction. *I didn't create slavery, I've never whipped anyone, and I've always shown kindness to the slaves.* Yet, deep down inside, she also felt a gnawing sense of culpability. In her heart of hearts, she believed she should have actively been taking steps to make a change. While he droned on about the impending surrender of Fort Sumter, she tried to comfort herself. *Besides, who would listen to a young woman anyway? What power did I have to make change?* The reassurances did little to quell her guilty conscience. Now that the first rebel shots had been fired, it was probably too late, and Louvenia feared severe consequences.

With an eagerness that was downright offensive to her, Jeb announced, "I'll be heading back to Baton Rouge to enlist today." Then, caught up in the madness, he added, "I can hardly wait to take down my first Yankee."

At that moment, Louvenia recognized she could never marry this man who carried so much hatred in his heart. Moreover, he had never even considered how his decision to leave would affect them or their relationship. It was apparent her feelings and thoughts didn't matter to him. The whole relationship ended at that moment for Louvenia, but she was too shocked by disappointment and the suddenness of it all to tell him.

Jeb wrote to her every day of the first week and eight times during the next three weeks. She dutifully replied each time because she didn't have the heart to break up with him in a letter. By the fourth week, only one letter came to Louvenia, followed by a welcome interruption for the next two weeks. Then another envelope arrived during the third week of the second month. She was feeling less burdened as the letters were an obligation she had come to loathe, and with that one, they stopped altogether. It would be yet another month until she got word he had been killed in a skirmish with Union troops—his first actual encounter with the enemy. Although Louvenia never expressed to anyone how her feelings for Jeb had changed, she had less trouble getting over him than a person in love ought to have had.

There were many social events on the McGee plantation during the first year of the war. Things were going rather well for the South, and there seemed to be great optimism and a celebratory atmosphere that ignored the awfulness of the rising death count. Like other pillars of Louisiana's aristocratic society, the McGee family hosted frequent gatherings that denied the perils of war and shored up, supported, and brightened the mood of the people. It was superficial and callous when contrasted with the travail facing so many, but society's unswerving posture was denial, and patriotism was the willingly expressed mantra. Of course, the mass delusion would be shattered for any individual learning their teenage child or spouse had fallen. In the face of such enlightenment, no amount of jingoistic rhetoric could cloud the sad reality of ultimate sacrifice.

The first year of the war had passed, and one such Saturday evening formal dinner dance was underway at the McGee plantation. Louvenia was about to make her strategically planned entrance, knowing she would look regal coming down the long, open, curved staircase in her flowing white-and-pink gown. It was her favorite, and her mother said it made her dark hair stand out. Had it not made her feel ridiculous, she would have worn the tiara with ruby stones and pearls. She had donned the crown before leaving her full-length mirror and deciding against it. *Who am I wearing this for anyway?* But self-conscious apprehensions aside, Louvenia knew everyone in the grand ballroom anticipated the appearance of this eighteen-year-old Southern lady.

Being a McGee, compellingly attractive, and unmarried made her one of the most desirable young women in attendance. Torn between her natural disdain for the affectation and another more complicated side of herself, Louvenia could put up with the pomp, mainly because it pleased her mother so much. It also felt good to know all eyes were on her, and it didn't even matter what the other young ladies thought—she was the center of the world for a couple of minutes at this event. Then, while making her grand entrance, she had her first glimpse of Captain J.R. Landers and froze about halfway down the stairs.

His dashing appearance, accented by the resplendent officer's uniform, was captivating. She was aware a lady shouldn't linger over her first glimpse of a young man. Yet the realization made no difference to her eyes, which unabashedly stayed transfixed on him. To the preoccupied mademoiselle, a full ten seconds passed instantly, while at the same time, Louvenia's rational side writhed in the onus of imprudence that felt like an hour. But her eyes would not budge, even as she consciously tried to force them to move. Finally, she whispered aloud, "Stop it, you fool!" By then, it was too late, her cover was hopelessly blown, and her interest in him was conspicuous.

Still motionless, she was composing herself when she heard her mother, who was two steps above her, say, "Lou, what's wrong, darling?" To make matters worse, her two younger sisters, standing at the bottom of the stairway, leaning on the dark wooden banister, were now giggling and pointing at her.

If ever there was a stereotypically handsome young officer in Louisiana's infantry, Captain J.R. Landers was he. The gleaming polished buttons on his dress uniform sparkled brightly against the field of gray, as did the scabbard hanging from his waist. Above its sheath, the sword's leather-wrapped handle was topped with a glistening, ornate brass guard and brass pommel. A well-trimmed beard served to make him look older than his twenty-one years might have without it, and his deep-set eyes and light brown hair framed a handsome picture. To Louvenia, his appearance was the perfect mix of a Southern gentleman's chiseled masculinity, refinement, and elegance. He carried himself in an erect posture befitting a leader who, in another setting, might have appeared too severe, but for this night of brass buttons and medals in the plantation ballroom, it was perfect.

Feeling an annoying warm flush in her cheeks, Louvenia answered her mother with the first ridiculous thing that came to mind. "Oh, I just remembered I forgot the tiara." Before all the words were out of her mouth, she wished she could pull them back.

On cue, Mrs. McGee quickly turned and dashed up the stairs. "Don't worry. I'll get some pins and bring it right down. Meet me in the library, and I'll set it for you." Not wanting to wear the tiara, the frustrated Louvenia wondered what else might go wrong.

There was nothing else to do but climb down the remaining stairs. Lou, who was wearing new heels, felt a worrisome wobble with every step. She slowly continued, fearing she might stumble and make an idiotic spectacle of herself. Louvenia's cautious movements raised the ire of her sisters, who interpreted her careful stride as exaggerated pretension. Continuing down toward the ballroom, Louvenia took a deep breath, put her insecure hesitations aside, and replaced them with a dignified attitude, reminding herself that everyone present knew she was the plum amongst the many young ladies in attendance.

There was extra tension in the air as a backdrop to the McGee's formal event. Having superior military leadership, the South had gained the upper hand. However, Lincoln, tortured by the fact that he could not seem to get his general-in-chief, George McClellan, to make decisive moves during the first year of the war, had a new strategy. The Confederacy was facing its first serious threat in early 1862 as Union forces under Admiral David Farragut were amassing for an assault on the vital port city of New Orleans. Given the North's industrial superiority, New Orleans was critically important to the survival of the Confederacy. Without it, the South would lose its best link to war supplies coming in from Europe.

With an enormous amount of Atlantic coastline to patrol south of the Chesapeake Bay, New Orleans was geographically too far for the Union forces to sustain a complete blockade. Moreover, denying access to Charleston and patrolling other Atlantic seaports had stretched the US Navy's capacity. The Confederates hoped to continue to attract support from Britain and other sympathetic Europeans. Still, the rebels must demonstrate that shipping to and from the other side of the Atlantic could be pursued safely and effectively. Maintaining a safe harbor deep in the South was essential, and Captain Landers would become one of the players as this drama unfolded.

Both sides knew Louisiana would be pivotal to the outcome of the entire conflict. Accordingly, the Confederacy organized Camp Moore just northeast of Baton Rouge in 1861. Located adjacent to the railroad, on high ground, with an abundant supply of fresh, clean water, it became the South's largest site for training soldiers. Additionally, it became a place of confinement for prisoners of war. Had the generals been able to gaze into a crystal ball, they would have seen the poignant aftermath since Camp Moore's most lasting legacy would be as a cemetery for soldiers.

Captain Landers arrived at Camp Moore on March 1, 1862, as the Twenty-Second Infantry Regiment was being assembled. He was proud to serve under Colonel L. Hebert, who charged the young officer with his primary duty, to oversee the training of conscripts. Twenty days later, while on his first leave from the camp, J.R. Landers was now attending a dinner dance at the McGee plantation, where he found himself falling quickly under the spell of Miss Louvenia McGee.

The captain was still in the front door foyer when he reluctantly turned his head to see what everyone was ogling on the stairway. Then he spotted Louvenia standing majestically on the curved staircase. Along with everyone else, his focus tarried there too. It hadn't yet dawned on the usually observant officer that her lingering gaze was riveted across the room where he and three other soldiers were standing. Slowly but surely, he understood the debutant was looking directly at him, and his heart nearly leaped from his chest. He stood there anxiously unsure about what, whether, and how to do whatever he was supposed to do, and it was a welcome relief when one of the other fellows shook his shoulder, demanding his attention to listen to a joke.

Meanwhile, Louvenia reached the polished floor of the ballroom and wove her way through the crowded room. She dashed into and across the dining room, then back onto the dance floor. Taking the circuitous route, she got to the opposite side of the crowded hall, barely avoiding her mother's persistent gesticulations. Louvenia pretended not to notice Mrs. McGee with the tiara in her right hand waving Louvenia over toward the library. Louvenia feigned conversation with another young woman to evade a determined mother on a mission, but not for long. Through the corner of her eye, she could see Mrs. McGee approaching. Seconds before her mother could grasp her arm, Louvenia escaped by brazenly walking right up to the four soldiers. Her eyes were on Captain Landers as she said, "Gentlemen, we're honored to welcome our brave defenders." She was laying it on thick but unable to think fast enough to come up with anything better to say.

Transfixed by her, J.R. quickly summoned every ounce of audacity he could muster, announced his name, reached for, and bowed a kiss to the back of her hand. The other soldiers stood their ground, seeing her interest was focused only on the captain.

"I'm Louvenia McGee," she hurriedly glanced at the other soldiers as she introduced herself. Then she bent forward toward J.R.'s ear and whispered, "Please rescue me with an invitation onto the dance floor."

He immediately took her hand and led accordingly. "What are we rescuing you from?"

"A maternal monster brandishing a tiara!" They laughed and began to dance.

They stayed together throughout the evening, dancing to the point of mutual exhaustion. Notwithstanding the few interruptions when other soldiers tapped J.R. on the shoulder to cut in, it became apparent they were interested in little else except each other.

The fireworks between them ignited quickly, and their relationship became intense. The inevitable separations from the young soldier during a time of war added urgency to the relationship. Over the next month, Captain Landers found numerous reasons to leave the encampment, some bona fide and others creative. Each case culminated in a visit to the McGee plantation and another opportunity to see Louvenia. Those visits became what they each lived for, and Louvenia found herself plotting to create opportunities to be alone with him.

Although he trained infantry soldiers, J.R. was also a skilled rider who, like most Confederate enlistees, had brought his own horse to serve with him. The horse was a Morgan, and the mount's name was also Morgan. He wasn't a huge creature, but he was powerful and well-defined with a compact body and a cleanly arched neck.

Louvenia knew several secluded places on the plantation's four thousand acres where a couple could embrace in broad daylight without her parents or anyone else coming upon them. She would anticipate each time he visited and ordered fresh mounts be readied upon his arrival. There would be the usual agonizing moments of pleasantries and conversation in the house with family members. The moments always included a discussion about the war, an obligatory dialogue her parents seemed to enjoy nearly as much as she detested. She impatiently tolerated it, watching for an opportunity to gracefully interrupt the conversation and say, "I've got two horses saddled and ready. I was hoping the gentleman might accompany me on a ride." They would then disappear for several hours.

Early springtime days in Louisiana could be warm, but it could also turn abruptly cool, and owing to the typically humid air, a person could quickly feel chilled to the bone. The first time they rode off together, she knew exactly where they would end up. The spot was about two miles from the McGee mansion, where an old barn stood near the edge of a swampy grove of Spanish moss-covered cypress. Adjacent to the south side of the barn was a large cotton field. A new, larger barn closer to the main home left the old one largely unused, except for storing bales of cotton, a cotton gin, a reaper, and some old hand implements that hung from the rafters and on the walls. The inside was far too dusty and dirty to be pleasant, but there was a delightful open grassy space behind the barn's west side, just above where the ground sloped down into the thicket of trees. She loved that spot because it was sunny, calm, and secluded. There a person could spread a blanket over the grass, stretch out, and listen to the peaceful sound of water coming from the nearby brook where it rippled over rocks on its way down to the boggy grove below.

Louvenia guided her mount to the southeast side of the barn. She rode nearly up to the large sliding door where she hopped down, handed the reins to J.R., and dragged off the leather bags from behind her saddle. "J.R., I'll spread the blanket and get our lunch ready out back. Why don't you secure the horses inside the barn?" He nodded while she added, "Would you mind unsaddling and brushing them down a bit for me? I don't want them wet and uncomfortable while we eat."

He walked the horses into the barn while she hung the saddlebags on the pole of a hitching post and followed him in. Louvenia took a five-gallon bucket from a hook on the wall next to an assortment of tack hanging in a well-organized row. Several fresh-looking, small bales of hay were on the wood floor nearby. While he was tending to the horses, Louvenia went to the stream and soon returned with water. Pouring half of it into another bucket, she said, "This'll give them something to do while you're brushing them out. I'm sure they'll be most appreciative." She hung the buckets, one in front of each horse. She also cut open one of the hay bales and placed a section of hay on the floor below each bucket, saying, "That ought to keep 'em happy. I'll be in the grassy clearing behind the barn getting our lunch readied." Then while he tended to the horse's comfort, she went back out to her favorite spot, spread the blanket over the lush grasses, and unpacked their lunch.

Louvenia removed her leather riding jacket and sat waiting for him on the blanket while the sun dipped behind a large fluffy cloud. A cool breeze supplanted the warm sunshine, and without the jacket on, she soon began shivering. As she reached for her wrap next to the blanket, J.R. approached and noticed her hand was shaking. Taking his cue, he bent in stride, grasped the jacket, and passed it to her. Instead of taking it, Louvenia grabbed him by the shoulders and drew him to her. Their first kiss, a pretense to warm her, fooled neither of them. She leaned back on the blanket, pulling his body over her, and there was no more shivering.

J.R. returned to Camp Moore that evening, and a self-satisfied Louvenia reflected on the events of the day, including the wily scheme to get him out behind the old barn. In retrospect, she felt immodest about going to such lengths to satisfy her cravings. But she resolved that lying under him on the blanket out in the open air was like a dream come true. At that moment, she had everything that mattered to her. Nevertheless, Louvenia had learned about a whole new side of herself—an obsessed person whom she never knew existed before becoming fixated on Captain J.R. Landers. He adored her too and could barely stand to be apart from her. Then, only one month into the courtship, J.R. said, "My life is meaningless without you. Louvenia McGee, would you consider becoming my bride?"

It was the end of April, and New Orleans had been lost to the North. People all over Louisiana were terrified. It was only a matter of time until Baton Rouge fell, but the Yankees seemed to be more interested in first securing the river fortifications and the area immediately around New Orleans. So the Confederate state government withdrew from Baton Rouge to Shreveport and decreed that all the cotton in the area be burned, lest it fall into enemy hands. That sad strategy was an act of desperation, and everything in life was now uncertain.

Even J.R.'s proposal of marriage took on a whole new urgency. Louvenia responded with an immediate, unqualified "Yes!" Against her mother's most vehement protests, a hastily planned wedding was held the following week. Instead of the grand social event her mother would have loved, the wedding was relatively small, although refined and beautiful.

They were married on May 5 at the McGee plantation. Lou and J.R. exchanged wedding vows on the large front lawn, framed between two large magnolia trees positioned at the end of a beautiful esplanade, surrounded by even rows of large, old oak and cypress. The photographer set his tripod just inside the front gate to secure a picture of the setting and the ceremony. His wide-angle composition classically portrayed the quintessence of Southern aristocratic life. At the center was the grand porch, and flanking the wide front doors sat a string quartet. The violinist held his instrument to his chin, his right elbow pointing to the horizon as if unveiling it. Spanish moss lavishly hung above the velvet lawn like curtains from the many deciduous trees, and a long white picket fence stretched in front of a thick row of blooming fiery-red azaleas that outlined the house yard. The scene, dotted with people dressed to the nines, focused on the couple standing before a tall, slender man holding a thick text. The image seemed to portray Dixie's finest, brought together as if for the last time in a spirited, festive occasion.

A phaeton carriage stood in front of the mansion, complete with its fringed top, and hitched to a noble black American Saddlebred. The carriage, trimmed in shining black, was exquisite with its body mounted high on large wheels, looking delicate with its matching brass lanterns adjacent to the edge of each seat. The carefully chosen Saddlebred presented an arresting profile. Accessorized with the finest harness to drive the carriage, the horse, with its beautiful, shining dark coat, was a picture-perfect match for the phaeton.

Everything was patrician, including the horse, displaying its well-bred lineage by holding its head high on a long neck, well-flexed at the poll, and showing off its distinctive high-stepping gait. Also known for its sure-footedness, the Saddlebred had become the horse of choice for wealthy plantation owners. Brandishing the breed had even become a show of patriotism since General Robert E. Lee was known to be devoted to his Saddlebred named Traveller. Lee's solidly built mount of sixteen hands had a distinctive grey coat contrasted with a long, dark mane and tail. Generals Stonewall Jackson and Ulysses S. Grant also chose Saddlebreds as their mounts. The horse and carriage were a regal match befitting the blue-blooded couple's first wedded ride, a traditional departure signifying the ceremony's close and the opening of a new life together.

During the lavish reception, word reached the plantation the Yankees had overrun Baton Rouge. With the enemy only sixty miles away, Captain J.R. Landers knew it was his duty to withdraw to Camp Moore. Louvenia's mother was furious but powerless when she learned of her daughter's plan to accompany him close to the fighting. They arrived before dawn and spent the short remainder of their wedding night in a small cabin on the military installation.

The ensuing weeks went by quickly in the modest officer's cabin as Louvenia fell into the role of an adoring young army wife. She tended the home and got to know some of the other soldiers and officers. Unfortunately, very few women lived at the camp, and Louvenia seemed to have little in common with anyone. Although not developing any friendships, she hoped things would improve with time.

Conversations with J.R. became superficial as he wanted to speak about the challenges of training recruits and the vision of an independent nation of the South. She quickly learned he was not ready to discuss the issue from any perspective other than extreme loyalty to the cause. Her arguments with Jeb Parsons had taught her that conversations skirting morality and politics would do little good in this environment. She cared about what J.R. thought but also recognized his convictions and did not want to jeopardize their relationship over it. Louvenia knew this was cowardly but did not allow herself to keep thinking about it.

Their home life fell into a rigid schedule formed by the military regimen, and they ended nearly every evening with an early bedtime and passionate lovemaking. She quietly worried about this because their birth control efforts were feeble at best, and she scarcely wished to become pregnant. Resigning herself to the possibility, Louvenia again rationalized against her better judgment by telling herself she loved him so much, bearing his child would be worth it.

She spent as much time as possible with J.R., and as long as she maintained an empty-headed patriotic façade, their time together remained happy.

Then, on August 5, 1862, rebel forces marched on Baton Rouge in a desperate effort to retake the State Capital. Leading a group of infantry trying to flank the enemy, Captain Landers was the first target, and he died that day along with the effort to regain Baton Rouge. When the news arrived back at Camp Moore, it gutted Louvenia to the core.

Unprepared for such grief, she could not think or eat, and drinking water became a mindless ritual. The remaining Confederate forces at Camp Moore were planning an evacuation. When notified it was time to move, she remained in the little cabin, unable to think about what she should or could do. Instead, she tortured herself, wondering why she hadn't talked some sense into him. She knew blaming herself was absurd, and nothing could have convinced him to leave the army. On the second day, the pangs of hunger hurt enough for her to eat some bread to allay it. But the self-indulgence of eating made her feel even worse, and she became nauseous. Her sole accomplishment for the day revolved around fighting off nausea. Grieving, nausea, and the whole ordeal left her in such despair, she cared nothing about anything.

On the third day, her mother arrived with Harry, their tall, soft-spoken house servant. They were such a welcome sight, Louvenia suddenly realized she missed home. Mrs. McGee went to Louvenia and hugged her, noticing her daughter had lost weight and seemed frail. "You're going to be fine, child," she said to Louvenia, then turned and went right to work. She opened her daughter's empty suitcase and said, "You lie down. I'll pack."

Oddly, just having an order to follow comforted Lou, who turned toward the tiny bed on the other side of the room. It was the first normal sensation she had felt in days. Lou thought to herself, *I feel like a little girl doing the right thing.* It reminded her of a particular moment in early childhood after a hair-pulling angry spat with her sister Audrey. Audrey had gotten the better of her and gone out to the stable in a huff. On that occasion, unlike most of her formative years, instead of administering the expected scolding, her mother smiled, stroked Louvenia's hair, and sat with her at the kitchen table. The two of them ate cookies, her mother told stories to her, and they laughed. But now, along with the fond recollection and a momentary sense of normalcy, came a crinkly feeling, then blackness as Lou passed out on the floor of the cabin.

Disoriented, she woke up in bed. Across the room, her mother commanded, "Just lie still. You haven't eaten. I'm fixing you some soup." Her mother's presence felt so good, bringing a sense of security and stability that had been sorely missing. Lou finally allowed herself to think of the future. *Okay, a new page has turned. There might still be life ahead.*

In the days after returning home, she continued to feel weak, with waves of nausea. She anticipated a great sense of relief when her period would finally come, confirming she was not pregnant. Instead, with each passing day, it became more and more apparent she was late for good reason. Soon a bloated feeling grew into a little bulge, and she started to think about how to break the news to her family. Everything in her world had changed.

The tragedy of losing J.R. shaped Louvenia's life in many ways. As the mother-to-be of a fatherless child, she felt no pride in his sacrifice. Her disdain for the insanity of war was reinforced, and her impatience with paternalistic Louisiana politics grew. She viewed their argument about states' rights as a ridiculous, devious excuse to justify greed and bigotry, and prolong slavery. Sadly, Louvenia felt like a traitor, wishing for the Confederacy's prompt defeat, even knowing there might be serious implications to her own family. Nevertheless, she felt that ending slavery was imperative. It was as simple as knowing right from wrong.

When October arrived, it had been barely two weeks since Lincoln issued the Emancipation Proclamation, a source of great consternation to the McGee family and their friends. Exactly how it might affect them and whether it was legal or temporary were all hotly debated issues. Still, one thing was certain, whenever the Yankees finally arrived at the McGee plantation, nine hundred soles living there in slavery would suddenly be free. On October 3, Yankee soldiers confiscated the plantation and arrested her father for resisting. It amounted to little provocation, but for spite, they went through their home, destroyed several oil paintings, and broke all the fine china in the dining room.

Louvenia stayed at home where she, her mother, and her sisters kept busy tending to injured soldiers, Yankee and Confederate alike. After a week, her father was allowed to return home, and for the first time, he was working shoulder to shoulder with former slaves in the fields, bringing in some of the late-season crops. It seemed surreal for them all to be working together. Most slave families stayed on at first because they had nowhere else to go, nor were they prepared to make a swift departure. No matter how one viewed it, the whole world had turned upside down. Yet for Louvenia, life was returning to normal, although she hardly knew what normal meant anymore. Her optimistic disposition had been challenged but not entirely subdued by the horrors of the vicious war. Within a few months, the McGees lost the plantation altogether and moved to Baton Rouge, where her parents were able to open a small shop selling tobacco and a few dry goods. They lived in modest quarters behind the storefront, and it was there, with her sisters tending to her, she gave birth to J.R.'s son. The baby was born at dawn, ending a labor that took all day and night.

"He's beautiful! What's the baby's name to be?" asked her sister Audrey.

"I'm going to call him Frank in honor of Uncle Francis," responded Louvenia.

The girls wrapped him in a soft blanket and took turns holding him. Then their mother opened the door for a first look at her grandchild.

Giggling, Audrey said, "Mama, meet Frankie!"

Louvenia watched as her mother reached for the baby. It was the most emotive face she had ever seen on the McGee family matriarch, showing tenderness that seemed so foreign, she looked like a different woman. The instant bonding between Louvenia's son and his grandmother was curiously unsettling, leaving Louvenia to wonder, *Why don't I feel anything magical? I don't feel anything except exhaustion. Shouldn't I feel some kind of connection? I adore him about as much as I would a scab falling off my skin after a wound heals.* The more she pondered, the worse she felt. *Even Audrey, the new aunt, seems to be more attached to this little person than his mother! What's wrong with me?* Everything felt so weighty, even thinking became too onerous in this physically and mentally drained state.

Louvenia's extraordinarily heavy eyelids closed, bringing peacefulness as she fell into a deep sleep. Then, after what seemed like only a few seconds, her mother brushed her cheek, saying, "Lou, Lou, wake up. It's been over an hour, and your baby needs tending to."

She knew the voice, but she wasn't sure where she was or what was going on. Like trying to climb up out of a deep crevasse, Louvenia slowly forced her eyes to open. The first thing she saw was her mother's face. Then the blanket was pulled aside, allowing insulting, cool air to waft over her. Groggily trying to pull the cover back over herself, she was befuddled that her mother was holding it down out of her reach. The confused young woman wanted only to stay warm and sleep. Finally, Lou remembered giving birth and grasped what was happening. Her mother placed little Frankie next to her chest. "Just love him, Lou," was all she said.

As the baby touched her, his faint whimpering and anxious face sent a pulse of reaction through her, quelling their mutual distress the moment his soft mouth latched on. Seeing, smelling, and feeling her baby at her breast completed her, cementing the elusive magical bond.

After the war, Louvenia found temporary work in several different Baton Rouge businesses. Her sisters helped with the baby during the day, and things worked out. In 1870 she was serving tables in a café frequented by carpetbaggers and prominent city and state leaders. Unlike most of her contemporaries, she did not find all carpetbaggers to be contemptible vultures, just there to reap the spoils of a defeated rebellion. Although some were there to plunder, many others were genuinely organizing the rebuilding effort. She appreciated their coalition with the Freedmen's Bureau, because the agency tried to help find and reunite family members of former slaves. It reminded her of Keesha, whom she often thought about, wondering what had become of Keesha and her family. Unfortunately, post-war Louisiana was chaotic, and she knew her chances of ever seeing them were slim at best.

While making a modest living in the café, she heard many conversations and saw the attitudes and behaviors of the community's movers and shakers. Her discontent grew as she often heard low road bantering and boasting. The theme was all too familiar, as pillars of society fashionably spoke about the stupidity of negros, who conveniently became the butt of their jokes. Louvenia expected more from these cultured upper-class citizens and wondered why they behaved so poorly. *Could it be the defeat of the South left white men feeling humiliated and impotent? Somehow the blacks make an easy scapegoat, conveniently available to allow the Southern white man to feel better about his lot. It's disgusting! Racism is alive and well in Louisiana. The defeat of the Confederacy made hatred toward the freed people even worse than when they were slaves.*

The biggest part of Louvenia's problem was she had done little to improve the situation. She wasn't sure what she should have done, but still felt as though she was as guilty as the people who had swung the whips.

She thought about it for three years. *I hear and see angry racialists in the café every day. I can't stand it anymore!* Finally, on Christmas day in 1873, she decided something different needed to happen and weighed her options. One simple fact stood out: her roots. *I'm part of the same society that has earned my disdain. I'm bound to the family, and that's the only thing keeping me here. They need me.*

That last thought crystalized it. *Do they really need me? No, not really, not like I need them.* She was face to face with the realization that neither her parents nor siblings depended upon her. She was the one with the modest income and little Frankie's needs. Then it all came to a head for her. *I have spent my whole life as a dependent. I've never achieved anything on my own. I've reaped the benefits of an immoral culture, received a good education, and enjoyed a thousand advantages denied to most others. I'm too dependent.* Knowing they would all be fine whether or not she was nearby, she made a difficult decision. *It's time to grow up. I'm leaving Louisiana.*

Louvenia's dream was to board one of the fabled Mississippi riverboats, set out, and seek her future. Up until now, it was just a fantasy. Now it was summertime, and she still hadn't acted on her yuletide resolution. With no idea what she would do upon arrival, she'd never find out by staying put. She made the impulsive decision to follow her dream to Illinois. Uncertain about what to expect, Louvenia envisioned a more progressive, enlightened place, fueling the romantic notion that she was going to start a new life in the footsteps of Lincoln.

She immediately began to question which was greater, her resolve or her fear. Although Lou dreaded telling her parents, she determined it would be the first apprehension to dispel. That evening she announced her plans to the family at dinner, and it felt like a weight coming off her shoulders. Of course, it wasn't going to change the situation in Louisiana, but at least it ended her complicity. The McGees were all distressed to learn of her plan, but they knew the strong-willed Louvenia would not be swayed once she made a major decision.

"Are you angry with me, dear?" her mother asked upon hearing the revelation. The question disappointed but didn't surprise Louvenia. Instead of considering what factors in her daughter's life had driven her decision, Mrs. McGee took it personally.

"No, mother, it's just time for me to stand on my own two feet." Louvenia might have liked to say much more or perhaps even berate her mother for who she was and the kind of life she and her father had led. But she didn't want to leave on an angry note.

Within a week, she made arrangements regarding the few responsibilities that wouldn't be traveling with her. "Father, may I take your leather portmanteau?" she asked the day before her departure. Ever since childhood, Louvenia had admired the large, leather-sided trunk. Back on the plantation, he had kept it in the library along with maps, globes, travel logs, and mementos. She hadn't given a moment's thought about how heavy it might get once she had her clothing and Frankie's things all crammed into it.

"¿Por qué no?" he began in Spanish then stopped, remembering Mrs. McGee's often repeated wish that everyone in the house speak only English. With a tear in his eye, he continued in English, "Of course you may. I can't tell you how much you'll be missed. I don't suppose we can change your mind?" he added.

"Father, I won't be changing my mind. I've finally decided to be honest with myself, so don't tempt me to get lazy and give up now," she answered.

Chapter Fifteen
LIFE ON THE PRAIRIE

"Love demands all, and has a right to all."
–Ludwig van Beethoven

It was a great relief when the family received a letter from Louvenia more than two months after she boarded the northbound riverboat. They had only heard from her one other time, fourteen days after her departure. In that hastily written note, she said she and Frank had arrived safely in New Boston, Illinois, a small river town where she intended to spend some time. However, this time the letter was much longer and contained big news. Louvenia matter-of-factly explained she had fallen in love and married Daniel Palmer, a smart, handsome, rugged man who was just perfect for her in every way. Her letter continued, proudly describing him in detail:

My Daniel's coal-black hair is thick, fitting his powerful frame. He's not afraid to wear it long, and when he combs it straight out, it reaches his waist! Hardly anyone ever sees that, though. I help him braid it at night, and it has a beautiful, curly wave in the morning. Although he needn't, he covers it most of the day with his favorite broad cowboy hat he likes to call his Stetson hat. Not only

*a man of great wisdom, but he also looks it too, with a broad face
and penetrating eyes set above his full, flowing beard.*

*Daniel loves to wear his soft leather boots, but I am trying to
train him to wear dress shoes when he walks around town. He
walks as if he is the tallest man you'll ever see, and I know he
would be surprised to learn his five-foot, six-inch frame is less
than average height. He is so confident, I'm sure he never gives
his stature a moment's thought, but I make sure not to wear shoes
that would make me seem taller than he. It seems funny it would
worry me and never him. Maybe it's because he is so intelligent
and people always ask him how to solve problems.*

*He loves a good joke, and when he hears one that catches his
imagination, his laugh is robust, jovial, and contagious. He's much
more the life of the party than a wallflower, but he has a somber
side too. Daniel never smokes, cusses, gambles, or wastes time.
He treats Frankie like he's his own, reads books on philosophy
endlessly, and can put away as much food at a meal as any man I
have ever seen.*

*It seems like I had to travel far and make many mistakes, but
finally, I feel as though I've found my home.*

> *With Love,*
> *Lou*

Never before had Louvenia referred to herself as *Lou*. When she
was a child, there were occasions when others tried to do so. She
would always promptly and firmly correct them by saying, "My
name is Louvenia." Mrs. McGee took this informality as a good
sign, suggesting Lou had finally found peace of mind. After so
much strife and disappointment, her daughter was happy and in
love, which lifted her mother's spirits.

Over the ensuing months, she sent letters back home regularly,
and the correspondence repeated the theme of devotion to the
newfound love of her life. She continued to go to great lengths to

explain just how different Daniel was from all the men she had ever known in Louisiana. His uniqueness, along with her desire for change, was a good fit. That, along with simple biological attraction, bonded them steadfastly. She was far from her high-born aristocratic past, a house of cards that had fallen all around the South. In the third letter, she tried to explain why she had left and what she had found.

I arrived in Illinois thirsting for truth, something real, ethical—and if I couldn't have that, then I would at least start with different. Daniel fit the bill in every way, and it didn't hurt that he's distinctive to the utmost, good-looking, and strong. True, his manner is unrefined. He's no Southern gentleman, and that's just fine with me too. I've found a man who's genuine inside and out. I don't mean to come off sounding like I don't appreciate all you have done for me, and I know the love of my family saved me during the worst of times. But I've been torn between the love of my family and abhorring the posh trappings of bigoted patricians. Since the war ended, all became very clear to me. Now in Daniel, I've found honesty and sharp wit in a hardworking, warm, sincere, kind person.

With Love,

Lou

Daniel and Lou grew a life together and, in less than a year, were blessed with their first child, a daughter they named May. Two years later, another daughter, Jessie, was born. Then 1877 ended joyously with the arrival of another baby girl, Audrey, named in honor of Lou's oldest sister.

Audrey was a beautiful child who didn't seem to thrive as their other daughters did. She had a soft, pastel complexion, and unlike her mother, had wispy, flaxen-colored hair. Her features were fine, almost too delicate, and her deep blue eyes made her skin look paler. Unfortunately, the child seemed to go from one bout of illness to another, and by the time she was five months old, Louvenia and Daniel were concerned enough to take her into town to see Doc Noble. They didn't like taking an infant out on the seven-mile trip, but neither of them knew what else to do. It was a mid-April morning and seemed like a good day to go since the sun was out and the temperatures mild for early springtime on the prairie.

When they expressed their concerns about the baby's marginal weight gain and how she tended to be fussy all the time, the doctor appeared to listen carefully. He took the child from Louvenia, held her out, and bounced her in his arms gently to gauge her weight. He stroked her face to determine her temperature and listened to her chest. "She is a lightweight, but her breathing is clear, and her heart sounds regular." The doctor's one-minute examination concluded with, "Everything seems fine with this one; some babies are just fussy that way. I'm sure as time goes by, her resistance will get better, and she'll start eating you out of house and home!"

"Isn't there something we should do?" asked Louvenia.

"You might want to start her on some solid foods to give her a boost. Nothing too heavy at first, you know," the doctor replied.

"No, I *don't* know," Lou replied. "We never had to give anything but mother's milk to the other children during their first year."

"Just grind up some rice or oats extra-fine, cook it up, and cool before feeding," the doctor answered as he dismissively stepped toward the door.

The Palmers found minimal reassurance from the doctor's blasé pronouncements, but he was the only physician in town, so they hoped for the best. Unfortunately, the next morning proved hopes weren't enough. Daniel's blood ran cold when he heard Louvenia scream out, "Daniel, my God, she's not breathing!" By the time he rushed into the bedroom, she was standing there holding Audrey's tiny, still body. It was too late to do anything, and they would never learn why she died.

The Palmer family again climbed to the top of the bluff, where they said their sorrowful farewells to Audrey. The tiny graveyard Daniel had cleared for baby Abba during a cold winter long ago had since become the final resting place for two other infants.

Louvenia began to read, "'The Lord is my Shepherd; I shall not want. He maketh me to lie down in green pastures'—" She choked up, stopped for a breath, looked at the three children standing beside her, and gained some strength to continue. "'He leadeth me beside the still waters. He restoreth my soul' ...." That was as far as she could get. She couldn't even catch her breath, so turning toward Daniel, she dropped the book in his hands, leaned on his shoulders, and wept while gasping for air.

Also grief-stricken, he didn't know how to comfort her. The two stood, her sobbing inconsolably, and Daniel choked up.

Finally, their three-year-old daughter, May, took Louvenia's hand in hers and said, "Don't worry, Mama. We'll take care of you."

May's half-brother Frank placed his hand on their mother's other shoulder, adding, "We'll tend to the flowers for you. This spot will always be beautiful."

Then Daniel picked up exactly where she left off reading the 23rd Psalm.

"'He leadeth me in the paths of righteousness for His name's sake. Yea, though I walk through the valley of the shadow of death, I will fear no evil: for thou art with me; thy rod and thy staff they comfort me. Thou preparest a table before me in the presence of mine enemies: thou anointest my head with oil; my cup runneth over. Surely goodness and mercy shall follow me all the days of my life: and I will dwell in the house of the Lord forever. Amen.'"

The children repeated *amen* in unison, then, hand in hand, the family started down the raspberry-lined path toward the house.

The day's chores brought a welcome relief from the quiet morning funeral. Will and Mary Kellogg came by that afternoon to prepare a meal and see to the children's needs. The Essleys also came to call, and by the time the day finished, Lou and Daniel faced the need to move on. Losing Audrey suddenly, for no apparent reason, just made no sense. Events blurred together, and friends helped them through it. Sweet Home weathered another tragedy, and there was lots of work to do every day. But they were still a family, and heartbreaking reality couldn't postpone their need to go on. Rural

Illinois families knew both joy and misfortune, and the Palmers, like other pioneering folks, had to rely on their strength, mutual support, and whatever the community might do to ease their way.

As Daniel and Lou approached their eighth anniversary, the newest little brother, Bart, was born on September 14, 1882. He joined his two sisters and half-brother, rounding out the family. They were now living in What Cheer, Iowa, near Daniel's parents and the rest of the Palmer clan. Their decision to leave Sweet Home wasn't easy, but natural events beginning with the winter of 1880–1881 would change the lives of many Midwesterners.

Winter had set in early, with snow flying by late October 1880. The first in a series of big blizzards came during the first week of November, and it remained extremely cold thereafter.

The fabled "snow winter" was unprecedented in every way. Snowstorms lasted for days on end, beating down the Midwest prairies and the spirits of all creatures unfortunate enough to be in winter's path. Railroads hired snow shovelers by the hundreds to dig out tracks buried so deep, adjacent telegraph lines also disappeared below the drifts. It forced some smaller rail lines to close service entirely until April. Deep drifts covered buildings too, and farmers had to tunnel down from the roofs of barns to gain access to the doors. The temperature stayed below zero throughout January, and it showed little sign of letting up in February. Keeping livestock was a constant struggle all winter, and Daniel was often outside for long hours, making sure the barn was secure, breaking out ice from the horse's water buckets, and sheltering the hives with an assortment of windbreaks. Mounds of drifting snow and bitter winds continued, and one had to cover their entire face to prevent frostbite.

It was just such a mid-February day, and dawn hadn't yet broken over Sweet Home when Daniel came in from early morning chores. He had begun to stamp his feet onto a rag rug in the adjoining mudroom when Lou, who was in the kitchen, looked at him in the light of the oil lamp and immediately broke out in laughter. "Daniel, you look like a walrus!" To Louvenia, the harsh prairie winters were still something of a novelty compared to the Louisiana of her upbringing. Never having seen snow back home on the plantation, she was mesmerized by its covering their Illinois farmyard, the rolling hills turning white, and the road drifting shut. It held a pleasing fascination for her the Canadian-born man just couldn't fathom. "Not so loud, walrus, you'll wake the children!" she scolded with a smile on her face.

He was trying to shake as much loose snow and ice off his outer clothing as possible before beginning to peel off the layers. His hands were moving slowly, not completely numb, but close to it. Not feeling particularly playful, he answered softly, "It's curious a wife would mock her hard-working mate this way." He moved toward the kitchen entryway where a half-length mirror hung. Daniel looked at his reflection and saw the large crop of icicles hanging from his mustache and beard, and he too fell into muffled laughter. "You're right. I do look like a walrus, but a damn cold one, who's looking for much balmier waters."

"I told you to wrap that wool scarf over your face!" Lou picked up the tightly rolled bright green scarf from the kitchen counter and threw it, hitting him square in the face as she admonished him further. "I don't know why I knit it for you if you won't wear it on a day like this!" The direct hit of the scarf knocked several icicles from his beard, making a minuscule clinking sound as they bounced on the nearby hard floor. The jingling icicles struck a chord as they both stood in opposite rooms, laughing until their sides ached.

Lou came to the mudroom and tenderly brushed the remaining ice from his face. She pulled on his sleeves, helping him yank his arms from the heavy sweater while they guffawed over the situation. His arms were finally free, but his fingers still hurt too much from the cold to consider undoing the laces of his boots. He wanted to get to the warm kitchen but couldn't step out of the mudroom because of the ice-packed boots. A wave of emotion came over him, and he pulled Lou close and hugged her. Her body felt so warm, it comforted him, and he just wanted to stay there, hold her, and think about how much he loved her. To her, all was now right with the world. She felt tiny, wrapped up in the big, damp bear hug of this man she loved.

Daniel felt so comforted, he didn't even think about moving. Louvenia's breasts were flattened against his chest by the unrelenting, strong hug, and she began to notice an unexpected stirring within her. Slowly she moved her hands from his back, forward to his sides, and gently pushed against his rib cage, separating the two of them while softly saying, "We've got something to take care of."

Too content to move, but intrigued by the look in her eye, he began, "My boots are still—"

Smiling a wily expression she hardly recognized on her, she interrupted, passing her index finger through wet facial hairs and putting it to his lips. "I'll take care of you" was all she said in a rare tone that sounded even more cunning than the look on her face.

She placed her hands on his hips to balance herself as she knelt in front of him. With her right hand, she grasped a wooden spoon they kept on the floor in the corner of the mudroom and began chipping the ice off of his boot laces. While seeing to the task, Louvenia glanced up at him, pleased he still wore a look of bewildered anticipation. Encouraged by it, she lightly stroked his hip with her left hand, which was still resting there, and repeated in a softer voice, "I'll take care of you." She playfully turned her hand, still resting it on his hip until her fingers pointed toward his center. The game was afoot with all the guile she could muster. She stretched her fingers over his pants, strumming her fingertips at whatever happened to be underneath and within reach. She could feel warmth growing under her fingers and decided the best move now was no move at all. So she kept her outstretched fingertips where they were, slowly and deliberately increasing and decreasing the pressure, as if she were operating some kind of pump.

Satisfied he got the message, she focused on the ice-packed boots, chipping ice with the spoon while her fingertips kept up the teasing, seductive cadence. Finally, the laces were loose. She placed his right boot in the crook of her right elbow, then immediately put her left hand back on his hip and said, "Okay, you can pull out now."

He looked her directly in the eye, smiling. "Don't you need two hands for what you're doing?"

She looked up at her left hand with its fingertips still dutifully performing their teasing assignment and giggled. "Daniel, do you mean I need two hands here?" she brushed her fingertips over the spot they had been prodding, "Or do you mean down there?" pointing at his boot.

Noticing her giggle still sounded seductive, he said, "I think you're right. We do have something to take care of!"

She grasped his boot with both hands, and he pulled his right foot out. They repeated the process for the left, and still kneeling in front of him, Louvenia reached up inside his pant legs and rolled down the wet socks, removing them slowly, one at a time. Meanwhile, Daniel's trembling fingers were fussing with the buttons on his shirt. Finally, she reached up and continued with the buttons on his trousers. While he wiggled out of the shirt, she undid the tight-fitting buttons on the damp, heavy fabric and pulled the trousers down off his waist until the heavy, wet material fell in a heap on the floor. Stepping out of them, he nearly lost his balance and placed one hand on her shoulder as she was still kneeling in front of him. She reached around him with both arms and drew him to her, hugging him with her head turned to one side while he struggled again to keep his balance. It was a curious situation to be standing in front of her, nearly undressed except for his long johns, while she knelt there, fully dressed.

The disparity made him feel ungainly, especially with Louvenia hugging him, her right ear firmly pressed against his groin. But the gawkiness quickly gave way to a lustier emotion. She felt it too, as the part of him next to her ear was responding. He moved his hands to her shoulders and tenderly pressed her head away from him. Making eye contact, he reached down inside her blouse with an ice-cold right hand.

Gasping when cold fingers touched her warm flesh, she rose to her feet. She pulled away in protest, and then pulled him to her in very rapid succession.

He repeated, "We *really* have something to take care of." Removing his hand from her blouse, he grasped the hem of her dress and began to lift it.

"No, not here!" She commanded, catching his arms before they got above her waist. "It's cold and wet."

He let go of her dress and followed her into the kitchen. Knowing she would lead him across the house to the bedroom, he decided this heart-pounding, lusty moment demanded something unique. She had started something special, something different.

When she was about halfway across the dimly lit room, he drew her hard against him and kissed her deeply. His back leaned against the kitchen table, he was intoxicated with the fragrance of her hair and the taste of her. The heavy oak table was the first new piece of furniture he had made right after they were married. It occurred to him there was something symbolic about it. With one arm firmly holding her tight, the other went for the oil lamps hanging above the table. With a couple of quick twists, the lights were out. Again, he reached under her dress and hastily raised his arms, pulling it over her head. Shaking it loose, he tossed it aside and leaned back onto the table, pulling her over him.

His hands were roaming over her back, devouring the feeling of her skin. He ran his hands over her legs and noticed goosebumps. He wondered if they were because of his cold touch or from chipping ice off his boots and laces. He rolled over until she was under him, safely in the center of the table, and they made love in a way they would both long remember. It excited him to think about her, who she was, where she had come from, and how unlikely it was for them to have ever gotten together. Yet, beneath him, this intelligent, refined, aristocratic young woman remained. So far from the plantation now, she still loved and understood the arts, could play music, and fluently recite poetry in three languages.

He wondered what she saw in him. In so many ways, she was his opposite, yet she loved him, and he loved her.

Less than an hour later, after the passions had settled, the two were sipping coffee together at the same oak table. "I'll never eat a meal at this table again without thinking about you and what we did here today," Daniel said.

She wasn't embarrassed, but her response was not about the table; she considered where and why they were there in this warm afterglow. Finally, she answered only, "I love you, Daniel Palmer."

A week later, Louvenia found herself wondering if it wasn't time for her period to start. But when another week passed, she was pretty sure about it. It was early morning, just before dawn, and much like that other memorable morning. Daniel had just returned from early morning chores, and the children weren't awake yet. Placing a cup of coffee on the table before him, Lou said, "Daniel, remember that cold early morning and what happened in the dark on this table two weeks ago?"

He looked puzzled. Then that big, broad smile returned to his face, and he waved his hand as if to say, *Go ahead.*

His reaction brought an unexpected blush to her face. Getting the best of her brought out his playful side, and he answered, "Oh yes, that's one cold, dark morning I'll never forget, especially the way you warmed it up!"

Trying to stay serious, she continued, "I think we might have made more than love that morning."

Perplexed when he should have seen the obvious, he asked, "What do you mean, sweetheart?"

Charmed by his naivety, she giggled, "You fool, maybe you're going to be a dad again!"

He asked incredulously, "Is it possible? Do you really think so?"

Nodding rapidly, Louvenia answered, "I never miss my time of the month, and it should have been here at least a week ago."

After a triumphant laugh, he said, "We've already brought our share of girls into this world. Would you like to give me a son this time?"

She was happy to hear his enthusiasm and see the joy on his face. Her response was both playful and to the point. "Well, Mr. Palmer, later tonight, after you've helped me with the dishes and read a bedtime story to the kids, you can join me in the room that's made for this kind of thing and set some more seeds for good measure!"

Over breakfast the next morning Louvenia said, "Daniel, you remember what I told you last night?"

He smiled, answering, "How could I forget?"

"Well, this morning I discovered that the stork must have already flown south for the winter."

He quietly took it in, then answered, "Well, that will give us something to work on, won't it?"

Chapter Sixteen

WHAT CHEER

"He who has never failed somewhere,
that man cannot be great."

–HERMAN MELVILLE

March comes in like a lion and goes out like a lamb, the old saying went. That generally reliable anecdote promised that harsh as March might begin, the temperatures would inevitably moderate, yielding to the comfort of April. But in 1881, March failed to bring its promised thaw, and on the few days where the temperature actually rose above freezing, it stayed damp, windy, and generally miserable. April was already beginning with more of the same. Daniel examined the hives every day, and he returned to the house that morning with rounded shoulders and a heavy heart. With tears in his eyes, he reported the news to Louvenia. "They're *all* dead."

There was such a heavy melancholy written across his face, she didn't know what to say. He continued through the kitchen without waiting for a response, sat at the small wooden kitchen desk, and scribbled a terse entry atop the blank page of his daily journal: *April 14, 1881, Winter kill, all bees dead!* He heavily underscored the word *all*, then added an exclamation mark. There were no journal entries during the next two days, a rare occurrence for the compulsive horticulturist—it was as if life froze.

The Palmers were nothing if not adaptable, and Louvenia was a rock when he needed her most. Throughout the ensuing days, she kept on encouraging him. "Daniel, we'll get through this," and "You started with nothing, and you can do it again." They talked it through for hours, but those conversations wouldn't be chronicled in his leather-bound notebook.

"Lou, you know the Mercer County School Board barely pays teachers. We really can't make it without the money Sweet Home honey brings in."

"You often get orders for Sweet Home raspberry nursery stock," she responded.

"But we can't make a living at it the way we could when honey production was good," he insisted.

Louvenia assured him, "You know we're going to be all right."

The proud, determined man interrupted, "Lou, I love you with all my heart, and I'll not have you struggling. Who would have thought I'd be starting all over again at this point?" His eyes glistened with moisture. "We have children to care for now!"

Louvenia, moved by his sadness, reflected quietly, *It's so rare to see defeat on this strong man's face.* She finally reminded him, "It's been almost seven years now, and in that time, we've never wanted for anything. We're both strong and healthy. We've been through worse, and you know we'll get through this. Perhaps it's time to think about selling and doing something else. It might be a good opportunity to move closer to your parents. I think that would be good for the kids."

Relieved by her positive tone and surprised by her willingness to make a change, Daniel asked, "Do you remember what Mother and Father said about What Cheer on their visit here before Christmas?"

"I remember them saying coal mining was still increasing and every business in town was booming because of it," she responded.

He added, "They also said the town needs another grocery because the old man running the general store barely keeps up."

They talked it out and agreed this was the right moment to move to Iowa. Besides, everyone would like the idea of bringing the children closer to their kin.

It was emotionally hard for Daniel to sell Sweet Home. He had built it up from nothing with his own hands. But he was devoted to Louvenia, and there was no doubt she would rather live in a town with close neighbors. Beyond that, the house out there on Sweet Home wasn't *really* her house. It had been built for Abba. Louvenia never let on if she felt any jealousy, but he was sure she would prefer to have a house of her own. For his part, he wouldn't miss the subtle reminders of that disappointing, unhappy outcome of life with Abba.

Once they decided, things happened fast. Telegrams were expensive, so he wrote a postcard to his parents in What Cheer. The missive said little yet said it all. So, to fit it all in, he wrote crisply:

Dear Mother and Father,

Selling Sweet Home. Lou, the kids, and me arriving next week.
Which does What Cheer need most, teacher or grocer— perhaps both? Have many raspberry nursery stock to sell.
Kindly provide a warm, dry, clean spot to stay 'til we're on our own.

As ever, Daniel.

That afternoon Daniel put on extra layers of clothing and a scarf over his face to keep the bitter late winter wind off for the seven-mile walk to New Boston. Although he could have taken a wagon or just saddled up, the Canadian frontiersman in him preferred the grounding of a brisk walk.

He stopped first at the home of his best friends, Will and Mary Kellogg, for a warming cup of coffee and to reveal the news. He had been dreading this moment ever since they decided to go. The walk to town had been particularly agonizing, mulling over what to say. *How do you bid farewell to such good friends?*

Looking Mary in the eye, he explained the Palmer family relocation plans. "Mary, it's time for us to join the rest of the clan out in What Cheer, on the Iowa side. This hellish winter has taken a heavy toll, and the apiary has utterly failed. You and Will have been like family to us, and I'll never forget you. I'll always be there for you, if ever—"

To make it easier, Will spoke up even before he could finish, "Daniel, what can we do to help?"

Daniel's warm, appreciative smile said more than words ever could. He grasped Will around the shoulders, giving him a big hug.

Their acceptance meant a great deal to Daniel, who relaxed and said, "There's not much that needs to be done. We'll be going within a week. I'll leave the farm up for sale, and I might ask you to check on things from time to time until it's sold. The house is a sturdy two-story, and there's a lot of interest in land these days, so we'll see how it goes. I'm going to the lawyer's office when I leave here."

"I know the children will benefit from being close to their grandparents," said Will. "What will you do for a living?" he asked.

Trying to lighten the atmosphere, an upbeat Mary passed a tray in front of them. "Daniel, I've got fresh molasses muffins. You need this to warm up good. And don't worry about us; you'll always have folks you can rely on here in New Boston."

"Thank you, Mary, I thought you'd never offer!" he said, taking a muffin with a smile. Then, turning to Will, he answered his question. "Coal mining has been booming in What Cheer for years now, and this horrible winter has increased the demand. All those miners and their families need to eat, be clothed, and support their households. My parents tell me there's already a great need for another grocery and dry goods store, and I've got some ideas on how to put one together."

Attorney Keele was seated behind his large oak desk when he heard a knock at the door of his one-room office. He called out, "Come in."

The door opened, and Mr. Keele promptly welcomed Daniel with a smile. "Hi, Mr. Palmer, it's good to see you again." Gesturing toward the four straight-back chairs lined up against the front wall, he said, "Please have a seat and make yourself comfortable. I'm just about to close up a project, and there's something I must not forget. I'll just be a moment." Daniel parked himself in the closest chair while the man wrote a couple of short sentences and signed the paper in front of him. Then he carefully replaced his long quill pen on the onyx pen rest that held a small glass ink well. After pivoting a large arced blotter over each wet place, Mr. Keele neatly rolled the document into a tight tube. Having disposed of the matter, he placed it into the documents box marked *outgoing* on the left-hand corner of his large desk.

Rising from his chair, he stepped over to offer his hand. "I'm truly pleased to see you, Mr. Palmer. What can I do for you?" Daniel accepted the handshake, noting Mr. Keele's firm, enthusiastic grip.

"Mr. Keele, my family and I are moving west to the Iowa Territory. I'd like to ask you to handle the sale of the farm."

"You better be careful about calling it the Iowa *Territory*. The folks living out there may take offense since they're all quite proud about having achieved statehood now."

"Thanks for pointing that out," Daniel said. "I'm sure you're right about that. I guess I've picked up the habit of calling it that from speaking with people on this side of the river. Starting now, I'll get myself used to just saying Iowa."

"So you need assistance selling your property?" the attorney confirmed.

"Yes," Daniel answered. "I have ten acres on River Road up over and including the bluff, almost eight miles outside of town on the main road."

Mr. Keele nodded. "I know the place well; you got it from Elisha Essley a bit over ten years ago. Old Elisha's got more land than you can shake a stick at." Then, respectfully looking down to break eye contact, Mr. Keele continued tentatively, "You remember, of course, that I handled Mrs. Palmer's sale of her half when she left."

Daniel answered, "Oh ... yes." He was uneasy and hesitated, remembering he had cared little about paying attention to the legal issues surrounding Abba's hasty departure. It also sounded bizarre to hear someone refer to "Mrs. Palmer" when they weren't speaking of Louvenia.

After briefly reflecting on what had transpired, Mr. Keele said, "I recall Abba's uncle purchased her portion—he's up in Minnesota, I think. It's my understanding he was trying to stake her relocation and getting settled upriver. I believe it was near Fort Snelling, but anyway, somewhere in Minnesota. I wasn't sure what to think when you didn't answer my letters back then. Then, finally, I had to get the sale recorded for five acres without a proper legal description of exactly what had been sold. She was in a hurry, and I remember her concern about not getting you riled up over the sale. It bothered me that the sale did not include a regular deed, nor complete clarity on what was carved out of the original parcel."

Daniel answered, "You know it's strange to me too, and I've never heard a thing from anyone in the Lord family about the land. But I would thrash any of them if they ever showed up on my place to make trouble."

The attorney assumed a proper straight-up tone. "Now, let's be glad nothing like that ever came of it."

He continued as though he hadn't heard Mr. Keele, "Well, now you're *my* attorney, so you can get this thing cleaned up, right?"

"Actually, it's not that simple," Mr. Keele responded. "One thing we'll need to do is draft a document describing my role, previously having represented Abba Lord in matters relating to this property. Then you will have to sign it, acknowledging you understand the conflict of interest implications for me to now represent you."

"I understand," Daniel said.

"Since we don't have a proper basis for the land, we'll need to finalize the whole thing on a quitclaim basis. That's also how I handled the Lord portion," Mr. Keele continued.

"Just what does that mean?" Daniel asked.

"Oh, well, the concept is simple enough. We'll issue a quitclaim deed when the farm sells, which essentially means what it sounds like. You will quit all claims of any sort on the entire property. So you'll *quit* your claim on the whole acreage because of the technicality that you can't provide the usual deed."

Daniel felt a wave of anger coming over him. He was in no mood to hear he didn't own the land he had been putting blood, sweat, and tears into for more than ten years.

The attorney, noticing Daniel was getting emotional, calmed him. "Mr. Palmer, don't worry, it's all water under the bridge now. You just focus on building a good future for you and your family, and we'll get the legal matters cleared up for you here."

That was all Daniel needed to hear, so he offered his hand to Mr. Keele, saying, "I'd be obliged to you." But Daniel Palmer wasn't one to just leave it at that. With a tear in his eye, he added, "Mr. Keele, make no mistake about it. Sweet Home is one of the best apiaries in Illinois or anywhere else. There's a good house with a deep well on a beautiful site, fertile soil, and scores of trees I planted to make it home. She's got a stream between the hills that never goes dry and a hundred excellent Thomas Hives, as well as over two hundred more assorted—some purchased, and some I made myself. The hives I built are the best because their design was based on years of experience, taking in the better qualities of all the others. All are clean and in perfect working condition. If the new owner gets blessed with serviceable weather, they'll be ready to produce like no other."

"Interesting, the way you said serviceable," said Mr. Keele. "The past two years brought the most brutal winters anyone around here's ever seen. I've been extra busy with folks' weather-related issues, and I've heard it called a lot of things, but mostly using four-letter words. The one thing it hasn't been for people in Illinois or Iowa is serviceable. I admit, it's helped my business some, and I'm sure the undertaker has been extra busy, but for most, well, it's sorrowful to think about it."

"We're leaving in three days, and I don't expect to be back. So just take your fees out of the proceeds and send whatever I've got coming to General Delivery, What Cheer, Iowa," instructed Daniel.

"I'll draw up the papers," the attorney responded. "You can put your mind at ease."

Daniel, Lou, and the children arrived in What Cheer the following Sunday. His parents met them at the train station with good news. His mother, nearly breathless with enthusiasm, began, "We've found a building three blocks from here with enough space for the family on the second floor and plenty of room for a store on the ground floor. T.J. contacted the owner, and the man is holding it for you to see."

"Catherine, it's wonderful to arrive and be made to feel so welcome," Louvenia thanked her as they loaded suitcases onto the wagon in front of the station.

"You're with family now, dear," was Catherine's response.

That struck an odd chord with Daniel as it dredged up old feelings of abandonment on the Canadian frontier. But not wanting to diminish the moment for Louvenia, he said nothing and tried to put it out of his mind altogether.

Catherine added, "We've made up beds for the younger children, and T.J. says if Frank would be interested in having his own room, then he'd be welcome to use the guest room at his house. It's just across the way from ours."

Louvenia glanced over at Frank, whose face lit up at the prospect. "What do you think, Frankie? Would you like to stay in uncle T.J.'s house while we get settled here in town?"

"I sure would!" the teenager blurted out. "This is going to be fun."

"I'm glad you're pleased. There may be some work too, you know," Catherine cautioned.

"I know. Uncle T.J. showed me how to play dominos, and now I'm getting good at it," the unaffected youngster answered.

Thomas and Catherine provided meals and a comfortable place to stay while the whole family went to work. First, Lou, Daniel, and their children scrubbed every inch of the building and painted it inside and out. Then, with furniture donated by his parents and lots of help from Daniel's brothers and sisters, they were moved in and settled upstairs in less than two weeks.

"It's been twelve days of hard work, and now I think we can call What Cheer our home," Daniel said to Louvenia. The Palmer family had been going at full speed that day and every day. Now, having finished supper, cleaned the kitchen, read stories, and tucked the kids into their beds, they sat together in the living room. Nearly exhausted, they relaxed over an evening's cup of tea.

Louvenia said, "Well, I guess it's time to make some decisions."

"You're right, dear. We've done our homework. What Cheer is growing in every way, and it promises to be a great marketplace. It's a certainty that this town has plenty of room and a strong need for our store."

"So now that What Cheer's ready, and we're ready, how do we get started? What are your ideas, and what's the next step?" Lou asked.

He answered assuredly, "It needs to be more than just another grocery store. I envision a broad range of staples, fresh foods, fish, and a wide variety of dry goods. And I think we need to do it sensibly."

"What do you mean by sensibly?" Lou chimed in.

He smiled his all-knowing school teacher smile as he answered, "We'll start a store that fits my personality—"

"Wait a minute," she interrupted. "How did we get from *we'll* start a store to fits *your* personality. Is it just you, or are we both working in this venture?"

Feeling the trap spring shut, he quickly retreated. "I'm sorry, dear; I didn't mean to diminish you by saying that. I meant it as a figure of speech and ..." No sooner had the words come out of his mouth than he realized it was not only a lame excuse but also simply untrue and wrong. He decided to admit defeat. "You're right, and I'm sorry. Sometimes I ... I act self-centered and egotistical. I guess I sounded as silly as, as Chauvin himself."

She laughed out loud at his stammering apology, and he breathed a sigh of relief. "I know you didn't mean it in the worst way," she said. "But I'm glad you at least can see a truth to which most men are blind. Oppression isn't always overt. It's most often sneaky and subtle. If I learned anything in Louisiana, it's that one mustn't stand by idly and look the other way." Her tone was distinctive, one he had heard before and only in her most serious moments.

"You're right, dear. *Our* store won't be the only one offering dry goods and provisions in What Cheer. But ours will be unique. It will run sensibly, economically, and responsively."

Lou asked, "When you say ours will be unique, do you mean the other What Cheer businesses come up short on those things?"

"Exactly." He held up his index finger. "And it's a problem going on all over. Here's what I've learned. The big general store, the livery, the millinery, and even the milkman run on credit. They don't get paid effectively, so they don't have the cash they need to respond to their customer's needs. So my idea is we do all of it better."

Knowing he wanted her to ask, she played along. "How will we do *all* that?"

He answered expeditiously, "We go strictly cash, and we sell at lower prices because we can."

"Why is it we can sell at lower prices?" Louvenia asked.

"Since we always stay in a cash position, we'll be able to afford to provide better products in bigger quantities. We get paid right away whenever we deliver any product or service. Since we don't have to wait for payment, we leverage our cash position to the benefit of our customers. I've even thought up a name."

Louvenia flashed an obligatory smile at him and responded on cue. "Okay, what's *our* new store to be called?"

"Palmer's Cheap Cash Store!"

Louvenia twisted up her face as she considered the name. "I like the idea, but I'm not so sure about the word 'cheap.' Couldn't that cause people to think our products are inferior?"

He confidently retorted, "We'll be working the principles of economy. They will quickly see the quality is there, and they'll consistently get more for less."

As she reflected, the furrow in her forehead smoothed out, and her eyebrows lowered. "I like it, and I love you. Now it's late. So let's call it a night."

Procurement of merchandise began the following day, and products were soon filling their shelves. Palmer's Cheap Cash Store opened for business before the fourth week came to a close. They offered an abundant variety of dry goods and groceries, and Daniel also wanted to develop a specialty the competition simply didn't have. He explored several options, and the day before the store opened, he said, "Lou, I want to go to Davenport today. I think fresh fish can become our hallmark." She gave him an incredulous look. "It's one thing people in What Cheer can't easily get, and I want to be the one who gets it for them."

"Have you thought about how we're going to be able to supply it?" she asked.

He laid out the plan. "Davenport's on the busiest river in the country, and we can get there in just over two and a half hours by train, including three stops! When I got the idea, I contacted Mr. Burkett. He runs a general store there. I think I've told you about him and his wonderful family. T.J. and I worked for him when we first arrived from Canada. They were kind in every way and even fed us when we didn't have a penny in our pockets. It was before we became schoolmasters. Mr. Burkett told me there's a Mr. Barr there in Davenport who supplies fresh fish to his store, and I can rely on anything the man says. Well, I heard back from Mr. Barr this morning, and he says he can provide fresh-caught fish from the Mississippi and exotic varieties of seafood brought upriver from the Gulf of Mexico."

Louvenia was intrigued. "Just how often would we need to make this trip?"

"Mr. Barr says if I come just once a week, he can have our order ready and iced up, enough to hold us for days. Of course, we'll run out during the last day or two of each week, but our customers will know when that is. Most of all, they'll know our products are first-class, affordable, and available."

She wasn't sure if he was right but knew he had thought it through carefully, and would trust his judgment. "Daniel David Palmer," she liked to use the long form of his name as an endearment, "I must say I'm impressed with how well you have planned this store, including so many details. You're amazing!" Her compliment was music to his ears, and he nearly burst his buttons with pride.

What Cheer residents, hooked on the fresh fish and other lower-priced groceries, happily returned, and Palmer's Cheap Cash Store grew into an overnight success. The family grew too with the arrival of a baby boy only five months after starting the new business.

The baby was born on a cool, comfortable evening, typical of September in What Cheer. The birth went smoothly, and half an hour later, a very tired Louvenia was sitting in her favorite rocking chair, nursing a baby whose tiny little body was wrapped up in a blanket, so only the crown of his head was showing.

Now that he was here, Louvenia said, "I've thought it would be a boy all along, but with two girls already, I didn't say anything to jinx it. I'm so glad I could give you a son too."

Daniel immediately thought about Frank. He had accepted him unconditionally and done everything he could to be a good, loving father to the young man. "Yes, now we're all evened up, two boys and two girls. The kids will want to know what to call their new brother. We better come up with something!"

They had thrown around a few possibilities during the summer months but never agreed on the perfect name if it was a boy. Had they been blessed with another girl, her name would have been Mary, in honor of Louvenia's maternal grandmother. "I'd like his middle name to be Joshua." Louvenia stopped for a breath and explained,

"It's biblical, and it would honor my brother. I never regret leaving Louisiana, but I was always close to Joshua, and I miss him."

"Well then, what's his first name to be?"

Louvenia smiled warmly at her husband. "Now it's your turn. Give him a name to go by."

Daniel pondered, staring at the floor. Then, after deliberating for a few seconds, he looked back up at mother and baby and gestured with his hands above the baby's head, "This is Bart, in honor of my brother." Louvenia's blank expression invited further explanation. Daniel hesitated, glancing to his right and left as if to make sure no one could overhear him before continuing, "In many ways, Bart is the least gifted of my siblings. He barely reads and writes, is terrible with numbers, and has all the eloquence of a turnip. But he makes up for lacking those skills with warmth, loyalty, and consistency. He is kind, and he's always been there for my mother and father." As if on cue, Daniel's mother opened the door. She entered with the baby's two sisters in hand and Frank right behind.

Louvenia said, "Everyone, meet Bartlett Joshua Palmer, your little brother and grandson! Bart, meet everyone!"

Many months passed, and the baby was becoming a toddler. It was early morning, and the family was seated around the kitchen table having breakfast. Daniel, gazing around the table at the beautiful faces of his wife and kids, was moved to say, "It's a truly golden moment in this beekeeper's life."

Louvenia laughed out her words, "Daniel, you haven't been a beekeeper for more than a year now. And, by the way, you're a mighty fine grocer!"

"True, I'm not tending to bees now, but one never stops being a beekeeper, at least not in spirit. I sell honey too, and symbolically speaking, only the hives have changed." He went quiet and added, "Lou, being a beekeeper transforms a man."

Louvenia wondered whether she should be worried about him but decided the contented smile on his face and twinkle in his eye indicated all was well.

Looking up at the place where the wall and ceiling met as though something were written there, Dan said, "This humble, yet nonetheless solid little house is our hive, and it serves us well. I am wealthy in every way that matters, even if I never become richer. I love you, Lou, my confidant, my partner, my wife." His trademark broad smile widened. "We are blessed with two beautiful little girls, a boy, and a baby son. I wouldn't take a million dollars for any one of these kids." His smile then turned mischievous. "Nor would I give a penny for another—so let's stop now!" They both laughed, and the kids, not really understanding, joined in their contagious laughter.

In a quiet moment later that evening, the contented beekeeper reflected on life in general. It led him to reminisce about how his childhood abruptly ended when thrust into adult responsibilities on the Canadian frontier. So much had happened since then. Picturing a large opened book resting on top of a library podium, he felt inspired to make a note in his journal:

I've seen and turned some difficult pages in the book of life. It's certainly different in the United States. I loved being a schoolmaster, even though a person can't make a living at it. The long, hard work hours on the farm were rewarding, although physically brutal, and the evenings were full of financial and emotional strain.

Peppering the days were so many unexpected events—even a slimy farmhand and a cheating wife. Yet through it all, we persevere, sometimes easily and sometimes hardly at all.

Then Louvenia arrived, and all became right with the world. We built a life, tasted love and loss, success and failure. When Mother Nature put an end to the thriving apiary, we found a way to go forward together. As a genuinely happy grocer, father, and husband, it's easy to put the dark experiences into perspective. It's all come together somehow into a delightful present. Given the opportunity to go back, I wouldn't change a thing.

Chapter Seventeen
MAGNETICALLY ATTRACTED

"Three things cannot be long hidden:
the sun, the moon, and the truth."

—BUDDHA

Bart was still a toddler when everything came crashing down. Louvenia, the busy mother of four, partner and proprietor of Palmer's Cheap Cash Store, and light of Daniel's life, died unexpectedly of a sudden illness in November 1884.

It seemed like she had come down with a common cold. Then, as the day went on, she became feverish. Her forehead glistened with perspiration, and damp strings of dark brown hair stuck wherever it touched. Dan was frightened because the fever seemed to be getting out of hand. "Hon, you need help. We've got to do something."

Lou had the shakes so bad her voice trembled. "What do you mean? I can hardly get out of this bed. Maybe it's something I ate."

"I don't know what it is, but you can't go on like this. I'm going for help," he said. "I'll tell Frank to keep an eye on the little ones and listen if you call for anything."

He called on the town's only physician to come to check on her. Less than an hour later, the doctor, Erroll Fishbein, MD, returned to the Palmer home with Daniel. Louvenia was in bed, covered with two extra blankets Frank brought to comfort her.

"Hello, Mrs. Palmer," the doctor said, reaching for her arm. She nodded a short smile of acknowledgment as he felt her pulse. The doctor observed a rosy color in her face, looked in her eyes, and listened to her chest. Then, arriving at a diagnosis, he turned toward Daniel and spoke about Louvenia in the third person. "She has plethora."

"What does that mean? Is it serious?" asked Dan.

Dr. Fishbein said, "I believe your wife is suffering from an excess of blood. I think we better take steps to relieve it."

Louvenia watched him open his leather bag and begin laying out several dreadful-looking metallic instruments on the table next to her bed. Fearfully she asked, "What are you planning to do?"

His nonchalant manner brushed her off as he responded, "We're going to drain off some of the bad excess from a vein." Then, with his lance in one hand, he began to lift her left arm with his other hand.

Horrified, she used all the strength she could muster to yank it away sharply. "You want to cut open my arm? No!" Louvenia was appalled. The usually tactful, polite woman showed no uncertainty. Her next command was directed at her husband. Weary as she was, it sounded more like a plea, "Send that quack away! If the Lord wants me to heal, I will, and if he is ready to take me home, I'll go as a whole person, not a drained shell."

Daniel, also aghast to think this was the best the doctor had to offer, refused the treatment on her behalf. "Isn't there something else you can do?"

Dr. Fishbein, whose voice was now edgy, capitulated. "Keep her warm, give her tea, and apply this poultice to her forehead whenever she perspires. We'll wait until morning, and if she's still feverish, I'll return with leeches to put on her skin to suck out some of the bad blood without using the lance. It's slower but generally effective."

"Are you sure about what's wrong with her, Dr. Fishbein?" her husband asked.

"It's hard to help people who question everything you do to try to help them! But if you decide to do things my way, come on by in the morning," he answered arrogantly, tipped his hat, and left.

As it turned out, a decision on the doctor's care plan wouldn't be necessary, because Louvenia passed away at 3:30 a.m. The family would never learn just why Louvenia had died. Daniel was as devastated by grief as he was filled with anger. He couldn't blame the doctor because he hadn't done anything, but that fact frustrated Daniel and made him furious.

He tortured himself with unanswerable questions. *What should I have done differently? Shouldn't the doctor have known what to do?* The more he thought about it, the angrier he got. *It's outrageous. Draining off her blood was the doctor's best answer to a woman who needed his help ... a mother with small children! I can't imagine doing that to a well person, no less a sick one!*

He was mad at himself too. As a learned man, wishing to be a shining example to his students, he'd studied mathematics, science, logic, and writing in ever greater depth. Yet none of it was of any help to his beloved. He chided himself. *Maybe I should have taken her to Dr. Caster for magnetic. But it all happened so fast. I wish I had done more for her.* There was no consolation, and the more he thought about the situation, the more perturbed he became over the uselessness of the physician.

Although Daniel was busy with arrangements, family, and friends, a seething ire about Dr. Fishbein repeatedly played in his mind in the ensuing days. Along with previous experiences with physicians, it all fostered a distinctly negative opinion of doctors.

A few days after the funeral, Daniel was back in the store, wrapping up some provisions for John Hart who operated one of the town's most successful coal mines. John said, "So sorry about your loss of Mrs. Palmer. I look for the day when doctors will be able to save a sweet soul like her."

The discouraged proprietor snapped back, "You have a much higher opinion of them than I can muster. I've become forced to see a bigger picture. The problem isn't just one incompetent doctor in What Cheer, Iowa. It's an unspoken deception involving every physician I've encountered. They're not only deceiving the public, but worse yet, they're also deceiving themselves by hypocritically claiming to be men of science. At the same time, any fool can see their practices with sick people are mostly barren superstition."

"I don't know about any of that," John answered. "But if there is anything I or my family can do for you and the children, please just ask."

Though he already possessed a hardening attitude toward the medical industry, the loss of Louvenia left an indelible impression on Daniel. He not only lacked aspirations about the healing arts, but also his inclinations leaned firmly in just the opposite direction. Having glimpsed multiple sides of it, he was utterly unimpressed with doctors of all kinds. Abba's spiritual gifts had led her to maintain a mail-order business as a clairvoyant physician. She would diagnose from a photograph or a lock of hair and capriciously offer up treatments for both body and soul. The surprising part was so many of her patients got better. On the other hand Dr. Fishbein, a shining example of modern medicine, arrived with a black leather bag and an even deeper layer of hypocrisy. He was good with a needle and thread to suture up injuries, but folks around town knew the odds were not in favor of patients seeing him for sicknesses.

Predispositions notwithstanding, even before he lost Louvenia, the hand of fate had already reached out to Daniel and inexorably begun to draw him in the most unlikely of directions. It had started in 1879, about a year and a half before their move to What Cheer. He had gone to town, seeking hinges and assorted small hardware needed to construct several new hives. Since it was early and he didn't come into New Boston often, he decided to drop in to see his old friends Will and Mary Kellogg.

It was mid-morning, and Mary, making tea when he arrived, was delighted to see him at the door. "Come in, Dan. You're just in time for tea!" Mary hugged him and walked him to the kitchen table while he glanced around, looking for Will.

"Where's Will?" he asked as she hastened to lift the whistling kettle and pour the boiling water over the strainer of loose tea.

"I'm so glad you are here. Will is in bed, taking a nap," Mary said.

Daniel looked at his pocket watch and responded, "I don't think I've ever known Will to be in bed at 9:30 in the morning."

Mary explained, "He's been feeling poorly for some time. After reading the paper at six o'clock this morning, he only sipped half his coffee and went to lie down thirty minutes later. I wasn't alarmed when he stopped to take some rest during the day, but his stamina seemed to be shrinking by the day. Today is the first time he couldn't make it through the morning."

"I had no idea this was going on," Daniel said.

"It has been for seven weeks now," Mary continued. "He has inexplicable hip and leg pains, no energy, and can barely walk or breathe. His short breaths are labored and so raspy. Doc Noble has tried several remedies but admits he has no idea what to do for him. The last time he came out, he said Will needed more sunshine. That may be, but he was out in the sun when he first started to feel poorly."

"I wonder what's wrong. Is there anything I can do?"

"I think my prayers have been answered," she responded. "I'm going to take him to see a special doctor in Ottumwa, and until you showed up, I just didn't know how I'd find the strength to get us there. We've never been to Ottumwa, but I know the Missouri and Mississippi Railroad goes there from Muscatine." She swallowed hard, building the courage to spell out what she was asking, "Dan, if you might travel there with us, it would mean the world to me."

He quickly answered, "You know I'd do anything for my best friends, but tell me, why Ottumwa? I know the town. It's fifty miles due south of What Cheer, the little coal mining community where my mother and father live. I know New Boston has only one physician, and I wouldn't give you a wooden nickel for him, yet I can't imagine that Ottumwa offers many physicians. Muscatine is much closer, you know, and I'm sure it has several doctors."

Mary donned her familiar smile, always a comfort to Dan, as she responded. "We're not going there to find *more* physicians. We're going there because there's someone who can help. I've come to learn how others have benefited there too."

He forced a smile through his skeptical face, "So just what goes on in Ottumwa?"

Mary took a deep breath. "Do you remember Madam Drury?" Before he could answer, she rolled her eyes, slapped her forehead, and added, "Of course you do. You've been to their place with us many times!"

Laughing, he chimed in, "Yes, I'll never forget. I thought we were entering an enchanted castle when you took me to my first meeting at Verdurette. I must admit, I was nervous and expected to see the most bizarre, spooky of things. I was intrigued by the Spiritualist philosophy but had no idea what awaited. Would there be doors with creaking hinges opening and closing by themselves, spells being cast, witches on broomsticks, or bats soaring about? Well, I learned a lot that day."

Mary laughed at the absurdity too. "I hope I'm not imposing on our friendship too much."

"Nonsense!" he retorted. "Ottumwa isn't even that far out of the way. Perhaps I can make a little detour on my trip back and see the family in What Cheer." Dan would do anything for the Kelloggs, especially now that Will needed help. "I just need to get word to Louvenia so she and the children are okay if I don't make it back by morning." Then, rising, he picked up his teacup and said, "Why don't you get Will ready while I stop by the telegraph office to get a runner out to Sweet Home with a message? Then we can get underway."

"Just a moment," Mary responded. "I didn't finish telling you about Madam Drury."

He lowered himself back into the chair, carefully replacing the China cup into the recess on its delicate saucer, and gave her his full attention.

"Dan, sometimes providence plays its hand when least expected, and I think you dropping in this way today is just that kind of situation. Yesterday evening was a similar circumstance. I was over at the general store when I ran into Madam Drury. She had stopped in to buy some coffee. She asked me where Will was, and I told her how out of sorts he's been and for how long. Without a moment's hesitation, she says to take him to Dr. Caster! So, naturally, I asked her, who is Dr. Caster? And that is how I found out."

Dan, not exactly sure what he had learned, retorted, "Found out what?"

"You asked me what goes on in Ottumwa," Mary responded.

"So just what does go on in Ottumwa?" he asked again.

Mary answered with conviction, "Madam Drury met Dr. Caster last summer. He was a keynote speaker at the annual Mississippi Valley Spiritualist Association camp in Clinton. Will and I were there, but we didn't arrive until the second day—not in time to hear Dr. Caster. She told me she went to his pavilion that evening to watch a demonstration, and she said it was simply amazing. People with all kinds of problems no one else could help had astonishing results right in front of her eyes. A child's fever was suddenly broken, a woman was able to put aside her crutches, and an elderly man could suddenly walk without pain. All kinds of real problems were being cured."

"It sounds like he's a miracle worker. Do you really think he can help Will?"

"I don't think bumping into Madame Drury was an accident. And one thing's for certain," answered Mary, "I won't sit idly by and watch him deteriorate when there might be help available."

A few hours later, Daniel was helping his ailing friend into the presence of this uncommon healer. He had to carry most of Will's weight as they entered the room. The doctor gestured toward a richly upholstered table. "Help him onto his back."

Dan helped Will to lie down. Will was so weak, it was an effort to lift any part of his body, and his right arm was just dangling down at his side.

The doctor said, "Let's position his arms at his sides with his palms down on the table." Then Dr. Caster said, "Thank you," while gesturing toward three upholstered chairs lined up against the wall near the door through which they had entered. He didn't speak to or ask any questions of Will, who seemed too exhausted for conversation anyway. Then, closing the door, he turned to Mary. "How long has he been like this?" It sounded as much like an accusation as it did a question.

She dutifully answered, "Seven weeks."

Not waiting for her to explain further, the doctor turned back toward Will and walked around the man lying nervously on the table. Dr. Caster gave Mary a reassuring smile and dragged a wheeled stool over to the head end of the table and sat on its swivel seat. Then, looking up at Mary, he pointed toward the chairs where Dan was now seated. "Please make yourself comfortable. This will take a little while."

He was now positioned just beyond the top of Will's head at a point where he could easily reach both sides with his hands. The doctor held his hands adjacent to Will's head without actually touching—positioned like one might hold an accordion. There, his hands stayed, completely still for what seemed like a minute, maybe two. The doctor then touched Will for the first time by reaching for the middle of his chest and rested both hands there, pressing lightly on Will's chest. His hands remained still for another minute or two, and finally, he began to move his hands from the center of Will's chest out toward the edge of his rib cage. He did this several times, almost like he was trying to brush dust or debris of some sort from Will's chest. Then, without getting up, he rolled his chair over to the side of the table. Now seated on his patient's right side, this time he placed one hand on the center of Will's lower abdomen and became very still. After a couple of minutes, he added his other hand and, as he had done on his chest, again began to make that sweeping movement from center to the sides of Will's abdomen. He did that several times and then, rolling his chair back to the head of the table, placed both hands directly on Will's forehead. Dr. Caster closed his eyes and again held very still.

Seeing tiny beads of perspiration appear on the doctor's forehead, Dan assumed the man was exerting inserting extraordinary concentration into this portion of his work. After several more minutes, the doctor's face looked drained. His hands slowly moved away from their direct contact with Will, and he held them alongside Will's head for about another minute.

Dan mulled over what he saw. *Oh, it's the accordion position again. I wonder what that does.*

Mary was also paying rapt attention, and she was delighted to notice Will's breathing was becoming regular and peaceful. Astonished, she whispered in Daniel's ear, "He's sleeping!"

Finally, the doctor pushed back with his legs, rolling the stool away from the table where Will was resting, and vigorously shook his hands in the air. It reminded Dan of someone shaking water off their hands before taking a towel to dry them completely. The doctor, who had been silent since asking that single, simple question and telling them to be seated, rose from the stool, turned to Mary, and said softly, "He'll be all right now. Sit with him until he wakes, then give him some tea. You can send your friend to Miss Hardy out front. She always keeps a pot of chamomile warming." The doctor smiled as he confidently handed Mary a neatly folded, large throw blanket before quietly leaving the room as if it was all in a day's work. He closed the door. Mary opened the throw and carefully spread the colorful blue, brown, and green knit woolen cover over Will.

In the course of about fifteen minutes, they had seen what appeared to have been a miracle take place. Then, leaning close to Dan, Mary said softly, "I haven't heard him take a quiet breath, without that raspy, raucous sound, since this all started. Look at his face; he's lost that pained look!"

To Daniel's amazement, his pale, weak friend was regaining his color. While Daniel couldn't put his finger on it, he could just feel life was right again in Will's body. Without doing anything except placing his hands near and on the man, Paul Caster had caused him to get better. Dan spoke faintly. "How can this be?" He didn't expect Mary to respond to the rhetorical question.

They exchanged perplexed looks, and on Mary's cue, they sat down in the sumptuously upholstered, overstuffed chairs near the table on which Will continued to sleep. In deference to Will's apparent need for complete repose, they did not speak anymore, just traded befuddled, expectant looks from time to time.

After a few minutes, Mary soundlessly stepped to the other side of the room, to a table loaded with reading matter. She took an almanac in one hand and a small, soft, leather-bound book in another. Returning to her chair, she kept the almanac and handed the book to Dan. He nodded his thank you in silence while looking over the simple softcover with its two-word title in the center, *On Magnetism*. Down at the bottom right, in smaller type, appeared *by Paul Caster*. He made a mental note of the unpretentious binding and reminded himself, *Don't judge a book by its cover!* Dan, always a voracious reader, now wanted to learn everything about magnetism.

Two hours passed while Dan read hungrily. Transfixed, he barely looked up, giving an appreciative nod and smile when Mary brought them each a cup of chamomile tea at the end of the first hour. Then, near the end of the second hour, she had just returned with two fresh cups. Dan was nearly through the book, while Mary had changed her reading material several times.

Suddenly, Will pushed the blanket aside, sat up effortlessly, and rose to his feet, saying, "I'm hungry."

Mary looked up from the pages of the *Saturday Evening Post*, and her jaw dropped. Standing before her was Will, strong and erect as if nothing had ever been wrong.

Feeling slightly disoriented, Will wondered why Mary wore such an astonished expression and looked around the room, soon remembering why they were in this unfamiliar place. He glanced back at the table he had slept upon, smiled at Mary, and offered, "That's one hard bed!"

Mary jumped to her feet, hugged her husband, and directed him to the chair where she had been sitting. "First, you'll have some tea."

Will sat in the comfortable chair, noticing he felt rested and surprisingly alert as he reached to accept the cup. "Thank you, sweetheart. Isn't life wonderful?"

Dan, confounded, said nothing and just stared at his friend for a moment. Then he finally asked, "How do you feel?"

Will quickly retorted, "Like new!"

Dr. Caster had taken nothing—evil or otherwise—out of Will's body, nor put anything into it. Yet his color had returned, his abdominal and leg pains had vanished, and he could breathe and move freely. Most of all, a twinkle of life had come into Will's eyes. It changed Will and sparked something in Dan, who felt a wave of hopeful optimism prompting introspection. *I wonder why this sense of lightness has come over me?*

Chapter Eighteen
TIME FOR A CHANGE

*"Those who cannot change their
minds cannot change anything."*
–GEORGE BERNARD SHAW

A roller-coaster of emotions gripped Daniel, bringing tears to his eyes. *What might have been the result if baby Abba had seen a confident, competent man like Dr. Caster instead of Dr. Noble?* That thought brought forth a surprising resolve. *I must learn how to do what he did for Will.* The great void losing children had left in his life would never and could never be filled. Nevertheless, a renewed purpose ignited the light of promise within him. While looking into the restored brightness of Will's eyes, Dan made a profound decision.

Mary was returning to Dr. Caster's treatment room with another hot cup of tea when Dan rose to his feet, declaring, "Will, Mary, I'm going to ask Dr. Caster to take me on as a student." Contrary to his expectation, neither seemed particularly surprised by his announcement.

Mary encouraged him, "Daniel, this is wonderful news. I'm going to mark it down in my journal. *In 1879 Will and Mary helped Daniel find a new path!*"

"It's no surprise either!" added Will, still a little dazed from the whole experience, yet not groggy for someone who had been in such a deep sleep.

"Well, it's a surprise to me," Dan responded.

"Shouldn't be!" asserted Will confidently.

Mary interjected, "Will, why are you being argumentative?"

"Because it's exactly what Madam Drury's friend said would happen! Even I remember that," Will answered.

"What do you mean?" Daniel asked.

"Don't you remember?" Will insisted, "I remember it like it was yesterday. It was the first time we took you to Verdurette. After introducing you and Louvenia to Madam Drury, she took us all across the room to meet her friend Mrs. Hart."

Daniel's nonplussed look indicated he had not made the connection, so Will continued, "You know, she wore a long, shiny bright-red robe, and he introduced her as Mrs. Hart, the Great Intuitive. Mrs. Hart shook my hand, then Lou's and Mary's, but when she took yours in hers, she stopped and said, 'It's an honor to meet such an important healer.' I laughed and corrected her, saying you were an important beekeeper!"

Mary chimed in, "Will's right. She would not relent. Dan, you insisted you were the New Boston headmaster and you also ran an apiary, but she claimed she could see it coming."

Will added more detail, "Yes, she said her vision consisted of two pictures. One was of a famous doctor, upon whose door was painted the words *Dr. Palmer,* and the other was of you lecturing before a crowded hall with an audience of hundreds glued to your every word." A look of recognition came into Daniel's eyes, which seemed to satisfy Will and Mary.

They waited for the doctor to finish his work with another patient who appeared to be the last. Betsy, who was in charge of running the infirmary, was tidying up the day's odds and ends, apparently getting ready to close. When the doctor returned to the large reception area, Dan approached him. "Dr. Caster, is it possible for an apiarian to learn what you do?"

The doctor looked Dan up and down, and his serious face gradually softened. "I don't generally take on st ... students because magnetism is a gift one must have inside." Again he looked Dan over, then said, "B ... but anyone who wishes to change the world must be willing to open the door when one who is worthy kn ... kn ... knocks, offering to take up some part of the load." The doctor was a man of few words, and this was the first time Dan noticed the man's speech impediment. Looking at the would-be student as if appraising a work of art, Dr. Caster added, "You say you are a beekeeper. Then you already know the most important part— we work with the essence of life. What remains is to u ... unite the material side of existence with that essence. We work with the subtle substance of the soul. It's the simple ability residing within that few are willing to embrace, to grasp what they already possess. I b ... believe you are ready to walk through that door, so I'll not block your way."

Like a giddy child, Daniel reached out, took the doctor's hand, and shook vigorously. "Dr. Caster, I'm now your student. When can I begin?"

The man responded, "You can begin immediately in two ways: first by releasing my hand before you sh ... shake it loose from the rest of me, and second by calling me Paul."

It felt oddly inappropriate, even disrespectful, to call his master by his given name. However, Daniel decided he'd better get used to it. "Paul, may I return next week?

Amused, Paul chuckled. "You mean you want a break so early in your training?"

Missing the intended humor, Dan explained, "I'm a schoolmaster, and I have children, and my wife and I run an apiary. So I'll need her support and about a week to figure some things out."

Now laughing amicably, the doctor said, "Of course, you must make arrangements! I'll see you back here in a week. If you need more t ... time, just let us know which day you'll be coming in so we'll be ready for you."

Dan decided that since the situation would be temporary, it would bring the least amount of disruption to the family if his mother could come from What Cheer to stay with Louvenia for a few days each week. He expected to be able to study with Dr. Caster all week and still spend weekends with the family.

The three arrived back in New Boston early in the morning, having boarded the train at 5:30 a.m. Daniel was home before lunchtime, sitting eyeball to eyeball before Louvenia. What had sounded so easy and obvious while experiencing a personal transformation in Ottumwa felt like a selfish demand to put upon one's spouse. He explained, "Hon, something different is going on there in Ottumwa. Do you remember meeting Madam Drury's friend Mrs. Hart the Great Intuitive at Verdurette? "

Louvenia was quick to answer. "Why yes, I do. She's the one who called you a great healer. And you just about told her you thought she was crazy."

"Yes." He was both surprised and enthusiastic that she remembered the incident. "I'd never given it another thought until Will and Mary reminded me about it."

"So are you going to tell me her prediction has come true?" she asked.

"Well, not exactly, but something remarkable has happened. Will was extremely ill, and I saw the most incredible healing take place. I don't know why, but I was shaken by it. What helped Will is called magnetic healing. And the doctor seems to think I have that capacity within me."

"Daniel Palmer, I know one thing for certain. You think things through, and if you feel called to do this, we better make it happen."

Moved by her selfless support, Daniel hugged and kissed her.

"It will require me learning at the doctor's side, in Ottumwa. I don't know exactly how much time, but I think I should ask mother to come help with Sweet Home and the children while I am at it," he said.

"Then you better get on tomorrow's train to What Cheer and see what she says," answered Louvenia.

He arrived in What Cheer the next day and surprised his parents with an unexpected knock at their door. His mother, who answered the door, was delighted to see him and welcomed him inside with a big hug. Then with a concerned look on her face, she asked, "Why didn't you tell us you were coming?"

"Everything's okay, Mother. There's just something I need to talk with you about, and this seemed like the best way," he responded.

She called out to Daniel's father in the next room. "Thomas, come here; we've got company. Hanna put on some more water. Your brother Daniel is joining us for tea."

Hanna and her father were instantly at the door, adding more jubilant hugs and kisses. When the door was finally closed, everyone moved to the parlor for tea. Hanna disappeared to the kitchen while he sat with his parents to explain the sudden visit.

"I've decided to study magnetic healing," he began. Silently they both watched as though he hadn't said anything yet and waited for him to add a meaningful thought. Then, realizing how peculiar that must have sounded, he remembered how strange it seemed to him, even after being familiar with the Drury's and *Spiritualism*. So, back-peddling, he explained, "It's a newer way of treating sick people, and it's really catching on. Dr. Caster in Ottumwa has an impressive clinic, and people travel from all around to receive his treatments."

"I've never heard about this," Thomas said.

"Why do you suppose the world needs more doctors?" Catherine asked.

"Mother, Dr. Caster isn't like the ordinary physician. He doesn't use potions or surgery, but he's able to help people—I've seen it."

Both parents were staring at him patiently but sharing the expression one might have while dealing with an intoxicated person. Knowing he hadn't reached them yet, he added, "Do you remember our friends Will and Mary Kellogg, from New Boston?" They both nodded affirmatively. "The day before yesterday, I helped Mary bring Will to Ottumwa. Will was terribly ill and so weak, I nearly had to carry him. His illness had been going on for nearly two months."

Hanna arrived with a tray and placed China cups for each person, filling her parent's cups first. They sipped tea while their son explained, "I've never seen anything like it before, but I saw Dr. Caster bring about an astounding change in Will in just a few minutes. I know this sounds wild coming at you this way, but I've given it careful thought."

"I'll look forward to learning more about it and seeing it with my own eyes," answered Thomas with a reassuring smile.

Dan pivoted in his chair toward Catherine. "Mother, do you suppose …" He stopped to consider his words, then began again. "May I impose upon your kindness to come and spend some time at Sweet Home? Louvenia will have her hands full keeping things going there, and she could certainly use some help with the children while I'm studying in Ottumwa."

Catherine didn't stop for even a moment to think about how much work or difficulty, or the length of time. Instead, lost time with the grandchildren is what flashed through her mind. It was simply a matter of geography and them being out of her reach over in Illinois. Without waiting for input from Thomas, she happily accepted the assignment. "Of course, dear." Her wide-eyed enthusiasm was overflowing. "This will be a nice opportunity for all of us. Our little Jessie likes handicrafts, but she wants to learn her way around the kitchen. The last time I saw her, she asked me to teach her how to make Grandma's favorite Sunday dinner."

Dan and his father looked at each other inquisitively, and their curious faces said they had no idea what Grandma's favorite was anyway. She glanced back and forth from Thomas to Dan and exclaimed impatiently, "*Hasenpfeffer mit lemon bars natürlich!*" She always said the spicy Bavarian rabbit stew reminded her of her youth back in Germany. Regaining her stride, Catherine continued, "Now we'll have time for some proper cooking instruction."

Gaining enthusiasm, she picked up her pace. "Jessie and May are both learning to knit, and I know they want more help. Louvenia, bless her heart, never learned knitting at home, so she's just taking it up herself, and May couldn't seem to get enough of it last time.

The kids are already adept at simple garter stitches. Their sweet little letters tell me they've been practicing since our last visit, so they'll be ready to learn some of the trickier work. Next, they will learn stockinette, and then I'll start them going on into decreases and increases."

Thomas, who had no idea about the intricacies of knitting or its lexicon, lacked the desire to understand and that tell-tale look of incredulity returned to his face. He struggled, forcing out an assenting nod to prove he was at least listening.

Not missing his deception, she took pleasure in elaborating, "Knitting is like any highly refined skill. You're certainly not born with it. Rather, one acquires it. A child has to learn the basics first."

Daniel enjoyed watching his father getting lectured at and barely kept the smirk off his face, thankful his beard hid some of it while his mother pontificated, "In stockinette, the first row gets knit, and the second row gets purled. The two rows are repeated, making a nice pattern, so the front side looks like a sequence of Vs, and the back looks like a bunch of bumpy ridges. None of it's too hard for these girls, but I know I'll have to work with those two until they get it. Increases and decreases ..." Catherine stopped, deciding she had gone beyond the extent of the men's attention span, took a short breath, and finished with, "And they both need a lot more time on my knee! We'll have a great time together. It will be perfect for them and me."

More than a little taken aback at her enthusiastic acceptance speech, Thomas and Daniel remained awkwardly silent.

Then Daniel said, "Mother, I can't tell you how much this means to me." He turned to his dad. "Father, I've already asked Bart to help you in the store. He says he'd be happy to cover part-time clerk duties."

"That's interesting," Thomas retorted. "Because up till now he's never shown any interest in the furniture business."

"Bart said he already knows how to keep the inventory up and seems anxious to help," Daniel answered. Then he turned toward his mother, to say, "I trust my sisters will keep up with things in the house—and look after Father."

Thomas nodded in agreement. "Daniel, you've been there for us. You can depend on us now."

It meant much more than just spending time with the grandchildren for Catherine. She had a gnawing soft spot in her heart for Daniel. Although she obediently went along with Thomas's decision to leave Daniel and T.J. in Canada when they emigrated to Iowa all those years ago, she had never felt right about leaving a twelve-year-old with so much responsibility. Even though he was strong and looked mature by then, she knew looking like a grown-up wasn't the same as being one inside. She always had a great fear something terrible might happen to them, and even though they grew up and safely arrived in Iowa, the guilt never left her. Times had changed since then too, and she lamented her lack of courage in failing to stand up to Thomas's patriarchal miscue. Now women were speaking up much more than before, but she distinctly recalled when he announced the unexpected decision. It threw her so off-balance, all she did was pose a mousy little question instead of resisting. "Dear, I'm happy to go south for a better life. But do you think leaving the boys here is a good idea?"

"I've given it a great deal of thought, and this is the best way," was Thomas's response. "It will get us firmly on our feet and give them a chance to become strong young men."

Catherine yielded without a fight—a choice she had never stopped regretting.

Now Daniel said, "This means a great deal to me. I'll be going to Ottumwa next week and hope to return to Sweet Home on the weekend. I don't know exactly how long the training goes on, but I expect to have it figured out after being there a couple of days."

Chapter Nineteen

THE TEACHER BECOMES THE STUDENT.

"Education is the kindling of a flame, not the filling of a vessel."
−SOCRATES

Arriving in Ottumwa early the following Monday, Dan knocked at the back door of the three-story infirmary where his new principal warmly greeted him. "Welcome young m ... man. Are you ready to learn?"

Dan again noticed Dr. Caster's minor speech impediment and decided it was the least important fact he had encountered since meeting the man. Recalling how the doctor had spoken very little when they were there with Will last week, he was struck with the notion that *what* one said mattered much more than the number of words with which they said it. Paul Caster took his hand and pulled him inside, closing the door before he had time to reply.

"Yes, sir, I've never been more ready to do anything!" Daniel answered. He then offered his hand to the woman at the doctor's side, adding, "Good morning, Miss Betsy."

She smiled and shook his hand. "Nice to see you again, Mr. Palmer."

"All right then, do you have any questions?" Dr. Caster asked.

Unsure where to begin, Dan asked the first thing to come to his mind. "Sir, how long have you been a magnetic doctor?"

He answered matter-of-factly, "More than fifteen years now. I've treated patients from every s ... state in the union and seven foreign countries."

Daniel's eyebrows rose, giving his eyes an unnaturally rounded, incredulous look.

Paul added, "I keep track, you know. We complete notes of record on every c ... case I see. You'll learn how to keep careful case records too. Anything else you'd like to know before we begin?" The minor stuttering seemed to come and go and had no noticeable impact on the doctor's self-confidence. Just the opposite appeared to be the case as he carried his tall, sturdy frame like one who was clearly in charge.

Dan felt a moment of panic, thinking there must be a thousand questions he should be asking. As nothing came to mind, he anxiously looked up at the ceiling, trying to think fast. "What should I do first?" he retorted.

"This morning, you should just st ... stand well aside and observe everything. Don't ask questions while I'm treating patients. I need my concentration. There'll be plenty of time for that later. If you need anything, just ask Betsy." He gestured toward the now familiar, friendly woman next to him.

Betsy gave Dan an "okay" hand gesture when they made eye contact. "I'll keep the tea and people flowin'."

It struck Dan that the team of Betsy and Paul worked like a well-oiled machine.

As Dan followed the doctor toward the first treatment room, another question came to him, and he hastily asked, "Have you taken students before?"

A now familiar soft smile came over Paul's self-assured face. "Yes," his teacher responded. "In seventy-six, I had three; in seventy-seven, I took on two more, now counting you, there's been seven. All, except my son and yourself, were physicians before coming to me. All of the physicians, except one, are now practicing magnetic."

"What happened to the one that's not practicing?"

"He was perhaps my brightest student. Yet he struggled more than anyone." Paul paused for further reflection.

Daniel asked, "Should I expect to struggle too?"

Paul's smile broadened. "When I say struggle, I don't mean financially or matters of competence. I mean grappling with the *big idea*. That struggle varies a great deal depending upon our view of life." Paul stopped walking and looked him in the eye. "I have studied this issue very deeply and conclude that life is undoubtedly the union of both the physical and the immaterial universe, the immaterial being the more profound of the two."

Dan listened carefully, eager to learn the philosophy behind what he had witnessed. He also noticed Paul seemed to have lost the stutter.

"Do you mean to say the essence of life is immaterial?" Dan inquired.

"Well, of course, it is," Paul said. "Consider this: when a person dies, they remain exactly the same size, shape, and weight as the minute before their death. What's missing at the moment after death is the all-essential, immaterial essence, which you call life. I have listened to the scientist whose philosophy depends exclusively on measurable material. His knowledge about the infinite will always dissolve in the finite. That's why he will always fail to answer the question, 'what is life?' On the other hand, the clergyman studies only the immaterial, spiritual side and can bring us only so far. Inconsistencies plague both groups—and most claim to have the one and only correct answer. It seems that those who neglect to combine the material with the immaterial are doomed to fail because they close their eyes to the whole picture."

The student then asked, "Are you teaching that healing requires both?"

"That's why I immediately accepted you to learn magnetic. Because as a beekeeper, you have already lived it and surely recognize this basic precept—perhaps better than most physicians I have encountered."

"It sounds like you have some experience in beekeeping yourself," Dan responded.

Paul thought about the patient waiting in the next room and said to Betsy, "Please tell Mr. Godfrey I'll be just a couple more minutes." He knew the points he wished to make were important enough to delay the start of the clinical activities a bit.

She smiled and nodded at him as she stepped toward the treatment room to deliver the message.

Paul began, "The ancient Greeks and Romans knew. Likewise, Hindu scriptures and Ayurvedic practices in India have recognized the importance of honey for four thousand years. The Egyptians, Native Americans, and Druids all knew it too. The Promised Land in the Bible was the land of milk and honey. Daniel, all the great ancient civilizations have recognized, revered, and celebrated the symbolism encompassed in this insect's organizational hierarchy and the fruit of their labor. Our modern Western mind stands alone in its unique numbness to that knowledge. Yes, I have shared time with bees. Theirs is the most self-absorbed of all altruisms. Individually, they work tirelessly bonded in a unison that demonstrates courageous commitment, unlike modern human beings. Their allegiance serves an immaterial purpose while their method remains of substance. They draw the essence of the flowers to serve the hive; they refine it into sustenance, an ideal, all of which is centered on its queen. Even the material pollination that perpetuates the food chain our civilization depends upon is made possible by their labor."

"As a beekeeper, I have been privileged to learn and see these things play out exactly as you say. But I have never tried to put it into words," Dan agreed and inquired further. "There seemed to be an unspoken, omnipresent something behind it all. How does this relate to your student who failed to practice magnetic?"

Paul's features hardened as he shifted his focus from the bees to his earlier student. "Andrew was deeply troubled. He carried crippling anger with him. We met by chance at a Spiritualist meeting at the home of a friend here in Ottumwa. He desperately sought peace of mind through spiritual pursuits when I met him, and his physical situation was poor. His legs were so lame, he had to walk with a cane. Dr. Still had been training to become a physician before the war, yet he learned most of his skills in those makeshift circumstances of the battlefield infirmary. But his anger grew on multiple failures that came later. His first wife, Mary, died after giving birth. Later, he could not save three of their children who became ill and died not long after his return from the war, turning his frustrations into intense anger. Later, tragedy struck his family again when yet another daughter, born to his second wife, died of pneumonia. Disillusioned with his vocation and dismayed by his inability to help those he loved, Andrew had rejected medicine. He asked me if I could help him that evening, and I consented to provide c ... care.

"I've seen many dramatic changes in people, but even I was surprised at how much he improved with a single magnetic treatment." Paul gestured toward the anteroom. "In that pile of canes lined up behind Betsy's desk, you'll find his, with the initials A.T.S. carved on its handle. Those canes and crutches were left here as testimony by those who no longer need them.

"It was natural for Andrew, a physician, to want to know how to do what I did. So he asked me to take him on as a student in much the same way you did. His intellect was outstanding. Although he readily grasped the ideas presented, he always remained profoundly troubled, torn by a deep-seated resentment, perhaps at his profession ...," he paused, glanced at the ceiling as if looking for clarification there, and then continued, "... and perhaps at life in general. I believe it resulted in a tacit, unjustified self-loathing. His acumen in all things studied was certain, but there was always a wall there. The barrier existed within him and served to keep him more concerned with methods than with the greater mission."

Again Paul contemplated the troubled man, searching for words. Then he explained further, "A bee attending only to the gathering of nectar would surely miss the point of the hive. And so it was with him. Magnetic healing and the glorious mission it serves could never be more than another technique in his ongoing battle with and hatred for illness. Centered on the battle, he forgets the mission. It left him unable to open himself up to see the biggest part of the picture. While he could understand we worked with a power greater than ourselves, for Andrew, the glory and goal has always been and always will be to find and exploit the next best material mechanisms. He could never fully come to grips with the notion that the immaterial is a crucial part of the whole picture."

Puzzled by the apparent inconsistency, Dan asked, "Why do you suppose someone so bright would miss something so obvious?"

Quick to respond, Paul said, "You may see how it fits together, but keep in mind, few people in my experience can see both sides, especially the tormented Andrew. Trained to be a medical warrior, he was the quintessence of a materialist who hated the failures of materialism. His intellect was superb; he could fully grasp but only effectuate the most fleeting embrace of things vital."

Dan felt compelled to offer condolences. "I'm sorry to learn such a great student failed."

His master threw up his arms to emphasize a swift reply, "Oh no, don't think for a moment that any of this means Andrew Still is a failure. On the contrary, it is rare to find one so driven. He will succeed in most any venture to which he puts his capable mind—except his own happiness. Unfortunately, however, his predisposition rules out endeavors dependent upon a functional depth of understanding of the immaterial universe. Some can imbue themselves with the intangible in a deeper, integral sense, to the point where it becomes part and parcel of their reality. In contrast, others can only glance at, label it *idealism* or *vitalism*, and move on.

"Andrew will always succeed, and I know we opened his eyes to a larger existence, but we must not expect to find the virtues of magnetic in his endeavors. In fact, since apprenticing here, he has become a physician of some repute. Although of the materialist persuasion, Andrew is at least aware of an immaterial something that will always elude his grasp.

"Dr. Still has devised a vocation called osteopathy, based on the relationship between the body's framework and its vascular system. It's a curious form of materialism combined with a magical philosophy. It proposes that the rule of the artery is absolute. It must be unobstructed, or disease will be the result. A critical look at his concept suggests one must believe in a doctor's ability to substantially direct and oversee the immaterial. Frankly, I don't see much hope for that proposition here and now in 1879, or at any time in the foreseeable future."

"Does tinkering with blood to alter illness make sense to you?" Dan asked.

The teacher methodically responded, "We can't deny the importance of blood, and Andrew does have a vision, albeit limited. There remains a problem. It requires an ongoing conceited overstatement of mankind's body of knowledge. However, it is arguably more enlightened than that of his colleagues, the ordinary, allopathically inclined medical doctors."

Lightening the now somber tone in the hallway, Paul added, "I am pleased to see he took one notable precept from his experience here. It appears on the cover of *The Announcement*, an advertising tract for his infirmary. If one opens to the inside of the cover page, it says, 'God or nature is the only doctor whom man should respect,'" Paul let that sink in momentarily before adding, "With that thought in mind, let's humbly step inside to see our first p … patient." Daniel followed, realizing Paul's stutter over the word "patient" was the first stammer he had noticed since Paul began to speak about the philosophical question.

Paul gave a polite double knock on the door, then without waiting for an answer, turned the knob and slowly opened it. Inside the room were seated a woman and her husband. As they entered, Paul greeted them, "G … good morning, my friends! I'm doctor Caster, and this is my protégé, Daniel. He'll be observing."

"I'm Jane Godfrey, and this is my husband, Mr. Phillip Godfrey."

Turning directly to the woman, Paul said, "Pleased to meet you. When did he lose his voice?"

She began, "Two weeks ago, Phillip came down with a fever. It was much later than usual when he arrived home from the mine. Usually, the evening whistle blows by five o'clock, but that day it was already six, and I was getting worried, so I went next door to Mrs. Efaw to see if her Jimmy was back yet. She was fixing stuffed cabbages and said she hadn't heard anything either. I had a stew warming on the stove, so I went back to stir it. That's when I saw Phillip coming down the street, and Jimmy wasn't too far behind. I noticed him when he was coming just past the Marks's house. It was cloudy, cool, and rainy that day—good for a soup or stew— and they never did blow the whistle. I never did figure that out, but from the moment I saw him close up, he didn't look right. His color was off, and he carried himself halfheartedly.

Paul broke in when she finally came up for air, "Okay, Mr. Godfrey, please lie down on this table. Just g … go flat on your back." Then, gesturing toward the row of chairs, he said, "Daniel, please bring Mrs. Godfrey some tea and sit with her."

Daniel soon returned with the tea. The doctor was turned toward the table just like he had been with Will, and was moving his hand and whole arm in a big arc. It almost seemed like he was trying to reach across the room to encircle a large space. His student wondered, *What could this achieve? Is he casting a sphere of some energy around himself and Mr. Godfrey?*

Pulling his wheeled stool toward the head end of the table, Paul remained standing, waved both hands over the entire length of Mr. Godfrey's body, and then he sat. Next, he placed his hands adjacent to both sides of Mr. Godfrey's head, just like he had done with Will. Dan remembered, *It looks like the doctor is holding an imaginary accordion again.* However, this time, he didn't stay that way long, perhaps thirty seconds at best. He then touched Mr. Godfrey for the first time, much like he had for Will, by reaching to the middle of his chest, resting his hands there, and placing light pressure on the center of his chest. He did this for what seemed like a much shorter time than in Will's case. Next, the doctor moved his hands from the center of the man's chest toward the bend of his rib cage. Dan noted, *It's that curious sweeping thing again. It seems like he's trying to brush dust or debris off of the patient's chest.* Some of it was quite similar, yet overall, it seemed like a much different treatment than in Will's case. Paul seemed to finish much sooner and with far less effort. There was no treatment of the lower abdomen nor placing hands directly on the man's forehead as he had done for Will.

Paul seemed to keep his eyes closed most of the time, but he wasn't working near as hard as in Will's case. There were no beads of perspiration on Paul's forehead, and while Dan was sure the clinician was concentrating, it involved far less effort overall.

A relaxed Dr. Caster rolled his stool back and shook his hands in the air in a cleansing gesture, similar to what he had done after treating Will. Only a few minutes had passed, and the room remained silent.

Paul stood and turned toward Mrs. Godfrey. "He may be a little tired, but he's fine. Miss Hardy keeps hot tea in the front room; you may wish to give him a cup. It's probably best if he sits a few minutes before you leave. I've someone waiting for me in the next room, so I'll leave you now. We might need to do a second treatment if he has any more trouble."

Paul signaled Dan to follow him as he turned toward the door. Then, noticing the doctor was about to depart, Mr. Godfrey sat up on the table with some urgency and robustly asked, "How will I know if it worked?"

Jane broke into gleeful laughter, through which she managed to say, "You foolish man, those are the first words you have uttered above a raspy whisper in two weeks!" Then she turned toward the doctor, whose hand was now on the doorknob. "I don't know how to thank you!"

Smiling, Paul guffawed back at her. "Hearing your happy laughter is p ... payment enough for me, but Betsy out front might want something more before you leave!"

Leaving Phillip and Jane, they stepped through the door, and Paul turned to Dan. The doctor's serene facial expression failed to conceal he had something purposeful in mind. Dan, still an educator, sensed a teaching moment was upon them, so he wasn't surprised to hear Paul ask, "What did you observe?"

Anxious to dive into the meat of his education, Daniel's compulsion was to answer promptly, even though he expected a knee-jerk response would likely be incorrect. Nevertheless, he offered, "I saw you heal Mr. Godfrey's voice."

Although the disappointment on Paul's face was obvious, the response was predictable since it was a leading question. Paul began, "*Daniel* ..." Calling his student Daniel, instead of the more familiar *Dan* modified the tone much like a parent addressing a child using both their first and middle name prefacing a reprimand. Paul was resolute, helpful, and sincere, setting the tone for a compelling lesson. "There is one basic principle at work in healing. It revealed itself in what you saw here today. To bear fruit in treating the sick, one must learn all healing ultimately comes from within the patient's body. And I know this may sound trivial when you hear me say it, but I assure you, it is one of the most profound concepts you will encounter. Now I ask you to contemplate that basic precept as we proceed."

Dan, who expected a rebuke, was pleased to be presented with an important principle. Remaining silent so the idea might sink in, Paul stepped down the hall to the next doorway. But before going in, he turned back to Dan. "Your first and perhaps only written assignment is to give me a narrative of how that great truth applies to each case we see this week. You can consider your homework due next week, or if you need lots of time, then let's say January 1st, 1880." Paul smiled and turned toward the next treatment room.

Again that polite double knock was followed immediately by turning the knob, opening the door, and courteously stepping inside. Paul began, "G ... good morning, my friends! I'm Dr. Caster, and this is my assistant, Daniel." Dan noted the greeting was nearly identical, including the elusive vocal falter, except the student had been promoted from protégé to assistant. Or perhaps he had just been demoted to assistant! Deciding his status was irrelevant,

Dan reminded himself to focus on what he was here for. He also wondered whether his teacher might use changing references like this as a clever way to size him up by reading his reactions.

Paul's side of the conversation continued as before. "Pleased to meet you. When did ..." Again the doctor's dialogue seemed to follow the same pattern he used for Will and Mr. Godfrey. The conversations varied little from hour to hour or from day to day. It went on that way for a week as he watched an endless string of hurting people flock to Dr. Caster. Most of them had tried to get help from ordinary physicians first. Having failed to improve, patients usually continued to suffer until someone finally said, "Go to Ottumwa and try Dr. Caster."

In an age when inventions were everywhere, and scientific discoveries were reported nearly every day, most hesitated to take such advice. They had no faith in someone they didn't know, with a method they couldn't see. Medicine was liberally claiming a relationship with science. While little evidence of it was found in the everyday practices of physicians, frustrated patients either gave up or tried another medic. The next doctor would try another tincture, potion, or lance. Desperate to get better, patients became bait for the snake oil salesman, and only when all else failed did they continue their search. Finally, these medical failures would arrive on Paul Caster's doorstep devoid of faith and expecting yet another disappointment. His simple, confident demeanor and warm, down-to-earth smile was a welcome change from the theater of the physician's office and the loud claims of peddlers selling bottles of mystical elixirs from the back of a wagon.

What amazed Dan the most was how often he saw dramatic changes in patients. He soon found himself expecting to see miracles in every case. Most responded quickly and assuredly. While a few didn't get well, none were injured by Dr. Caster's treatment.

Each day he watched in awe as his master worked case after case. It was nothing short of amazing to see him awaken the innate ability of patients to heal. On weekday evenings, Dan would usually have supper with the Caster family. He always insisted on helping clean up after the meal and would typically engage in social chat for a while, but not too long. Soon the houseguest would thank the Casters for sharing their home and observe it was time to retire to his upstairs bedroom. He felt it was most polite to leave the family some time to attend to their own business and pleasures.

His room was clean. It had two inviting gable windows, a comfortable bed, and a wingback upholstered chair. Within the dormer to the right of the door were a small writing desk and a matching straight-back wooden chair. Before the other fenestra stood an armoire with open doors, providing a place to hang his jacket, shirts, and trousers. It also had two drawers at the bottom to accommodate folded items. The bed occupied the center of the room with a simple headboard up against the exterior, south wall. Dan found that the wingback chair fit him perfectly, and he liked to sit there and reflect on all that had gone on during the day. In these quiet moments, he would relax into that chair, close his eyes, and think about the cases they had seen that day.

Can I believe my own eyes? was the burning question. Studying Spiritualism had opened him to the idea that there was indeed a non-material facet to the universe. Nonetheless, he was a learned man and didn't want to be duped into believing some flim-flam. Magnetism was different, but still, he had witnessed how easily some had debased Spiritualism, turning a quick buck by selling séances of spooky gobbledygook to vulnerable grieving widows and other sorrowful souls. His moral sensibilities would not allow him to foster any dishonest business or swindle on defenseless sick people, making these quiet moments of reflection particularly solemn.

He devised a basic question. *If I were now a practicing magnetic, with what I know and have seen, would I send my mother, father, sister, or brother to me for help?* The answer was always the same. *Of course, I would! They deserve the opportunity to get well and be well.* No matter how many times he allowed himself to entertain this question, the conclusion was always the same.

Nevertheless, qualms would fearfully return—never in the light of day while watching the extraordinary events unfold in the clinic, but always alone in his room when he allowed those moments of uncertainty and doubt to creep upon him. He would sit quietly, trying to grasp how a material person with a real malady could get well without some temporal intervention. Dan had learned that whether preparing lessons for students, keeping bees, or working out a problem, writing in his journal always helped to put things in perspective. Studying magnetic made him feel terribly out of step with the rest of the world, so he opened the soft-cover volume to describe his perceptions. He began by inserting a title at the top of the page.

Leaving common beliefs behind.

The whole world is seething, searching for the right pill or potion, seeking a panacea in a pill bottle. For thousands of years, physicians have always tried to put something curative into the sick body or take something evil out of it.

Their approach never seemed to work out so well for my own family. Could a better answer really exist in an immaterial something no person can see or feel?

Incorporeal answers grant little solace to my insecure mind.

Is my finite intellect trying to answer infinite questions?

Every evening the struggle played out. Dan contemplated similar questions and found no peace. Then, on Thursday night, during the second month of apprenticeship, he sat in the wing-back chair and asked himself one of those questions with a different spin. The new twist was just what he needed to change his thinking. Instead of struggling to fight illness, the question morphed into, *Where does health come from anyway?* That question seemed to crack open a door, and new thinking rushed in. He hastened to the desk, opened his journal, and dipped his quill. At the top of a blank page, he wrote a new title in all uppercase letters.

WHERE DOES HEALTH COME FROM?

This is the unasked question.

Perhaps this is the bigger question.

Do healthy bodies get sick?

It would seem so, but if that's true, is there a consistency problem?

Why do only some people get sick when others in the same family, eating the same food, and living in the same circumstances don't?

Healthy bodies must have something inside them that withstands illness.

I deduce that whatever that something is, it can be thought of as the cause of health.

He underscored the last thought, thinking it was an idea he wished to explore. *It's not a big breakthrough, except perhaps in thinking.* It prompted the next profound question, which was even harder to answer. He skipped down a few spaces in the journal and added.

Week seven in the study of magnetic brings one certain conclusion: health must come from within.

If health comes from within, then is it material or immaterial? Is it both?

Maybe we're finally asking the right questions.

He decided to take the thought to bed with him. But, despite his hopes that the answer would come without a struggle, it was still unanswered when he awoke.

The next morning's clinic activities were brisk, with little time for conversation between patients. However, the lunch break brought an opportunity to talk. Dan said, "Paul, I'm fascinated by this entire experience. You never promise any cures, but somehow the work you do brings people to heal. Every evening when I retire to my room, I contemplate the day's work. Then I do what I always teach school children to do. I write down what was presented that day. Journaling identifies my thoughts and questions." Dan paused for a bite of an apple.

Paul responded, "Where have these reflections taken you?"

He swallowed and answered. "It seems like everyone is seeking a way to conquer illness. Unfortunately, even if they win a skirmish, they lose the bigger battle anyway. It's a noble cause, but a war against disease eventually becomes a losing proposition. I wonder if it's even the right question, so I keep asking myself if it makes sense."

"All great breakthroughs begin by changing the question," Paul offered, then matter-of-factly assaulted his own apple.

"Now I've started thinking about what causes health. That brought me to the next question, and frankly, I'm not sure how to begin to answer it," Dan added.

"Tell me about the latter question," the teacher said.

His student eagerly answered. "I think the greatest change this study has made for me is from a practical point of view. I now understand that the immaterial side of the universe is real." Paul nodded his agreement without interrupting. "Knowing this and seeing how health comes from within the patient, the question arises: is that inborn something of the material or the immaterial?"

Daniel saw the broadest smile come over Paul's face, and he watched in anticipation while Paul finished chewing some apple. Paul seemed to be savoring the morsel as if he enjoyed both the fruit and the philosophy. Finally, he swallowed and smiled. "Daniel Palmer, you've just asked a question you will work on every time you practice your art. A young man may someday ask you the same question, and your answer will exist in the knowledge that the essential part of that man's education is complete because he is now asking the right questions."

Keeping his excitement subdued, Daniel asked, "What does that mean for me, here and now?"

"You just graduated!" was Paul's answer.

They quietly sat together, finishing their lunch. Finally, Daniel asked, "What happens now?"

"How do you mean, what happens now?" Paul responded.

Dan, still taken by surprise, followed with a succession of short questions "Am I finished now? Will I get a diploma? Is there anything I must do?"

Paul responded with a most self-satisfied expression, "The answer to all three questions is no."

Playing on the student's anticipation, he paused, adding emphasis and a little drama to what would follow. "As you well know, a person never finishes an education. They merely qualify to move forward. No, I do not issue diplomas. You already have a diploma issued by heaven on high, and no, there is nothing you *must* do, but you will feel compelled to do that which matters."

They completed the day's clinical work as usual. It was a busy day. Yet, in Daniel's mind, a bittersweet tone of finality surrounded everything said and done that afternoon. Dan followed and closed the door when Paul stepped out of the treatment room. Then he turned to his teacher, offered his hand, and said, "This experience has been a rare, great honor for me. I'll forever be in your debt."

Paul held back his smile. "Well then, why doesn't your face portray cheerful enlightenment?"

The student realized his countenance displayed sadness. The teacher had imparted a small but valuable lesson in that simple question. The downturned corners of Daniel's mouth began to rise, along with his eyebrows, into a smile that better fit the situation.

Paul accepted the handshake, offering both of his in a warm, uplifting two-handed shake, adding, "I have also benefitted in this apprenticeship."

"I suppose I'll return to Illinois now," Dan said.

"Yes, but you'll probably want to catch tomorrow morning's early train. It's too late to catch the five o'clock, and it's just as well because the family would miss seeing you at supper tonight."

The following day they were up and at the station before sunrise. Paul's final comment was, "Be sure to keep me apprised of what becomes of our work together."

The trip back to Sweet Home was another time for uninterrupted introspection. Dan was pleased to be returning to Louvenia and the family. There was much to do, and no doubt Louvenia would be happy to see him picking up his share of the burden again. It was time to consider issues that would impact the family's future.

Travel by rail always seemed to be a good time for contemplation, so he took the opportunity to summarize the experience. *There was far less actual hands-on activity than I expected—well, it was hands-on to the highest degree, but those were mostly Paul's hands.* There had been some technique training, including direct observation and critique relating to Daniel's application of the art, but most of the preparation was conceptual. Self-doubt began to creep in. *Did I learn enough? Do I dare go into the world and try to take care of people?*

It occurred to him that if the training had been more technique-oriented, it would have understated the importance of the immaterial aspect. In watching his master care for patients, formulating questions, and struggling to answer them, he had gained an understanding that the immaterial facet was the key objective of the instruction. The unspoken but obvious implication was that working with the material side of his patients would be an art he would refine in practice.

Now that he was deemed ready to go forth, a practical question came squarely into view. *How can I realistically add this work to an already full life? Are not my obligations toward the family paramount?* But, no matter how he tried to figure it out, at this time, there was no way the answer to his questions included the practice of magnetic healing.

His aspirations about Sweet Home and his leadership role in the apiary world hadn't changed. *I'm serving as president of the state apiary association, and I've promised to write a column for every edition of the apiary journal.* That thought jolted through him, and he slapped himself on the forehead with the palm of his hand. *The editorial for the fall 1879 issue is due next week! I'll have to carve out some time to finish my essay on practical measures to control swarming. I still love teaching too. Am I to leave all that behind? Am I ready to take on an entirely different role? Am I really suited to be a healer?* He recognized that answering that question would be a struggle, and he looked forward to having a conversation about it with Louvenia.

While the train rolled across the Iowa prairie, he watched the steady parade of countryside go by in the faint, early morning light. The sky was still brighter than objects on the ground, so he gazed up more than down. Against that dimly lit sky, he glimpsed a huge flock of small birds that demanded his rapt attention. Spellbound, he watched their strange-looking maneuvers. Their flight was such a convoluted ballet, the performance must have been carefully designed. The synchronous movement was a spectacular sight, so rapid, he wasn't sure just which kind of birds they were. The enchanting murmuration whirled about, spinning and rolling dramatically. It moved in the same general direction as the train, allowing him to watch the show. Their tiny bodies, dark blue wings, and heads resembled those of the barn swallow, but it wasn't the individuals that attracted his attention. It was the group's magnificent choreography that seemed out of this world. It reminded him of the many similar collective behaviors of bees that revealed the presence of an intelligent but inexplicable design that transcended the action of each individual. Observing this phenomenon brought tremendous comfort, and he once again yearned for his life as an apiarian.

Dan blinked, recognizing the serendipitous performance had helped him make a decision, and spared Louvenia the task of being the sober one who would have to point out all the problems and risks such a career change would entail. He wasn't sure what he would do with the new knowledge, but it was time to return to his life at Sweet Home—as a beekeeper and teacher of New Boston students during the academic term.

Chapter Twenty
BECOMING A HEALER

"You never know how far-reaching something you may think, say, or do today will affect the lives of millions tomorrow."

–B.J. PALMER

It was late December 1884, five years since Daniel had decided to continue life as an apiarian, and there were no regrets. Life at Sweet Home with Louvenia had been wonderful, although not without challenges. They worked hard growing a life together, and when severe weather brought circumstances that forced a change, they bravely did what was necessary. Moving to What Cheer was not the end of the world, and they quickly built a successful business together. Daniel would not have even considered starting a magnetic practice had the shocking loss of Louvenia not jolted him into reassessing everything.

He wasn't yet ready to embark on a new career, nor did he have a great vision to change the world. Dan and the children were at his parent's home in What Cheer, where the entire family was gathered for Sunday dinner. Noting he was reticent, Catherine asked, "Son, what are you thinking about?"

He responded, "I've never put my study with Dr. Caster to work."

She answered, "Well, that may be true, but Daniel Palmer has done little except work since our dear Louvenia left us."

"Mother, she never leaves my mind entirely, and I keep thinking about what happened." He searched for words to describe what he felt. "Dr. Fishbein angers me. The superstition angers me. When she was sick, I called on the physician, expecting him to help Louvenia." He said her name softly, with reverence. Then his tone shifted, resentfully spitting out, "Helplessly struggling with illness in a bed, she needed care, but this learned man's only answer was to drain her blood!" A tear fell as he looked down at the floor to hide his emotion and faintly added, "These children lost their mother that night."

Catherine said, "We're *all* deeply saddened by this loss. But let's not forget what matters now. She brought joy to this family and blessed you and us with these beautiful children."

Thomas spoke up, "Dr. Fishbein doesn't matter, son. What matters is how this family goes forward."

Dan forced the frown off his face and dabbed his eyes with his shirt sleeves. "Mother, Father, I believe it's time to put my training to work."

Pleased to see his mood lightening, Thomas put the finishing touch on the meal. "Okay, kids," he looked Catherine in the eye and raised his glass of water. "Let's all thank Mother for a lovely dinner."

The children and grandchildren all recited the customary, "Thank you, Mimma!"

It didn't matter to her daughters, Lucinda, Catherine, and Hanna, that they had also worked hard to prepare the feast because thanking Mother for supper was a Palmer family tradition. Catherine had done little of the work that day, although she had been there orchestrating every step. She, the artist, coordinated the timing and movements just as carefully as a conductor standing before an orchestra. Dan had watched the performance. To him, that moment's warmth, comfort, and spirit made all seem right with the world, and everything in life that had come before seemed worthwhile. It was almost as if the great estrangement on the Canadian frontier had never happened all those years ago.

Always ready to scrutinize, his thoughts returned to the difficulties of life on the Canadian frontier. *Running Palmer's Cheap Cash Store contrasts quite favorably with the hardships of the past.* He glanced over at his closest brother, T.J., and wondered just what he might be feeling right now. There had been many cold, lonely nights when he sat up frightened, wondering if he was really up to caring for the two of them—but it always seemed better in the light of day.

The grandchildren watched for a nod from Catherine, which their smiling Mimma gave as she rose from her seat, admonishing them, "Not too loud, children." They bolted from the table and scattered while Thomas stepped into the parlor, where he always went after Sunday dinner to sit and finish reading the newspaper.

Hanna handed Catherine a steaming hot cup of tea and took her mother's glass and silverware to the kitchen sink. Catherine followed her husband to the parlor, where her latest knitting project waited on the end table beside her favorite chair. She loved these most relaxing moments when she could sip her tea, listen to the sounds of family activity coming from various corners of the house, and gaze out the window while her hands busily produced works of art.

Hanna and her sisters, Lucinda and Catherine, were soon giggling playfully, poking at one another in a well-worn lighthearted verbal joust as they dutifully cleared the table. Finding a morsel of mashed potatoes remaining on his plate, T.J. placed it in his mouth. Before he could return the fork to the table, Lucinda wrested it from him and lifted his plate too. Standing there putting on a show, she held the dish vertically, inspected it, and exclaimed, "This plate is so clean we may not need to wash it." Before T.J. could come up with a clever retort, Dan caught his eye with a waggle of his head and gestured toward the den where they might talk.

The best T.J. could come up with was, "Just doing my part to keep the chores minimal." He rose from the table to follow Dan without waiting for a response from her, but as he passed through the den's doorway, he heard Lucinda's voice leading a trio of loud cackling.

T.J. entered the room smiling. But even before they sat down, a serious-faced Dan spoke, "I have a question." Intrigued, T.J. locked his gaze onto his brother as he eased himself into the soft green upholstered Morris chair in front of the window. With T.J. now sitting straight up and the daylight of a bright afternoon bursting through the window directly behind him, Dan could no longer discern any of T.J.'s facial details. Unfazed, he continued speaking to the featureless head. While maneuvering into a high cane-backed chair opposite the window and his brother, he said, "You've been publishing the *What Cheer Patriot* for nearly five years now, and I think you've surely learnt something of what makes people tick. You've seen all kinds of businesses boom along with this town, while others don't have the knack. Some of your advertisers flourish, continuously buying pages of publicizing year in and year out. Then some arrive, make a big splash, and then go out like a grease fire. I want to know why some make it while others shrivel up and go away."

The enthusiastic older brother hadn't paused long enough for T.J. to get a word in. T.J. knew his brother's style well, and he enjoyed patiently listening while Dan made his point.

"Now," Dan continued, "D.D. Palmer comes to town with a new magnetic message, and I need to know what it takes to reach the people who need to hear it. Selling fish, some confections, a few dry goods, and the like was easy. They wanted a grocer, and I provided things effectively and more efficiently than anyone else. But now"—he paused to highlight the importance of what he was about to say—"now I'm selling something they can't taste, feel or see. I don't want to waste time. There's too much to get done. How would you do it?"

When Dan finally took a breath, the younger brother was pleased to play the role of learned confidant. T.J. relished his assignment and gazed out the opposite window toward the sky in careful reflection. He soon responded, "You already know what it takes to reach people; you simply provide them with what they want." Then the publisher in him grew a slight smirk, quickly adding, "And you make sure they know about it!"

Dan protested. "This is different. I've watched Dr. Caster change lives! And the people never even knew they needed what he gave them."

"No!" T.J. insisted. "The formula is no different when it comes to their ailments. Oh, they may be a bit more desperate, which makes it all the more important you can deliver the goods.

"Big brother, this part's important." T.J. illustrated by holding up his index finger and pointing it toward the ceiling to underscore his point. "About six months ago, Asher Headley advertised hunting knives for half-price in his general store. I asked him why, and he told me he had a box of fine steel blades but hadn't sold a single one in over two months. The advertising worked better than expected, and he sold the whole box of twenty knives the next day. The problem came the day after when six more people asked for half-price knives he couldn't deliver. I received a letter to the editor that week, complaining about Asher Headley's unscrupulous business practices. Frankly, it surprised me anyone would get so upset over the matter. Ethically speaking, if someone felt so strongly about it, then I should print the letter; otherwise, I would be guilty of hiding the thing. Neither did I want it sprung on Asher, so when I was in his store, I told him what he would see in tomorrow's paper. Asher knew what this thing could do to a businessman's reputation, so he assured me he would order more knives. I asked him if he thought his customers would be happy to wait. He said not only would he pay the express charge to get them in soon, but he would also put matching leather sheaths on half-price to go along with them. So I asked if that might leave the first twenty customers unhappy because they had to pay full price for the sheaths. Mr. Headley could feel himself getting in deeper and deeper, so he decided to solve the problem by offering the sheaths for free to everyone who bought the blade, including those who bought the first twenty. He also bought extra ad space from me on the opposite page. He asked me to write a paragraph on his behalf in the three-by-four-inch box, explaining the whole situation, thanking the person who brought their concern forward, and making it clear to everyone how important each customer is to his business. Even though he had to give away a few leather sheaths, just last month, he told me it was one of the best things he ever did to promote goodwill and increase trade."

Dan argued his case, "T.J., I agree with all you are saying. But now I'm telling you, I have seen miraculous things happen! People need this, and I can give it to them."

A smiling T.J. stood before his chair, waving his arms in a big arc, and drew a semi-circle in the air saying, "The answer's clear, then. All you need to do is put the conviction and the passion you just showed me into words. That together with results in people will sell 'em."

Dan, a bit nettled, also rose from his chair and placed his left hand on T.J.'s right shoulder. "You make it sound simple."

"That's the secret of the whole thing, brother," T.J. added. "You keep it simple!" Daniel's skeptical face told T.J. he needed more encouragement, so T.J. said, "Let's take a walk."

They stepped toward the door, and each pulled their light jackets from a row of metal hooks mounted on the wall adjacent to the door. Thomas had artistically repurposed six worn cast-iron horseshoes into coat hooks by fitting them to a red cedar timber. The wood was varnished, and the glossy black paint over rounded iron edges made for a smooth, decorative, yet functional ornament. Their father had a penchant for creating useful things from materials others might have just discarded.

Once outside, they traversed the small house yard, approached the short white picket fence, and opened the gate. Stepping onto the wooden sidewalk, T.J. continued as if the discussion had not been interrupted. "It really is that simple. First, tell the people what you want to show them; make sure it's the truth, because they'll never forgive you if they find you unreliable; then tell them repeatedly."

They took a few steps without speaking while Dan took it in.

Then T.J. offered, "Here's the thing. I receive enlightening information when you and I talk about what magnetic offers and the wonderful results you've seen. That's good, but five hundred other people in town still don't know. When you help one of them, that individual enthusiastically tells their family members and a few others. That's all good too, but it happens slowly. But when we put that message in the paper, we reach hundreds immediately."

The word "hundreds" resonated with Daniel. While listening to T.J. expound upon advertising concepts, he scrutinized their surroundings. What Cheer was typical of those small coal mining towns dotting the central Iowa prairie. He gazed across the road at his grocery and remembered the town's economic base, centered on the hard-working miners and their families.

The structure housing his business and family residence was a two-story wood-frame structure with a stone façade covering the lower half and horizontal wooden timbers painted white covering the upper half. Three wooden steps and a wide recessed landing led up to the front door. The landing was flanked by large plate glass windows diagonally directed toward the street. The entryway effectively provided a preview of the merchandise and a flood of additional daylight for the interior.

Behind the shop, a sizeable storeroom separated the grocery from the lower portion of the family's modest living quarters. They had a large eat-in kitchen, living room, and a den, and in the upstairs were four bedrooms. It was fully adequate to their needs, and the family had been quite happy there while Louvenia was with them. Dan reminisced about how he and Louvenia had worked so hard to build up the business—he full-time and then some, while she divided her time between the store and seeing to the needs of the children.

Bringing Dan back to the present, T.J. said, "I could help you with a fair amount of free editorial space, and you could—"

Realizing he had zoned out of their conversation, Dan interrupted, "Sorry, T.J., I've been thinking about how it was when Lou was still here. And I think you've helped me to recognize something."

He paused only long enough to gulp down the words that were about to follow, then resumed with a shaky emotional voice, "This thing will take a completely new start."

"What do you mean?" T.J. asked.

"There are too many old memories, too much to undo here. Besides, What Cheer is too small for what I need to do." Dan continued apologetically. "Brother." He stopped and looked T.J. squarely in the eye. "You, Mom, Dad, Bart, and the girls have all been great for the kids and me. Nevertheless, it's time to move on. I can see it clearly now."

"I didn't say anything about you leaving," T.J. insisted.

"No, you didn't, but you helped me think it through, the way you always do," Dan answered, adding, "I need to put this before more than a few hundred people."

A frenzied T.J. fired, "Are you sure? Where will you go? Who'll take care of the kids? What about the store?"

"I don't know the answer to any of that," Dan responded. "But it becomes obvious when you get the facts out in front of you. What Cheer is great, and leaving the family again will pain me. But I've got to do this thing." He looked directly at T.J. and said, "The kids will adapt, and we'll visit What Cheer often."

T.J. argued, "You're still mourning her loss. Take some time. Tomorrow you may see it differently."

"No, brother, I'm sure," Dan said. "And I've been starting to grasp it for some time; I just wouldn't let myself see the whole picture till now. I can't make a significant impact from here. What Cheer is just too small and out of the way for what I need to do."

Stunned, T.J. went quiet, and so did Dan. They walked together, feeling the sadness, like something bigger than both of them had taken control of the situation. Two blocks later, they reached the train station. It was quiet there, so they sat together on a wooden bench beside the tracks in the sunshine.

After a couple of silent minutes, Dan finally spoke. "I'm at peace by the river. I think the Iowa side is better for me, so perhaps I'll try

Burlington. It's a large town growing into a city now. I've visited there many times, and I like how it looks."

Once the decision was made, things began to happen fast. The grocery business was doing well, but Dan wanted to free himself of entanglements. His first idea was to offer it to his youngest brother. "Bart, you've worked here part-time for quite a while. How would you like to take over the store permanently?"

Always short on ambition, Bart quickly decided he didn't want it for himself and said, "Don't worry, big brother. It should be easy to sell. I bet you John would jump at the chance to own the business. Besides, he knows all the customers and understands the business as well as anyone."

Dan followed with, "Bart, if you'll work with him temporarily, see to the sale and transition, you could take a fair share of the proceeds and use it for any venture you might be interested in going with."

Bart answered, "I've already got plans of my own. I've been thinking of getting a pair of first-rate carriages to provide a fine-quality funeral service. There's a profit to be made, and I wouldn't have to work every day."

While disappointed to hear the latter part of Bart's reasoning, the naturally ambitious older brother nodded affirmatively. "There should be adequate proceeds to buy your carriages and provide the furnishings to get my magnetic practice started." The two shook hands, capping it off with a big hug.

Wishing to be close to the Mississippi River and all the goings-on continuously surrounding its commerce and commotion, Dan firmed up his decision to relocate his family to Burlington. The fast-growing river town on the Iowa side was about forty miles downstream from New Boston, Illinois. He had visited Burlington to deliver honey several times while running the apiary and was always impressed with its picturesque setting. The formidable body of water dotted with small islands bounded the community on one side. Nearly a mile across, the Mississippi's rapidly flowing waters were awe-inspiring. The hills seemed to spontaneously rise like an extension of the river in a semicircular fashion, prompting its earlier inhabitants, the Sac and Fox tribes, to name it Rock Hill in appreciation of its natural beauty.

It was now Monday evening. Having decided Burlington was full of potential, a daunting step was before Daniel. It was time to tell his parents about the decision to move. He was angst-filled because it meant taking the children away from them. It would be a distance of a hundred miles, which could have been covered by train in two hours, except the train didn't run directly. The best route involved a connection in Ottumwa, which turned into a half-day journey, even by rail.

Nevertheless, he summoned the courage and came out with it. "Mother, Father ..." His serious tone brought their full attention. "The Chicago, Burlington, and Quincy Railroad started in Burlington, and it's growing like gangbusters. I think I can grow there too."

A teary-eyed Catherine spoke first, "Son, T.J.'s been speaking to us while you were talking with your brother Bart. We understand how difficult this time has been for you."

Seeing the tears overflowing from her eyelids and rolling down her face, Thomas said, "You have something to do that's important to you, and we're behind you. The Palmer family will find a way to bear up, and we may have to become regular visitors to Burlington."

With Bart overseeing the business transfer, Daniel was free to get the family relocated. They were at the station three days later, preparing to board the train. Many of their crated-up possessions were already en route via freight. Hugs were given to the grandparents, aunts, and uncles. Daniel and the kids disembarked in Burlington late that afternoon. They proceeded four blocks from the depot to their new home, a building he had leased sight unseen on Jefferson Street.

He and the children explored their new home together. The kitchen, dining room, and living room were on the ground floor. The entryway was through an expansive porch in the rear of the building. It was clean and pleasant, and the living quarters included an upstairs with two large bedrooms for the kids and one for Daniel. Out back was a large fenced-in yard, complete with mature oaks and walnut trees for shade. In the front portion of the building was a commercial entrance with a large window of the storefront type. It opened into an attractive anteroom he envisioned as a reception area with seating. Adjoining was a larger space, which he had earmarked for his clinical work.

Daniel declared his practice was to officially open on Friday, September 3, 1885. While getting settled and preparing to open the practice, he needed a source of income, so he signed on to teach the spring term in Burlington.

During the summer months, the family worked together to organize the practice. He designed and placed an order for two thousand printed circulars, and he and the children made the dissemination of the brochures a family event as they walked all over the city and stuffed mailboxes, screen doors, and flower boxes with the announcement. Its bold title line read: D.D. Palmer cures without drugs. He also put a dignified, simple message in the newspaper in which he announced D.D. Palmer would be opening his magnetic healing practice on Jefferson Street in Burlington, Iowa.

It had been eight months since he'd first told his parents of his plans to move to Burlington. The business began well, and a month went by in a flash. Then, on the first Sunday of October, Catherine, Thomas, and T.J. came to visit Daniel and the kids in Burlington for the first time. They all met amidst hugs and kisses at the depot and walked through the warm, breezy streets back to the Palmer home and clinic. Frank was happy to see his favorite uncle, and he monopolized T.J. with questions about goings-on back in What Cheer. May and Jessie were skipping along happily as their big brother, twenty-three-year-old Frank, carried little Bart most of the way. His sisters had begun to call Bartlett Joshua by his initials, but the tag hadn't yet stuck. Even their father reluctantly came out with the occasional "B.J.," although he preferred the long form of the name for his child.

Their visit was one of those great family moments where everyone was happy, healthy, growing, or already grown. Daniel was proud his practice was rapidly increasing and enthusiastically relayed stories about successful cases he had treated.

His father said, "Daniel, I have to tell you when you first said you were planning to give up a successful business to go into this curing venture ..." He stopped to consider his words, shrugged, and continued, " ... I thought you had gone loony. But I've got to hand it to you. You've created something here."

Dan, unaccustomed to receiving heaps of praise from his father, was now wearing a large but not quite bumptious smile.

Seeing things from a mother's perspective, Catherine chimed in, "Son, this is the first genuinely happy smile I've seen on your face since we lost Louvenia."

The smile fell from his face like a stone. But he caught himself by glancing at the row of children surrounding his parents. Their happy faces, so at ease with their grandparents, lightened him and restored his smile. The children were all the evidence he needed to know life must go on. Dan swept his hand toward them, saying, "They keep me moving forward."

The Palmer family repeated these visits to Burlington once a month, usually arriving by mid-morning on Sunday. Catherine and Thomas would come each time, and depending upon what was going on back home, at least one or more of the siblings would come along. They would have dinner, a short visit together, and be off on the five o'clock evening departure, arriving back in What Cheer later that evening.

By the waning months of 1887, two years had flown by, and the Palmers reunited at the station for another visit at ten o'clock in the morning on a Sunday in Burlington. This time Hannah and her brothers Bart and T.J. came along too. Their sisters, Lucinda and Catherine, stayed in What Cheer, ostensibly to clean the floors at home and in their parent's furniture store. They also planned to be visited by a certain pair of What Cheer's eligible bachelors— something they had somehow forgotten to mention to their parents.

The family enjoyed dinner and an afternoon of pleasant conversation in the spacious living room in Burlington. A steady hum of background squeals confirmed the children were happily cavorting somewhere in the house with their uncles. Then, as the bright afternoon sun began to wane, Daniel made a surprise announcement. "I've made a decision that involves another move."

"Back to What Cheer, I hope," his mother interjected buoyantly.

Patiently acknowledging her, he said, "No, Mother, not back to What Cheer." Then, looking serious, his eyes darted between his mother's and father's searching for a reaction. "As you know, the magnetic practice has been catching on well. I've taken on many kinds of diseases from minor to serious with great success, and frankly, I think it's time to take the next step."

Hannah barked, "Can't you ever stay put, Daniel?"

Knowing it was more of a judgment than a question, he patiently explained, "Burlington is a good community, but I think this thing is too big for me to stay here. Besides, Paul's son Jacob lives in Burlington. I've visited with J.S. many times, and he plans to open his own magnetic practice here. Paul has passed away, and I think it would be most respectful of Paul's memory if I weren't in competition for patients with his son." He paused to emphasize that point and then continued, "Beyond that, I find Burlington neither big enough nor progressive enough to fit my vision of where this is all going."

"Just what is your vision? What's your next step, son?" asked Thomas.

"I've looked around carefully, Father, and I find that the most progressive, fastest-growing city on the upper Mississippi is Davenport. The downtown is flourishing, and it even looks and sounds like a real city," he answered.

"Do you think you will be able to find a good place to start up there?" Catherine asked.

"Yes, Mother, there's a perfect location, and I've struck a deal to rent two treatment rooms, and three others for residence, on the top floor of a great stone structure called the *Ryan Building*. It's on the corner of Second and Brady, right in the center of the downtown, and there's plenty of room to expand as and how I need it."

Daniel unrolled a document and handed it to his parents. At the top was a the title *Lease*. Immediately below was *Effective Date: November 23, 1887.*

His mother read the date. "So it looks like you'll be moving by year's end?" she asked.

"I hope to have the practice up and running in January," Daniel replied.

It's all-new, so we're getting in at just the right time to be a part of the most prominent office building in the city, and it's even got an elevator! The owner has promised to give me top priority regarding the entire floor as the practice grows. There're forty rooms on the fourth floor, so plenty of opportunity!"

When he came up for air, his father said, "Well, it appears you're off and running."

"I am, Father," he answered.

The family returned to the station for their trip home, and when Thomas checked the train schedules he said, "The train from What Cheer to Davenport is an hour and a half shorter than the one we're taking today."

"Good, these weekend visits are a joy, but the travel is tiresome," she answered.

Before another month passed, Dan and the children were living on the top floor of the Ryan Building in Davenport. Having begun practice just two years ago, the process to create the business was fresh in his mind. Daniel was already seeing his first patients on January 15, 1888, less than a week after they arrived. This time the practice grew even more rapidly. When he wasn't seeing patients, he circulated throughout the downtown, meeting people and making connections.

Mr. St. Onge, the owner of a large, busy dry goods store on the ground floor of the Ryan Building, greeted him on the sidewalk during the third week. "Young man, you have quickly developed a steady stream of clientele flowing up and down these stairs."

"I'm pleased to have a chance to visit with you, Mr. St. Onge," Dan responded. "It's great to be here, and by their referrals, I believe the community is pleased too."

Revealing he didn't expect the man's clinical prowess to be extraordinary, St. Onge added, "You must know how to market."

Daniel pretended not to notice the backhanded compliment. "The business strategy is simple; it's a combination of newspaper announcements to inform and referrals from patients who get well where other methods failed them." Now thinking he perhaps sounded a bit cocky, he decided to soften his bearing. "In reality, I'm not doing things much different from you. I offer a high-quality, affordable service people need, want, appreciate, and are willing to pay for." He emphasized the final phrase.

"Mr. Putnam introduced you as Daniel, but I see your sign says D.D. Palmer. Which do you prefer to go by?" The store owner's tone was friendlier, even conciliatory.

"My given name is Daniel, but when I first started practice, I put up a sign that read, *Dr. Daniel D. Palmer*. After that, patients started calling me *Dr. D.D.*, which seems to have stuck. I don't mind if you prefer to call me by my given name, but others may not know who you're referring to."

"Well, D.D., I'm glad to have you as a neighbor. Just let me know if there's anything I can do for you," Mr. St. Onge said.

The practice grew rapidly, as did the children. Without Louvenia's presence, the family often struggled with the demands of everyday life. Ironically the former schoolmaster's children, now enrolled in the city's schools, were getting sporadic education. Their father, busy in his practice and spread thin when not caring for patients, failed to notice attendance and performance issues soon enough to stay on top of the situation. Still grieving the loss of his wife, Daniel wasn't thinking about getting married again. He hired a series of housekeepers to help keep things together, but the work was demanding and the pay modest. As a result, they rarely stayed on for more than a few months.

During their second year in Davenport, a young woman named Alvilla Thomas came under Dr. Palmer's care. Her legs were paralyzed, she was in constant pain in her upper body, and no one seemed to be able to help her. Villa's physician had been giving her morphine for more than a year, but nothing he or several other doctors tried brought any healing. The morphine gave temporary relief, but when it wore off, the unbearable pain returned. Having already seen disappointment under the care of all the best doctors on both sides of the river, she had low expectations about seeing the unusual magnetic practitioner.

Upon arrival for her first visit, two family members helped her onto the treatment table. Dr. Palmer began in his usual manner by sitting on his rolling stool while holding his hands adjacent to her head. His hands were close but did not touch her. It became quickly apparent to him this was one of those situations where he must apply all his concentration. Perspiration soon appeared on his forehead, and when a drop rolled down onto his nose, he thought, *This must be what Paul Caster felt like that first time in the Ottumwa infirmary when he treated Will.* It was the first time a patient's treatment had demanded so much of Daniel's energy.

After treating patients, he frequently felt revitalized, almost as though the process gave him more energy, but not in her case. Instead, he was exhausted after completing her first treatment. After the treatment, he stood and slid the rolling stool to the side of the room, then asked, "How do you feel?

She answered, "I'm not sure, just exhausted."

"That's what I expect. You should stay here and rest in this room for an hour." He covered her with a blanket and said, "Just relax. I'll return to check on you."

He went across the hall to his private office, sat behind the desk, put his head back, and almost immediately fell asleep. After only fifteen minutes, he awoke feeling invigorated and returned to work. Daniel treated two more patients before returning to check on Alvilla.

He spoke softly, "It's time to wake up."

She opened her eyes and smiled. "That was refreshing."

It was the first time he had seen her smile. "You should go home now and take ample rest this afternoon. Try to sleep again first," he said. She nodded in agreement. Then he added, "Afterward, if you feel the urge try to stand on your legs, then try it for only a moment to see what happens." He wasn't sure why he felt compelled to make such a suggestion to someone whose legs had been paralyzed for so long. But he had learned to trust conceptualizations that just came to him that way, so he said it. "I would like to see you again before the end of the week, and we'll see just what your body can do."

Two days later she returned for the follow-up visit. While she was being helped onto the treatment table the doctor asked, "How have you been doing?"

A more talkative Villa responded. "After I got home, I went to bed like you told me. But I was surprised not to wake up for three-hours. Whatever you did made me really tired, and I went into a deep sleep."

"Well that's a good reaction," Dr. Palmer assured her.

Villa continued, "Something strange happened. When I woke up, my upper body pain was only a dull ache. But what surprised me was these numb legs. They were giving me a distant tingling on the bottoms of my feet. I mean it's been so long since I'd felt anything there, the prickliness felt like it was coming from far away."

The doctor said, "This all sounds encouraging."

"Well here's the good part," Villa added. "I laid there for a couple of minutes, and then I remembered what you told me to try. No one was in the room at the time, or I would have felt foolish trying it. I rolled on my side, reached for the crutches, and struggled to my feet. Then standing there and feeling stronger than usual, I leaned less on the crutches. It amazed me that I didn't lose my balance. So I gradually took more and more weight off the crutches, until finally, those useless legs were holding all of my weight. I'm so weak that after a few seconds, I started wobbling, so I just eased back onto the mattress."

Villa had experienced a breakthrough. Later that day, she tried it again and was able to stand for almost a minute, then several minutes later, she did it again. Finally, about an hour later, she could stand for three minutes. Over the ensuing days, she carefully began to use her legs. Within a month, she received three more magnetic treatments and regained her ability to walk without assistance.

The life-changing experience marked a turning point for Villa, who soon invited D.D. to dinner. Before long, she was seeing him regularly, and four months later, they were married, on November 6, 1888. Villa, suddenly finding herself in charge of a ready-made family, loved her husband unconditionally, but affection for the children didn't come spontaneously or without challenges. Bart was only six, and the girls were entering their teens.

Although she regained her ability to function, some of the damage was permanent. Despite incredible overall progress, the habit of treating pain with morphine continued. The children grew up seeing this. They often spoke of their stepmother as either an angel or a devil, depending upon the availability of morphine. Mostly they viewed Villa as the classic evil stepmother, partially because she had a generally stern disposition and was unrelenting in her demands regarding their household chores. From Villa's point of view, the children had been let to run wild for the past four years, and reining them in was no easy task, especially for someone having limited physical capacity.

Their chores also included tasks related to the family business. Within four years, the Palmer Infirmary had grown to occupy eighteen rooms, and by 1895 occupied the entire fourth floor of the Ryan Building. Being the only doctor for such a large infirmary, Daniel worked long hours. His clinical help was limited to two nurses who moved patients about and saw to scheduling and clerical matters. Forty-two rooms meant a lot of upkeep, especially cleaning. Although there was hired help, Villa felt the children needed to learn responsibility and saved the dirtiest jobs for teaching them. In the ongoing tug of war between the children and their stepmother, Villa received the nickname "Villa the Villain," a designation they would never dare utter within earshot of their father. Often frustrated, she complained to Daniel that the children would not mind her. Deeply engrossed in his practice, he cared little for refereeing. His impatience about it, and loyalty to his wife, often caused him to unfairly side with her, disciplining the children without even considering their side of the contest. Punishment in the Palmer family was corporal, which led to growing resentment on the part of the children and a growing tension within the family.

However, not all the children's memories were bad, and one of their fondest recollections of stepmother Villa involved a family vacation in 1889. Villa often spoke proudly of her uncle, a general, who became famous for his exploits during the Civil War. Although he was a Southerner by birth, his loathsome regard for slavery caused him to remain with the Union Army. General George H. Thomas gained national attention in 1863 with his strategic regrouping of Union forces in the face of defeat during the Battle of Chickamauga. However, his nickname, the Rock of Chickamauga, became permanently stuck to him when his troops routed the Confederates under General Braxton Bragg the following month during the Chattanooga Campaign. The outcome of that Tennessee victory opened the door to the well-known invasion of the Deep South.

When the opportunity for a train trip and family vacation arose, Villa was keen to include the Tennessee battlefields. Always the school teacher, Daniel loved the idea of having a historical element to the trip. The children were most impressed by Terry, an elderly guide who showed them around the site of the Battle of Nashville. The kindly old black man explained the battle by showing the children how the battlefield's terrain became important in formulating strategy.

Terry seemed to be reliving the experience before the young people, who better understood his enthusiasm when he told them he had served under General Thomas. He seemed to have no end of stories to tell, and Terry enthralled the children throughout the tour. He also charmed them with an anecdote involving the former soldier's experience as a prisoner during the war. "Once, when

I was a prisoner, President Abraham Lincoln called to look over the prison." The man paused, adding special reverence to the fact that the martyred emancipator had touched him personally. He looked up toward the sky as if he were reading words written on the clouds. "Our great leader took time to confide in me, a soon-to-be emancipated negro. 'This is the first prison I have ever been in,' Mr. Lincoln said.

"To that, this old colored man …," Terry raised his left hand above his head and pointed down at himself, "… gave him a snappy answer, 'I've been in all the rest!'

"That was all I said, and Mr. Lincoln laughed one of those big hearty laughs he was known for—the kind my momma always called a belly laugh. Then he slapped me hard on the back and said, 'You've suffered enough. I'm going to see to it you are out of here today.'

"I was out before sundown with a new shirt and pants and a gold piece in my shirt pocket!"

The now excited eight-year-old B.J., blurted out, "Why were you in prison?"

Terry tipped his hat lower on his forehead and lowered his chin, implying he was about to share a secret. "Most us guests were living there as prisoners of war, but I was there for another reason."

"Did you kill someone?" B.J. quickly asked.

"No, nothin' like that. It seems I possessed an abundance of foolishness in a white man's world that spared little of it for colored folks," Terry answered.

The girls wore puzzled looks, not really understanding his crime, while B.J. followed enthusiastically with another question. "What else did the president say?"

B.J.'s older sister, May, elbowed him hard. "You're being rude now. You know you don't speak to an adult unless they talk to you first!"

Unfazed, the boy gave it right back to her. "He did talk to me first. And he said the president talked to him, and if he can talk to the president, then I can talk to him!"

Laughing a belly laugh himself, the elderly gentleman said, "Now that's okay, kids, lemme tell you what else." The children instantly gave the man their fullest attention. "Mr. Lincoln had a soft spot for the underdog, an' if the Lord ever made any underdogs, then I was sure one of 'em. But this great leader of men made me feel like I could talk to 'im just like anyone in my own family—I think that was part of his greatness. And there was a sad side to 'im that made me think he wanted others not to feel as sad as he was."

B.J. interrupted again. "Why was he sad?"

Catherine elbowed him again, harder this time, but saying nothing.

Keeping the peace, Terry hurriedly responded to the little boy's question. "Mr. Lincoln's eyes seen a lot of suffering, and he was tryin' to make a difference. I was in awe, but somehow I found the nerve to ask, 'How do ya bear up with all the trouble in the country?'

"He didn't think long and just answered like he had already been studyin' it. Mr. Lincoln said, 'When I have a knotty problem, I often try to think of how Mr. Jefferson might have dealt with it. If one wishes to get anything done, the weight of holding this office can be extraordinary. I read one of his letters, written before he was elected president. In that letter, Mr. Jefferson wrote:

"*No man will ever leave that office with the reputation which carried him into it. The honeymoon is short, and its happy moments are ransomed by years of torment and hatred.*

It became true for Mr. Jefferson, the greatest leader this country ever had, and it became true for me, a much lesser man, within the first week of moving into the White House."

Terry straightened himself, looking even taller to the children than before. "I tell you, children, I could feel Abraham Lincoln's sadness at that moment. He seemed to know he would never, and couldn't never, give up, and it brung great pain onto himself and everyone he cared for."

Villa had only been their stepmother for a little over a year when she took the children on that trip to Nashville. Daniel, busy in the practice, had stayed in Davenport. Traveling together gave Villa an opportunity to bond with the children in ways that didn't come as easily at home.

Chapter Twenty-One

THE ROCK ISLAND LINE, 1914

"The civilized man has built a coach,
but has lost the use of his feet."
–Ralph Waldo Emerson

The train slowed and whistled its way into the city. Great plumes of steam shot like white billowy arms, embracing the ground along each side of the locomotive. The hot whistle screamed its shrill warning before rolling through every crossing. This Rock Island 930 locomotive was a powerful 4-6-2 type whose state-of-the-art coal-fired power plant could propel her up to one hundred miles per hour. Built ten months earlier by the American Locomotive Company in New York, the spotless engine approached Davenport's Chicago-Rock Island and Pacific Depot from the east.

Two hours earlier, at LaSalle, Illinois, B.J. had boarded the train, which was already en route from Chicago to Des Moines and points west. Upon entering the coach, a uniformed porter greeted and directed him. The refined black man said, "Sir, please proceed right down the aisle, gesturing toward the interior. You'll find *very*"—he slowly articulated the word for emphasis—"comfortable seats in this coach." B.J. wasn't sure why he was privileged to be in this car but readily accepted his good fortune.

As the door behind him slid closed, he was surprised to notice how silently it floated. *It must have precisely machined, smooth bearings,* he thought. Standing at the end of the aisle, he took in his surroundings. With only eighteen seats in the luxuriously configured car, it felt expansive. There were six rows of double-width upholstered chairs on the right and a corresponding row of single seats on the aisle's left side. Running the Pullman's length was a line of ornate brass chandeliers attached to an indented tray ceiling. The ceiling, covered in navy-blue embossed paisley paper, effortlessly coordinated with the thick blue carpet below. The walls were trimmed in oak, richly stained a light reddish-brown, and superbly sealed with a satin varnish. The well-cushioned seats had soft upholstery with a light orange-colored print. The silky fabric was reminiscent of the muted hue of autumn leaves still on the tree—that hard-to-capture and short-lived color trees display on their way between green and brown.

The only other person in the car was seated in a unique section of the coach with a convenient work table. More than a handy fixture, the desk was a beautiful piece of furniture, constructed with highly variegated bird's eye maple, inlaid near the edges with mother-of-pearl purfling. Glimpsing out the window, B.J. noticed the train was already moving. That was another extraordinary feature of this particular train. Its movement lacked the usual sudden lurch forward that signaled the beginning of travel. Instead, it just began to glide effortlessly and quietly. B.J. approached, pointing at the single empty seat across the table from Robert's, and asked, "May I?"

Robert gestured at the seat with a robust, assured voice. "Of course!"

B.J. added, "This has got to be the finest, most beautiful coach I've ever seen! There must be royalty aboard."

Glancing up from his desktop, Robert forced a smile to acknowledge the comment. Evidently intrigued, Robert looked at him again. B.J.'s intense blue eyes and friendly smile did have a way of disarming strangers, and his presence had a larger-than-life quality that made him seem a much bigger man than the slender five-foot-six he was. With a thin, dark-brown leather headband traversing his forehead, long, dark, wavy hair, and a neatly-trimmed Van Dyke beard, B.J. had a very distinctive appearance: someone it would be difficult to forget having met.

"My name is B.J. Palmer. I seem to recognize you, but I can't place you. Have you been in the newspapers lately?"

The question brought another smile to Robert's face. "I'm Robert." The mature man withheld his last name for the moment, seemingly enjoying the hint of mystery. "I served as Secretary of War, and I've been an ambassador too." B.J.'s eyes widened as Robert spoke. "But that was some years ago." Robert gestured with both hands encompassing the entire Pullman. "Now I'm in charge of building this car you're sitting in."

B.J. tried to take it all in, realizing the man he had interrupted was a celebrity. Moreover, there was a much greater sense of familiarity about him than what some faraway newspaper stories or photos might explain. Robert reached into his vest pocket and pulled out an elegant, heavy-parchment business card, which he passed to B.J. with a polite nod of his head. B.J. examined the card identifying Robert Lincoln as an attorney, businessman, and chair of the Pullman Company.

Robert continued, "I'm on my way to Des Moines for a meeting about supplying custom Pullman cars to the Rock Island Line. They're preparing to open that new Twin-Cities to Kansas City route and would like to do it in style."

"I live in Davenport, and I've already heard about this worthy project. I hope the meeting goes well. I'm sure it will be good for Iowa," B.J. replied.

Robert added, "Well, my wife, Mary, and I have a soft spot in our hearts for Iowa. Her people are from Mount Pleasant, Iowa. She's a graduate of Iowa Wesleyan College and stays most interested in anything that affects her alma mater."

"It's a fine institution," B.J. responded. "Several Wesleyan graduates have come up from Mount Pleasant to attend my school. They've been among the best-prepared students we get."

Their rapport was growing, as was the warmth in Robert's tone. He reached into his briefcase and pulled out a rolled-up leaflet printed on a hefty, rich-looking, long photographic bill. "I'll let you in on a little secret. Here's an interesting project bearing the name Pullman." He proudly unrolled and suspended the large, glossy sheet for B.J. to behold.

A bright orange border wholly framed it. The upper third portrayed a black-and-white image of a four-door automobile. Above, in big, bold black letters, was emblazoned: *It has taken us eleven years to produce this car.* B.J. was impressed by the stylish wooden spoke wheels surrounded by bright, wide, white-walled pneumatic tires. The company logo appeared below the picture, composed of a much larger brilliant orange script that matched the handbill's perimeter color. The emblem consisted of the name Pullman written in beautiful calligraphy. Its final letter "n" looped into a broad underscoring of the entire surname. Then, below the logo was a table, framed in orange, with a bold heading: *There will be a big demand for the right sort of six-cylinder makes this year. If the one you represent is minus just one of these popular features— what will you say?* The full-page advertisement continued with paragraphs of fine-printed specifications. Then came the four-figured dealer's price list, bold and proud. Finally, the advertisement ended with simple, black lettering at the bottom: *Pullman Motor Car Company, York, Penn.*

After a quick scan of the flyer, a bemused B.J. exclaimed, "York, Pennsylvania? I thought Pullmans were built in Chicago."

Robert's answer was indirect. "B.J., you have just seen something none of their dealers have even laid eyes on yet—they'll have to wait thirty more days!"

"Your secret will be safe with me," B.J. said. "But it won't be easy because one of my good friends is Willard Velie, owner of the—"

A now broadly smiling Robert interrupted, "The Velie Motor Vehicle Company in Moline! I know Mr. Velie, and his company is a lot like Pullman." Robert hastened to add, "And to Pullman, he wouldn't be a competitor. He'd be a colleague, interested in crafting quality, not just fast and cheap like our friend Mr. Ford."

Tapping a finger to his lips with a small smile, B.J. nodded. "My lips are sealed."

Robert chuckled and said, "I'm sure the Pullman Motor Car Company would appreciate your discretion, but let me tell you something else interesting. The Pullman Company, formerly the Pullman Palace Car Company, builds railroad coaches. We have never designed nor built an automobile!"

Dumfounded, B.J. began, "Then how is it they call this automobile—"

Again Robert enthusiastically cut him off. "That's an excellent question, my friend. They're the York Motor Car Company. Mr. A.P. Broomell, York's founder, will also see me in Des Moines this evening, where he plans to convince me we shouldn't file a lawsuit against them. According to Mr. Broomell, they just chose Pullman's name"—Robert slowed his speech and softly articulated the final part of the sentence for emphasis—"in *our* special honor. The implication is their quality and luxury parallels that of a Pullman railroad coach."

"It seems like preposterous usurpation to me," B.J. said.

Robert, still having a good laugh, answered, "Ludicrous!"

B.J. responded, "I'd love to be a fly on the wall for tonight's conversation."

Robert and B.J. had discovered they were kindred spirits. The conversation continued for nearly two more hours while they enjoyed each other's company, ranging from the impacts of new manufacturing processes on handcraftsmanship; rapidly evolving know-how vis-à-vis transportation, especially automobiles; business ethics; parallels in their professional and personal lives; and especially the uncanny similarities in relationships between themselves and their respective parents.

The train was crossing a large wooden trestle above a lake when B.J. saw something flicker across Robert's face. "Are you okay?" B.J. asked.

"Huh? Oh, sorry, I guess I had gone somewhere else for a second—actually, seeing this Illinois countryside makes me think about my father," he explained. "But you wouldn't be interested. I mean ... we're not talking about him now."

B.J. felt a familiar pang in his gut. "No, not at all," he replied. "I'd love to hear about him. In fact, I'd be honored."

"When I was little, mother was my rock. I never doubted my father's love, but he didn't have time. She was always there for me. However, the distance between my mother and me increased as I grew up. I've always blamed the *guests*." Robert held up two fingers in a pantomimic for quotation marks on each hand. "They were the strangest of friends she seemed to attract with increasing frequency."

B.J. listened and fidgeted, nodding encouragement as Robert confided in him. His face drew still and tight as some of Robert's threads were eerily comparable to the Palmers' father/son experience. Robert went on, "Most of them were there trying to leverage her position for political favors. She wanted to have close friends, but she was too naïve. Mother couldn't distinguish between the genuine and the schemers. And the Spiritualists proved to be a great distraction from her real life. She was especially vulnerable when my little brother Willie died of typhoid. Falling into a deep melancholy, she was desperate for answers. Father believed in a hereafter, but not in those people whom Mother brought in for meetings. He would have done anything he could to help her. It put him in a difficult position when people asked questions like, *Why are séances being held in the White House?* Those charlatans feed on personal tragedies, and they're quick to seize an opportunity for profit."

B.J. said, "My father was a Spiritualist too, but only as a religion. He believed there was something profound about life. It was about much more than just the material substance making up people and things around them. Although a Spiritualist, he had no regard whatsoever for the séance crowd. He fancied himself a 'buster of the frauds.' He was good at it too. There were even occasions when he received death threats for it!"

The two were becoming fast friends. An hour ticked off in a flash as they spoke about their life's journey. Robert talked about the plans his father had made for after his second term. "Father said we'd return to Illinois. He said he was going to start a farm and it would teach responsibility to my brother Tad, and resourcefulness to all of us."

Startled, B.J. leaned back and slapped both hands on his thighs. "Amazing. That was like having my father right here in this car with us. He was the epitome of a self-reliant person." Then, on a more somber note, he added, "Back home, I'm facing the greatest confrontation of my life, and when I boarded this train, I wasn't sure if I could pull it off. Here, in this short stretch, your presence reminded me that I can."

"How so?" Robert queried.

B.J. swallowed hard before answering. "It's not easy to express, but I'll try to explain. My sisters May, Jessie, and I, grew up under the watchful eyes of the least affectionate stepmother you might imagine. Alvilla Thomas married my father a few years after my mother died. And my father was obsessed with his science, only finding rare snippets of time to give to his family. She seemed jealous about sharing him with us and always found some way to tie up his time like she was competing with us.

"There weren't many, but in those times when he was alone with us children, it was just magical. He wasn't overly warm and didn't do a lot of hugging and the like, but we honestly knew a father's love. Unfortunately, in recent years my father and I became estranged. We had some thorny disagreements, and last year he passed on. I've felt a great void, and I regret we never reconciled. But somehow, you remind me of the best part of him." B.J.'s eyes were tearing up, and he tarried while he again swallowed at the lump in his throat. "Thank you."

Robert placed his right hand on B.J.'s left shoulder, patted it, and responded simply, "I'm honored to have played that role."

The train was gliding to a stop. B.J. reached for his leather grip from behind the seat. Dropping it in the aisle, he looked directly at Robert, concentrating as if to memorize his face. That scrutiny revealed the extent to which Robert actually resembled D.D. Palmer. They were about the same age, with a similarly stocky build; both had broad faces with a full beard and a high forehead. *Well, perhaps the resemblance is mostly physical*, B.J. thought. *True, both men epitomize strong intellect. But where Robert carries all the culture and refinement of an aristocrat, Father's character was rugged, more like a lumberjack.*

The rhythm of wheels on rails slowed, signaling their imminent arrival. B.J. Palmer reached out to shake his distinguished seatmate's hand while rising from his seat to gather papers and repack his attaché.

Robert received his hand graciously. "It seems we have had much in common, particularly when it comes to relationships with our fathers."

While lowering himself back onto the seat, B.J. watched his eyes as Robert continued, "In my childhood, Father was always gone, attending court or making speeches. When I first applied to Harvard and got rejected, I needed to talk. But he was so busy pursuing the White House, there never was a suitable, quiet moment left for me. I understood he had a big job to do, but still, there was anger seething within me. I was jealous of his time—the one commodity he seemed to have the least of.

"After he got elected came an endless stream of politicians vying for his favors and attention. Then the war came. I don't think I got ten minutes uninterrupted with him before"—Robert paused briefly, and a genuine reverence entered his voice—"I don't think I got ten minutes uninterrupted with him until the end." Robert gazed out the window as the elegant stone station came into view. "I remember sitting by his bedside in that little bedroom in the boarding house across from the theater. It was the longest night of our lives. Mother wailed inconsolably while physicians mopped and kept digging at his bloody wound. They were of no help, and sometimes I think he would have been better off if the guards had kept them out entirely.

"The gut-wrenching night seemed to go on forever. Oddly enough, I feel guilty for remembering this was the longest time I had been able to spend next to him since my earliest childhood days." With rapt attention, B.J. listened while Robert continued. "It seems great men often give their magnificent gifts to the world at the expense of their loved ones. Perhaps we should honor and respect their decision to do so rather than resent them for it."

The train stopped, so B.J. gave the older man's right hand a firm two-handed shake. "It's been an unforgettable visit." He reached into his vest pocket, pulled out a business card, handed it to Robert, and said, "If there's anything I can ever do for you, just get in touch."

Robert smiled. "Likewise."

B.J. stepped to the end of the Pullman where, feeling recharged and inspired, he bounded down the steps toward the familiar platform.

Standing on the wooden boards, he glanced at the three parallel sets of tracks and then shifted up to the three-story depot's tile roof. Finally, his gaze fixed on a tall spire towering over the courthouse several blocks away, which reminded him of the telegram in his shirt pocket. B.J. unfolded and read the off-white paper. It had shaken him with mixed emotions when he first received it, but now, he reread it with renewed confidence.

Western Union Telegram
November 23, 1914
Received at LaSalle, Illinois

To: Dr. B.J. Palmer, c/o the Paul Carus House, LaSalle, Illinois.
From: Frank Elliott, Davenport, Iowa.

"I'm summoned to testify about you at grand jury tomorrow. Please return to Davenport."

Frank

Chapter Twenty-Two
SCOTT COUNTY COURTHOUSE

"One ship drives east and another drives west,
with the selfsame winds that blow. 'Tis the set of the sails,
and not the gales, that tell us the way to go."
–Ella Wheeler Wilcox, "The Winds of Fate"

B.J. knew what Frank meant because this wasn't the first time a jury had assembled on the matter. Saddened to learn it was happening again, B.J. was especially irked. He had been in LaSalle taking care of patients and planned to stay for two more days. In his element there, he enjoyed the people and accommodations of the beautiful Carus home. Not just a stately mansion, its fifty-seven rooms offered a backdrop for philosophical discourse and publishing. Its grandiose double-door, second-story main entrance set the tone. In an experience not short on pomp, one approached via a choice of twin rounded staircases leading up to the home's vast, ornate porch. Picturing that grand entryway, B.J. capitulated and made a mental note, *I'll surely return for an extended visit when time allows.*

Folding the telegram back up, he stuffed it back into his shirt pocket, glanced up at the sky, and started down the stairs to the street, where he set his sights on that tall spire above the courthouse.

He would have liked to stop home first to see his wife, Mabel, and the baby, but the grand jury could already be in session.

The atrium was silent. Its monumental proportions were cold and intimidating. *I wonder if it's intended to daunt the visitor without an inviting handshake or any sense of welcome,* B.J. thought. Every little jangle reverberated, making the empty hall seem eerie and menacing—perfectly designed for generating apprehension.

He strode briskly through the foreboding façade. The vestibule's tall, brass-trimmed double doors provided a weather-tight aperture. As he crossed it, he looked down, grinned appreciatively, and said, "Hello, Iowa," as he spotted the Great Seal of the State of Iowa, inlaid at the center of the white tile floor.

Loaded with symbolic imagery, the seal's focal point, Old Glory, waved in a wheat field bordered by the broad Mississippi River. Over her dark waters chugged the river's fastest steamboat, the renowned side-wheeler, *Iowa.* A citizen-soldier stood proudly supporting the flagpole at the center of the seal. Perched on top of the pole was a felt liberty cap. Its conical-shaped design, an ancient icon of freedom, adorned the centerpiece. Boldly affirming Iowa was the gateway, it stood like an oasis at the edge of slavery's great moral wasteland. The soldier's wide-brimmed hat resembled cowboy garb more than military attire, and the plow at his side attested to his actual identity. An eagle soared above the river, soldier, field, and flag, clutching a streamer in its beak. Emblazoned on the ribbon were the words: *Our liberties we prize and our rights we will maintain.* The state motto so lucidly cast her ideals, only the most unobservant could enter there, failing to recognize the values held dear by Iowans.

After the principles portended in the portico came the main concourse. Its high ceiling, wreathed at the perimeter with a carved egg and dart border, was ideal for generating echoes. A massive brass chandelier with lots of crystals hung in the center. Bright shimmering splashes of light projected around the hall from its many prisms. But the kaleidoscope of color did little to warm the big room, so sedately accented by a hard, off-white marble façade. The cool stone layer covering from top to bottom added an imposingly harsh, albeit opulent, touch.

Solemnity and ceremony notwithstanding, B.J. boldly entered the empty lobby. His unconventional, self-assured presence seemed effortless. Frank had complained in a private meeting the week before, "You know, chief, it's not fair. Some of us have to muddle through life, always struggling, but you have this gift. I don't know what it is, a charisma that charges a room just by your being in it."

B.J. chuckled back at him. "Well, keep in mind that things aren't always what they seem, my friend."

Remembering Frank's comment now, B.J. mused, *I hope all that's charismatic works well today.* Then he traversed the concourse, straightened up, and stopped to read the chalkboard before entering a long corridor. At the top was written November 24, 1914, and in the center it said, *Grand jury ahead*, with an arrow pointing down the hallway. He strode on down, unfazed by his surroundings, almost regally, as he reached into his vest pocket.

Glints of sunlight sparkled over the ornate face of the gold pocket watch he now clasped in his left hand. The dependable instrument pointed at 4:20 p.m. The late afternoon sun was at a perfect angle to send strobing shafts of light over its jeweled face each time he passed by another tall, narrow window. He held it longer than necessary to enjoy sparkling red flashes reflected by a deep crimson ruby. The jewel marked the sixth hour at the bottom of the timepiece's face. Bright sunlight always brought out its brilliant red color and inspired him to put Burma on his list of places to visit soon.

As of late, B.J. had been dreaming of taking Mabel on a trip around the world. His plan, revealed to her at breakfast earlier this week, was becoming very specific. "Mabel ..." He took in a sip of java, sniffed, and savored its aroma while lifting the solid gold chain that arched across his vest. The golden object rose from its pocket and twirled slowly.

Watching his flair toward the dramatic, Mabel smirked. Both knew it was little more than a maneuver intended to get her full attention.

Gesturing toward the gyrating watch, he declared, "This ruby speaks to me, and it has convinced me we must see the famous mines in the Valley of Mogok."

She knew full well he was referring to the gem he oft admired at the six o'clock spot. But while he pointed, she playfully rolled her head as if connected to the rotating watch dangling at the end of the chain.

With his eyes fixed on hers, he somehow missed the humor. Taking the challenge, he produced a resolute expression to show he was dead serious and said, "It will surely be one of our first stops in Siam."

Poking fun at his clumsiness, Mabel looked at him as if he'd gone daft and burst into laughter. "Dear, I've seen that stack of travel brochures sitting on your desk for more than a week. I'd hate to see you in a situation where you had to keep a secret! Now tell me what's on your mind."

A tad annoyed she had taken the drama out of his proclamation, B.J. explained, "First, we'll clean up Joy's malicious mess. Then we'll turn a new page by boarding the finest steamer available. I've been settling my mind a bit by reading those brochures, and I've concluded that Cunard's newest, *The Laconia,* is the cream of the crop. We'll book into her best stateroom." His enthusiasm swelled. "On her A deck, *The Laconia* has a library with electric lights and a thousand volumes." Not wishing to get it wrong, B.J. pulled a folded sheet from his pocket and continued to read directly from the brochure. "'The select library, accessible to only first-class passengers, includes many rare volumes. Our guests enjoy an exclusive reading room, decorated in Georgian style with chaste white Greek columns.'" He turned the handbill around so she might glance at the picture. Then he read on in his best stage voice. "'Picture yourself happily seated here on the port side next to the window in a comfortable cane chair before an elegant mahogany writing desk.'" Knowing she wouldn't remain patient much longer, he skipped ahead, varying his pitch, pace, and intonation. "Oh, and the caption brags about your many comforts: 'the chairs in the library have loose cushions covered in rose velvet; Persian carpets over an Austrian oak floor; tapestries on the wall; and green juopé embroidered curtains.' They also have—"

Mabel interrupted, her face softening with a smile. "I know you're a passionate man, but such zeal about a vacation? And I definitely wouldn't have expected you to give a hoot for green juopé embroidered curtains!"

"You're right, hon," he responded. "But it's something we've earned and need. Lord knows how you've pushed yourself to the limits for the past five years. Running the entire anatomy department would be a handful for anyone. But you're tied up caring for little Davey, not to mention how all the boys and girls at the school seem to think you're their mother too!"

"So you're saying this is all for me?" Mabel asked, wearing her most suspicious mien.

B.J. knew it was time for a tactical retreat, and he also knew she was too bright to be trifled with once she put her cards on the table. Nor did he desire to be condescending anyway. Knowing the best tack with Mabel was always to be straight out, he offered, "No, not at all. We both need this, and so does the profession. This thing we have belongs to the world, and since the world isn't yet beating down my door to ask for it, I'll have to bring it to them. We'll take the best of chiropractic into every corner of the globe and show it to them."

Their personal and professional lives were so intertwined, it was often difficult to distinguish between them. Now that the conversation had become more like one of their typical strategy sessions, Mabel responded. "So this is for both of us? Or should I say *all* of us?"

B.J. ignored the hint of sarcasm and answered with a soft, simple "Yes." Then his dreamy side resurfaced. "I have to work on my next book, and I can already feel myself writing it there on the deck of *The Laconia*. The ship will be leisurely ambling along, cutting through small waves lapping against the high-sided steamer. I'll be feverishly dragging my fountain pen over paper, sipping espresso on the veranda, and taking in the fragrance of salty, clean air. But none of this could be right without you by my side."

Her eyes darted back and forth between his, as if mystified. She knew he was under enormous stress and cut him some slack by simply saying, "Yes, I'd love to accompany you on a steamer to Siam. By the way, what are juopé embroidered curtains?"

B.J. answered, "Darned if I know; I was going to ask you." He gurgled with enthusiasm, "I suppose they must be extraordinary, though!"

He had envisioned precisely how it would all unfold. The first week they would sail away from the world's troubles, enjoying each other's company and the indulgences bestowed upon those cruising on *The Laconia*. The following week would find B.J. and Mabel standing before a marble hillside entrance to one of the legendary mines at Mogok. This time he'd make sure she didn't preempt his moment of theater. In that exotic place, he would draw out the timepiece. Then, while holding her hand in his, he'd use her finger to point to the superb ruby on its face and say, "Now, from this place, let's choose a fantastic big sister gem for you to wear on your finger." It was a plan he knew would come to pass—perhaps just a bit delayed owing to the current tribulation.

Chapter Twenty-Three
KEEP SMILING

Darkness falls wherever there is no light.

B.J. continued down the hallway of the Scott County Courthouse while focused on another majestic jewel. A fiery diamond replacing twelve on the timepiece glistened in the sunlight. *Funny how a diamond is the most precious of all gems, cherished through the ages. But the greater warmth of the red ruby wins my heart.*

Returning the watch to his vest pocket, he remembered why he had entered the building. It sparked a much different thought: *This exquisite timepiece is always reliable, precise, and faithful— qualities often lacking in people.*

A drab picture came to his mind's eye. It was the image of Joy Loban. Far from prodigious, Joy's homely visage featured a narrow baby face. His small, close-set, beady eyes had trifling irises in the dullest shade of brown. His hair was dark, almost black, and Joy's nose was oversized more than a smidge, giving the face a too-pointy look. Beauty only being skin-deep, its absence is surmountable with loads of personality, but unfortunately, neither genetics nor providence had occasioned that attribute in Joy's case. Neither was it helpful that his parents chose to give him a girl's name. Joy was brilliant, one of the most promising of the Palmer School's faculty members, but unfortunately, he also had a penchant for being insufferably self-centered.

It saddened B.J. to think of how bright and articulate his friend could be, while at the same time, Joy had a propensity for missing the bigger picture. However, all those negative notions stopped flashing through B.J.'s mind when he caught sight of Frank seated near the end of the stark passageway.

With its high ceiling, marble walls, and hard tile floor, the Spartan setting echoed every step he took. The wide hallway felt distinctly narrow with an overriding, wintry atmosphere. His thoughts shifted. *If I had a long, stone corridor like this, I would line it with plants, pictures, and ideas.* But nothing was being done to warm up these surroundings. The only objects affixed to the austere walls were signs, with black lettering painted on pale yellow, prim-looking plaques. All in the same severe formal uppercase lettering, their inscriptions identified what lurked behind each door. They seemed to shout: MAGISTRATE, CLERK of COURT, JURY ROOM, TREASURER, COURTROOM.

A row of stark, straight-backed wooden chairs lined the hallway to complete the effect. Their darkly-stained backs contrasted coldly with the white marble chair rail. Combined with their lack of padding, they could only foster an uncomfortable experience.

B.J.'s footsteps came closer to the only man seated in the hallway. He was leaning forward with his head in his hands. To his right hung the last black-on-yellow sign, which read GRAND JURY. Frank didn't look up to see who was coming but just sat there looking dejected, as though it were he who was in jeopardy rather than B.J.

As he walked closer, B.J. pictured Frank in a blissful moment at last summer's all-school picnic. Frank was seated at a long wooden table, sublimely enjoying a large slice of watermelon, which he held in both hands right below his chin. Frank's great big smile framed the moment. This pleasing picture was evocative of how the personalities of Frank and Joy were nearly opposites. B.J. valued consistency and reliability, both qualities that defined Frank.

On the other hand, Joy had a great intellect, debased by a lack of character. It brought to mind something B.J.'s close friend, the noted writer Elbert Hubbard often said: "An ounce of loyalty is worth a pound of cleverness."

When Frank noticed the familiar footsteps, he knew without looking it was his teacher, boss, friend, and mentor. The fact that Frank's cousin Mabel was B.J.'s wife didn't win him any points with The Chief.

B.J. was ambivalent about the nickname bestowed upon him by the staff of the Palmer School. But since it never obstructed progress, he was okay with it.

Frank knew nepotism didn't get him the job, and any advancement would depend upon actual merit. He wanted it that way and appreciated The Chief's singular vision. All activities supported the mission and an overarching vision. Frank loved going to work each day because employment at the Palmer School embodied teamwork.

The present situation was tense, and it was hard to know what to say. When close enough to speak, B.J. softly uttered a well-rehearsed, "Keep smiling."

Frank looked up, his high forehead giving way to serious, close-set eyes. His Roman nose, surrounded by high cheekbones and a strong jawline, bolstered a thin upper lip. Frank's features gave the impression of a kind, intelligent fellow who was somewhat fatherly looking. "I don't know what to say," Frank began tentatively, "except I think the whole world has gone mad! Accusing a righteous man of murdering his own father! What could be lower than that?"

B.J. answered simply, "Well, I don't know, but give destructors enough time, and they'll always come up with something. It's what they do. Joy is no exception, but he's in for much more of a fight than he thinks!" B.J. laid his hand on the seated man's shoulder and patted him for reassurance. "Well, I can see a real friend seated here in this hall of hell—or justice." He looked up at the sign above the door to the left of Frank's chair. "I guess the grand jury will determine which it is. But whatever they say, you are loyal and true."

Frank, comforted by B.J.'s words, wasn't seeking reassurance. Looking up at B.J., Frank shook his head negatively and, with a pained look, said, "Losing a parent is hard on anyone. But to maliciously drag your good name through the filthiest of gutters at a time when people should be rallying around and giving you support. It should never happen this way."

B.J. was calm, "Frank, it's a fact that when any man takes up the mantle of leadership, he puts a target on his back. When we do ... " He paused to choose his words carefully. " ... It's good we don't have a crystal ball to see what those slings and arrows will look like, because if we saw, we might not have the courage to go on. Life is just like that. Some days we find ourselves in the lap of luxury, maybe visiting with the president's family, and other days fighting for our lives. Today we just happen to be doing both!"

Not easily consoled, Frank added, "I hate to think what might happen to the school if this hits the papers. D.D., you and Mabel, Martin, and everyone have worked so hard to build it!"

Both men silently stared at the somber, unadorned hallway.

Frank broke the silence to make an announcement. "B.J., this may not be the best time to mention it, but I've decided to run for the legislature. Maybe I can do something good—bring honest, straight thinking to Des Moines."

B.J.'s fierce eyes widened revealing his fighting spirit. "Frank Elliott for Congress! You'll have my support every inch of the way!"

"I really mean it," Frank insisted. "I'll tell you one more thing too. I won't rest until I pass a chiropractic law in the State of Iowa."

"Frank, you have the vision, and that's why I called you back from California to help me run the school," B.J. continued. "But first, we need to clean up Loban's dirty little mess. Have they called you in to testify yet?"

He answered in a quieter voice, "No, but they said to be here at three-thirty, and I've been sitting here for an hour waiting."

Frank looked intently into B.J.'s eyes as though they contained the secrets of the universe. The Chief's eyes revealed no secrets, but they seemed to transform in a flash. The striking blue spheres encircling the intense dark pupils were surrounded by a softer green halo yielding a gentler twinkle.

B.J.'s whole face became cheerful as he spoke again. "Frank, don't worry, just stick to the truth like glue. Darkness can't cover daylight. We'll keep on and get through this until we ignite a spark that will overcome, transforming Joy's rivulet of urine into an ocean of change. The Palmer School will not end now, not here, and not with me. It's going to go on to improve the lives of millions!"

Chapter Twenty-Four

HARVEY

"Little deeds are like little seeds—
they grow to flowers and weeds."

–D.D. Palmer

Still a slave state when he was born in 1857, Missouri was Harvey's birthplace. He was nine years old when his mother, Esie Lillard gave him a folded, worn copy of Lincoln's Emancipation Proclamation as a reading assignment. He never forgot her tone and the reverence and determination in her face at that moment.

Esie's friend, Juanna Smith, who passed it on with a whisper in her voice and fear in her eyes, said to Harvey's mother, "Esie, this an' the Bible's what he needs to read."

It was less than two years since the war had ended. Juanna had summoned the courage to travel with her Davenport neighbors, Abe and Vera Jackson, downriver to Canton, Missouri, about twenty-five miles north of Hannibal. Fear had become a prominent part of her life, her first response to everything that happened.

When the Jacksons encouraged her to go on the trip with them, her first thought was of the recent *Sultana* disaster near Memphis. There was still a lot of mystery and rumors about it, but there was no mystery about the misery inflicted. It festered in the country's consciousness, especially in river towns like Davenport. Lots of speeches were given, articles written, and countless conversations buzzed in taverns and around fireplaces in folks' homes.

The two-year-old steamboat was licensed to carry 376 persons, including the crew of 85. But on that fateful day in April 1865, it was jammed with over 2,000 when her boiler exploded. The *Sultana*, a typical side-wheeler with classic twin smokestacks, looked like she could have been plucked from a Mark Twain novel. Yet, rather than simply depicting life on the river, it became the backdrop for a tale of horror. More than 1,500 people died, and adding a bitter irony, about 1,100 of those were Union soldiers returning home after surviving the hells of war. The majority had boarded the ship in Vicksburg, where many former prisoners of war were brought for the repatriation process.

Many of the liberated prisoners were ill or wounded, having survived a stint at Camp Sumter, which became known as the infamous Andersonville Prison. Despite their disheveled condition, they were in high spirits because they were going home. Only a few years earlier, the young soldiers leaving their homes, singing and marching through small mid-western towns, had been a rousing spectacle. Complete with parades and brass bands, proud mayors gave speeches and spoke of glory and patriotism. Now they might sing songs, but of a much different type. No longer emblazoned with visions of grandeur, the ugly truth of war had caught up with them. The insanity of it all could no longer be hidden from them by any drumbeat, nor could the silver-tongued deceptions of politicians ever again incite them to mindless patriotism. They had seen war's horror and degradation, and they knew its lunacy first hand. In a cruel twist of fate, these survivors thought they were lucky. An hour before the explosion, the ship's Captain J.C. Mason paid homage to them: "These veterans looked the devil in the eye, spat at him, and now they're going home."

The carnage on board the *Sultana*, not unfamiliar in those times, boosted the United States to the dubious distinction of having hosted the worst maritime disaster in recorded history. Soon rumors began to circulate suggesting the explosion was an act of sabotage by frustrated Confederates seeking revenge. However, the record showed the *Sultana* had trouble with leaking boilers and had repairs twice during the week preceding the explosion. There was a certain amount of anxiety to get underway in Vicksburg, and perhaps the repairs were made too hastily. Two days later, more repairs were made on leaky boilers in Memphis. Sabotage could not be ruled out, but either way, it was a dark day in a divided country—albeit a day sandwiched between many dark days.

General Lee had already surrendered, and the day after General Johnston's surrender, the disaster took place amid anticipation of peace. It was ten days after Lincoln's assassination. And his murderer, John Wilkes Booth, had been caught and killed the day before the *Sultana* exploded. Bleak times of conflict in the country were well-reflected by these events in the murky waters of the Mississippi.

Juanna was determined to overcome her fear, so she agreed to go, not unhappily, because it had been so long since seeing her old friend Esie. It was to be her first riverboat excursion. She had heard much about the elegant staterooms with etched-glass windows, beautiful carpets, and toilet stands. She looked forward to seeing the gilded saloons and dining rooms with prism-fringed chandeliers, ornate pianos, and colored fanlights, not to mention the bathhouses with hot and cold water. But her illusion of spending a day in a floating palace was quickly shattered. When she and the Jackson's boarded the 330-foot colossus, they were promptly directed to the Bureau.

The Bureau turned out to be a third-story cabin for negro passengers located behind the officer's quarters, aptly named, the Texas. Perched above the Texas and the Bureau was the rectangular Pilothouse.

Steamboats began to have "Bureaus" after the war. These humiliating accommodations marginalized the newfound status of their race. The name Bureau was acquiescent to the new federal agency, the Freedmen's Bureau, whose charge was to manage issues pertaining to the rights of former slaves. Compliance in this manner was more derogatory than affable. Located high on the third floor, the view from the Texas was good on three sides, but behind it, the Bureau only offered an aft view.

Juanna lived in Iowa now. Even before the war, Iowa was a free state, but it was never free from hatred and injustice. The war was over, and Juanna's people down South now lived without masters. But that never extracted the fear forever imposed deeply in Juanna's being. When she was a little girl in South Carolina, she saw Uncle Willy Smith lynched for "attacking" a white woman. Everyone knew he was innocent. She felt the same fear when her mother took her by the hand later that night, and they started their secret trip north. Her whole body never stopped shaking for nearly a month while they traveled from one stop to another—always hiding, always afraid. She vividly remembered the moment when the shaking stopped too. It was their last stop the night before coming to Davenport. The small village got its name in honor of an Ohio church, the West Branch Friends Meeting.

Mostly Quaker, West Branch, Iowa, was on the prairie about fifty miles west of the Mississippi. There she found peace in the home of Eli Hoover and his quiet Quaker family. Eli had moved his family west from Ohio to a small farm on the edge of the settlement in 1854. His son, Jesse, who apprenticed with a blacksmith, was beginning to build his trade there in the tiny town. Jesse was courting Hilda Minthorn, a teacher from Ontario, Canada, whose Quaker family had also found their way to the peaceful Iowa village.

The Quakers seemed strange to Juanna. They didn't fight in the war, but not because of fear. They said the war was wrong but slavery was wrong too. The Hoovers and Hilda sat with Juanna Smith and her mother in front of a warm fireplace where they explained their beliefs. Jesse said, "Instead of violence, there're always better ways to solve problems."

That was the moment when the shaking finally stopped. Juana suddenly felt safe. It was strange; she knew the Quakers wouldn't get their guns to protect her, but she felt profoundly safe there anyway. It was a kind of safety guns and violence could never afford. By their activist role in the Underground Railroad, this Quaker family wordlessly set an example, revealing their commitment and leadership.

It was a blessing when the shaking stopped in West Branch, but the veiled fear would live with her forever. The uncontrollable fear returned to her in its most overt form, the shaking, from time to time. Once, she and her mother traveled way into Illinois to pay their respects to Abraham Lincoln. She would never forget her mother's words, "Horrific murder, so senseless!" When Juanna glimpsed the president's body, the shaking began again. She thought, *If hateful devils can murder this kindly leader, they could hurt anyone, anywhere.* The shaking only lasted a couple of hours, but it didn't feel any different than seeing what they did to Uncle Willy or secretly traveling the Underground Railroad.

Boarding the steamboat and being directed to the Bureau rekindled the feelings Juanna had during those days with her mother. It hadn't been long since Uncle Willy's lynching, and she remembered that she was elated when her mother told her they were leaving the South Carolina plantation that quiet night in 1859. Abolitionists had already worked secretly with safe houses and furtive stations for years. Yet Juanna was puzzled when they slipped away because it seemed like they were going in the wrong direction. Her mother said they were going to find freedom in the farmlands of the prairie, so Juanna expected to journey toward the Smokey Mountains and then Midwest, but instead, they boarded a small boat and went south toward Savannah.

Before dawn, she was shaken awake by her mother and ushered quickly from the docks to a construction site. After a breakfast of bread and molasses, Juanna's mother told her to rest while she started to work making bricks. To Juanna, it seemed foolish to spend precious time doing anything but running during their escape. But there they were, mother making bricks, a skill she had learned on the plantation. Juanna wondered where all the urgency had gone. It still felt a lot like working for the master.

Many of the out-buildings on the plantation were made of brick, because the plentiful red clay was of a near-perfect consistency for forming into construction quality brick. Soon Juanna was well-rested and began to explore the building site. She learned that colored folks actually owned this place.

They were building a church, but not just a church, *their* church. The congregation had existed since Revolutionary War days when British occupying troops allowed a freed slave to build his church just outside town. It was then called the First Colored Church. Years later, in 1822, it changed its name to the First Colored Baptist Church, and now, in 1859, they were working together with the parishioners of the Second Colored Baptist Church to build this most special place of worship, the First African Baptist Church.

As Juanna wandered around inside the structure, a man with a deep voice spoke to her. At first, she was frightened but soon determined that he was kindly and meant her no harm. "What's your name?" he asked. "I'm Pastor Campbell." She stared, wide-eyed, while he spoke. "It's evidence of God's grace that right here, on Franklin Square in Savannah, Georgia, colored people are building this great structure right in front of everyone, even those who hate us."

"I'm Juanna. Mama, an' me, are goin'," was all she said, mustering all the bravery she could find within her.

Pastor Campbell, who took an immediate liking to Juanna, told her the story of the church and its congregations, and even showed her some secret places in the building. The sanctuary floor was cleverly designed like an African tribal symbol. The emblem itself was a camouflage whose function was to provide air holes in the floorboards. Below it was a space where runaways could hide since the church served as a stop on the Underground Railroad.

He walked Juanna over to a small, unfinished room in the back of the site where several ladies were seated, their laps full of fabrics, threads, and notions. The room was light with song, chatter, and laughter, and the ladies quickly invited Juanna into their cluster.

Before lunchtime arrived, Juanna had learned the rudiments of quilting and had already helped to connect several squares.

Juanna's mother joined them for lunch, and Juanna enthusiastically told her all about what she had seen and done that morning. First, she talked about the kindly Pastor Campbell and explained how she had learned the secret significance of quilting. Then Juanna took her mother by the hand, led her to the center of the building, and pointed up. "See the pattern of nine squares in the ceiling? Mama, that's a sign. It stands for the nine-patch quilts that the women are making. Folks are s'posed to look for quilts hangin' in the yard of safe homes on their path to freedom."

Juanna and her mother stayed in the church for nine days, making bricks and sewing quilts. Finally, they left again at night in a small boat, but this time up the Savannah River toward freedom.

A shocking, shrill scream of a steam-powered whistle quickly brought Juanna back to the present, reminding her that she was no longer on the plantation, no longer in Savannah, and no longer in the South. She was a free woman riding on a great steamboat on the upper Mississippi.

After leaving for freedom and arriving in Iowa, Juanna occasionally exchanged letters with her good friend Esie in South Carolina. Her writing skills were minimal, but she got by. Esie and her folks later came north and settled in Missouri. Canton, a busy little river town, being just a day's ride by steamboat, certainly wasn't like going back to the old South again. But Missouri had been a slave state during the war, and that alone was enough to scare Junanna's fear-ridden soul.

Juanna could never just hand her copy of the Emancipation Proclamation over to Esie Lillard as she would any newspaper or a book. The document made her feel empowered and reverent—two values that helped her control the ever-present, albeit repressed, terror. She had folded the paper into quarters and sealed it in an envelope, although no one could know what was inside the envelope. Rather than simply place it in Esie's hand, she stood close and stealthily passed it to her. She could not help but look around to see if someone was watching her, as if they were ready to send her and her mother back to the plantation. Ridiculous, too, because Mama Smith had been gone for some time and the old plantation was burned to the ground by Northern troops—that's what Syrophenia Smith, Uncle Willy's sister-in-law, had written in one of the few letters that Mama Smith used to get.

Later that afternoon, Esie called Harvey to her side, and together they read the document. She was determined to teach Harvey about the harsh realities of life for colored folks. She wanted him to know who he was, but more importantly, she wanted him to know what he could be. Harvey was going to learn to read and a whole lot more.

They pushed through word by word, and Harvey repeatedly protested, "I don't understand this, Mama."

She forced him to continue right to Lincoln's last sentence. *I invoke the considerate judgment of mankind and the gracious favor of Almighty God.* Then Harvey asked, "Why ain't we on this list?"

"What do you mean, son?" Esie asked.

"Why ain't Missouri on the list?" he persisted.

"Oh, it's complicated," she explained. "Missouri kept slavery, but it didn't join the rebellion." She thought about it for a moment and then tried to explain, "Harvey, 'tain't easy for people to change things, even righteous people. This document was a big *first* step toward freedom—unthinkable just a few years before. It wasn't easy for Mr. Lincoln to do it either, so he wrote it only about the states in rebellion against the country. Missouri didn't get free until we had the Proclamation of Freedom done here after the war."

"I still don't understand," was all Harvey said.

"Son, the entire business of slavery was of the devil, and the devil never gives up easily. That's why the whole country's Constitution was changed after the war. It's called the Thirteenth Amendment." She turned the paper over and said, "Now read this to me."

Harvey began to read the short handwritten statement on the back:

"'*Neither slavery nor involuntary servitude, except as a punishment for crime whereof the party shall have been duly convicted, shall exist within the United States, or any place subject to their jurisdiction.'*"

"*There's an extra lesson in this one for all of us, including the white folks.*"

She watched for his reaction, then seeing only confusion, she added, "It warns us not to get convicted of a crime because the punishment is slavery, all over again!"

He reassured her, "I won't never, Mama!"

Harvey knew the best and worst of both worlds. From his family, especially Mama, he learned warmth, love, and caring on the deepest human level. However, having a white grandfather had left him with lighter skin, straighter hair, and a too-narrow nose that announced to the world that he wasn't pure anything. Mama knew that his mixed appearance would be a peculiar cross to bear, so she was determined that Harvey would learn to read and write and that he would be taught the importance of learning itself.

Harvey's father, Solomon Lillard, was the bastard child of the English nobleman Sir Benjamin Lillard. Solomon never knew his father because their masters in Virginia split up the family when they sold his mother Creola and her family to a plantation owner from South Carolina.

Sir Benjamin did nothing to provide for his son, Solomon, the product of a long-term relationship with Creola, one of his slaves. The affair came to an end when Creola gave birth to Solomon. Until that time, Lady Lillard had only had suspicions, about which she chose to look the other way. But she became distraught and obsessed with jealousy when faced with the unavoidable evidence of his dalliance. She made such a stir that it forced Sir Benjamin's hand to take steps to have Creola and her entire family removed. In a pathetic act of defiance, Sir Benjamin arranged for Solomon to keep the good name Lillard.

Fair-skinned Solomon grew up in South Carolina, where he worked the fields on a plantation. He and his mother arrived there soon after having been sold when he was a baby, so the plantation was the only home he ever knew. His mother told him that he had an older brother and a sister. Unfortunately, both were lost to them forever when the family got split up by Sir Benjamin's brutally selling them to different owners.

Solomon fell in love with Esie the moment he laid eyes on her. They both remembered and often reminisced about that mid-July afternoon. Standing in the hot, humid vegetable garden with sweat dripping off her, Esie noticed Solomon walking with a bushel basket. It was loaded with produce destined for the summer kitchen, a detached building only a few steps behind the big manor house. Muggy summer days in South Carolina's low country made a summer kitchen an absolute necessity to keep the heat produced by the large ovens and stove out of the manor house. She had seen him before, but this was the first time he seemed to notice her, and there was magic when their eyes locked on to each other.

There were more than a hundred enslaved people at Beaufort Manor, and Solomon and Esie had never spoken before. Their first words came out clumsily, two nervous teenagers wanting but not knowing exactly how to strike up a conversation. Finally, Solomon placed the basket on the ground next to Esie and said, "I don't know why so many of us folks have come and gone lately. The masters think nothing of splitting up families."

Esie looked around before answering, "JayRon, a strong man my same age, and his eleven-year-old sister, Jayde, were both sold last month. They disappeared from Beaufort Manor about a week apart, and their mama's still here with a broken heart.'

Solomon said, "My mother told me that we'd already been sold from the upstate of South Carolina three times before ending up here. She said that it made her less desirable to keep 'cause I was so tiny back then."

"Well, you ain't so tiny now," she said with a glint in her eye and a coy smile making him gasp, and his heart skipped a beat.

When Solomon finally caught his breath, he answered, "The whims of the master make it difficult to keep up with who's who. Now tell me you're gonna stay put, 'cause I hope to see you around."

"I might not have much say in the matter, but if anyone asks me, I'll tell 'em that I'd just as soon stay right here," Esie said.

Unbounded love belonged not only to privileged masters. Whether prosperous or wretched, love was impartial to one's station in life. Slaves fell in love and felt love, perhaps even more deeply than the well-heeled master in his opulent mansion. Neither the indignity of their plight nor the pain of the whip could take their freedom to love or be loved. If love was different for the enslaved people, then perhaps their close, frequent acquaintance with suffering allowed them to appreciate and be sensitive to life's most profound meaning. No doubt it drove some to become hardened to the world too. However, one thing was for sure: Esie and Solomon couldn't keep their eyes off each other from that day forward. They married in 1856 and were blessed with a son less than a year later. They named him Harvey.

Colored folk gave Harvey a cautious eye because of how he looked. His skin was of a distinctly lighter tone than his mother's, and while his facial features were African, they were subtle owing to Grandfather Benjamin's contribution to his lineage. He grew up being called "boy" along with various deleterious labels by whites.

It seems like I've spent my whole life trying to prove myself to somebody. It makes me weary sometimes, thought Harvey. But when those times came, he tried to think of Mama, her values, and her high expectations of him. *Bless her for insisting that I become educated. I'd never have amounted to much without her.*

As a child, he often wondered about the different worlds of light- and dark-skinned peoples. At age twelve, he asked his mother a profound question. "Mother, what do white folks feel?" He didn't have the eloquence or finesse to articulate the question more clearly. Since life seemed so unfair, he wanted to understand why; and perhaps by knowing whether white people, living without the pain, hardship, deprivations, and many other adversities of colored folks, understood what it felt like to be colored. "Do you suppose they don't value living in peace with dignity the way colored folks do?'

She replied, "I don't know what you mean for sure, but let me tell you that most of them don't have any idea what life is like for us. And make no mistake about it, most of 'em don't care anyway."

He pursued the idea, "Mama, why don't they know that we want a good life too?"

Esie gave a thoughtful reply, "Our families got torn apart by hate and brutality. But the more they slash at the heart and soul of us, the stronger our substance gets. When a church is burned, we feel loss, and people get hurt. But our faith gets stronger, not weaker. When brothers and sisters are beaten, raped, robbed, and killed, those of us who survive grow stronger. Baby, it's like an endless circle. When they do their worst to us, it brings out our fierce love for life. We rise up from the ashes, and it mocks 'em because their burning hatred nourished that love."

"But why is it like that, Mama?" he asked.

"Harvey, no one breathing can answer that question," Esie answered. "But you can take strength in knowing that our people always rise above."

The year was now 1895, and Harvey, a grown man, lived in Iowa. He continued to ponder the same injustices he asked his mother about all those years ago. Since then, finding precious few earthly answers, Harvey had relied upon his strong faith in God in their absence. He was also learning to be patient, mainly by making his share of impulsive mistakes as a youngster. Later, Harvey came to Davenport, where jobs were easier to find. He found work as a floor sweeper and gradually developed his own janitorial business. It was a day full of anticipation for Harvey, who was at the station, awaiting the arrival of Uncle Jim.

Mama's brother Jim had always been kind to Harvey. Jim's affable personality made him well-liked by everyone who knew him. He wasn't really Mama's brother, but they had adopted one another as children back at Beaufort Manor. She saw little of him after going to live in Missouri, where life wasn't near as hard as back in South Carolina. Uncle Jim stayed on the farm down South, but he managed to come to visit in Canton at the Lillard home for a month or so every couple of years. Harvey remembered those times fondly. Uncle Jim had a distinctive laugh, and he loved to tell jokes and spend time with Harvey. So it deeply troubled Harvey when Uncle Jim didn't step off the afternoon train.

Uncle Jim hadn't been to see the Lillards in recent years. His last trip north had been for Esie's funeral, and now that Mama was gone, he just didn't seem to get back for those precious visits anymore. Uncle Jim would send short letters occasionally, and in the last one, he wrote that he had moved farther south into Florida, where he was making a living working in the booming citrus business.

Harvey knew that traveling to Iowa wasn't easy for Jim, so he was excited when he got the letter saying that Uncle Jim was taking the train to Davenport. The letter, which arrived on September 16, read, *Nephew, it's been too long, I'm coming for a visit. It'll be the afternoon arrival on September 17th. Please meet me at the station.*

Harvey got the extra bed ready at home and even arranged to have a few hours off so he could meet Jim at the Rock Island Station. That was yesterday, and now feeling very uneasy, Harvey took off more time today and waited, hoping to see Uncle Jim step off the train at 4:00 p.m. He mused about what their visit would be like. *Will Uncle Jim still like to go fishing? Will he have a lot of new jokes to share? Will his hair be all gray?*

Four o'clock came and went again, but Uncle Jim's warm, familiar face was not among the passengers who disembarked. Harvey's concern was growing deeper now. He didn't know what might have gone wrong, nor did he know how long it would be before he might hear anything from Uncle Jim. He knew that he couldn't keep finding ways to explain to Mr. Putnam that he must excuse himself to go to the station every day. Even though Harvey ran his own janitorial service, his assistants, Tamika and Demetrius, were working out on the farm this week, getting tomatoes and a few delicate vegetables in before preparing to harvest the corn in just a couple of weeks.

Cleaning in the Ryan Block was the mainstay of Harvey's business. The four-story brick structure was one of the biggest buildings in town. Located at the corner of Second and Brady Street, it was the busiest spot in town. The bottom floor was occupied by St. Onge's Big Busy Store, a large dry goods and department store. Mr. St. Onge assigned cleaning and general maintenance to his own employees, leaving the upper three stories to Harvey and his assistants. Those three floors were mostly offices and administrative workplaces, leaving plenty for Harvey to keep after.

Mr. Putnam managed his building fastidiously, and he would not tolerate excuses, even from Mr. Lillard. Harvey's crew set three whole days aside every month, except in winter, just to keep up with the windows and trim connected to the brick exterior. Harvey had a strong work ethic too, and he was confident that his crew always left the building spotless. But one thing was certain: Harvey could ill afford to displease Mr. Putnam.

Resolving to head back to work, Harvey turned toward the door of the depot. He noticed a newspaper folded in half on the bench closest to the exit. Harvey absentmindedly picked up the litter and scanned the front page rather than just tossing it in the trash. He read the big, bold letters at the top, *The Democrat,* and below that in smaller type, *Today's Date: September 18, 1895.* His eyes flashed over the middle of the page, stopping to read a short column announcing that Booker T. Washington was scheduled to give a speech that day opening the Cotton States and International Exposition in Atlanta, Georgia. Then at the bottom, on the right-hand side of the page, his gaze caught the word *Florida.* A sickening chill ran down Harvey's spine even before he forced himself to read the terse copy.

The dateline said *Jacksonville, Florida.* Nearly frozen with dread, Harvey read and then reread, *Jim Brady, a negro, was shot in West Palm Beach last evening by deputy Torbett while he was trying to escape.* There wasn't any detail, no explanation, nothing at all. It was as if the paper was saying, *That's the whole story.* Why burden the reader with more specifics? It was common knowledge that negroes were often incarcerated, especially in the South, and they must be dealt with if they tried to "escape." Nothing more needed to be said.

Harvey's anger, frustration, and pain welled up inside. Yet despite his ire, feelings of helplessness, and despair, Harvey knew he must finish the day's work before he could even think about what to do. Fighting off the rage and waves of strangely empty nausea, he left the station and returned to the corner of Second and Brady.

A sudden flash caught the corner of Harvey's right eye. The glint of sunlight reflecting off the head of a rivet startled him, and he knew that he better move fast. Harvey quickly darted to his left as the object came into full view. He felt a puff of air hit his right cheek as an iron horseshoe flashed swiftly by his face. The hoof barely missed him by less than an inch! Angry fists shook at Harvey while the animal flounced, gradually calming down until all four of the horse's hoofs were down on the pavement. The rider, an out-of-towner, didn't know he needed to watch out for Harvey as local folks did.

Locals were well aware of Harvey, who occasionally got so wrapped up in thoughts that he sometimes just walked right out in front of the noisy horses and wagons. Traffic was dangerous for everyone, but it could be treacherous for Harvey, a deaf man. "I'm so sorry, sir!" Harvey apologized and wisely turned back toward the Ryan Block while the driver hurled a string of profanities spiced with racial slurs after him. The stranger never knew how wasted they were on Harvey's deaf ears.

Several hours of cleaning lay ahead of Harvey before he could call it a day. Only then could he take time to think and try to make sense of it all. He got to work and made up for the lost time by moving his broom quickly but deftly. When he finished the third-floor offices and hallway, he climbed the stairs to the fourth floor to repeat the ritual.

Since it was late, he proceeded past the main entrance, choosing to sweep the smaller private office at the end of the hall first. The door's upper half was of smoked glass with stylishly painted, large black letters *Dr. Palmer, Private Office.* He gave the glass panel a brisk knock to announce his entry more than seek permission. The door shook, the glass shuddered, and then Harvey turned the knob and entered. Expecting an empty room, he worked his broom, proceeding through the doorway as usual without even looking up. Then there came a vibration that he felt much more than heard. A booming voice shouted, "Good evening, Harvey!"

Chapter Twenty-Five

HARVEY AND D.D.

Davenport, Iowa, September 18, 1895

It had been one of those sultry mid-September days in which the heat of summer hadn't yet yielded to the lower temperature and humidity that the calendar promised would soon arrive.

Dr. Palmer, shuffling some papers at his desk, had already lit an oil lamp as the daylight was fading. Realizing he wasn't alone, Harvey contritely said, "Oh, I'm sorry, Dr. D.D. I didn't know you were still here."

Dr. Palmer, now sidetracked, was in just the right mood for a diversion, and the two began to chat. Being deaf and preoccupied, Harvey was an unlikely candidate for a tête-à-tête. Nevertheless, Harvey was always polite, especially to one of Mr. Putnam's best customers.

Dr. Palmer was nearly shouting as Harvey strained to listen, his eyes fixed on Dr. D.D.'s lips. "How long have you been deaf, Harvey?"

Harvey looked up at the ceiling, quickly doing some math in his head before answering. "Over seventeen years, Dr. D.D.," he responded with absolute clarity of speech, suggesting to D.D. that this man grew up able to hear.

"How come you're deaf, Harvey? Just what happened?" Dr. Palmer inquired.

A thoughtful Harvey reflected, momentarily surprised by the question. Then he answered, "I don't know why, but I know exactly how it happened. One day, all those years ago, I bent over with a scrub brush, struggling and reaching down into a corner. Then, while cleaning the baseboard above the floor, I felt something snap in my neck. It was a queer sensation, and nearly all sounds were muffled by the time I turned around and got up. It only got worse. Now I don't hear folks talking to me, a trolley rumbling, or even a passing horse or racket of a wagon!"

Numerous Davenport residents could attest to his situation, as Harvey was a known traffic hazard. "I can't use one of those inventions—not loud enough," Harvey added, pointing at the candlestick-shaped telephone across the room.

Its black vertical cylinder topped with a pivoting mouthpiece rose out of a round molded base. Below the microphone, about one-third of the way down the cylinder, a switch arm extended horizontally from it with a rounded fork-shaped hook to hang the receiver on when not in use.

D.D. Palmer was the first Davenport doctor to have a telephone right in his office. Although it represented the leading-edge of progress, it wasn't used often enough to deserve a seat of honor next to his blotter, quill, journal, books, and typewriter.

Harvey's story piqued Dr. Palmer's interest, and he asked, "Harvey, would you like me to take a look at your neck?"

Harvey wasn't apprehensive. He knew that Dr. D.D. Palmer was an eccentric man, but he also knew that Dr. Palmer had the busiest practice in town. People flocked to him from all over for his special kind of treatment. Harvey reasoned, *I've seen so many doctors about my hearing, and none of them could help—I guess I don't have anything to lose. If Dr. Palmer has helped so many people, then maybe ...* Harvey was tired, physically and emotionally, so he simply ended the deliberation with a smile and an affirmative nod.

"Have a seat, Harvey," Dr. Palmer said, waving his hand over a stool. After the man was seated, the doctor embarked on a robust probing, touching gently but deeply along Harvey's neck with strong, perceptive fingertips. As he scanned Harvey's neck, something felt odd, and he kept returning to one place near the top of his neck, just slightly below Harvey's head and to the left side. Finally, he paused, pressed very lightly, took his fingers away, and then came back as though something at that one spot was calling to him.

It wasn't supple like other parts of Harvey's neck. It felt thick, chunky, and full, causing the healer to think, *Something is just not right there.* He also noticed that the small muscles attaching to the right side of that vertebra were pulling hard in a sustained tug toward Harvey's skull. Keeping his volume well above normal, with his face close to the man's ear, Dr. Palmer barked, "Harvey, you've got a bump there! Does it hurt when I touch it?" he asked while deliberately probing the spot again.

Harvey shrank away from the doctor's finger, hesitated, and nodded. "I guess I just never paid it any attention before."

Then Dr. Palmer boomed, "Give me a minute, Harvey. We've got to figure this thing out." He patted Harvey's shoulder like one might to bring reassurance and stepped to the secretary desk. He picked up a donut-shaped bone, sat down, and stared at it intensely while twirling and turning it about with his fingers. Harvey felt strangely abandoned. After a couple of minutes, Harvey shrugged and pivoted around on the stool, preparing to get up and return to work. Dr. Palmer noticed the movement and held up his hand, waving it downward while hollering, "Please, Harvey, just sit tight a minute."

Harvey shrugged again and waited.

After flipping through his journal and reviewing several pages of his hand-written notes, D.D. pondered some more and reached for a thick book. He scrutinized a page of anatomy drawings showing the details of neck vertebrae. Glancing from the page and then up at Harvey, he envisioned the structure as if he could see inside the man's neck. Restraining his excitement, he hastily scribbled in his journal. *I've finally seen the missing link!*

With his heart pounding like a fortune hunter about to open a treasure chest, he noticed a cool wetness, sticking his shirt to him. *I'm breaking out in a cold sweat!*

As one of Iowa's most successful healers, Dr. Palmer already knew that what he did was real, though he could barely come to terms with the non-material part of it himself. What he did could not be measured, poured into a jar, or sold as an elixir. Observers could not see, feel, taste, weigh, or smell it. Patients couldn't either. They just got better. So it never surprised him when other doctors in town failed to grasp that magnetic healing was responsible for cures where their ordinary methods had failed. He even felt that some measure of his exceptional success was attributable to the fact that his method did not cause harm—a virtue that was lacking in the other doctors' practices.

Thinking and acting quickly, he concluded, *It doesn't matter whether or not my method is misunderstood. How could others comprehend what I am still coming to grips with?* Those thoughts evoked a vivid recollection in D.D. Palmer's mind. It was as though he was there again, on the first day he entered the impressive infirmary of Paul Caster years ago, and it brought back the same feeling that he had had then.

Even more impressive than Caster's facility, a modern four-story brick building, were the results of his practice. Throngs flocked from far and wide to receive treatment from Caster.

Staring at his journal in deep contemplation, D.D. seemed nearly oblivious to Harvey, who fidgeted around again and sighed deeply to keep his presence felt. Finally, D.D. looked up inquisitively, and when his eyes met Harvey's, he realized that his self-absorbed behavior was becoming rude. He said to Harvey, "I'm sorry, but I think we have found something important. Please have a comfortable chair. I just need another minute."

Gesturing toward an armchair on the other side of the room, D.D. rose and picked up a small box wrapped in brown paper, decoratively tied with a fluffy-looking string. He walked over to the chair and gave it a robust pat on the seat, and when Harvey followed, D.D. handed him the package. "The best cookies in Davenport are in that box. Please relax a minute, try some, and tell me if you agree." Harvey shrugged his shoulders, smiled, and remembered that he had missed lunch. The baked goods were too appealing to pass up. He sat down and pulled at the string, and the knot bounced open.

D.D. smiled back, returned to his journal and quickly found the section describing that first visit to Caster:

- Will sought relief from multiple symptoms led by lethargy, vague pains, weakness, and a nagging digestive disturbance.
- It was getting worse, and the doctor's remedies seemed to be making him more and more miserable.
- The Kelloggs had heard of Dr. Caster through Madam Drury and some of their Spiritualist friends.
- Paul Caster was a prominent disciple of the famous Franz Anton Mesmer.

Gazing at his desk blotter, D.D. reflected on those entries. *The Spiritualists hold a vitalistic philosophy and appreciate immaterial things. It's also how they conduct their whole lives.*

Even before arriving in Ottumwa, he knew that magnetic healers were a breed apart. In the context of the times, neither magnetic healers nor medical practitioners were all that highly regarded. However, Mesmer had advanced magnetic healing in Europe, and his work gave birth to the science of hypnosis. Having caught the imagination of both the popular and scientific worlds, the word *mesmerize* was coined in his honor. Caster's natural ability, hard work, and charismatic personality soon brought him fame as the nation's leading magnetic practitioner.

D.D. Palmer was impressed that Caster got great results without resorting to surgery, toxic drugs, or brutal bleedings—all commonly practiced by the medical doctors.

Palmer, always a stranger to self-doubt, had decided then and there to study magnetic healing and learn the art directly from the master, Paul Caster. Now, nine years after learning and practicing the art, and despite seeing many dramatic results, to D.D. Palmer, something important was still missing. His thoughts raced. *My training delivered little on methodology and much more on why we do this. I had to develop most of my technique on my own. Although I felt mildly short-changed at the time, in retrospect, it worked out because necessity opened the door to innovation.*

Other magnetic practitioners imparted their "magnetism" to the entire body, but D.D. explored improving efficiency through more precision. He called his technique *specific* and delivered his energy right to and only at the sick parts. His unique style involved placing his hands above and below the ailing body part and then coursing his magnetism between his hands to elicit a change in the sick tissues. It improved the results and led him to the forefront of his art, which got him noticed in his community. Instead of calling him Mr. Palmer, or by his first name, out of respect and admiration, people soon referred to him as *Dr. D.D.*

But D.D. Palmer could not be satisfied with being the best magnetic healer around. Magnetic healing helped people but always left D.D. with an elusive, gnawing question, and he was troubled that everyone else was content to let it go unasked. He was thirsting to understand why some people get sick while others, living in the same conditions, eating the same food, and leading seemingly parallel lives, do not. Why does one family member get the flu and another not? Why should one be in bed for twelve hours and another for many days? *Why did our baby die when the rest of the family lived?* How could the whole family be okay when his beloved Louvenia suddenly, mysteriously, and senselessly succumbed to a fatal illness?

He had been reading, experimenting, taking notes, and studying these confounding issues for years. He turned the page in his journal and quickly slid his finger down that page's entries:

It can be deduced that the difference comes from within the individual.

- *Davenport's medical doctors superstitiously let bad blood.*
- *Physicians try to drive sicknesses out of their patients chemically.*
- *They play the role of warriors, jousting with their elusive enemy, disease. A few battles are won, yet they always lose the war.*
- *Why doesn't anyone study the cause of health?*

D.D. studied anatomy voraciously. He became fascinated with the body's nerve pathways as he tried to understand the cause of health. D.D. considered it to the point of obsession. Often he would wake up in the middle night when a piece of the puzzle would come to him.

One night he had awoken with such a realization. Like any leap in awareness, it had been right in front of him all along. He awoke from a dialogue with Dr. Jim Atkinson, former Davenport physician, whose ignominious reputation did not preclude him from showing up in Daniel's imagination. Daniel liked to sleep on it when stymied by a problem or deeply troubled, hoping that the answer might come to him. Atkinson never gave answers to questions, but his inimitable style was to draw out or provoke solutions. Rather than a homily, Atkinson would pose questions that seemed to be intended to chafe Daniel. The latest annoying but probing query was, "If you look at a problem only from where you are, then why expect to see what is going on where you are not?" The dream had ended, and a new discernment began.

It was well before dawn, and the darkness helped Daniel think. *I've practiced magnetic healing for nine years. It hasn't brought many answers, but it's opened the door to new questions. True, I've been honored to help many people, but the magnetic energy work is limited and not always reliable.* Many results were achieved by sparing the patient from their doctors' harsh drugs and surgical treatments. This thought had always troubled Daniel because he knew that his work did more than just save patients from their physicians. And he didn't believe that one should build a life based on the shortcomings of others.

He wrote the next series of journal entries early that morning:
- *We must find the key to what's missing.*
- *Magnetism is isolated to only a part of the person.*
- *It gets outstanding results in part because other doctors are oblivious to and fail to address the immaterial side of patients.*
- *But magnetism is just as one-sided as what the medical people do!*
- *It reaches only the immaterial side of our patient's needs.*

While Daniel reviewed, he was distracted by a nagging awareness of the present and called out, "Harvey, we're getting somewhere. Have another cookie."

Anxious about Harvey across the room, he sprinted back through those thoughts of the wee hours before dawn:
- *Magnetism is not physical, at least not the meaningful part. Neither are words.*

As he reviewed the notes, he remembered that he had been trying to sharpen his thinking by creating a model:
- *The physical parts, the mouth and throat, make words, but the immaterial ideas conveyed are what matters.*
- *Accordingly, that which has no substance is of greater importance.*
- *Thinking in words makes this challenging.*
- *Finding words that adequately describe the immaterial makes it more elusive.*
- *Words like "mystical" make it sound unreal, magical, or religious. Yet magnetism is real, not paranormal, nor magic, and it isn't religious at all.*
- *Let's refer to it as the immaterial side of existence.*

Several more short statements in the journal notes shaped a model to explore the idea:

- *Immaterial does not imply mysticism or religion any more than the word "love" does.*
- *Love is genuine in this universe, but it certainly does not exist as a material substance.*
- *People can experience love, but they can't touch it with a finger, weigh it, measure its temperature, length, or depth.*
- *One can love a physical object, but the love itself remains immaterial.*
- *Love as a model expresses the thought. Still, it does not account for the union of this immaterial idea of love with the material person feeling and expressing love.*
- *Experience leads us to understand that the human being is a combination of the physical matter and the immaterial portion of life.*
- *This immaterial essence requires the physical body to be expressed.*
- *Where then does the body gain the ability to connect the material with the immaterial? How does it do that?*

Recollecting how that question helped him come up with an apt model, he reviewed the next entry with greater anticipation because it provided an essential, profound part of the model:

- *Begin by holding a finger out in front of your face in this moonlit room.*
- *Now think about moving your finger, but don't do it.*
- *Consider how still your finger appears. Yet physical science assures us that its molecules are consistently in motion.*
- *Think again about moving your finger, but this time, actually wiggle it.*
- *This model demonstrates that we can combine an immaterial idea, the thought of movement, with a material action, the finger's movement.*

- *If conscious thought can cause the union of an immaterial idea with the matter, must not the same thing be going on unconsciously, regulating all of the complex internal functions?*
- *Truly, this joining has to be one of the key characteristics of life itself.*
- *The dim quiet of a bedroom can reveal and enlighten.*

Daniel believed that he did some of his best thinking during these sleepless hours of darkness. He also had a habit of writing in his journal every day because he had learned that the act of writing clarified thinking, sometimes immediately and sometimes later when he reviewed previous thoughts. Given the light of a new day, the mistakes of yesterday's ideas often showed up.

In those restless hours, he'd mull an idea over and over. Although productive, he knew that he needed the lost sleep. Eventually, he figured out that if he kept some writing materials next to his bed, he could jot down a few key ideas in the moonlight so that they would not be lost. Once that was done, it often gave him enough peace of mind that he could return to sleep, assured that those gems were not lost. Finally, he summarized the last page in that section of the journal and underscored it:

- *The key is connecting the material with the immaterial. Thus, health comes from within.*

In that sentence, Daniel felt confident that the idea was now securely locked in a safe place, and he could now go back to his welcome rest.

But no additional rest would come to Daniel that night. Instead, his mind raced continuously until dawn. *The key is connecting the material with the immaterial. It's so apparent that I feel stupid for not seeing it sooner. But how do we utilize the conclusion that health comes from within? The reasoning that led me to it was sound, but why am I so sure?*

Lying there in the dark, Daniel repeated the key phrase to himself over and over again, whispering, "The key is in connecting the material with the immaterial; therefore, health comes from within. I'm back on the merry-go-round, and it won't let me sleep. The key is connecting the material ..." Finally, no longer whispering, he said it aloud, with a slight modification. "The key is *reconnecting* the material with the immaterial; restoring health from within. The intelligence residing within the body connects the material with the immaterial. It provides the opportunity for expression." Putting the prefix "re" in front of the word "connecting" made the breakthrough, and he could see how it worked.

Sleeplessly tossing and turning in the dark, he realized that something else was bothering him and sat up to write on a new page:

- *Operating on the immaterial side of existence, magnetic practice lacks a consistent and predictable way of relating to the material substance of a person.*
- *The medics, who have such disdain for our successes, work only on the material substance of their patient. They're blind to the vital immaterial essence at the core of every human being.*

The obviousness of the answer was stirring, yet he felt embarrassed that it had taken him so long to notice. He continued writing:

- *As long as a healer only asks one side of a two-sided question, they can only expect to see shadows of the answers.*
- *How did hosts of healers fail to see the chasm between their practices and the needs of their patients?*
- *Moreover, how did I fail to see it too?*

Revolutionary new thoughts were triggered by changing the basic question. Instead of battling sickness, he could now explore what health was and where it came from. He scribbled more notes as thoughts came quickly:

- *Sickness doesn't thrive in the presence of health.*
- *A scattering of light always chases away the darkness.*
- *Sickness isn't an entity at all; the life within is the entity.*

That health comes from within the body itself appeared to be a subtle enough conclusion. But it was startling because the idea was so simple. Asking a new kind of question changed everything. Seeking answers to different questions reminded D.D. of observations and insights gained in early childhood.

Daniel had learned how to hunt for food at age seven out on the Canadian frontier, and that experience provoked his obsession with anatomy. However, what fascinated him most wasn't the predictability of animals' insides but rather the uniqueness of each one's structural makeup.

Many believed that the heart was the core of life and that it vivified all other parts. Hence blood was considered the essence of life. Accordingly, superstition, medicine, and folk tales were rooted in that deeply ingrained belief. Popular stories about vampires and other supernatural legends attributed magical properties to blood. Daniel grew to understand that it wasn't so mysterious. He had seen animals die many times and always felt reverence that his companions either concealed or simply lacked. Quarry lost blood, and the red fluid wasn't supernatural. He had cut them up and found that hearts weren't enchanted. They were pumps.

Intrigued by the mysterious lore attributed to the vital fluid, he decided to look into it after completing his training with Paul. That quickly revealed that the role of blood was a matter of controversy, and the myth about the supremacy of blood in the bodies of humans and animals had deep roots. In 1628 English scientist William Harvey demonstrated that the blood was circulated through the body. For unveiling that information, the scientist was ridiculed, having blasphemed against accepted ancient wisdom. As was taught by Galen more than a thousand years before, the enduring belief was that blood originated in the heart and the liver, then merely consumed by other body parts.

During the Crusades, western scholars were exposed to enlightenment about blood circulation in the published works of philosopher and scientist Ibn al-Nafis. Al-Nafis wrote in defiance of the assertion that the soul originated in the heart, a widespread belief in Europe since Aristotle. Unfortunately, substantiation was not enough to overcome belief. Authorities quickly buried his work in Europe.

When William Harvey rediscovered and documented those principles in 1628, western thought was no more ready to accept new ideas than during Ibn al-Nafis's time. James I, the fatally ill king, had been under the care of Harvey, and his failure to cure the monarch probably didn't do much to enhance Harvey's credibility. Ultimately, the tradition of blood-letting went on unmolested long after Harvey's death.

Two hundred fifty years later, the fact that the heart pumps blood was generally understood, yet a twisted, bizarre belief remained. The popular notion was that the circulating blood possessed some kind of supernatural enchantment. In that setting, Paul's former student, Andrew Still was hawking the practice of osteopathy and catching interest amongst physicians with his method based on the primacy of the blood vascular system. However, in the age of electric lights and telephones, Henry Gray and other anatomists were cataloging anatomical knowledge. Provoking a deeper study of function, the conviction that physiology was controlled by the blood vascular system was making less and less sense. Instead, increasing anatomic and physiologic knowledge suggested that life in animal bodies was regulated intelligently, with the brain coordinating function in the body through a scantily understood network of nerves.

Putting his hands on Harvey Lillard's neck, D.D. Palmer had seen beyond the stifling horizon. A new attitude and perception derived from changed thinking came upon him. He used deductive reasoning. Function depended upon an internal intelligence to coordinate everything. Without full expression of that intelligence, life's processes were vulnerable to all manner of difficulties. He was delving into whether life itself was being choked off within his patient.

The bump on the neck of this humble deaf man had helped to crystalize nagging questions into a leap of awareness. D.D. finally saw *how* the expression of life could be distorted within the body. The epiphany revealed that interference could occur, distorting the flow of life's information.

Now he had a theory about how to release the current. *Perhaps we can free up the flow of information.* Thinking it through to the point of taking action gave him chills and made his hair stand up.

The cold sweat, which now engulfed him, was derived from anticipation and excitement mixed with more than a little anxiety. He was about to try what hadn't been done before. What's more, D.D. Palmer was vulnerable.

He had little respect for the medical doctors in town—and he never tried to hide it, believing that his methods were superior to their ineffectual, frequently harmful, and often superstitious practices. Like his teacher Paul Caster, D.D. enjoyed spotlighting his successes, especially where the medics had failed. He mimicked Caster's hobby of collecting crutches and canes from patients who no longer needed them after magnetic treatments. Caster even made a point of being photographed while sitting amidst the collection for publicity.

D.D. exposed his gruff side by building a collection of no longer needed canes and crutches to testify his successes and as a monument to medical failures. He liked going out of his way to rub their noses in it. But he also knew that his competitors would just love to point the finger of blame if this experiment should injure Harvey. Then a stray thought flashed across his mind at the brink of the experiment. *I wonder if publishing my picture, surrounded by those canes and crutches, might just come back to haunt me.*

He finally composed himself and rose with an air of majesty and conviction on his face. Then, making eye contact with Harvey, who was still seated with the package of cookies in his lap, D.D. boomed loudly, "Would you like me to try to help you?"

Normally Harvey would have been afraid and more cautious. Normally he would have asked for details, taken more time to think it over, or even refused treatment without more to go on. But today was not normal. He was in an unusual frame of mind, owing to the day's confusion, anger, and frustration. He kept thinking about Uncle Jim. *It was surely murder because that man would never have broken the law. If people can do that to Uncle Jim, then the whole world really is mad. And so what if Dr. Palmer is weird? The more peculiar, the better! The less this man is like the rest of the hateful white man's world, the better.* Harvey's grimace was subdued as he raised his eyebrows, rose to his feet, and nodded. "Yes, Dr. D.D."

Waving his hand over a sturdy wooden bench, Dr. Palmer stridently instructed, "Harvey, please lie face down." As Harvey lowered himself, D.D. placed a purple horsehair cushion under the man's chest and a soft, clean folded towel under his head and chin to provide support and cushioning. He gently turned Harvey's head to the left so the side of his neck with the bump was up. Then carefully probing the upper neck, the doctor pressed the bump just enough to outline the prominent vertebra. Using his highly developed sense of touch, he formed a mental picture of the bone and did the same with the vertebra below, confirming that it was misaligned with the adjoining ones.

The moment of truth was upon them. D.D. fastidiously contacted the skin and soft tissues on the edge of Harvey's vertebra using the heel of his left hand, just below his little finger. Holding it securely with gentle pressure, he was prepared to carry out the test. He planned to impel the vertebra back toward its proper position. Then doubts crept in. *How much force? How fast? How deep? What if it's too slow or too fast?* D.D. froze, terrified at the very idea of what he was about to do.

It horrified him to know that he allowed fear to take over. *I've conquered fear many times before. I thought I'd put it away permanently.* Instead, it had whispered itself back into his life and stared him right in the face. His focus was shaken. *That mischievous sprite must have been there all along, just waiting for the right moment. Don't let him win!* he chided himself. *We're on a precipice, requiring all my focus—what better time for it to lurch out and seize control?*

After a few seconds, he decided. *No, I'll not give in!* D.D. pushed all trepidation aside, dispatching it with a triumphant strike, as sure and steady as a samurai warrior's blade. Fear was displaced by a different state of mind. *I've spent nine years learning to work with the immaterial side of life. Mastery is the next step. With Harvey's help I'm going to see if we can successfully reunite the immaterial with the material.* With those thoughts, D.D. entered an unfamiliar mindset. Like a perfect union of the mental and physical realms, it was a dimension of courageousness without recklessness, and a place where hesitation, fear, and faltering no longer exist. Unshakable calm and determination had come over D.D. Palmer, whose head and heart became unmovable, focused totally on what he was there to do.

Then came a light, fast, precise movement of Dr. Palmer's hands. D.D. straightened up and cautiously watched for Harvey's reaction.

Harvey felt a snap, not unlike many years before when he had lost his hearing. Harvey's first thought was, *No, it didn't hurt, but it didn't feel like anything normal either.* He wasn't sure whether he was supposed to do something, so he waited for instructions.

Trepidation aside, D.D. was pleased that while his hands were on Harvey's neck, all went exactly as he had pictured in his mind. *Yes, the movement of my hands was rapid and controlled. However, this is uncharted territory, and nobody knows precisely how it should be done or what it should feel like.* He hadn't even given a moment's thought about what it should feel like. *Harvey's vertebra moved just a little; a bit like the popping of a knuckle on a person's hand, but different in that it moved less; it glided in the intended direction, returning to a position where and how it fits nicely.*

D.D. stood silently, waiting to see Harvey's reaction. That moment seemed to last a very long time. He did not want to suggest anything to Harvey, so he just waited as the seconds ticked in agonizingly slow succession. While he waited, D.D. felt a chill and realized that his shirt was drenched to the point that it felt heavy. It wasn't a particularly hot evening. By mid-September, those oppressively hot Iowa days began to give way to more comfortable, dry air that was particularly refreshing at dusk. No, it wasn't the heat of the day causing his shirt to be wet. *It's my great enemy, fear.* With anxiety getting the best of him, D.D. called out, "Harvey?" as a wave of uncertainty chilled him to his core. There was no response. D.D. put his mind to work on the big picture of what was happening.

He banished the trepidation as thoughts spurted through his lips in a murmur that was surely too quiet for the deaf man to hear. "So this must be what it feels like to make history." The idea brought a smile to his motionless face, although he still didn't know what to expect from Harvey.

Harvey remained still and thought about what had happened. *Was it good or bad when I felt my neck snap?* He apprehensively opened his eyes and gazed at the large clock displayed on a heavy wooden shelf across the room. The timepiece had a warm-looking, darkly stained wooden case, making its bright white face look conspicuous. The relentless, unmistakable movements of the second hand stole attention by quickly jumping once every second. Its skipping contrasted with the minute and hour hands, also constant, albeit imperceptible motion. Staring at the clock, Harvey continued to reflect on what had occurred. *Dr. Palmer's hands were steady, just like the hour hand on that clock.* The hour hand pointed at the five, and Harvey tried but could not see it move. Next, he locked on the longer minute hand, pointing steadfastly at the nine. Although it was moving much faster than the hour hand, its movement was also imperceptible. Then he focused again on that second hand. It moved so quickly that it shook as though an earthquake shook it once every second. It jumped so fast that he could not *see* the movement, just the shaking as the second hand momentarily tried to stop and collect itself for the next spasm announcing the passage of yet another second. The performance played in Harvey's mind as he thought. *Dr. D.D.'s calm, sturdy hands suddenly jumped, but not very much.* He pictured them vibrating like the second hand on the clock, but their next jump never came.

Seconds passed, and no more movements came from Dr. D.D.'s hands. Of course, the doctor's hands were not on his neck anymore.

They had left him with the speed of a lightning bolt, and there he lay, with his head still turned to one side. Not stunned, yet he felt like he was vibrating, just like the second hand on the clock, anticipating the next bolt of lightning, which also didn't come. Although something very unusual had just happened, he felt sure that he was unhurt. On the other hand, he was unsure about how he was supposed to feel.

As the apprehension faded, a peculiar, tremendous wave of well-being came over Harvey. He knew that something extraordinary had taken place, and while he didn't understand it, he sensed that it was good.

When he began to raise his head, Dr. Palmer placed his hand over Harvey's head, loudly saying, "Please be still for a moment." Then, after about a minute, he said to Harvey, "Let's have you sit up now. Try to keep your movements easy." As he rose, he could feel the doctor gently supporting his head.

Harvey used his arms to push the upper part of his body off the table. Then while rising from the bench, he unconsciously rolled his neck from side to side, as if to test it.

D.D. boomed, "Go easy with that neck!"

Harvey moved it more gently, noticing that it glided smoothly and comfortably. *This seems strange*, Harvey wondered. *Why should my neck be feeling better, moving so effortlessly, so right? After all, it wasn't hurting, just that spot that felt tender when Dr. Palmer pressed on it.* Harvey also felt mildly warm and relaxed—something unusual had happened.

Then he felt a strange compulsion to walk to the window. Dr. Palmer looked on anxiously as Harvey peered out the window. Seeing a horse and buggy rounding the corner directly below the window, Harvey threw up the sash and stood dumbfounded. Harvey muttered something to himself first and then repeated it aloud. "No! No! How can this be?" He didn't just see a horse and buggy. He *heard* iron horseshoes slapping cobblestones. He *heard* iron-rimmed wagon wheels bouncing loudly over uneven pavers! The familiar rhythmic sound, absent for so very long, uniquely combined the deep thud of hundreds of pounds of force through each leg of the draft horse's massive body, with the high-pitched collision of its iron shoes hammering the rounded cobblestones. It was astonishing.

Although he was unsure why, Harvey felt obliged to walk across the room to that clock on the shelf, and the unimaginable came to pass. A rhythmic, metallic clinking now accompanied the movement that had transfixed him a minute ago. Then, knowing that his own faithful timekeeper would never lie to him, he reached into his pocket, pulled out his watch, placed its familiar worn face next to his ear, and shrieked, "I can hear!"

Dr. Palmer's eyebrows raised and a great smile came across his face, but he remained silent acknowledging and observing that this was Harvey's moment.

He was hearing everyday sounds for the first time in seventeen years! *Perhaps not as completely clear as the sounds I remember from many years ago, but this is amazing*, Harvey pondered. *It's like someone has removed heavy mufflers off my ears.*

Removing heavy mufflers triggered a curious memory, drawing him to another time and place in a flash. Since this day had produced one shocking event after another, he barely paused to second guess it. Crossing the room, over to the bay window again, he listened for more sounds emanating from the busiest corner in town. Part of him was overseeing the activity below Dr. Palmer's window, while another was mysteriously reliving a distant memory with such intensity as to seem real.

He pictured his mother scolding him when he was five years old. He had tried to leave the supper table without observing a traditional family sacrament. The ceremony was a three-pronged routine. It began with a "thank you" to Mama for preparing the meal, a kiss of appreciation on her cheek, and a request to be excused. His faux pas prompted a litany of adjectives about gratitude and respect to spew from her. Meanwhile, Harvey tested her by rhythmically inserting and removing his index fingers from his ear canals. It entertained him as much as it infuriated her. Harvey also recollected the familiar behavioral tweak that usually came from the business end of Mama's broomstick becoming acquainted with his backside. He vividly remembered his fingers' soft popping sound when he rapidly removed them from his ears, intermittently interrupting Mama's thunderous words. The defiant act toggled her reprimand on and off in staccato fashion until Mama's broom decisively ended the game. Harvey smiled to himself, thinking how ridiculous he must have looked. He knew that a familiar fragrance or the aroma of certain foods could spark a memory, but he had forgotten that one could have the same experience with sounds.

He noticed the eager expression on the face of D.D. Palmer, but the doctor would have to wait while Harvey ruminated. *I feel lightened, even joyful, especially compared to the anger, despair, and bitterness of a few minutes ago.* The profound sadness about Uncle Jim hadn't gone, nor had the empty feeling, still in the center of his chest. But it was transcended by the wondrous miracle of restored hearing. That gift, coming from such a strange character— the contrast fascinated him.

Such a day, thought Harvey. *Heartbreaking news about Uncle Jim and now this unexpected, sensational cure. What next?* Harvey didn't consider himself philosophical, but this surrealistic event made him wonder, *Are all of life's important events supposed to come with a punch and a kiss?*

His thoughts returned to his childhood when Juanna Smith told him about the lynching of her Uncle Willy and how her mother decided it was time to flee. He remembered the look in Juanna's eyes when she spoke of their trek toward freedom. *Juanna may have been a child, but she knew that the Underground Railroad was to be their deliverance—and she understood what would happen if they got caught. So why shouldn't she have shaken with fear amidst the nightmarish thoughts of Uncle Willy's murder?* The disparities tore at Harvey. *How do I celebrate this part of the day while lamenting the earlier?*

A most unlikely individual, D.D. Palmer had mollified the awful news, at least in part. D.D., who had neither put anything into

Harvey's body nor taken anything out, had just succeeded where all the others had failed. While the others had all the ceremony, tools, and credentials, Dr. Palmer used only his hands! With all these thoughts flashing through his mind, Harvey could not find any words to speak, so he uttered what sounded to his ears like a lame, inadequate, and insufficient, "Thank you, Dr. D.D."

Harvey was again surprised, having heard his own words. Somehow life had been breathed into those numb vestiges that had silently mocked him for years, stubbornly refusing to impart even mundane, everyday sounds, the ones that seem to matter most only when they are lacking. The absence of sound had often angered him, while it frustrated everyone around him. The veil had lifted as if the sparkling light of life had finally displaced a long, dark night.

Author's Commentary

Historical facts inspired this work of fiction. Yet as an amateur historian, I've found that the closer one looks at history, the murkier *facts* become. Furthermore, if twentieth-century experiences taught us anything, we should know just how fragile history can be.

For a case in point, at this writing, controversy exists in Japan over whether integrity demands revision of the historical record. At the close of World War II, the Japanese people resoundingly renounced the imperialism that led to a vast Japanese military expansion in the first half of the twentieth century. However, some Japanese academics and politicians are now questioning how to teach that portion of the country's history.

The prevalent dialogue does not question whether millions of Chinese, Koreans, and others were victimized or whether a devastating sneak attack on Pearl Harbor took place. Nor does it suggest that alignment with Hitler wasn't immoral or disastrous. However, it questions content taught to children in Japanese schools since the war. Revisions now inching their way into Japanese textbooks present another perspective on the events leading up to Japan's invasions in Asia and the attack on the United States. They have dared to delve into previously taboo questions about the economic and political pressures that led Japan to make fateful decisions. Judgment aside, having endured defeat, accentuated by the desolation related to the events of Nagasaki and Hiroshima, the Japanese culture required time and healing.

Time brings about data loss, contextual distortions, and reliability issues. Coupled with political sensitivities, we get censorship, manipulation of facts, overstatements, and understatements. The tweaking of historical facts isn't a new phenomenon, nor is it unique to any particular culture. Some suggest that every generation revises history according to its perspective. As the saying goes, *history is written by the victors*, and the final product reflects the interests of those in power. It seems fair to say that epistemology has been a struggle for the human race since before we began to write on papyrus.

Archeology and history have always been confronted with the challenge of finding and deciphering clues into meaning. Records are often lost or destroyed, and scant information easily lends itself to misinterpretation.

Imagining the excitement felt by the first archeologists to view Peru's Nazca lines from the air, one is struck by how the breakthrough opened up so many new questions. The lines were invisible on the ground for hundreds of years until the twentieth century, when the advent of flight changed everything. Distant viewing from airplanes offered a broad enough perspective to see the fascinating shapes. In that vast desert, these wonderfully preserved ancient drawings remained unmolested despite the fact that they were constantly exposed to the elements. Perhaps the greatest beauty in that rare discovery is that it revealed itself openly, suddenly, and completely. It hardly allowed ideological distortion and provided no sudden riches.

Technological advances of the information age have created a far more complex set of problems in that we are inundated with enormous amounts of information. The sheer volume of it has made evaluating and cataloging data a daunting task for the most sincere of record keepers. Separating fact from fiction used to be far more black and white; it was either true or false. Now there are millions of shades of gray.

Simple geography is a factor in the integrity of history too. Children learning about the Civil War in America are presented with differing points of view. A child learning about the period in a classroom in New York might take away key concepts like *freeing the enslaved people* and *saving the Union.* In contrast, one in Charleston, South Carolina, might have learned about *economic domination* and *states' rights.* Deep in the South, some adults, without tongue in cheek, still refer to the *War of Yankee Aggression.*

Time also plays a role in recording facts surrounding conflicts, as evidenced by two and one-half years of further enslavement forced upon families in Texas. There are various versions of why and how news about the end of slavery was withheld until June 19, 1865, even though the Emancipation Proclamation became official on January 1, 1863.

Seeing may not mean believing. Books have been written, movies produced and watched, and testimony has been studied. Yet millions of us who viewed the murder of President Kennedy are nevertheless left uncertain as to the truth of the matter.

Portraying the whole picture is another problem. Beyond the difficulty of merely *getting it right,* there is the challenge of context, especially with regards to the personalities of the history makers. The Civil Rights Movement in the United States provides an example. Church bombings, demonstrations, angry rhetoric, fear, racially motivated murders, marches, riots, and the like were all in the news as a daily event. Dr. Martin Luther King Jr. was a focal point. The visionary leader who led the March on Washington, won the Nobel Peace Prize, and taught non-violence was, in one of those irksome twists of fate, murdered by a racist. While the facts of his murder remain uncertain in the face of allegations of conspiracy, his contributions to the Civil Rights Movement and the country's social fabric are a certainty. He became larger than life, which made a meaningful understanding of the human side of his personality unfeasible for most of us.

Many years later, while perusing his famous "Letter from Birmingham Jail," I finally saw the essence of King as an individual. His words, composed under the distinctive circumstances of a person incarcerated, brought forth a profound new understanding. Each idea spoke as though he were there, alive and in person, with an enlightening message.

King firmly believed in a simple yet powerful idea—that every individual has a moral duty to oppose unjust laws. He considered it an ethical imperative and conveyed it in a way that resonated with his readers. It's a message that can change attitudes. The letter offered a glimpse into what drove him, revealing his true self in a way that headlines are doomed to miss.

While it is important to document human events, conflicting data can make even a trusting person skeptical. This problem highlights the valuable role that works of fiction can play. Apart from its usual functions, fiction can be liberating. Scholarly peer review occurs in an environment populated with well-meaning individuals, each bringing a predisposition to favor the existing standards. The hope is that these values guide the expansion of knowledge. Yet, practically speaking, a tyrannical side to the system exists as it tends to perpetuate the politics of those doing the review.

Unencumbered by the need to conform to any system, storytelling can provide a rich view of people's lives and events. It can build context-specific backdrops, and it might even provide a forum to air a taboo perspective or open the door to an awareness of another point of view, excluded in nonfiction.

It is axiomatic that an author's slant, view of life, expressive skill, and the limits of his/her imagination will all impact the value of such a work, and the one before you is no exception.

Scholarly research into the life of the founder of chiropractic inspired this writing. It also revealed much about the veracity of available information, especially from observing how Palmer's words have been used to further particular agendas. In numerous cases, it turned out that the representations were blatantly opposite and conclusions contrary to the actual beliefs and objectives of the profession's founder. In that regard, isolated passages from his writings have often been taken out of context to justify therapeutical practices that were antithetical to Palmer's ideas.

This author's passion for the philosophy and history of chiropractic fed an interest in telling the story of these fascinating people and events. Where the particular facts were unavailable or unknowable, imagination based on the author's view of the personalities was called upon. Where this took place, the fabrications were consciously constructed in harmony with the overall spirit and desire to render the essence of the personalities. In a small profession such as chiropractic, some may find this storytelling heretical, especially as it deals with persons and ideas enveloped in controversy. Those taking offense are reminded that this is a work of fiction.

All of the inspiration for the story is based on the lives of real persons who participated in developing a new profession. However, the reader is cautioned to realize that this remains a work of fiction. Many of the events and characters in this story are depicted factually and others imaginatively. I've woven the details in the story together as a combination of unfeigned and fabricated features intended to form a tapestry that is plausible in some parts, probable in others, and occasionally outlandish.